I0818326

THE LAST NANNY

REBECCA TAYLOR

OPHELIA HOUSE

www.rebeccataylorbooks.com

Sign up for Rebecca's Newsletter

Thank you, Rod. I love you.

CHAPTER 1

I stood, my hands sweating and clasped in front of me, waiting for Nicola Drake to finish typing on her computer and tell me why I'd been summoned to her home office. I'd only been a nanny for Nicola and her husband, Damion, for six weeks. When I arrived at their Upper East Side apartment, which was larger and grander than any home I'd ever seen during my whole life in Nebraska, including Warren Buffet's, I knew immediately that I'd made a terrible mistake coming to New York.

This city I'd always dreamed of living in was too big, too busy, too expensive, too out of reach for a girl who had lived her whole life in a two-bedroom apartment in a town with a population of less than two thousand.

Within one week, I knew for sure I didn't belong here.

Now, six weeks in, I wasn't sure I would have the chance to stay if I wanted to.

Nicola typed out her last line and, with a profound sigh,

turned her always-piercing gaze onto me. She stared at me for several seconds before saying anything. The critical arch of her perfect eyebrows made me squirm like always.

"Libby," she began, tilting her head slightly to the right as if a new perspective of me may improve her view. "I'm sure you know why I've asked you to come see me during my working hours?"

I wasn't exactly sure, but if I had to guess... "The vase?" I asked.

Nicola closed her eyes and nodded once. "The Baccarat vase, Libby."

Yesterday, their son George, who was eight and had a terrible habit of running everywhere, limbs flying while he played pretend war with both a NERF gun and the most realistic lightsaber I had ever seen—a game that was expressly forbidden by Nicola—had chosen the area beneath the foyer table as his encampment. The foyer table that supported a crystal vase filled with the enormous fresh bouquet that was delivered and arranged by their florist every week. The foyer table that, while extremely sturdy, was apparently still no match for a hyper eight-year-old boy hopped up on the pancakes loaded with syrup I had made him for breakfast.

I had been minutes away from getting him out the door and down to Central Park so he could run wild. I only needed to clear away the breakfast dishes, when I heard the ear-shattering smash of crystal hitting Italian marble flooring. By the time I had dropped the dishtowel and run from the kitchen to the scene of the disaster, George was crying, his head buried in his knees, hugged tight to his chest, as he rocked back and forth amongst all the sparkling shards of broken glass.

I swooped him up and rushed him to the family room, just in time for Nicola to come storming in.

"What the hell happened? I was in the middle of a critical business call!" She glared at us, the anger radiating from her eyes like laser beams set to kill. George, now standing beside me, shrunk further into my side. "Well? Is one of you going to tell me?"

I put my arm around George as he started sobbing and buried his face in my sweatshirt. It had become clear to me over the past month and a half that George was afraid of his mother. Especially when she was angry, and she was angry a lot.

"It was my fault," I said. "I was trying to fix the arrangement in the foyer. I lost my balance and knocked the vase off the table." George stopped crying. I could feel him holding his breath, waiting for what would come next.

But Nicola only stared at me, her face expressionless, her voice silent. Her eyes flicked briefly to her son, hugging my side, and then back to my face.

"I'm so sorry, Nicola." I shook my head. "I'll clean it up right now…and pay for it, obviously."

At this, Nicola scoffed. "You're going to pay for it?"

"Well…" Based on the tone of her voice, the vase was probably more expensive than I had imagined. "Maybe you could take it out of my wages? Until it's covered?"

Nicola laughed and now shook her head. "Sure, Libby. So let me see…" She placed her long, manicured fingers on her sharp hips and shifted her gaze to the ceiling. "Now, if my calculations are correct, if we hold back all your wages to pay off that antique Baccarat vase that was a wedding gift from Damion's great-grandmother…let's see, that means you'll be all paid up by this time next week." She centered her gaze back on me. "Two years from now."

I gasped. How was it even possible that some glass could cost that much money? "I...Nicola, please." I sent nearly every penny I made home to Nebraska to pay for my father's care. There wasn't any way I could afford to fix this mess. I glanced down at George. At least, not without throwing the kid under the bus.

"Just get out of here. Both of you. Call maintenance to come clean up the mess. We'll decide next steps once I've discussed this with Damion. Right now, I have work to do."

That was yesterday. Now, as I stood in front of her, sitting behind her glass desk, the expanse of sky that hung over Central Park framed in the floor-to-ceiling windows behind her, I waited for Nicola to deliver her verdict.

My one chance was that Damion would have been a voice of reason when she spoke to him. Damion was the one who had hired me, after all. And while Nicola would have preferred to hire and import a French au pair, Damion, who had grown up in a Colorado ski town before moving to New York to attend Columbia, had advocated for someone more authentic, someone more like his own mother and sisters and less like a European socialite.

Unfortunately, Damion was out of town for work. And while he had been the one to hire me, it looked like Nicola would be the one to—

"We're letting you go, Libby."

CHAPTER 2

I felt every last drop of blood drain from my body. Helpless, I stared at my feet. I didn't want to cry in front of her, but the tears were rising in my throat. I hated New York, and Nicola quite frankly, but I needed this job—badly. The Drakes paid me three times what I would make as a nanny back home. And since I lived with them, it also saved me from paying rent and utilities. Even still, it took nearly every dime I made to pay for the nurse who took care of my dad. If I didn't work for them, I wouldn't be able to afford his in-home care anymore.

He'd have to go into a nursing home.

And his Medicaid wouldn't be enough for one of the nice ones.

"Nicola...please. I'm so sorry about the vase," I said as the tears filled my eyes.

"Yes, the vase. About that." She reached for her computer

screen and turned the monitor so we could both see it. She clicked her mouse, and a video began to play.

It was from one of their in-home surveillance cameras, which was mounted above the cabinets in the kitchen. In the video, I stood at the large center island while George sat eating on one of the high counter chairs. Confused about why Nicola was showing me this, I glanced up at her, but she kept her eyes glued to the screen.

A second later, Damion walked into the kitchen. There was no sound, but he smiled when he saw George and me and started chatting with us while making coffee. George finished his meal. I cleared away his dish, rinsed it, and put it in the dishwasher. George jumped down from his chair.

When I passed by Damion on my way out of the kitchen, he leaned in toward me. It was slight, nearly imperceptible. Once I had left the room, Damion closed his eyes and appeared to take a deep breath. He shook his head once, glanced out the door George and I had just left through, then took a long drink from his coffee.

Nicola clicked her mouse, and the video stopped. I shifted my gaze from the screen to meet her eyes. Her expression was ice. "Oops," she said, her voice laced with sarcasm. "That's not the video I meant to show you. This one is."

While she clicked through a list of video files, I knew for certain that the video that seemed to suggest Damion was interested in me being more than just a nanny was exactly why I would be losing my job today.

I sat, frozen on the outside but swirling on the inside, as I watched the video of George playing and knocking that ridiculously expensive vase off the table. The video proved that I didn't break it without me having to personally tattle on George. Nicola stopped the replay right as I saw myself rushing into the frame and swooping George into my arms.

"So, as you can see," Nicola said as she turned her monitor back around. "The proof is here. You've literally forced our hands, Libby. You only have yourself to blame."

Because of how Damion reacted to me in the first video, I knew I'd be losing my job today. But Nicola's statement still confused me. "Proof of what, exactly?" I whispered.

"Proof that you're a liar. Proof that you are not to be trusted." She shook her head in mock sadness. "Clearly, George is the one who broke that vase, and yet you thought the wisest course of action was to teach my son not to accept responsibility for his actions. Instead, your behavior would suggest to him that blaming your mistakes on another person and lying are how a problem should be handled." She shook her head again. "Libby, I had my reservations when Damion hired you. I felt, even then, you weren't appropriately trained or psychologically equipped to help raise our son. But I will confess I never thought you lacked a moral center."

What frustrated me most was how I just sat there, speechless, tears running down my face, not saying a single word to defend myself or contradict Nicola. I was being fired because her husband looked my way, never mind the fact that I had no idea about it and had never, ever done a single thing to encourage it.

"And now, I see clearly that allowing you to stay one more minute under our roof will likely result in the most dire consequences for my family." Nicola took a breath, lifted her chin, and stood from her chair. "Please pack your things, Libby. You have one hour. I will call the garage and have them bring your vehicle up. Your final check is already at the bellman's desk downstairs."

Stunned, it took me several seconds to process what she had just said and collect myself enough to realize I'd been dismissed from her presence, their lives, and this home.

I was out of a job. I had nowhere to live, nowhere to go, and no one on this side of the country I could even call. I managed to stand on shaking legs and make my way to her door. With my hand on the doorknob, I whispered, "I'll just say goodbye to George."

"That won't be necessary. He's been told you're leaving, and I've had the new nanny take him out of the house until after your departure."

I looked back at her, standing at her desk, backlit by the view of this city that both revered and rewarded women exactly like her. Beautiful, thin, rich, well-bred, and cruel. "Don't worry, Libby. You are a capable young woman. I'm confident you'll land on your feet."

I turned back to the door and opened it. I was only two steps outside her office when I heard her add.

"Or on your back."

CHAPTER 3

I sat behind the wheel of my ancient, beat-to-death Camry, turning the key again and again while praying the engine would turn over. I hadn't even been inside the car since I came to work for the Drakes. Along with room and board, they had also paid to keep the car I'd driven out from Nebraska housed in the garage deep below their Park Avenue building.

After my sixth time listening to the engine gasp and choke, the valet who'd brought my eyesore of a car to the surface leaned into my driver's side window.

"Try giving it a few pumps of the gas," he offered with an empathetic smile.

I gave him a frantic look, and he backed away slowly, but his advice worked. I pumped the gas a few times, turned the key, and after only one small engine gag, the car came to life.

I breathed a sigh of relief and even managed to say a quick

thank you to the attendant before pulling out of the garage and into New York traffic.

Without any idea where I would or could go, I simply followed the brake lights in front of me for several blocks and tried to think.

I had my last check from Nicola in my pocket, but nearly every cent of it needed to be sent home to Nebraska. Dad's in-home care cost a fortune, and I had barely kept up with the payments before being fired. I had forty-seven dollars in my checking account, a quarter tank of gas in my car, and no idea where I would be sleeping tonight.

To top it all off, I'd left the Drake's in such a hurry I hadn't even had breakfast. It was nearly eleven o'clock, and I was starving. I wish I'd thought to grab some food from the kitchen on my way out the door.

One thing was for sure, I couldn't keep burning gas I couldn't afford to replace. I took the next right, drove several blocks away from the traffic-heavy Central Park area, and found an empty parallel parking space on the street in a residential area.

I switched off the engine and fell back against my seat. I needed to find another job immediately. But another job as a nanny would take time. It was unlikely Nicola would give me a reference, and there would, of course, be the background check which could take a week or longer. I could try to find a place washing dishes, cleaning rooms, or waiting tables, but a different job was unlikely to provide me with a place to live and food.

Nicola's parting words rang through my head. "I'm sure you'll land on your feet. Or on your back."

I closed my eyes and tried to scrub her implication from my mind. It was an insinuation that had haunted me since I'd hit puberty full speed at twelve years old. Full-chested and curvy, an aura of sexualization had hung on me long before I even really knew what sex was or how it happened. I'd endured jeers and cruel remarks from the boys in middle school, lies and gossip about me through high school, and now, assumptions about who I was and what I'd do with essentially any man that had a penis—married or not.

Nicola, who was so slick, tight, and small she could easily be mistaken for a Parisian runway model, was threatened by the way her husband had looked at me in the surveillance video.

Would it make her feel any different to know that my looks had always made me feel threatened in this world, too?

I doubted it.

When Nicola fired me, it made me upset. The unjustness of it had burned like hot coals at my core. Sitting here now, my chest felt tight, and I was having trouble breathing. The panic was setting in.

I grabbed my backpack from the seat next to me and got out of my car. A walk and some fresh air were exactly what I needed to clear my head enough to think straight and find a solution.

On the corner two blocks from where I'd parked, I ducked inside a coffee shop and found an empty table for two at the back. I pulled my laptop from my bag, opened it on the table, and searched for their free Wi-Fi signal.

When I saw it was password protected, I died a little more inside. I would need to spend money I couldn't afford on their cheapest menu item. I got up and headed for the counter.

With a small black coffee, which still cost me nearly five dollars, and the Wi-Fi password, I logged onto the internet and pulled up the listing service I had used to land the job with the Drakes, find a nanny dot com. My profile was already set up here, and while it would likely take some time to get matched up with another family, interview, pass the background, and fill out all the other paperwork, getting the process moving as soon as possible was my best next move.

After this, I'd work on finding a job I could start immediately while waiting for another placement.

I took a sip of my boiling hot coffee, grimaced at the bitter taste, and then realized the carafe of free creamer was at the end of the counter, along with packets of sugar and sweeteners. At the very least, I should enjoy my overpriced coffee while I searched for jobs.

I typed in my criteria: full-time, room and board, and pay range. I left the location open—I didn't care at all about staying in Manhattan. I clicked the search button and took my coffee over to make it taste better while the program did its thing. With any luck, hundreds of results would be listed by the time it was done. Tons and tons of families all over the nation who needed a nanny right away.

By the time I had added a heavy pour of creamer and four packets of sugar to my cup and returned to my table, find a nanny dot com had a list on my screen waiting for me to review.

I had hoped for hundreds and been given four.

Three weren't looking to hire anyone for three to six weeks.

Which left one option.

One family in New Hampshire looking to find a live-in nanny, room and board provided, for their six and twelve-year-old sons, hiring Immediately.

I sat down, clicked open the listing, and prayed their definition of Immediately meant today.

CHAPTER 4

I positioned my laptop so that the camera would face the wall next to my table instead of the hallway to the bathrooms and shifted my chair into position.

The older barista was giving me the side eye from behind the counter. I lifted my now long empty coffee cup to my lips and pretended I was still enjoying the drink I had purchased from them almost three hours ago. The barista sighed and shook her head. The shop was busy, and I was taking up space.

After responding to my only option, I couldn't believe my luck when the New Hampshire family messaged me within minutes to ask if I had time for a virtual interview. Today!

Given my own personally horrible history in life, I wasn't generally the type of person who felt that the universe ever had my back. Maybe it was the depth and degree of my present desperation, but the powers that be sure seemed to be at least willing to give me a chance right now.

If all went well, I'd vacate this table within the next twenty minutes with a solid solution for my current troubles.

I clicked the virtual meeting link from find a nanny dot com and waited to be connected with Doctor Jacob North and his wife, Alexi North.

A man appeared on my screen before I even had my earbuds positioned. They were early. I hadn't expected that. Nicola Drake always kept me waiting.

"Hello," I said. "Sorry, just a second." I held up one finger as I put in my second earbud. "There." I sat up straight. "Doctor North?"

"Hello, Libby," he said. "It's nice to meet you."

He was sitting directly in front of a brightly lit window, making it impossible to clearly see his features. It was like I was meeting his shadow for the first time instead of him. One thing was certain, I didn't see his wife in the frame.

"Thank you so much for responding to our listing and being able to interview so quickly."

"Of course." I managed to restrain myself from saying any more. If they asked outright, I wouldn't lie about being fired by the Drakes. But I wouldn't just offer up the information either, especially since I'd done absolutely nothing wrong.

"Both Alexi and I reviewed your profile on the site. I see you are from Nebraska originally. My aunt lived in Omaha...before she passed away."

"Really?" I said, trying my best to sound thrilled by this random fact. "Well, it is a beautiful state." It wasn't. It was just a polite thing to say. While it turned out I had no love for New York, I wasn't missing anything about my home state either—except my father.

"Really? Well, I'll have to try and get out that way sometime myself."

It was difficult to tell because he was so dark on screen, but it seemed like he kept glancing up at something in front of him.

"But how about we get down to the details here."

"Sounds good."

"As it turns out, my wife and I are in a bit of a bind. We basically need someone who can get here and start yesterday. I'm a professor at Eastbridge University, and my wife is a documentary filmmaker. She's just had an opportunity come up that she can't turn down, but it means she'll be out of the country for the next several weeks. We lost our last nanny quite unexpectedly... she quit without notice, that is. Basically, we're looking for someone to start immediately. Is that something that would work for you?"

I nodded while my brain worked to process everything he'd just shared. They were as desperate as I was. If I played my cards right, I might never need to reveal my own dire straits. "So, essentially, if you were to hire me, I'd need to be there by..."

"Today," he said. "If that's possible. Or tomorrow...or the next day. Really, just as soon as you can get here."

I nodded. Today? Even if I walked out of this cafe and started driving immediately, I had no idea how long the drive between New York and New Hampshire would take.

"We have a couple more questions, but to be honest, everything in your profile looked great. I could book you a plane ticket for the next flight out of New York."

I completely understood their circumstances, but suddenly, something about his tone and frank desperation gave me pause. Almost like a silent alarm was sounding throughout my nervous system and making me reluctant to just go charging into the situation. What exactly was making me nervous now? After all, this was precisely what I needed to solve my problems, and it was happening much faster than I could have dreamed possible.

Was it the fact that I couldn't really see his face?

That I hadn't met his wife?

Or that, as of yet, there was no evidence that there were even children in the home who needed a nanny.

What if this was all some sort of ploy to get a young woman, alone and disconnected, up to some psychopath's lair in the middle of nowhere New Hampshire?

Also, was it just the lighting, or did he keep looking at someone or something beyond his computer screen.

"I...um. I actually have a car here. It's just parked on the street right now and I don't have anyone I could leave it with. I'm not sure how long it would take me to drive up there." Or even if I should drive up there.

It was Doctor North's turn to nod, but he seemed really distracted now. I was about to ask if he wanted to finish the interview a little later when I saw him motion with his hand, waving someone towards him. A small person came into view a second later and crawled onto his lap. "Libby, this is Daniel. He's our youngest—six. Our other son, Garrett, is twelve." Doctor North leaned his head close to his son's. "Daniel, meet Libby."

The little boy leaned in very close to the computer screen, making it easy to see his inquisitive eyes and big smile, even with all the bright backlighting.

So, all creepy feelings aside, at least there really was a child that needed a nanny. "Hi Daniel," I said, and gave him a little wave.

"Is she the new Jessica?" Daniel blurted.

Doctor North shifted in his seat. "Well, buddy. We're hoping so."

I watched as Daniel also looked up and past the computer before them. Because he was a child, his actions were more obvious than his father's. Clearly, someone else was in the room.

Was it the other kid, Garrett? Or the wife and mom, Alexi? And if so, why didn't whoever it was just introduce themselves?

CHAPTER 5

The additional questions Doctor North had for me were both minimal and basic. He asked me to tell him more about my hometown.

"There isn't much to tell. Hallsworth's tiny. So small, the elementary, middle, and high school are all in one building," I said.

"Will you need much time off to visit family and friends?" he asked.

I shook my head. "I don't have any friends," I blurted out before realizing how colossally sad this statement was. "I mean, not any that I'd plan to visit. And my father is the reason I need this job. I send home almost all the money I earn to pay for his in-home nurse and care."

At this, Doctor North cocked his head and again glanced up at what I now assumed was Mrs. North behind the computer. "I see. And what about your mother? Other family?"

"My mother passed away when I was eight. And growing up…well, there wasn't any other family around. At least my father wasn't in contact with anyone. So, if I have any, I don't know them."

There were a few other questions that, in hindsight, I didn't feel were exactly pertinent. When I interviewed with Damion Drake, he had a list of questions about my experience, education, temperament, and beliefs about childcare.

By comparison, Doctor North's interview was more personal. Almost intrusive, really.

Why am I talking about my dead mother and disabled father? What do they have to do with getting this job and my ability to care for their sons?

Before ending the meeting, he officially offered me the job and asked if I could start right away. But despite seeing that, yes, there was at least one actual child in the home, there were enough weird flags about the interview that I said, "Thank you for the opportunity. I'm interested…but can I have some time to think it over?"

"Um…" He again glanced up. "I mean, sure. But how long do you think you'll need? We really do need someone up here right away."

"I know." I felt so pressured to give an answer immediately that part of me almost just blurted out, "Yes." Because I really, really needed this too. But another part of me was holding back. Asking me to think it over. "If I could just sleep on it? New Hampshire would be a big change for me. I just want to make sure I've considered all the possible…" Red flags. Weird vibes. Concerns I was having. "Logistics," I said.

Doctor North nodded. "Yes, of course. Let us know tomorrow morning. That's fine," he said, even if his tone conveyed that it was actually not fine. He wanted this locked down now.

"Thank you for understanding. I'll be in touch very soon," I said, and we ended the meeting.

As I packed my computer away and got ready to finally get up and leave, the look of relief on the barista's face was obvious. I picked my empty cup off the table and took another long, fake sip from it—I'm sorry it took me over four hours to drink one cup of coffee, jeez—before depositing it in the recycle bin on my way out the door.

Now that I was back outside on the mid-afternoon New York streets, my next problem presented itself. It was a relief to know that I now had a job again, should I take it after thinking it over. But where exactly would I go while I did all this thinking? Since I was fired and kicked out of the Drake's luxury home on Park Avenue, I didn't have anywhere to go besides my car.

I couldn't afford a hotel. Not even one of the super crappy places that were both filthy and infested. I had heard about people in the city who were forced to sleep in their cars—now I would be one of them.

I headed up the street to where I'd parked. I walked several blocks, my mind running through the interview and my very limited options. I walked even farther, my brain spinning, before I stopped and realized I had come too far.

I had missed my car.

I turned around and went back. Paying closer attention and

scanning the street. I didn't see it, but I felt pretty certain it was on this block—wasn't it?

Distracted by being fired and panicking about what I would do, admittedly, I hadn't been paying close attention. I pulled my key fob from the side pocket of my bag and began pushing the emergency horn button. This was how I always found my car back home when I couldn't remember exactly where I'd parked.

I expected to hear it start blaring any second. There wasn't any way I was more than a block away. Nothing. Just the regular traffic and occasional horn from the busier cross street.

"You're that girl that parked her car in the no parking zone!" Someone called out from above me. When I looked up, I saw an old woman leaning out of her second-floor window. Her brows were knit together, and she pointed a bent and arthritic finger at me.

Confused, I turned around to see if maybe she was hollering at someone else.

"Yes, it's you I'm talking to. You left your car in the no-parking zone." Now, she pointed to her right. A street sign was attached to the light pole.

No Parking Zone. An arrow indicated the zone started there and extended to the end of the street.

I looked at the empty space in front of the sign and realized that was exactly where my car had been.

"They've come and towed it!" she called, shaking her head. "You shouldn't park in the no-parking zone!"

I looked up into her disapproving expression and watched as she closed her window with purpose and then took a seat. Her chair was positioned right at the window, and I couldn't help but assume that monitoring the no-parking zone in front of her building was what now gave her life meaning.

My shoulders sagged as I stared at the empty space. I couldn't afford to get it out of the impound, and everything I owned was in that car.

What the hell was I supposed to do now?

CHAPTER 6

The person sitting directly across from me had a sticker plastered to their open laptop.

Sometimes, the Universe makes decisions for you.

I stared at that sticker for several minutes while trying, and failing, to process the bizarre events and circumstances that had occurred in my life since waking up this morning.

"Flight 485 is ready to board. We'd like to invite our passengers in boarding group number one to approach the podium at this time."

I looked down at the boarding pass on my phone. I was in boarding group one, seat number 3A. I stood up, slung my ratty backpack over my shoulder, and got in line behind the people scanning the QR codes on their phones and entering the jet bridge.

I had never been on a plane before.

After learning that my car and nearly everything I owned were locked behind a chain-link fence at Izzard's Impound and that it would cost me five hundred dollars to get them out, I called Doctor North.

"I've thought about it. I'll take the job. I can leave today if you send me the plane ticket."

"That's great news," he said, although his tone of voice was flat and didn't sound like he actually thought it was great at all. Based on our previous conversation, I thought he'd be thrilled. "Give me a few minutes, and I'll email you the itinerary and ticket."

"Okay. And thank you," I said, trying to still sound professional and not like I was on the verge of tears.

"Of course. But, if you don't mind me asking, what will you do about your car?"

I looked at the empty space where it had been parked and then up to the window where the woman still sat staring. She was somehow managing to pretend she didn't see me down here struggling with life. "It's not a problem I have anymore," I said.

The line was silent for a moment. A surge of panic ran through me—I needed this job and the place to stay that came with it. Had I sounded too frantic? Was Doctor North having second thoughts himself?

"Well," he finally said. "It sounds like everything has worked out for us all then."

I was afraid of saying anything more, anything that would or could inadvertently wreck this for me. "Yes."

I walked the streets of New York for the next fifteen minutes, frantically refreshing my email every few seconds, waiting and watching for the airplane reservation to come through. If he didn't send it, what would I do? I was just imagining myself trying to get comfortable on a Central Park bench for the night when, finally, I got the email.

I headed to the nearest subway station as fast as possible and figured out how to get to LaGuardia.

As I boarded the flight with the rest of the passengers, I watched the man in front of me cross himself and then lay his hand on the outside of the plane nearest the open door before crossing the threshold. I wasn't necessarily afraid of flying; at least, I didn't think I was. But the man's actions made me wonder if he knew something I didn't.

Did I, too, need to pray for safety?

When I stepped aboard, the flight attendant greeted me with a smile. I wasn't sure what to do or where to go, so I showed her the pass on my phone.

"Hello, Ms. Luck. You're joining us in 3A today."

She must have figured out from the look on my face that I didn't understand exactly what that meant.

"And that's just right here," she said, pointing to a wide leather seat three rows from the front of the aircraft door. "In first class," she added with a smile and an excited shimmy of her shoulders.

It must have been painfully obvious to her that traveling in first class would be an extra special treat for a girl who looked like she needed a shower and whose only luggage, a ripped backpack, might have been pulled from a nearby dumpster. I was shocked and certain that it showed as I stood frozen and staring at the large seat next to the oval window.

"Are you sure?" I asked the flight attendant.

She smiled and nodded. "Yes, dear." She glanced at the

annoyed-looking man behind me. "Why don't you go ahead and sit down."

I nodded. "Right. Sorry," I tried apologizing to the man, but he only furrowed his brow further and pushed on through, past a divider curtain, and onto the back of the airplane.

I sat down, shoved my backpack under the seat in front of me, and stared out the window at the ground crew loading bags on the plane next door to us. Doctor North had surely made a mistake buying a first-class ticket for me. I had no idea what it must have cost him, but I hoped he wouldn't be taking it out of my paychecks.

"Would you care for a pre-departure beverage?" a voice to my right suddenly asked.

Startled, I jumped in my seat. When I turned, I saw the flight attendant holding a tray of beverages before me.

"Sparkling wine? Water? Or orange juice?" she asked.

"Um." I was thirsty. Also very, very hungry. I still hadn't eaten anything and only had my expensive coffee to drink. "How much is it?" I asked.

"Oh, no!" she exclaimed with her generous smile. "It's complementary. Everything up here is." She winked at me.

Free? That I could afford. "Can I have all three?" I asked.

The thinnest of clouds passed over her expression, but she never lost her smile. "Of course, you can," she said, placing napkins first and then the bubbly wine, water, and orange juice onto the small, square table built into the armrest. "And here is the menu for today's service. It's a short flight, so only a light snack," she said, handing me a half-letter-sized piece of cream-colored card stock. "I'll come get your order once we're in the air."

I nodded as she moved on to the passengers in the row behind me. I picked up the water and downed it in one long swallow while reading the food options. I would also get to eat! Maybe it was a mistake, maybe Doctor North would pull the cost of this first-class flight from my paychecks for the next ten years, but right now, I felt so—

"Ms. Luck?" I was yanked from my thoughts by a different flight attendant. An older, sterner, less smiley flight attendant. Given how she asked me my name, I guessed they had discovered the mistake, and I was about to get kicked out of my posh seat. I glanced at my untouched, golden sparkling wine. I should have drunk it down when I had the chance.

Embarrassment crept up my chest and lit my face bright pink. All the other first-class passengers, the ones who truly belong here, were about to watch me and my crappy backpack get kicked out. I couldn't speak, so I only nodded at her.

The barest of smiles forms on her lips for the briefest of seconds and then evaporates. "Would you care for a pillow and blanket?" she asks and holds up a plush folded gray blanket, topped with a plump crisp white pillow, all tied together with a dark blue ribbon like a gift.

"Oh!" I was completely shocked. "Yes, please," I say and take it from her.

"You're welcome, Ms. Luck."

"Thank you," I say, and for the first time in my entire life, I actually feel like my last name fits. With the blanket draped across my legs and the pillow propped behind my head, I sip my sparkling wine as the plane pushes back from the gate. Having long suffered the bad variety, I felt it was about time I had some good luck for once.

I didn't know what I was getting into on the other end of this flight, but I would enjoy this moment while I had the chance.

If my life had taught me anything up to this point, it was that any good fortune I may experience would certainly not last long.

CHAPTER 7

He was standing in baggage claim holding a sign: Ms. Libby Luck

Only as the plane was landing did I realize Doctor North and I hadn't communicated about how I'd be getting from the airport to the house. I couldn't afford an Uber, and even if I could, I didn't have their address.

As the runway lights sped past my oval window, a profound sense of dread settled into my gut.

I was so desperate after being fired by Nicola, kicked out of the Drake's house, and having my car towed that I'd rushed into this situation without any planning or sense of what I was getting into.

I knew nothing about these people, and I'd be sleeping in their home tonight. It didn't feel possible.

As I descended the escalator leading to the airport exit, I saw him with the sign. I was relieved to see there was a plan to pick me up, even if I hadn't known about it.

He was tall, broad-shouldered, and had a full head of dark hair. As I got closer, more details about his features came into focus. It was impossible to tell from our poorly lit video meeting this morning, but now I saw him clearly.

He's good-looking.

He has dark brown eyes and a square jaw with a slight scruff, like he might not have shaved today. He's wearing a loose flannel over a black T-shirt tucked into jeans that look like they were both thrown on and designed for him.

He's watching me as I come down the escalator, and I can tell he recognizes me, but he doesn't smile. Good-looking or not, his gaze reignites the nervous dread I've felt since exiting the plane.

"Hello," I say, pointing to his sign when I reach him.

"Libby Luck," he says it more as a matter of fact than an actual greeting.

"Yes." Seems the only appropriate response. It's like I've been summoned from the waiting area of a dentist's office.

To our left, the conveyor belt that will deliver the bags from my flight starts up, and the crowd pushes closer to watch and wait.

"I'm parked in short term." He nods and starts walking over to join everyone else. "I'll help you with your bags."

"I don't have any," I blurt.

He stops and turns back around, his eyes boring into mine before briefly glancing at my backpack. "That's it?"

I nod. "It's a long story, but yes. This is it. I'll have to replace some things when I have the chance."

He stares at me a moment longer, like maybe he, too, is just now wondering what exactly he's gotten himself and his family into by hiring a woman who shows up with nearly zero belongings.

He lets out a small sigh. "Okay. Well, let's get going. It's a long drive."

I follow him through the automatic sliding glass doors and exit the airport. The humidity and heat mix with the scent of jet fuel, and I feel lightheaded. Admittedly, having three glasses of free sparkling wine on the flight was probably not the best idea. I felt the charcuterie plate I'd chosen off the first-class snack menu churn in my stomach.

Do not get sick, I ordered my body. That was the last thing I needed right now.

The first thing was a shower. The second was a toothbrush, which I no longer owned thanks to a nosy, grumpy, bored old lady and Izzard's Impound.

Doctor North pulled a key fob from the front pocket of his jeans and pointed it at the dark garage ahead of us. A double beep echoed throughout the concrete structure, and the lights of an expensive-looking black pickup truck flashed. He opened the passenger door for me, and I watched as a running board automatically extended for me to use as a step.

"Thank you," I said and slid onto the taut black leather seat. It may have been a pickup truck, but the interior rivaled any luxury car on the market. Years ago, when he could still walk and speak, and we both assumed he always would, my dad and I visited the Ford dealer closest to our town. We had sat inside a new truck, not unlike this one, and my father had nearly wept when he saw it cost twice as much money as he made in a year.

No matter what type of person Jacob North was, I figured it

was highly unlikely he'd mess up the interior of his brand-new truck by murdering me inside it.

He opened his door and slid behind the wheel, his profile illuminated by the high-tech dash in front of us. Plus, did murderers ever look as good as this man?

Although, I suppose it would make it easier for him to get away with it.

CHAPTER 8

He was right. The drive was long. Nearly two hours of uninterrupted, awkward silence. The only break was when we pulled off the highway and into a Walmart parking lot so I could buy a few essentials.

I was thankful Doctor North decided to wait in the truck while I bought toiletries and new underwear. I also grabbed a couple of cheap T-shirts, a pair of jean shorts, and rubber flip-flops. It was still warm outside, and these would have to do until I could build my small wardrobe back up. But if everything worked out with this job, I would need significantly warmer clothes for autumn in New Hampshire.

After leaving the store, we drove for miles down several roads flanked by the tallest, densest forest I had ever seen. The sun was setting as we pulled off a main road and onto a dirt one. There was no marker for it that I could see, and it seemed like we had taken a random left turn directly into the woods.

I assumed the turn onto the dirt road meant we were

nearing the house, but we continued to bump and bounce down the rough road for another ten minutes before I saw even a hint of light in the distance.

"You guys really do live out in the sticks," I said, trying to keep my tone light and breezy—like a joke. But it was impossible to miss the nervous tremor.

If he heard it, Doctor North didn't give any indication or offer any reassurances. "Yes," was all he said as he continued to stare out the windshield. His profile, handsome as it was, looked eerie lit only by the blue lights emanating from the truck's console.

"Do you own much of the land around the house?" I asked, now that I could see more lights and the outline of their home coming into view.

"Yes," he said again.

I worried this was all I'd be getting from now on. These creepy one-word, monotone responses that for sure meant I was going to get killed the moment he could drag me from his expensive truck so my blood and guts didn't ruin the new car smell.

"It's just over a thousand acres. We've been on the property since we turned off County Road 12. It's very remote, which is one of the reasons we needed you here so soon." He now glanced in my direction. "It takes a long time to drive the boys to and from school every day. And it's in the complete opposite direction from the university where I work."

I stare at him, my relief washing over me and making me feel stupid for being paranoid. I couldn't drive his kids to school every day if he killed me.

"Alexi." He glanced at me again. "My wife," he clarified. "She's leaving tomorrow. Her flight is very early, and she'll be gone for several weeks."

"She's leaving?" This news surprised me.

Doctor North took a deep breath. If he was trying to act like this fact didn't bother him, he was failing at it. "Yes. It's for work...something she can't pass up. She makes documentaries, and this one is her most ambitious project so far. When our last nanny left, Alexi was between jobs and was able to pick up the slack. But then, she got a call last week about an opportunity that could change everything for her. Let's just say we didn't have a good plan in place for a lightning strike like that. You're the fifth nanny we interviewed."

"Let me guess," I said. "No one else could start as quickly as I could." This better explained their desperation to hire and get me here so quickly.

"That's right," he said as he pulled the pickup to a stop on the circular drive in front of the largest home I had ever seen.

It was nearly night now. As I got out of the truck, I looked up to see that the sky was dark blue, lit only by the barest remnants of daylight as the sun receded over the horizon that couldn't be seen from inside the depths of the surrounding forest. The moon was up, half full, and hung alongside more stars than I had seen since leaving Nebraska.

I'd spent less than two months in New York, but I'd already forgotten how much I loved being able to look up and see the universe. It was magnificent to see, but also reminded me of how small and insignificant we all were.

I imagined Nicola Drake, and self-important people in general, didn't like being reminded they were actually quite small and insignificant.

I slung my backpack over one shoulder, grabbed my two plastic Walmart bags from the truck's backseat, and followed Doctor North up the drive to the stone steps leading to the massive front door.

"Do you need a hand with those?" he asked as he reached for my bags.

"I'm good, thank you."

He nodded and opened the right side of the double front door, then stood to one side to let me pass in front of him. The house was dark, quiet, and felt like no one was home.

Doctor North closed the door behind us and reached for the wall to our left. Lights, warm and bright from the chandelier high above our heads, now illuminated the entrance. No doubt, it was a mansion, but it was a country mansion. All big beams, rustic hand-scrapped wood floors, and cream-colored plaster walls. At the center of the large foyer, an enormous table made from an intact slice of a tree that was five feet in diameter supported a massive floral arrangement that incorporated long twigs and flourishes of bristle cone pines amongst the white and yellow flowers I couldn't identify.

I was just about to ask where the kids and Mrs. North were when I looked up to the top of the grand staircase in front of us and saw a small face peering down from the shadows of the landing above .

Doctor North tossed his keys into a tray on the table next to the door and followed my gaze to the second floor. He leaned closer to me and whispered, "That's Daniel. He can be a little shy when first meeting new people, but he'll warm up."

In the car, all I could smell was the scent of new leather and carpet, but being this close to him now, I noticed that, in addition to being ridiculously good-looking, Jacob North also smelled amazing. I didn't know if it was shampoo, soap, or a special cologne, but Doctor North had a warm, woodsy scent. It was soothing, and I imagined what it might be like to curl up next to someone like him.

It was not exactly the thing I needed to be thinking about, but it was a far cry better than being worried I was maybe about to die.

"Are you going to come down and say hello, buddy?" Doctor North called up.

Daniel shook his head, but a few seconds later seemed to change his mind because he stood up and moved to the top of the stairs.

He was already in his pajamas, his hair drying from a recent bath. He held the banister as he descended the large steps that seemed like a lot for his little legs to navigate. When he reached the bottom step, he launched himself into his dad's open arms. Held by his father, Daniel turned and gazed at me for several seconds. It felt like he was trying to figure something out, and then he asked, "Do you know where Jessica is going?"

CHAPTER 9

I smiled at Daniel but turned a questioning gaze to Doctor North.

"No, buddy," Doctor North said. "Remember I told you. This is Libby. She'll be your new nanny."

"But maybe she knows where Jessica is going," he said, looking at me like I could confirm this was true.

Doctor North looked like he was at a loss for words, so I decided to take a stab at helping out. "I'm sorry, I never met her. But she sounds like she was a pretty great nanny."

Doctor North looked at me and said, "He was very attached to Jessica. She was with us since before Daniel was born."

I raised my eyebrows. Compared to my six weeks with the Drakes, over six years with one family seemed like an eternity. Especially when it was a family that lived in the middle of nowhere. It made me wonder what kind of personal life Jessica could possibly have had way out here.

And, more importantly, what kind of life would I have? I

suddenly wanted to ask why she had left but figured the question might upset Daniel, who was clearly not over her leaving.

"Aren't you supposed to be in bed?" Doctor North asked, and Daniel nodded his head. "That's what I thought. Let's get you back upstairs, and we can show Libby your room."

Still holding Daniel, he started up the stairs, and I followed. "After we get him tucked back in, I'll show you your rooms and a little bit of the house."

"But those are Jessica's rooms," Daniel protested as he looked at me from over his father's shoulder, his eyes filling with tears.

Doctor North didn't argue with his son, but I did hear him let out a long sigh. "It's going to be okay, buddy," he said, rubbing Daniel's back as we reached the top step and the second floor.

Daniel looked at me, with several tears running down his cheeks, and shook his head. It was clear that I would have to work to win this kid over. Whoever Jessica was, Daniel still loved her and missed her a lot. I'd have to remember to ask the Norths what sort of things Daniel liked to do with Jessica. Even still, I'd likely need to take it slow with him. Unlike the Drakes' son, who was so rambunctious and had barreled right into a relationship with me on day one, I could tell Daniel was quieter and maybe more sensitive.

We stopped at the first room in a very long hallway. There were three other closed doors, but Daniel's door was open. It was a huge room for such a small boy. There was a double-sized bed, bedside tables, and a dresser on one side, and what looked to be an entire playroom on the other side. It was dark, with only a rotating nightlight of constellations and stars projected onto the walls and ceilings for light. Still, I could see that the sheets and comforter had been thrown back when Daniel had gotten out of bed to investigate my arrival.

Doctor North lowered Daniel back into his bed and pulled the covers up over him. He leaned in and kissed his son on the head, "Goodnight, buddy."

"But Dad," Daniel protested, his voice still shaky from crying.

Doctor North brushed Daniel's hair back off his forehead and wiped the tears from his cheek with his thumb. "You're tired. It's been a big day. Go to sleep, and everything will be better in the morning."

From the doorway, I could see Daniel give his father an angry scowl before rolling away from him and pulling his covers over his head. Doctor North stood up, stared at his son for several more seconds, then turned back to me. His eyes met mine, and I could see his son's pain was also hurting him, but he shook his head, joined me, and closed the bedroom door.

"He's tired. We all are, quite frankly. Jessica's leaving was unexpected. It threw us all into a tailspin."

"Doctor North?"

He held up his hand and shook his head. "Please, call me Jacob. Only my students call me Doctor. Plus, if you're going to be living here, I don't think I could deal with that level of formality every day." He gave me a small smile, the first I'd seen on him since picking me up at the airport. It was evident that Jessica's departure was causing him a lot of stress.

"Okay," I said. "Well then, Jacob, I just want you to know, I'll do everything I can to help Daniel feel better."

Jacob nodded. "Thank you. I'm sure it will all work out. It's just going to take some time...for all of us." He nodded his head to the right. "I'll show you your rooms, Garrett's room, and some of the house."

I nodded but was honestly surprised that he didn't mention introducing me to Mrs. North. I couldn't imagine any mother allowing a stranger to be around her kids without at least meeting them first.

CHAPTER 10

My room was at the end of the hallway, two doors down from Daniel's and right next door to Garrett's. The boys shared a bathroom, which was the other closed door between their bedrooms. When we passed by, Jacob knocked lightly on Garrett's door and tried the doorknob.

It was locked.

Jacob stared at his son's door, and for a moment, I thought he was going to call out to him and ask him to unlock the door, but he didn't. "He's probably already asleep," Jacob explained. "He had...well, it was kind of a stressful day at school for him," he finished in a whisper, like he was maybe afraid Garrett might hear him. "It's better to let him rest. You'll meet him in the morning."

I nodded and followed Jacob further down the hall to the door at the end. I had never been in charge of a kid as old as Garrett, but I actually remembered, vividly, what a nightmare middle school could be. To top it off, this kid was getting a new nanny, and his mother was leaving the next day—when I was twelve, I probably would have locked my door, too, if I'd been allowed.

I had imagined the room I'd be living in would be smaller than Daniel's room—the help's quarters. But when Jacob opened the door and flipped the light switch, I actually gasped. It wasn't smaller; it was even larger. It was so large I couldn't even see the whole space from the doorway because a separate room was closed off by a set of double wooden doors.

Jacob walked into the room. First he turned on two table lamps, and the chandelier hanging from the ceiling, throwing the whole room into a warm and welcoming glow. This was a living room with a plump white couch, white wood tables, and a bookshelf that filled one entire wall from floor to ceiling.

"I hope this will be okay," he said as he crossed the room and pulled open the heavy, pale pink silk drapes, revealing the expanse of windows across from where I still stood at the door.

I watched as he walked to the closed double doors and opened them before disappearing into the next room. I stood, shocked by what I was seeing and wondering if it could possibly be true.

"I know your last placement was probably pretty fancy, so I hope this will be okay," Jacob said in the next room. "But please don't hesitate to let me know if there is anything you need or want to change. We want you to be comfortable." He poked his head through the double doorway a second later. "Libby?"

Speechless, I stared at him. A shadow of worry crossed his face. "Is something wrong?" he asked.

I shook my head. Wrong? I hadn't even seen the whole place yet and still couldn't believe this was where I would live now.

"Do you want to see the bedroom and bath?" He gestured to the space in the other room. "Or, you know, if this isn't okay—"

"It's amazing," I blurted.

With this, his shoulders dropped, and his relief was obvious. "Oh good," he said. "Cause for a second there, I thought...well, never mind. So long as you're happy. I don't know what I'd do at this point if you changed your mind."

I followed Jacob into the next room. It was the bedroom, equal in size to the living room, complete with a king-sized bed, a large armoire, and another small couch that matched the one in the front room. The bed was framed in dark wood, hand-scraped like the floor, and had a mountain of pillows in a variety of sizes that complemented the pale blue comforter.

When I lived with the Drakes, Nicola had several subscriptions to fancy home and decor magazines. Gazing into this room felt like standing in one of those pictures. I never, not in a million years, imagined I would ever see one of those rooms in person.

Now, I would be living in one.

"Like I said, if this isn't your style, or you'd prefer something else—"

"It's perfect," I said. "I don't want to change a thing." I couldn't even imagine how I could make it any better.

"Okay...well, if you change your mind once you settle in..."

Jacob opened another single door and flicked on the light. I could see it was the bathroom. It was stunning, with dark wood cabinets, white marble floors, and countertops. But by far, the most beautiful thing in the room was an enormous soaking tub right next to a large picture window draped in the same pale pink silk curtains that were in the front room.

"And your closet is also in here," Jacob added as he opened yet another door next to the glass shower.

I followed him and saw the walk-in closet with more hanging rods and built-in shelves than even Nicola Drake had in her posh bedroom suite. I envisioned my four Walmart T-shirts hanging in this expansive and beautiful space and nearly cracked up laughing.

When Jacob turned to me, cocked his head, and gave me a worried look, I realized I was standing there with my mouth hung open. I snapped my jaw shut and tried to find words for this experience.

"It's amazing," was all I managed to get out.

Jacob blew out a breath and nodded. "I'm so happy you like it, Libby." He gestured for me to head back to the bedroom and then turned off the closet light. "I know you're probably exhausted after such a whirlwind day. I'll just show you the kitchen, the car you'll be driving, and oh, before I forget." He reached into his back pocket, pulled out a cell phone, and handed it to me. "This is already set up and this is the number." He handed me a yellow sticky note with the ten digits. "I realize you already have your own, but I feel it's only right that I provide and pay for the one you'll need to manage the boys and stay in communication with me."

I nodded and placed the phone and note in my own pocket. The Drakes had also given me a phone that was on their family cellular plan—it was one of Nicola's old phones that was so dated it wasn't worth her trading in. But I noticed this phone was much nicer, maybe even the latest model. "Thank you," I said.

"Of course." Jacob nodded and gestured for me to follow him.

Back in the hallway, we passed Garrett's locked door and then Daniel's, which was still closed. Presumably, and hopefully, he had fallen back to sleep despite his tears. We also passed by the grand staircase we had come up before.

"This house is a little bit of a maze," Jacob explained. "Don't worry if it takes you a little while to get the lay of the land. There are several landings, hallways, and staircases that lead downstairs. I'll show you the one that goes directly into the kitchen."

I followed, keeping pace as Jacob quickly navigated. We took several turns and passed even more dark hallways that branched off from landings and two more staircases that were apparently not the one that led to the kitchen. I was just thinking that this house reminded me of a spider's web when light through a cracked door at the end of a hallway caught my attention.

Jacob didn't stop, and I didn't want to get lost, but I took a moment to stare into the space. For a singular moment, I saw a figure pass by the opening. They were dressed all in black and had long brown hair—it was only a split second, and then they were gone.

"Libby?" Realizing I wasn't behind him, Jacob had stopped on the landing ahead.

"Sorry, I'm coming," I said as I jogged a few steps to reach him. "I just thought I saw someone," I said.

Jacob nodded once and headed down the staircase in front of us. I expected my statement would lead him to explain about his wife's presence and the fact I had yet to meet her. Something logical and mundane, but he remained silent as we descended the wide circular steps that spiraled into the kitchen below.

He was probably just as tired and overwhelmed as his son—in a single day he had interviewed, hired, and transported a complete stranger into their lives and home. Since he didn't think to offer up the information, I decided to help him out.

"Was that Mrs. North?" I asked.

Jacob stopped in the middle of the dark kitchen, his hand resting on the edge of the large island. He didn't answer or even turn around to look at me.

"I saw someone," I explained. "At the end of that last hallway. The door was cracked, and a light was on. I just assumed—"

"Yes," Jacob answered. "That was Alexi. That's her office down that hall."

CHAPTER 11

I woke to the sound of the alarm on my new phone. I rolled over, plucked the device from the bedside table, and shut it off. It was six a.m., the time Jacob suggested I get up and meet him, Garrett, and Daniel downstairs as they got ready for school.

The boys would need to be driven to Westbrook Academy.

Jacob would be heading to Eastbridge University.

Before getting up, I lay flat on my back and stared at the ceiling high above my head—I simply could not believe my luck.

If I had woken up in my car parked on some sketchy street in downtown New York to discover all my good fortunes had been a dream, I would have been less surprised than I was right now, realizing that this beautiful room, in this beautiful house, was my new reality.

Everything was perfect. Even the bed was comfortable—which was making it hard to get up.

Last night, once Jacob had finished giving me a very basic tour of the house, I had been unable to fall asleep despite my utter exhaustion.

Partly, it was excitement about my unbelievable luck. Partly, it was being in a new and unfamiliar place. But mostly, it was because I fully expected Alexi North to come knock on my door as soon as she had finished packing for her trip.

She never did. Finally, after several hours of waiting, I couldn't fight off the sleep my body so desperately craved. Once I allowed my eyes to close, I instantly fell into a heavy, dreamless sleep. I couldn't remember stirring even once all night.

But right now, I couldn't afford to make a bad impression on my first day. I picked up my new phone and checked the time. Six-o-five. I sat up and swung my legs over the edge of the bed and onto the plush white rug.

The room was dark, thanks to the heavy silk drapes blocking the light from the windows. I crossed the bedroom and pulled one drape to the side, checking to see if the sun was even up yet. It wasn't; only the predawn light could be seen illuminating the sky above the dense forest visible from this view, but it was enough.

I gaped at what I saw before me.

It had been pitch black outside when Jacob had shown me my room last night. Now, in the early morning light, I could see the view.

I pulled the curtain all the way back to the adjoining wall and did the same on the other side. Soft gray light spilled into the room behind me as I stared out into the new life before me.

They weren't windows, I now realized, but sliding glass doors that led to a balcony off my bedroom. I flipped the latch on the handle and slid the heavy glass door open. Unlike the sliding back door in my father's house, that rattled in its frame and was frequently stuck or off its track, this one glided smooth and soundless.

This door was money.

It wasn't until I went to work for the Drakes that I was even aware of such things, largely because I had never in my life encountered luxury. But I learned quick; you could tell a feature was expensive by the quality of the details. Like this door, or the decadent waft of a fabric, the texture and finish of a table...all tell-tale signs that signaled extreme value to those who knew what to look for.

By and large, six weeks at the Drakes hadn't taught me much. I had no idea a crystal vase could cost more than most people in my hometown made in a year. But it did begin my education. At least enough to know that I probably had no idea how much money the Norths had invested in the creation of this house, on this land, and with a view as phenomenal as this.

I did know it was more money than I would ever experience in my lifetime—beyond being the hired help in their luxury worlds.

I stepped onto my balcony and felt the chill morning air ripple across my bare legs and arms. Inside my room, with the door closed, I heard nothing but silence. With it open, the sounds of the forest, birds chirping, and the breeze through the pines were like listening to nature's orchestra.

I could see where the forest ended and the perfectly trimmed lawn began. As I stepped closer to the wrought iron railing, more of the yard below me came into view.

There was concrete decking that surrounded a large rectangular pool and pool house.

In the water, Jacob North was swimming laps. His muscular and tanned body cut through the water fast and sleek. His arms propelled him with a grace and expertise I'd only ever seen when watching the Olympics. His back muscles flexed and released like a machine while his feet broke the surface like a rhythmic propeller. He alternated breaths every five strokes—I counted—and when he neared the pool wall, he never slowed as his body folded forward, flipped, turned, and launched back in the opposite direction.

Hypnotized, I watched him cross the length of the pool two more times before remembering I was supposed to be downstairs learning about the boys' morning routine and getting ready to take them to school.

I turned away, reentered my room, and leaned against the glass door once it was shut behind me. What was I doing? What was I thinking? I just got fired from my last job because Nicola only suspected something might happen between her husband and me.

Finding Jacob North even slightly attractive was the last thing I needed to be thinking about.

Because there simply wasn't anywhere for me to go if I lost this job too.

CHAPTER 12

It was now a quarter after six. I grabbed my Walmart bag off the chair in the corner of my room and tore the tags off a pair of underwear, shorts, and a t-shirt. I pulled my one and only bra from the tangle of sheets—I'd taken it off in bed last night—and threw everything on. I slipped on the rubber flip-flops I'd also bought at Walmart, only a dollar fifty, and headed for the bedroom door.

I didn't shower, brush my hair, or my teeth, but I figured there'd be a few minutes for all this before driving the kids to school.

Right now, I just needed to make an appearance. Let Doctor North, Jacob, know I was here, and I was serious about doing a good job. I assumed the first thing I would need to do was make the boys some breakfast.

I headed out my door, walked to the end of the hall, and stopped. Which direction had we come from last night? I turned right, took several steps, but didn't recognize where I was or see any stairs.

Multiple staircases led to the bottom floor, and one went directly to the kitchen...but which way was it? This house was enormous and confusing, and it would definitely take me some time to get used to.

Ten minutes later, I finally arrived in the kitchen feeling frantic. I had gotten so turned around upstairs, I half worried I would have to call Jacob and ask for directions.

Not that he could have answered his phone while working out in the pool.

Except, when I entered the kitchen and looked up, I saw Jacob. He was no longer in the pool.

He stood at the kitchen counter, still in his wet swim trunks. He'd thrown on a t-shirt that clung to his damp body. His hair looked like he'd just dried it with his towel. He pulled a mug from the espresso machine and turned to me. His blue eyes met mine as he took his first sip.

"Did you sleep okay?" he asked.

I glanced over to the kitchen table. Still in his pajamas, Daniel was slumped over a cereal bowl. When he saw me, he sat up a little straighter—he was curious about me, but there wasn't any smile.

I was not Jessica.

"I'm sorry I'm late," I said, realizing Jacob must have gotten Daniel his breakfast. "I did sleep really well. Too well. I think yesterday—"

Jacob held up his hand. "Don't worry about it. It was a long day...for everyone. And we were up earlier than usual."

I nodded and ventured another glance at Daniel. Of course,

they had said goodbye to Mrs. North this morning. How was Daniel handling his mother's departure so soon after his beloved nanny quit?

His eyes remained glued to the remnants of floating chocolate puffs in his bowl.

"Coffee?" Jacob asked. "Or something else? I'm pretty sure this machine can outperform a Starbucks. Although I admit, I don't know what half these buttons and levers do."

Suddenly conscious of my cheap t-shirt and overall disheveled look, I folded my arms over my chest. "Um, yes. Coffee…please. That would be really great."

Jacob nodded and went to work making my coffee while I stood, unsure of what to say or do. I knew it would eventually get easier. I would learn their routine, this house, and how I fit into it. But this morning, I felt like I could squirm out of my skin from the discomfort.

"Anything in it?" Jacob asked.

"Cream and sugar?"

He opened the industrial-sized fridge and added cream to my coffee. Then opened a draw, pulled out a spoon, and handed it and the mug to me. He pointed to the sugar bowl on the counter.

"Thank you," I said, and turned to add three heaping teaspoons of sugar to my cup. The heat from the mug felt comforting in my hands.

I took a sip and closed my eyes. It was the most delicious coffee I'd ever had. "This is so good," I gasped.

Jacob nodded. "It's only ever the best for Alexi."

Was it my imagination, or did I catch the faintest hint of

sarcasm in his tone? It made me wonder if everything was okay between my new employers.

The Drakes were my first intimate and behind-the-scenes view of another couple's marriage. While on the outside, they presented as a perfect, beautiful, successful, wealthy, and influential couple, six weeks of living with them taught me that not everything is what it seems.

Especially when it came to a marriage between two people with much to lose.

From down the hall, I heard a door open and close. Jacob and Daniel directed their attention behind me, and when I turned, I saw someone walking towards us.

"Garrett," Jacob said, getting his oldest son's attention.

Garrett looked up from the phone in his hands. He glanced briefly at his father before his gaze settled on me. He was tall for twelve. Solid and slightly overweight. He looked more the size of a fifteen- or sixteen-year-old but had the slumped and rounded physique of the boys who spent long hours glued to gaming monitors while eating bags and bags of potato chips and guzzling gallons of soda. His face sported a smattering of inflamed acne across his forehead and chin, while his eyes were hollow and rimmed in dark circles. Given the guarded and slightly aggressive vibe he put out, it wasn't hard to imagine why he'd had a bad day at school yesterday. And while I knew it wasn't fair, based on this first impression of him, I also imagined that whatever had happened was probably Garrett's fault.

"Is this the new one?" he asked, his tone was flat and disinterested. It was like he was asking his father if I was a new household object, like a couch or a lamp.

"Don't be rude," his father said. "And where have you been?"

"Out," Garrett shrugged. "I went for a walk."

Jacob and his son stared at each other for several seconds. I could feel the unspoken tension radiating off them but had no idea why or where it was coming from. I assumed it was most likely Garrett's way of being disappointed in Jessica quitting and his mother's abandonment—but being twelve, he couldn't dissolve into tears like Daniel had last night.

"Come and say hello to the new nanny. Her name is Libby."

Garrett raised his eyebrows in a sarcastic arch. "Hello, Libby," he drawled, then turned to leave. "I'll be in my room," he added, then disappeared around the corner.

Jacob stared after Garrett for several more seconds, and I wondered for a moment if he was going to call his son back and make him apologize or something. But instead, he let out a sigh and redirected, "Now, about today." Jacob ran both his hands through his still-wet hair. "Unfortunately, I have a packed schedule that involves teaching three classes, mentoring four doctoral candidates, and appearing at a mandatory cocktail party for a colleague who recently published his latest eight-hundred-page tome. A book he will undoubtedly only sell to the students unlucky enough to be required to take his class."

He took a long swallow from his mug and then placed it on the marble counter. "All that is to say…how do you feel about getting dropped into the deep end today?"

Still processing and trying to connect the dots on Garrett's attitude and Jacob's schedule, I nodded. "Yes. I can do whatever you need. If you could just point me—"

"Perfect," he said, finishing his coffee and placing the cup in the sink.

He then spent the next fifteen minutes giving me the cliff

notes version of an onboarding session. Along with the rapid-fire explanation about what needed to happen today, I received the address to Westbrook Academy, the keys to the car I would be driving—a white Jeep Wrangler—and a guided escort up to Daniel's room so I could help him get ready for school.

After Jacob pulled a couple school uniform pieces from the closet and tossed them onto his son's bed, he headed out of the room. "Got it?" he asked as he backed out the door and gave me an expectant smile.

"Um," I said, glancing at Daniel, who looked as stricken as I felt at the sight of his departing father. "Yes," I said. "I think so?" I took a deep breath and tried to pull myself together. "I'll figure it out," I added with a confidence that I certainly didn't feel.

"Jacob nodded once and glanced at his son. "Bye, buddy. You're in great hands, and I'll see you later tonight."

Before Daniel even had a chance to respond, Jacob was striding down the hall. "Oh," he added. "Just bang on Garrett's door when you're ready to leave." Then he disappeared around the corner and out of sight.

I stood staring at the empty hall for several seconds. I was trying to understand how both Jacob and Alexi could just dump their sons into the hands of a complete stranger when I heard a small sob beside me. When I turned and looked, I could see little Daniel, his arms hanging limp at his sides as tears ran down his face.

Obviously, he was wondering the same thing about his parents.

I knelt and took his little hands in mine. "It's going to be okay," I whispered. "I promise."

Daniel looked into my eyes. I hoped my words and body language would help to calm him down.

I watched as his expression changed. The sad downturn of his mouth hardened into a flat line as his brow furrowed deeply.

"I hate you!" he yelled as he ripped his hands from mine, ran into his bathroom, and slammed the door in my face.

CHAPTER 13

As I pulled the Jeep up to the front of Westbrook Academy, I glanced at the clock on the dash. We were almost an hour late.

Given the morning we'd had, I didn't really feel like I was at fault.

I turned off the engine and glanced at Daniel in the rearview mirror. It didn't matter what tactic I'd tried over the course of our long drive. "Want to talk about it? Do you have a favorite TV show? I bet you're amazing at video games! Do you want me to bring a special treat when I pick you up today?" Nothing had cracked Daniel's sullen disposition. He'd remained silent, staring out his window for the entire forty-five-minute drive.

While not at all friendly, Garrett had at least lifted his head from the depths of his phone every time he felt the need to criticize or correct me.

"You know, Libby, you really shouldn't be on your phone while driving," he'd said from the front seat beside me the moment I picked up my new cell to check Google Maps. "I doubt my dad would like to hear about how you don't take safety seriously," he added as he returned his attention back to his own phone.

Feeling ashamed and slightly terrified that Garrett would tell his parents, and I'd get fired, I lowered the device and placed it on the center console between us.

It was impossible to miss the self-satisfied smirk on Garrett's face.

I took a breath, gripped the steering wheel until my knuckles turned white, and focused all my attention on the road ahead. I had only been in the kid's presence for a little over an hour, and I already knew I was completely out of my depth with Garrett.

And he absolutely knew it too.

I not only needed to work to win Daniel over, but I also needed to figure out, and fast, how to establish some authority with this preteen monster.

We drove for the next thirty minutes in silence. Once we were in town, I realized I was completely lost. Since Garrett wasn't exactly offering up any hints about where the school was, I caved and picked the phone up again to check the map.

As I had feared, we'd passed the road I'd needed to turn on a mile back.

"You know, Libby, if you're not able to control yourself when it comes to your phone, it might be helpful to put it out of reach when you're in the car. That's what Jessica used to do. I mean, unless you're trying to drive us all into a ditch on your very first day."

I sighed and put the phone back down, but I could hear

Daniel crying again in the backseat. When I glanced in the rearview mirror, his eyes met mine. "I want Jessica," he sobbed.

"She's gone," Garrett said matter of fact. "So, you might as well stop crying about it like a baby."

Which, predictably, only made Daniel cry harder.

I didn't know what to say about any of this. So I didn't say anything and my silence was me losing ground with both of them. Ten minutes later, we'd reached the school—an hour late.

Garrett was unbuckled and out of the Jeep the moment the tires stopped moving. He didn't say a word to me—not goodbye, see you later, or even go to hell. He just left, and I watched him go as a sense of fear took root in my gut. I had no idea how to be a nanny to a kid like him.

I turned my attention to Daniel in the backseat. "Ready?" I asked.

And, also without a word to me, he unbuckled his booster seat, grabbed his backpack off the seat beside him, and opened his door.

"Do you need help?" I asked, rushing to get out of the car before him. By the time I made it to his side of the vehicle, he was already halfway up the brick walkway to the school's front door.

Since we were so late, the front door was locked, which slowed them down at least. They waited, staring straight ahead while I pushed the intercom button and waited for us to be buzzed in.

"May I help you?" a woman's voice came over the speaker.

I leaned in. "Hello, yes. I'm dropping off Garrett and Daniel North."

"Oh yes, their father called. You must be the new nanny."

A moment later, the door clicked, and before I could reach for the handle, Garrett grasped it and pulled. He shoved his little brother through a crack in the door and quickly followed. Before I could grab the handle, Garrett had the door shut behind him.

On the other side of the again locked glass door, I saw them walk up the long hallway. When they reached the first cross hall, Garrett grabbed Daniel's backpack and pulled him close enough to say something in his ear. He let him go a moment later, and they parted ways, heading opposite directions.

I was in a war, and I'd just lost this battle. I shook my head and buzzed the office again.

"May I help you?" the woman asked again.

"Um, yes. Sorry, but the kids slipped through the door before—"

"Oh yes, we saw them and marked them present. Although they are tardy," she chastised. "School does begin at eight o'clock."

"Yes, I know…I'm sorry." Why was I sorry? It was their fault we were late. Actually, it was probably the entire North Family's fault they were late. It certainly wasn't my fault Daniel was upset or that Garrett was acting like a jerk. I was just the one stuck dealing with the emotional fallout their parents had inflicted.

"Yes, well," the woman continued. "Pickup is at three-thirty. Please be on time."

I nodded at the speaker. "I will. And again, I'm sorry."

More apologizing! It was a bad habit, born from anxiety, that reared its head whenever I was in a stressful situation. I had even apologized to Nicola Drake as she was firing me for something that wasn't even remotely my fault.

God. I needed to work on being more assertive and less of a doormat.

I fished the keys to the Jeep out of my pocket and used the fob to unlock the door. It was just after nine o'clock. It would take me forty-five minutes to drive back to the North's house, and then I would need to leave again by two forty-five to be back at the school on time to pick them up.

As much as I relished the idea of getting back to the house to have a moment to myself, settle in, and familiarize myself with my new home, there were also some things I needed to take care of in town.

The most important thing was depositing my last check from the Drakes into my bank account so that the payment to Dad's in-home care nurse didn't bounce. It would also be nice to check the town out and get the lay of the land.

The North's house, tucked away in the depths of their forest, was so far from civilization, I worried I might get completely swallowed up into that sequestered life if I didn't make an effort to learn about what was outside of it.

I again wondered about Jessica. I assumed she was young, like me. Had she felt alone? Isolated? Maybe she had friends. People she knew from town. Or had she felt trapped in that huge, beautiful house? It was certainly an idyllic and luxurious home, but I couldn't honestly imagine living out there for as long as she had. I wouldn't be surprised if that was why, after six years, she had finally left the Norths.

I would never know what motivated Jessica to leave, but I didn't plan on staying here for more than a year. I had plans—

things I wanted to accomplish, places I wanted to travel. I was too young, and life was too short, to get shackled to a family that chose to live like hermits.

Never mind how gorgeous the house and surroundings were. If New York was too busy and too much, then the North's home presented a polar opposite problem. It was far too isolated for me.

I shifted the Jeep into drive and pulled away from the school, confident that, one day, I'd find my happy middle ground.

CHAPTER 14

The town was like somewhere out of a Hallmark movie. Main Street consisted of five blocks flanked by brick, two-story buildings that housed several small businesses. There were cafes and restaurants with outside seating, a bookstore, a toy store, numerous clothing boutiques, a bakery, a sandwich shop, a candle and soap shop, and even a store that sold specialty pet supplies.

It seemed busy for nine o'clock in the morning. People sat at tables, sipping coffee and eating croissants while their dogs slept in the sun or begged for leftovers beside them. In New York, people swarmed the street in the mornings on their way to high-rise offices. Here, people strolled, shopped, and generally left me with the impression that they were either retired or independently wealthy enough to not bother working.

At least not at a typical nine-to-five, I realized.

I pulled the Jeep into an open parking space on the second block, turned off the ignition, and flipped down the visor.

"Oh my god," I said as soon as I saw myself in the mirror. It was only then I realized, in my rush to get Daniel ready amid his resistance and silence, that I had neglected to even brush my hair before leaving the house.

I pulled my brush from the depths of my ratty backpack and attempted to at least tame my wild appearance. I piled all my hair up into a messy bun on my head and secured it with the hair tie wrapped around the brush handle.

I sighed at my reflection and flipped the visor shut in disgust. It was the best I could do under the circumstances.

I slammed the Jeep door, swung my bag over my shoulder, and headed for the nearest coffee shop. I wanted to check and see if my bank had a branch in this town, but I needed more caffeine first.

The carved oval wooden sign hanging out front read: The Coffee Klatch. I was about to enter when I noticed a guy halfway down the block. He was stopped right in the middle of the sidewalk—staring at me.

He was rail thin with a gaunt, haunted look. His hair hung, overgrown and limp, down the sides of his face. A scraggly, short beard hid his mouth and chin. But I noticed his eyes the most, two bright, crystal blue marbles. They were sharp and seemed to pierce me with the intensity of his gaze. When he saw me staring back, he looked away quickly, shoved his hands deep into the ripped pocket of his threadbare hoodie, and made an abrupt right turn to cross in the middle of the street.

It wasn't a big deal; he was probably homeless or an addict high on something. Still, he gave me a weird vibe. When he was halfway across the street, he glanced at the Jeep I was driving, then back at me once more before he picked up his pace and began to jog. He headed up the opposite side of the street.

Seeing the Jeep and me getting out of it, did he think I had money? Had he been just about to mug me or something? Possibly, but as I watched him hurry away, I realized his expression had been more surprised than anything else. Like maybe he had recognized the Jeep and was confused when he saw me driving it.

Did he know Jessica? Had he been expecting to see her, not me, getting out of it? And if so, did he not know Jessica had quit her position with the Norths and moved away?

I looked back up the street and tried to get another look at him, but he had disappeared amongst all the other people coming in and out of the shops and restaurants.

I pushed through the cafe door and was greeted by the rich scent of freshly brewed coffee and the warm, sugary aroma of hot baked goods.

I got in line behind two elderly ladies scanning and discussing the chalkboard menu hung high on the wall behind the counter.

If I saw that guy again, maybe I would try to speak with him. If he was Jessica's friend, he'd probably like to know about her leaving the nanny position with the Norths.

Then again, if Jessica was his friend, why wouldn't she have told him herself? He was super sketchy-looking, and it was hard to imagine that someone who had worked for the Norths would be friends with a guy who looked like he probably spent most of his nights looking for his next fix.

It seemed more likely that if he was someone Jessica knew,

she had likely left without telling him because she didn't want him to know her plans.

While I waited for the women to place their orders, I turned and stared back out the glass doors.

Maybe that guy was the reason Jessica left.

CHAPTER 15

"Heeelllllo?" someone said behind me.

I turned to the counter and saw that the two elderly ladies had finished ordering. The barista was waiting on me with an undeniably annoyed expression.

"Oh, I'm sorry," I said as I pushed up to the counter. It seemed that even in the middle of nowhere New Hampshire, I irritated baristas. "Um," I said, only now really looking at the menu. I'd been so distracted with my thoughts about the guy and Jessica that I hadn't decided what to order. "I'll just take a vanilla latte."

"What size?" the girl asked me, her voice seething with impatience.

"Right, sorry…um, medium. No, make it a large, please."

The girl sighed loudly. "One large vanilla latte. Coming right up."

I moved over to the end of the counter, where the other two ladies were also waiting for their orders, and watched as the barista pulled levers, steamed milk, and poured all three drinks. The women paid for their drinks and left the shop, so deep in conversation the whole time that they didn't seem to notice the barista's angry glare.

But I felt bad. I always hated feeling like I was the reason someone was upset—even though I knew I hadn't done anything all that wrong. Why were coffee shops always so rushed and fast-paced, even when they weren't busy?

The girl behind the counter looked like she was having the worst day of her life. When she called me over, "Large latte," her voice flat and all business, I stepped up to the counter and tapped my debit card to the terminal.

"I'm sorry," I said as I pushed the twenty percent tip button.

Her head snapped up, and she looked at me with a confused expression. "For what?" she asked.

"Earlier, ordering, taking too long. I wasn't paying attention. I know it's annoying when customers do that. I used to work at a McDonalds in high school." I shrugged. "So, sorry."

Now, her facial expression completely changed as her shoulders sagged. "Oh god, I was being a bitch. I'm sorry." She shook her head and handed me my drink. "It's been a crappy day," she continued. "Actually, strike that. This whole week has been complete shit," she finished in a whisper, even though we were the only two people in the building. "So, if I bit your head off earlier…I'm really sorry. God was I also being bitchy to those two?" she nodded her head in the direction of the plate glass windows where I could see the other two women had taken up one of the patio tables out front.

I shook my head. "Honestly, I'm not sure. But they were so busy talking I don't think they would have noticed anyway."

The barista let out another huge sigh. "I hope so. Because if they complain to Trisha, she's going to be pissed. She's already told me off once this week for having a shit attitude."

She didn't say, but I assumed Trisha was the owner or manager.

"I'm Kyra, by the way," she said as she reached below the counter and grabbed a metal water bottle covered in vinyl stickers.

"Libby," I replied.

"Are you visiting or new in town? Because I know I haven't seen you around before."

"Um, new, I guess. I just started a nanny position."

"Shit!" Kyra said, making her way to the end of the counter and over to my side. "Are you the new North nanny?"

Her question took me by surprise. "Yes," I blurted while my mind cartwheeled through the potential reasons Kyra may know this. "How did you know?"

Kyra waved me over to one of the tables and took a seat. "It's past the morning rush, technically my break time anyway. Come sit down," she ordered with authority, which made me realize Kyra was one of those girls who was used to having others listen to her and do what she asked.

I sat in the seat opposite her and held my scalding hot coffee cup between both my hands. She flipped open her water bottle and took a long pull from the built-in straw before gazing back at me. "I knew their last nanny," she said.

"Jessica," I stated.

"Yes. She came here practically every morning after dropping off the kids."

"Garrett and Daniel," I said.

Kyra gave me a confused look. "That's their names? Huh. Anyway." She waved her hand before her face, like pushing aside irrelevant information. "Like I said, she came in here every day and then last week." She lifted both her hands and popped her fingers open like an explosion. "Poof! She's just gone."

"Yes," I said. "She quit."

Kyra leaned in conspiratorially. "That's what they say." She raised her eyebrows.

I sat back a few inches. "Wait…what do you mean?" I thought about the weird guy I'd seen out front. "You were her friend. Did she tell you something else? Was something wrong?" I thought about how devastated the North family would likely be if something bad had happened to Jessica.

Kyra shook her head. "I mean…yeah, I knew her." She shrugged. "But I didn't know-know her. You know?"

I didn't. "You were friends?"

"Well, not exactly friends. We would chat a bit when she came in. But Jessica mostly kept to herself. Trisha thought she was a stuck-up bitch. But that was only because she was so ridiculously gorgeous. I never could understand why she had tied herself to some family that wasn't even hers in the middle of nowhere New Hampshire when she obviously could have been a model or something in New York or Hollywood. It just seemed like such a waste to me." Kyra shrugged. "But I didn't *necessarily* think she was a bitch. She was usually nice to me. And she tipped really well, too. I did think maybe she was a little lonely. I mean, you'd have to be, right? Out there at that house all alone, day in and day out. I mean, there's nothing out there. Literally. Sometimes, I wondered if I was the only other person she spoke to every day other than the kids and their parents."

I took a sip from my latte. So, Kyra wasn't really Jessica's friend. It sounded more like she was an acquaintance. "But, if she didn't say anything to you, there must be a reason you think she didn't just quit."

Kyra nodded. "Well, she never said anything, and I never said anything, but everyone in town knew she was fucking around with a married man."

CHAPTER 16

The shock of Kyra's announcement hit me like a blunt instrument. For several seconds, all I could do was stare at her, numb and silent, not knowing what I should say. Thankfully, Kyra continued without needing any response from me at all.

"I mean, that was the rumor anyway. But honestly, who knows what's true. Some people think she ran off with him."

"Who was the married guy?" I asked, wondering about the guy I'd seen out front. Although, he didn't really seem type.

Kyra leaned in. She was in full gossip mode. "That's the thing. No one really knew. Several dads at the elementary school were suspects. Trisha is certain it was the fourth-grade teacher, Mr. Evans, who quit one week before Jessica left. But it's all conjecture if you ask me.

"Earlier, when I was coming in, there was a guy out front. He seemed surprised when he saw me getting out of the North's Jeep. It was like he was expecting to see Jessica."

"What did he look like?"

"White, tall and thin, but with these crazy blue eyes. But honestly? Kinda homeless."

Kyra shook her head. "He doesn't sound familiar. But I do think Jessica once mentioned to me that she volunteered at the shelter. So probably it was someone from there that knew her. She's one of those girls that people, especially guys, just sorta fall in love with."

Remembering what she'd told me about her boss's feelings about Jessica, I said, "Except Trisha, of course."

Kyra snorted and water shot out of her mouth as she laughed. "Yes, definitely *not* Trisha. Or probably any of the other women who had to deal with the rumors of their husband being the one that was sleeping with Jessica."

I opened my mouth to ask her why there were so many rumors about Jessica but was interrupted by the sound of the bell hanging over the cafe door. When four new customers entered, Kyra stood up.

"Breaks over, I guess. But hey, welcome to town. And if you ever want to hang out or anything, just let me know. I can show you around and introduce you to some of my friends."

"Thanks," I said as I stood up myself and headed for the door and the Jeep parked outside. "I will."

I WAS in line at the bank when I realized two things. One, Kyra hadn't given me her cell number. So, if I was going to get in touch, I would have to either go back to the cafe or call her there. And two, I never got an answer as to why there had been so many nasty rumors about Jessica. Kyra had made it seem like Jessica was one of those people you just couldn't help but love.

Certainly, Daniel did. So much so that I worried I wasn't ever going to be able to measure up in his eyes.

And yet, there was also a faction of people that disliked her enough to spread toxic gossip about her. They mistrusted her enough to feel like she was the kind of woman that was a threat. The kind that ran around sleeping with husbands.

I deposited my last check from the Drakes, got back in the Jeep, and headed back to the house. I watched the town recede and the dense forest rise up, trees flying past the windows in a deep green blur.

I didn't know Jessica, but I did know what it felt like to be an outsider. To be accused of something you not only didn't do but would never do. If she was as beautiful as Kyra described, it was easy enough to believe that there was probably some degree of ill will toward her simply born of jealousy. I would reserve my own judgement until I was presented with something bad enough, and credible enough, to change my mind.

I had just lost a great job simply because another woman believed her husband was attracted to me. It was entirely possible that Jessica had felt driven out of this town by the gossip alone.

I pulled the Jeep onto the expansive driveway on the side of the house. Jacob's truck was gone. He said he would be at work for most of the day and evening and, depending on how soon he could escape the faculty cocktail party, to not expect him before nine tonight.

Which meant, I had the whole house to myself until it was time to go pick the kids up.

CHAPTER 17

From the little I'd already seen of it, the house, when taken room by room, was both opulent and warm. Its smaller parts were inviting and luxurious. But overall, it was confusing and made me feel like I was trying and failing to navigate a complex maze of hallways, rooms that led to other rooms, and dead ends that seemed incongruous.

Who on earth had designed this house? I couldn't even begin to imagine builders trying to follow the blueprints.

For my first hour alone, I treated myself to more coffee from the North's De'Longhi espresso machine. The steel monolith, with its multitude of buttons and levers, would have intimidated me six weeks ago. Thankfully, the Drakes owned this exact same machine, and Damion had been kind enough to teach me how to use it the morning he found me looking lost in front of it.

Damion had always been kind to me. From the day he hired

me to the day Nicola fired me. I couldn't help but wonder what he had said and maybe felt when he learned about what Nicola had done.

What reason had she given him, I wondered. Had she also shared with him the video of us together in the kitchen? Or, more likely, made up some lie about me?

I shook my head; it didn't matter anymore. That was my past. This place, and the North family, was my future. And given my precarious circumstances just yesterday, I was unbelievably lucky to be here.

I opened the fridge, added cream to my coffee, and helped myself to one of the raspberry Danishes that looked like they had come from a local bakery.

My goals this morning were simple. I wanted to figure out how to navigate this house, and explore some of the grounds. One of the things I was most excited about was that I had immediate access to fresh air and nature just out the backdoor. If my six weeks in New York had taught me anything, it was that I was not meant for city life. The miles of concrete and view-altering skyscrapers had left me longing for the open sky and the sights and sounds of country life. The constant sound of human activity that never stopped in New York had weighed on my nerves and left me in a state of continual anxiety. The city I had grown up dreaming of ended up leaving me overwhelmed and oppressed.

With my plated Danish and coffee in hand, I wandered the first floor of the Norths' home. There was the kitchen and foyer I had seen last night, and I managed to locate all three staircases leading to the second floor. There was also a spacious sunken living room with the largest sectional I had ever seen. I could imagine as many as fifteen people lounging comfortably across its cream leather as they watched a movie or a sports game on the massive television mounted to the wall.

Which made me wonder if the Norths entertained many people out here. The house certainly seemed set up for it, with a bar cabinet and wet bar tucked against the far wall, sumptuous seating, pillows and throws, a huge television—and that was just this room. The dining room had a solid mahogany table with sixteen chairs. The kitchen was equipped with all the best appliances and enough workspace and room for a catering crew.

And then, there was the pool.

I stood outside on the stamped and stained concrete patio and surveyed the pool, pool house, fifteen lounge chairs, and the five canopy umbrellas that surrounded it.

To my right, the patio continued toward the lawn to a separate covered, entertaining space. The latticed portico was entangled with lush green vines that were currently in bloom with bright orange flowers I didn't recognize. From where I stood, I could see there was a built-in grill attached to a granite counter with a smaller fridge underneath. There was enough space for a long outdoor table with ten chairs and another shaded seating area with an outdoor couch and chairs. There weren't currently any cushions on, but I assumed they were stored in the pool house.

With a home like this, it was clear the Norths must do a lot of entertaining. Maybe Jessica's life hadn't been as isolated as I imagined.

Which meant mine wouldn't be as isolated as I feared.

The thought brought a smile to my face. I envisioned myself lying on a pool lounger in the sun, sipping a fruity cocktail, while parties of people came and went, eating, drinking, laughing, and dancing.

And I was getting paid to be here.

The job, which had yesterday felt only like a timely life preserver, was turning out to be the opportunity of my lifetime. Suddenly, I completely understood why Jessica had stayed with the Norths for six long years.

But, given all the perks, I was now more curious than ever about why she would leave all this behind. It made me wonder if there wasn't some truth to what Kyra had told me. Because if she didn't leave this place for love…then what?

Maybe I could try to find a way to tactfully ask Jacob. I should have thought to ask during the interview.

Movement in the distance caught my attention. I looked up. Across the expansive yard, at the very edge where the professionally manicured lawn met with the forest's wild and shady tangle of trees, a deer stood, head lowered, eating grass. I froze, but she seemed to sense my stare because she stopped eating and raised her head to stare back at me. I held my breath, awed by the sight of her and hoping my presence wouldn't scare her off.

We stood still, gazing at each other for several seconds. I felt like we were casting some spell of connection between us. I half wondered if she would allow me to come closer if I tried to approach.

Then, as if she could intuit my thought, she leaped away, back into the shadows and safety of the dark forest.

The woods were probably teaming with wildlife, and the

thought made me smile. I realized I was grateful for the accessibility to the natural world that surrounded my new home. I looked forward to exploring the wooded acres and knew I would spend at least some of every day taking long walks through the woods.

But not today.

Back inside, I closed the heavy sliding glass door behind me. There was one more room on this floor I hadn't yet explored.

Double doors were closed at the end of a long hallway to the right of the foyer. I was expecting maybe a main-floor master bedroom, so when I opened them, I was so surprised I gasped.

It was a library.

The ceilings were very high, at least thirty feet or more. I could tell that the library was composed of what would be the first and second floors in the rest of the house. Every wall was filled with books, top to bottom. Halfway up, a wooden catwalk allowed you to walk around the second level and browse the shelves.

I stood, shocked and staring. It was like something out of a British period show. I walked into the room, spinning slowly so that I could take it all in. Near the far wall, there was an enormous mahogany desk. It was piled with papers, folders, and stacks of books. There was also a large silver computer monitor and a sleek, low-profile keyboard.

The wood floors were covered with decorative rugs. Upholstered chairs and small sofas were tastefully clustered into seating groups around the room.

The only part of the walls not filled with books was the large stone fireplace opposite the desk.

Behind the desk, one shelf held several framed documents.

When I was close enough, I could see that they were Jacob's framed degrees: a Bachelor of Arts in literature from New York University and his Ph.D. in literature and creative writing from Duke University.

I inspected the desk more thoroughly and realized this wasn't only a library. It was also Jacob's office. I knew he was a professor of literature at Eastbridge Universtiy, but had he actually read all these books?

I liked to read and had been excited to see such a large collection. But as I scanned a few of the titles, I realized that what I usually enjoyed reading was definitely not the type of books Jacob had on these shelves.

A History of Midcentury Spanish Authors

Collected Poems of W.B. Yeats

Studies in Classic American Literature

It wasn't surprising, but it was slightly disappointing. I wondered what Jacob would think of me if he found me lounging next to his pool with the latest paperback by Colleen Hoover. Because I would bet a million dollars there wasn't a single copy of any of her books within a mile of this house.

Except for the one in my backpack, of course.

I gazed up at all the collective knowledge around me. Maybe it was time to expand my horizons. I had always wanted to go to college. But with the death of my mother and then my father's illness, even the idea of it had always been a ridiculous, out-of-reach pipe dream. There wasn't any money for me to go to college, and since I had to work full time to support my father now, there wasn't any time either.

People like the Norths and the Drakes were successful and

well-educated, but they had probably also always been well-supported by other successful and well-educated people.

It was hard to see how and where to start on a path to a better life from nowhere and no one. I'd never had anyone in my life that could even point me in a direction.

Now, I would be living with a university professor—maybe there were some opportunities I'd never considered?

CHAPTER 18

Even though I now felt like I had a better sense of direction on the first floor, it still took me five minutes and several wrong turns to return to my bedroom.

One of my wrong turns was down the hallway that led to Alexi's office.

I recognized it from last night. Gazing down the dark hallway to see the light through the cracked door and Alexi passing behind it.

Only today, the door was closed.

Without really knowing why, I found myself heading down the hallway anyway. I was curious, I suppose. Having seen her husband's elaborate office space, I wondered what Alexi's looked like.

His work was books.

And hers was film.

His space housed the most impressive private library I would probably ever see in my whole life.

What wonders would Alexi's hold? A high-tech film studio? A plush private theater? Since hers was already on the second floor, I suspected it was not as grand as Jacob's. There simply couldn't be the space for it.

Feeling nervous, I reached for the door handle. I had started out simply exploring my new place of work, but this definitely felt more like snooping. Was I wrong to poke around in Jacob and Alexi's personal spaces? Stumbling into Jacob's library was an honest mistake.

What I was doing right now, this was intentional.

I hadn't even met the woman yet. I had no sense of how she might feel about me looking into her world.

I should turn around and wait until she was home and invited me in.

My hand turned the handle anyway. Excessive curiosity had always been a personal weakness of mine.

It moved a fraction of an inch and stopped. I tried the other direction and was also stopped.

It was locked.

I bent low, looked at the handle, and saw a keyhole.

Maybe the key was somewhere in the house, but that was definitely going too far. Alexi had locked the door for a reason. She obviously didn't want anyone, including the nosy new nanny, going into her office when she wasn't around.

"Message received, Alexi," I whispered and turned around to leave. I was just about to turn the corner at the end of the hall when I heard a loud thump behind me.

I froze. The unexpected sound from an empty room ignited a glimmer of fear in my gut. I turned and faced the door again, watching it carefully for any sign of movement—anything that would indicate I wasn't alone.

Jacob was at work. The boys at school. And Alexi...where was Alexi? I realized at that moment that I didn't actually have any idea where she was.

Jacob had explained she was leaving on a trip for work. But where? Shouldn't I know? What if there was an emergency with the kids, and I couldn't reach Jacob?

The handle didn't turn, and no other sound came. So, I walked back, slow and hesitant, to the door. There was likely some logical explanation, I reasoned. When I reached the door again, I placed my palms flat against its surface and pressed my ear against the cool wood.

At first, I didn't hear anything. Or so I thought. I listened harder, closed my eyes, and focused on anything that might be amiss in the room. I hadn't imagined the sound; I was sure of it. It was loud—a heavy thud.

There weren't any more thumps, but I could make out a soft, electrical hum. Like a machine was running in there. I pulled my head away from the door and tried the handle again—still locked.

I walked away, glancing back every few feet. A new feeling settled over me like an expectation. As if I might turn my head and suddenly find that not only was the door now open, but there would also be someone, or something, peering out at me from the crack in the door.

"Ridiculous," I whispered to myself. But the declaration brought me no comfort. When I reached the end of the hall, I stopped and waited to see if maybe the sound would happen again.

After a full minute of silence had passed and my overactive nervous system had nearly returned to normal, more logical thoughts prevailed.

It had mostly likely been a precariously balanced book tumbling from a shelf. Or even a framed picture falling off the wall. Heck, these were things that I had seen happen before. Once, I had used only a thin nail to hang a framed family picture on the wall of our apartment back home. After a week, the picture's weight had finally proven too much for the nail, and the whole thing had come crashing to the floor. Shards of the broken glass had damaged the photo and left a deep gouge right across my mother's face.

I was six in the picture, and we were all dressed in our best Christmas clothes. My mother had made an appointment for us to have a professional family photo taken. We had gotten up at five in the morning to get ready and then driven two hours to the JC Penny in Omaha for our appointment at the portrait studio. It was the last photo taken of us all together before my mom died.

She could only afford one copy of the eight-by-twelve-sized photo, and I had been sick for weeks over the damage. My mother's face was ruined because I'd been careless.

It was the last picture she'd ever taken.

I turned in what I thought was the direction of my bedroom and sighed at my own stupidity. The sound was nothing. I was simply tired and overwhelmed by the sheer amount of change I'd undergone in the last twenty-four hours.

What I needed, more than anything, was rest.

When I finally figured out the way to my room, I crawled into the sumptuous bed, rolled onto my side, and hugged one of the soft pillows to my chest. This bed felt too good to be true. Like the best dream I'd ever had.

A nap. That's what would be perfect right now. To just close my eyes and drift off for twenty or thirty minutes. I hadn't realized how exhausted I was until just now. I allowed my muscles to relax, my eyes to close, my body to sink deeper and deeper and deeper...

* * *

"LIBBY?" someone's voice called to me from far away.

"Libby? Wake up." A hand rocked my shoulder roughly. I opened my eyes to a blurry image. I didn't know where I was. The room was gray from a fading light streaming through two giant windows.

A man was standing over me.

"Libby. You forgot to pick up Garrett and Daniel."

As understanding broke through my sleepy fog, adrenaline shot hot and fast through my system. I sat bolt upright. "Oh my God," I said as I looked into Jacob North's concerned expression. Beside him, Daniel stood glaring at me with hatred in his eyes and tears running down his face.

"Jessica never forgot us!" he screamed, then turned and ran from the room.

CHAPTER 19

I took small bites of the cheeseburgers and french fries that Jacob had bought at a fast-food drive-thru in town after he'd picked the boys up at school.

Two hours after the kids were released for the day.

When no one arrived to collect them after school, the woman at the front desk called Jacob and Alexi. Alexi hadn't picked up her phone, and Jacob was in the middle of teaching a class. Once he checked his messages thirty minutes later, he immediately drove the hour and a half from his campus to the boys' school—Garrett was annoyed and surly, but Daniel was distraught and sobbing.

"I tried calling the cell," Jacob explained. "When you didn't answer, I panicked and worried something had happened."

I didn't know it, but the ringer on my new cell had been set to silent. So, while Jacob had called me numerous times, I had continued, unbothered and dead asleep in my new luxurious bed.

"I'm so, so sorry," I whispered for what must have been the tenth time. It was now me who felt like crying, and I wasn't sure I could stop the rising tide of tears in my throat. The guilt and shame I felt—how could I have possibly let this happen, and on my very first day.

Jacob let out a sigh. "Like I said, it's okay. It was an honest mistake, especially considering how exhausted you probably are after uprooting your entire life and transitioning into this as quickly as you did."

The fact that he was being so nice about the whole thing only made me feel worse. If this had happened back in New York, Nicola would have spent at least an hour lecturing me while I stood hanging my head in her office. I couldn't help it; several tears rolled down my cheeks, off my chin, and landed on the greasy paper wrapper of my mostly untouched burger.

"Don't cry," Daniel whispered.

When I glanced at him, I saw he, too, was staring down at his uneaten meal. I doubted that he had completely forgiven me, both for forgetting him and for not being his beloved Jessica. Still, at least he didn't seem quite as angry.

"I'll try," I whispered back, and the barest hint of a smile lifted one corner of his mouth. He reached for one of his chicken nuggets and finally took a bite.

"See," Jacob said as he finished his food and crumpled the wrapper into a tight ball. "Everything is fine. Plus, this was the perfect excuse to escape suffering through Professor Thatcher's congratulations cocktail party. I should be thanking all of you," he finished as he attempted a hook shot with his garbage that missed the trash can on the other side of the kitchen by about ten feet.

"You missed Dad!" Daniel laughed.

Jacob swiped a dismissive hand in the direction of the garbage. "I wasn't half trying. If I wanted to, I could make that shot with my eyes closed."

Daniel smiled and shook his head. "You never make it," he said and stuffed another nugget into his mouth.

"Dude!" Jacob faked offense. "You don't need to tell Libby that. You're making me look bad."

And just like that, Jacob had shifted the whole mood of the evening in a few minutes—well, almost. Garrett still sat slumped in his seat, silent and uncommunicative. He stuffed the last bite of his burger into his mouth and was up and out of his seat with his own garbage in one swift movement. He placed it in the can and left the room without uttering a sound.

He was clearly very pissed off with me, and I would definitely need to find a way to make it up to Garrett. But I was grateful to see both Jacob and Daniel smiling. I resisted the urge to provide more assurances that what happened today would never happen again.

Words were cheap. It would be better to prove my reliability by just doing my job and doing it well.

"Can we call mom?" Daniel asked. "To say goodnight."

"Sure," Jacob said as he cleared the empty soda cups from the table. "I mean, we can try anyway. She did tell me that her cell service isn't that great where she's staying."

"She makes movies," Daniel turned to me and explained.

I nodded. "Your dad told me they are documentaries." Suddenly realizing how little I knew about Alexi, I turned to Jacob, who was washing a plate in the kitchen sink. "What is her movie about?"

Jacob's hands stopped moving. He opened his mouth as if to speak, then closed it again. Even in profile, I could see the shadow of concern cross his features. He glanced at his son, who was too busy dipping fries in ketchup, to see that something was distressing his father.

"Yeah...how about we chat a little later?" Jacob said as his gaze shifted to me.

"Um, yeah. Sure." I shrugged. I hadn't thought my question was a big deal, but based on his reaction, it clearly was. I couldn't imagine why, but whatever Alexi was working on was clearly a secret from Daniel.

Did she film porn or something? Which was a totally weird thought, but also, honestly, it was the first taboo topic that popped into my head. As far as I was aware, Alexi was a respected documentary filmmaker—maybe it was a documentary film about the porn industry?

I was pretty sure I'd seen something like that advertised on Netflix once.

Whatever it was, Jacob's dodgy response definitely piqued my curiosity about Alexi and her work even further.

Once we had all finished eating, I followed Jacob and Daniel upstairs and hung back as Jacob moved Daniel through his bedtime routine. Bath, teeth, pajamas, and apparently, they usually read a book or two, but tonight, they were going to call Alexi together. Jacob said it would be early morning where she was—somewhere in Europe. "So don't be disappointed if she doesn't answer. Mom works long hours when she's on location and gets tired, so she might still be sleeping."

Daniel nodded while his father pulled out his cell.

"Goodnight," I said and backed out of the room to give them some privacy.

Jacob raised his hand as he listened to his phone. I was surprised when Daniel looked at me and said, "Goodnight, Libby."

Was it possible that, despite my colossal screw-up today, Daniel was beginning to come around? I realized it was most likely because he'd seen me crying at dinner, but whatever. I'd take it.

"I'll see you in the morning," I said and closed the door as they continued to wait for Alexi to pick up on the other end of the call.

I headed down the hall to my own room. When I passed Garrett's closed door, I paused and considered knocking. I could let him know that his dad and Daniel were calling Alexi—surely, he would want to speak with his mom, too. I raised my fist to knock but stopped when I heard Garrett's voice on the other side.

"You idiot!" he screamed. "I said, circle around to the north, you fucking idiot! You missed the pistol! You missed it!"

I lowered my hand and listened to the stream of profanity Garrett was screaming for several more seconds before I realized what was happening.

He was gaming, obviously. What was less obvious was how Jacob and Alexi felt about his language while gaming and whether I should or would be expected to do anything about it. For half a second, I considered going in and saying something to him. Then I realized, given his cursing dexterity, this was unlikely to be the first time or a rarity.

I had already gotten off on the wrong foot with Garrett.

Reprimanding a middle school boy about his language would likely earn me even less respect and an eye roll. I decided to ask Jacob about it and how he'd like me to handle it in the morning.

I backed away from his door and headed down the hall to my own room. Since I had already slept away most of the day, I was nowhere near tired enough to go to bed myself.

I grabbed my backpack off the floor next to the bed and carried it into the sitting area of my room. I fell back into the plush couch and placed the chenille throw over my bare legs as I pulled my laptop from the bag.

Once it was open and connected to the Norths' WIFI, I typed "Alexi North documentary filmmaker" into the search bar and hit enter.

As the first page of results loaded onto my screen, I immediately knew why Jacob hadn't wanted to discuss Alexi's new film in front of Daniel.

Whatever it was that I imagined the woman was into, it certainly was not this.

CHAPTER 20

The first picture I clicked was of Alexi standing with her crew on stage as she accepted an Academy Award for Best Documentary Feature Film. The women all around her were draped in designer dresses. Alexi wore a blue tuxedo jacket without a shirt. The jacket's opening cut low between the swell of her small but perfect breasts. The matching pants accentuated her long legs and stopped just above her black stilettos.

She looked stunning and powerful, like she could just as easily be starring in films as creating them. She was so glamorous; Alexi looked like she lived in the Hollywood Hills, not the middle of the woods. As beautiful and elegant as this home was, it was difficult to picture this version of Alexi living here.

And yet, this wasn't what surprised me the most.

It was the subject matter of her film. Or rather, films plural, because it wasn't only the film she had won the Academy Award for five years ago. It was the fact that Alexi had, according to her Wikipedia page, created and filmed fourteen films. And every single one of them was centered on the same subject.

Serial killers.

Apparently, each of her films focused on a different killer.

That was why Jacob didn't want to discuss Alexi's current film with me in front of Daniel. How do you explain to a six-year-old, not only what a serial killer is, but also why it is your mom is making a film about them?

Fourteen films.

A knock at my door startled me and made me jump.

"Libby? "Jacob asked on the other side of my closed door.

Feeling guilty that I had just been searching for Alexi online, I snapped my laptop shut. "Just a second. "

As I went to open the door, I couldn't help but wonder if Jacob was now rethinking his previous good-natured response to my mistake today. It was possible he hadn't wanted to reprimand me in front of Garrett or Daniel—who was clearly already upset because I forgot him.

As I opened the door, I braced myself to gracefully accept whatever lecture I may be about to receive.

Jacob stood there with one hand resting against the door frame. If he was here to give me a talking-to, his body language certainly didn't show it. If anything, he looked sheepish and somewhat embarrassed to be standing there.

"I hope I didn't wake you," he said.

"No, I was just about to get ready for bed." I pulled the door open wider and stepped away from it, allowing space for him to come in if he wanted.

He looked past me into the room behind me and seemed to be thinking about coming inside. He then leaned back as if thinking better of it. "Since Daniel's in bed now, I thought I'd stop by and answer the question you asked at dinner. Sorry if my response was strange, but we don't talk about Alexi's work in front of the kids. I guess we've never really figured out how to explain it all to them."

He had no idea that I had just basically answered the question for myself by stalking his wife online—and I certainly wasn't about to admit it.

"The topics of Alexi's documentaries… they're a little unorthodox, I guess." He ran a nervous hand through his disheveled hair. I got the impression he was anxious about confessing to me what her films were about. Maybe he feared it would scare me off, and he'd be left high and dry again without a nanny.

"I probably should've told you this earlier, and I hope it doesn't freak you out. Although I'm sure it might freak you out a little."

His eyes met mine, and I found myself again considering just how handsome Jacob North was. The pictures I'd seen of Alexi made me think she was glamorous, beautiful, and powerful in the Hollywood way. But Jacob North had that rugged, outdoorsy, and yet still intellectual vibe. He had changed out of the sports coat and oxford shirt that he'd worn to work and was once again wearing a loose flannel over a black T-shirt that, unfortunately, fit perfectly over his chest and showed exactly how well-muscled he was from all the swimming he did.

He didn't come right out and tell me about Alexi's work. He was hesitating. Maybe he was waiting for me to reassure him that I was here to stay no matter what he told me.

Because the truth was, I was here to stay. Even if my first guess had been correct and Alexi not only documented porn but created it, I didn't have anywhere else to go. I needed this job. Jacob North may be afraid of running me off, but he didn't know how dire my own personal situation was.

"You don't have to worry about freaking me out. I'm sure whatever it is, I'll be fine."

He looked away and nodded. "It's just… I guess, not everyone is that understanding. Especially in some of the circles I run in. The academic ones, I often find I have to defend Alexi's chosen subject matter."

"Well, I'm certainly no academic."

Why had I said that? It's not like I wouldn't want to be an academic if I'd been given half the chance. I didn't want to leave Jacob with the idea that education wasn't something I didn't care about. "I mean, maybe I am more open-minded than you may imagine?"

He took a deep breath. "Alexi's films, they're about…serial killers. And I suppose it would be one thing if she made documentaries about other topics too. But her films are exclusively about serial killers. They always have been, and sometimes, well, other people find that very strange. Some people, both in her world and mine, have suggested that it's…well, a weird obsession, I guess."

He held up both of his palms to me like he was taking a secret oath. "And I swear, it's nothing as nefarious as that. It's a topic she finds interesting. And she's always been exceptionally good at getting them to speak to her candidly. Which is, of course, what makes her films so good."

"Them?" I asked.

"Sorry, what?" Jacob looked at me with confusion.

"You said she's good at getting them to speak."

"Oh, yes. The um…subjects. The killers, I mean. That's what she does. She interviews serial killers from all over the world and somehow manages to get them to open up to her. In ways they probably never even opened up to their own attorneys…or themselves, quite frankly. Which is why, of course, her films are so popular."

And award-winning, I thought, but did not say it. That would be a dead giveaway that I'd been researching Alexi online.

Jacob suddenly smiled at me. His grin was undeniably sheepish. "So that's it," he said. "Our dirty little secret. Hopefully, you can understand why we don't openly speak with the boys about their mother's work. At least, not yet."

"Of course." I nodded but privately wondered if Jacob and Alexi had any idea how soon their sons would likely be hearing the truth from friends at school. In my experience, like when I was a kid, children tended to find out the truth much sooner than parents would like. Especially secrets as public as Alexi's success. In fact, it seemed impossible that Garrett hadn't already dealt with this. Did the Norths seriously imagine that Garrett and every other middle schooler at Westbrook Academy didn't already know?

"Well, I can promise they'll never hear it from me."

"And this doesn't make you feel too uncomfortable?" Jacob asked.

"No." I smiled and tried my best to look reassuring. I did think it was pretty weird, although seeing that Alexi had won an Academy Award for her work certainly made me feel better.

Her work was obviously legitimate and well-regarded by the film industry. "I look forward to watching some of her films."

Jacob nodded. "Any time. We have them all, obviously." He took a backward step away from my door. "Well, I should let you get your rest. We'll see you in the morning?"

I nodded. "Good night."

"Good night, Libby." Jacob pulled my door closed, and I headed back to the couch.

As I was about to reopen my laptop, I thought about the conversation I just had with Jacob and wished I had someone in my life I could talk it over with. The few friends I'd had in high school had long ago left our small town for either college, careers, or to start their own families. I was connected to a few of them on Facebook, but aside from liking the occasional pictures of their achievements or life milestones, we didn't keep in touch—not really. I couldn't just call them up out of the blue and begin telling them about how much I'd screwed up my life.

I still had Dad. Sort of. But he hadn't been able to form a coherent sentence for almost a year, thanks to the stroke that left him partially paralyzed. He understood what I said to him, I could see the alertness in his eyes. But telling him about pretty much any aspect of my life right now would only make him feel worried...or, more likely, guilty. That was the last thing I wanted. He knew that my whole life had been put on hold when he got sick—and I knew he hated that.

CHAPTER 21

It had been two weeks since I overslept and had not picked up the kids. Since then, I've had zero slip-ups. The boys were dropped off in the morning and picked up every day, on time, and with no yelling or drama. However, Garrett still only communicated with moody silence or snide comments.

Daniel, at least, was coming around. My teary regrets over dinner that night had gone a long way to earning his forgiveness.

But not necessarily his love. Daniel did what I told him to—put on the clothes I laid out for him, ate the food I made, and always did his homework at the kitchen table right after school. But anytime I asked if he'd like to play a game or go to a park the answer was always, "No thank you, Libby."

At this point, Daniel was resigned to me being his new nanny…but it seemed like it was going to take a lot more time before he liked it.

After dropping them off every morning, I parked the Jeep outside the Coffee Klatch. The little shop and my visits with Kyra were becoming a part of my morning routine here in Walford. She worked most mornings, and if the shop wasn't busy, she'd spend a few minutes, and once even half an hour, chatting with me while I sipped my drink.

It was maybe too soon to call her a friend; she was really just an acquaintance. But I liked her. Kyra was funny and vibrant and always spoke her mind.

I thought maybe if I stopped in the shop enough days in a row, we would eventually become real friends.

In addition to learning as much as I could about Alexi and her film career, I spent many of my late mornings and early afternoons trying to find information about Jessica.

Which was difficult since I didn't even know her last name. I was reluctant to ask either Jacob or Kyra because I was afraid they would instinctively know that I was snooping around online, trying to find information about people that were not really my business. There wasn't any way I'd ask Garrett. He was already distant and suspicious of me. I had considered asking Daniel. As much as I hated to admit it, I could probably find a way to get a six-year-old to give me some information without him becoming too suspicious of what I'd be doing with it.

I was, yet again, letting my curiosity get the better of me. I had settled into a routine at my new home and job. Get Daniel ready, make breakfast, get the kids to school on time—easy enough considering I had all those hours between drop off and pick up to do as I pleased. Usually, I poked around the house, watched Alexi's films, or took long walks into the woods around the house.

But regardless of what direction my days took, they always started the same. Every morning, my alarm went off, I hit snooze for another ten minutes and thought about the last person who had slept in this bed.

Between what Kyra had told me about the town gossip, and Alexi's documentary subjects, I wondered about why Jessica had quit. I turned over again and again the reasons she might have left this family, this beautiful house, and a ridiculously good paycheck.

I never landed on a conclusive answer but was leaning more and more toward the town gossip being the reason. Maybe she had, in fact, run off with the married fourth-grade teacher.

When my alarm went off a second time, I would make my way toward the windows in my bedroom, pulling back the heavy floor-to-ceiling drapes and allowing the first morning light to flood the room. Most mornings, because it was still warm and autumn hadn't yet settled in, I slid the large glass door open and crept onto my balcony.

It was a beautiful view of the forest, yes. But I also regularly watched Jacob swim his laps in the pool below.

I was careful not to head out onto the balcony before he started and doubly careful to make sure I left before he finished his last lap. The last thing I wanted him to know was that I spied on his daily exercises.

Another curiosity...why did I do this?

I wasn't stupid. Although actually, if I thought about it, maybe I really was, in fact, very stupid. Because after having been here for two weeks, it was glaringly obvious to me, and even more to my nervous system, that I was becoming very attracted to Jacob North.

Of course, he was handsome—that was the easy part. And it would have been the quickest variable to get over. If it was only that. Unfortunately, it was also the way he was with his kids. It was clear that Jacob was a patient and kind father.

Much like my own father, actually.

Additionally, Jacob was a very intelligent man. If only his good looks were hindered by a stupid brain. Sadly, I was now confident Jacob had read nearly all those books in his elaborate library. Almost every night after Daniel was in bed, if I happened to pass by his open office door—I did this frequently —Jacob could be seen with a book in his lap, sitting in his leather chair nearest the fireplace, under the warm glow of a nearby lamp.

I never interrupted him.

I did find myself walking a little slower each night past that door. Hoping for what? I didn't know. Or didn't want to admit. But deep down, I knew. I wanted Jacob to invite me into his library, his world, his work.

And his arms?

His bed?

No, no, no!

I was being ridiculous. He was a married man. Not only a married man, but a married man who happened to be my boss. Married to my other boss. My other boss, who was statuesque, beautiful, successful, famous, and also intelligent. And it was this thought, I suppose, that allowed me to brush away my growing attraction towards Jacob.

You only needed to look at his wife one time to realize how

utterly and absolutely ridiculous it was for me to even fantasize that Jacob North might find me attractive, too.

This thinking allowed me to laugh about it. To realize what a child I was. It was barely anything more than a schoolgirl crush, I reasoned.

Because of this, because I believed my attraction was neither serious nor dangerous, not really, I allowed myself to watch him swim every morning.

Because it was beautiful, and he was so good at it. Strong, confident, capable. There was nothing really wrong with admiring him from afar.

There were so many obvious boundaries between us...there was nothing to worry about.

So why, I wondered, did Nicola's parting words continue to ring through my mind. I was a capable young woman, she said. A woman that would land on her feet–or on her back.

When her curse sprung up in my mind, usually after I caught myself daydreaming or fantasizing about Jacob on the long drive to and from town, I pushed it aside. Clung to all the very concrete reasons why there was nothing to worry about.

At least, that was what I did until Jacob finally told me the truth about Alexi.

CHAPTER 22

I had been working for the Norths for nearly three weeks when Jacob asked me to meet him in his office after I'd put Daniel to bed.

We had, all four of us, settled into a pretty regular routine. Each night, after Jacob got home from work, we would sit down at the kitchen table to eat dinner. Either something I had made or he had picked up on his way home. Then Garrett would retreat to his bedroom behind his locked door, and Jacob and Daniel would hang out alone for an hour or so before it was time for me to make sure he took his bath and got ready for bed.

Some nights, Jacob would come upstairs and either take over the bath duty so he could have a little more time with his son or read to Daniel one or five of his favorite bedtime books.

Then, every night, once Daniel was in bed, Jacob would go back downstairs to his office. I would head to my own rooms to watch TV or continue my fruitless search for information about Jessica. Sometimes, I spent the evening watching one of Alexi's documentaries, which admittedly were fascinating but far too disturbing to watch right before bed. Jacob was right; Alexi had a natural talent for getting these complex, dangerous, and deeply disturbed individuals to share detailed information with her.

All of which left me shaken and terrified. On the nights I stayed up watching her films, I was unable to fall asleep for hours. All I could think about were the victims, tragedy, and torture they had endured at the hands of a monster who was behind bars but also enjoying a cult-like celebrity of followers.

And while it was true the victims weren't around any longer to have to endure this – their families and loved ones certainly were.

What must it be like to turn on something as universally popular as Netflix only to have your own worst nightmare thrown into your face again and again and again?

On those nights, I lay awake, staring at the ceiling, wondering if a family ever survived such a thing. If they ever would know anything near normal again.

I doubted it.

But on all the nights I had spent at the Norths' house thus far, never, not once, had Jacob asked me to meet him in his office until now.

Even though everything had been going well between us since my first mistake, as I stood outside his office door, my palms sweating, a nervous dread ran through me. I couldn't help but think about being in this exact position three weeks ago when Nicola Drake called me into her office to let me go.

I clenched my hands at my side and shook them out before knocking on his door.

There was no reason for me to feel this way. I knew it. I was confident that whatever the reason Jacob was calling me into his office, it was not to fire me.

Still, this summoning was more formal than our previous conversations, and just the fact that it was different made me nervous.

"Come in," I heard him call from the other side of the door.

I turned the knob and pushed the double doors inward. I glanced at first to where I usually saw Jacob in the evenings, in the high-backed leather chair near the fireplace with a book opened in his lap. But he wasn't there.

"Hi, Libby," he said.

My head swiveled in the direction of his voice. Jacob was sitting at his desk, his large computer monitor blocking him from view. "Please come in," he added. "I'll just be one more second; let me finish this email."

I wandered over to his large desk and listened to the clicking of his keyboard as his fingers flew over the surface, typing out his message. I hung back several feet to avoid seeming intrusive as he finished his work. My eyes scanned upward at the shelves upon shelves of books towering above him.

There were two final clicks of the keys. "Send," he said. I heard the click of his mouse, and then Jacob stood up from behind his desk. "Thank you for coming, Libby."

As I stood facing him, I couldn't help but notice this was a different Jacob from the one I had gotten to know over the last three weeks. A more formal Jacob, I realized. I imagined this is what Jacob was like at work. He'd been home for hours but hadn't yet changed out of his coat and tie.

This was Doctor North, as his students and the other faculty saw him. My biggest question was, what was coming? He needed to speak with me, he said. But why in his office? I felt like one of his students called in to discuss poor course progress or a bad grade on a test.

"Please take a seat," he said, gesturing open palmed to one of the plush chairs positioned to the side of his desk. I did as instructed and lowered myself into the cushions. I immediately wished I'd remained standing. The chair was too soft, angling me back into what, under normal circumstances, would've been a comfortable position. But at this moment, all it did was make me feel vulnerable.

Jacob looked at me for several uncomfortable seconds, took a deep breath, and sighed loudly. "I'm sorry, I'm not entirely sure how to begin. Honestly, I've run through this scenario several times in my mind, trying to imagine the best way to tell you."

Oh my God, I was getting fired. I wished more than anything that I had remained standing for this.

"And I guess I had figured, doing it in here, more formally, maybe...well, it had seemed like the best version of all the terrible options I thought through. But looking at you now, I think maybe I've just made you nervous."

I swallowed hard. I realized he was waiting for me to give him some sort of reassurance that I was fine. But the fact was, I was nervous. Very nervous. If I was losing this job, I literally had nowhere to go.

"OK, well, I'm just gonna say it. But please know, Libby, all of this was still very tentative when we hired you. We weren't sure, not at all. So...I guess I'm just really hoping you'll understand that."

I could hardly stand this any longer. "Please, Doctor North, just tell me," I whispered.

He nodded. "Alexi and I... we're getting a divorce."

The entire time he'd been speaking, my eyes had been low, focused on the circular knot of wood on the side of his desk. But now, with his declaration hanging in the air between us, I finally raised my eyes to meet his. "What?"

His expression looked helpless. "Please don't make me say it again. It was hard enough to get it out the first time."

I shook my head. "I'm sorry, of course I heard you. I guess I just can't quite believe it. I thought maybe you were about..." The rest of my sentence died on my lips.

"What?" He asked.

I shook my head again. "To fire me," I breathed.

He pulled his head back in surprise. "Are you kidding?" He stood up from his desk and came around to where I was sitting. I watched as he knelt before me. "Libby, please know I cannot even begin to imagine what I would do, how we would even survive if you weren't here. You've been nothing but amazing since you got here."

My eyes met his. "Except for oversleeping and forgetting to pick up the kids," I reminded him.

He smiled and looked away. "Well, that was just that one time." He returned his eyes to mine, and then, to my surprise and shock, he moved his hand to where mine rested on the rolled arm of the chair and placed his on top of mine. "If anyone should be doing any firing around here, it's you. Firing me, a terrible and chaotic employer, too lost and floundering to even disclose the most basic of information to you before you uprooted your whole life and moved to a whole other state." He gave my hand a gentle squeeze and then pulled his hand away. "I'm the one who should be terrified. Terrified that you'll decide you've had enough and quit."

Just like Jessica, I thought.

CHAPTER 23

That night, I again lay awake staring at my ceiling. But instead of thinking about serial killers or speculating about why Jessica had left, I couldn't stop thinking about Jacob's confession.

He and Alexi were getting a divorce.

Jacob had explained how they'd been having a rough time in their marriage for years. "In part, it was both of our careers. Alexi traveled so much with hers. And me." He gazed at one of the nearby bookshelves. "Well, if I'm honest, I tend to get lost in my studies and writing. So, I can honestly say it's not ultimately her fault or my fault…but neither of us was probably grounded enough to be the full-time caregiver to children while the other pursued an ambitious career."

He was once again seated at his desk. He looked lost and was obviously feeling confessional. I could only assume that's why he told me what he did next.

"I think we both honestly thought we could make it work.

Even though everything changed between us once Garrett was born, I guess I just chalked that up to typical family growing pains." He shook his head, his eyes unfocused, his mind contemplating the downward trajectory of his relationship. "We leaned on Jessica a lot. Too much, probably. Looking back now, with her gone, I realize neither one of us was probably equipped to become a parent. So, yeah, I have a lot of regrets."

"Regrets?" I blurted before thinking better of it.

"Alexi never wanted children. Not really. Don't get me wrong, she loves the boys and would do anything for them... I'm almost certain of that. But the fact is, I pressured her. In those early days when we were first dating and then engaged, she said it more than once. Her career was what was most important to her; she never had the desire to have children. And it's not like she didn't tell me that. She was always very honest and upfront with me about that. Alexi is always very honest and upfront about everything."

Lying awake in my new bed, Jessica's old bed, I rolled onto my side as my mind ran through Jacob's admissions.

He didn't explain exactly why Jessica left, but it gave me a pretty good idea. It was easy to imagine. Being a young woman stuck in between two people whose marriage was falling apart, this job likely became more than she wanted to deal with. I didn't know how old Jessica was, but she was probably about my age.

As a nanny working for a family, when one parent, admittedly, didn't really want to be one, and both parents were so super focused on their careers, it was clear that a lot of the parental expectations must have been put onto her shoulders alone.

And this wasn't speculation. Jacob had admitted as much just moments ago in his library.

While it was normal for kids to get attached to their nannies, it was now crystal clear why Daniel was so heart-broken over Jessica's leaving. I wondered if he wasn't as close to his own mother as he had been to Jessica. This may also explain why Alexi hadn't seemed overly concerned about even meeting me before placing her kids under my trust and care.

As I closed my eyes and finally felt sleep pull at me, I wondered if Alexi and the boys had much of any relationship at all.

Because it occurred to me that in the three weeks I had worked here, I had hardly heard Garrett or Daniel even mention their mother.

Only Jessica, Jessica, Jessica.

CHAPTER 24

By the first week of October, the days were chilly, and the nights were cold. I had purchased some more clothes over the past few weeks, but I still needed some things for the approaching winter weather.

So, after my morning coffee with Kyra, I headed down to the second-hand boutique store on the next block. Kyra said she always shopped there and that it was a great place to find some really good clothes at cheap prices. Apparently, this is where all the wealthier local women came to get rid of the things they didn't think they'd be wearing anymore.

But as I flipped through the rack of puffers and all-weather jackets, even these heavily discounted prices were still more than I could afford to spend. The Norths were paying me well, but there still wasn't much left over after I made the weekly payments to my dad's in-home care nurse.

I was likely going to have to find a shop without the word

"boutique" in the title. Something like the Salvation Army or Goodwill was where I would need to go next.

I was about to get up and leave when I glanced up from the rack of sweaters and saw a man standing next to my Jeep parked outside. His hands were cupped around his eyes, and his face pressed against the driver-side window, as he peered into the car.

I froze and watched as he lowered one hand and pulled at the door handle, checking to see if it was unlocked. My heart beat hard, and my mind scrambled to remember if I had locked the doors.

It was such a small town; I had more than once wandered away from the Jeep without bothering to lock it.

Thankfully, the door didn't open for him. But what should I do? Scared, I wandered over to the large plate glass window that looked out onto the street and watched as he scanned the front seat, then moved his search to the back window. He also tried the handle on that door. Now that I was closer, I recognized him.

It was the same man I had seen as I was walking into the coffee shop on my first day in town. I noticed he was wearing the same ratty hoodie he had that day. His greasy hair was now pulled back and held by an elastic tie.

I watched as he pulled away from the window and looked around, checking to see if anyone on the street was watching him. I could see his crystal-clear blue eyes when he looked in my direction. This was definitely the same guy.

He then started searching the street and sidewalk. A moment later, he picked up a fist-sized rock from the plot of dirt surrounding a tree on the sidewalk.

He was going to break the Jeep's window.

I needed to do something. How could I just stand here and watch this man break into the vehicle the Norths had given me to drive? I was too scared to run out there and confront him, and when I looked around the store, the lone saleswoman who had initially greeted me was nowhere to be seen.

He was already heading back to the car with his rock.

"Crap," I whispered. Then an idea occurred to me. I fumbled around in the small pocket at the front of my backpack where I kept the keys to the Jeep, pulled them out as fast as I could, and hit the emergency horn button.

Just as the guy raised his hand to break the window with his rock, the Jeep's lights started to flash, and an ear-piercing repetitive siren broke the sleepy early morning silence of the street.

Surprised, he fell back a step and dropped his rock immediately. Realizing he'd been caught, his head whipped back and forth, scanning the street and sidewalk all around him. That's when his eyes met mine through the window.

When he saw me, he clearly knew it had been me who had sounded the car alarm. He took a step back, getting ready to run away, but before he did, he lifted his arm and pointed his finger at me. Then he turned around and ran, faster than I thought he looked capable, up the street before disappearing down the next alley.

For several seconds, I didn't move. I didn't breathe. All I could think of were his electric blue eyes, which were dead focused and determined, and his finger pointing at me as if to say, "I see you. And I'll be back."

CHAPTER 25

I didn't stop shaking until I pulled onto the dirt road that led to the house. As the Jeep bumped and rolled along the deeply rutted road, I felt like it was shaking some sense into me.

What had I been thinking? I ran out of that shop, my heart racing like I was the one who had done something wrong. I should have told someone. I should have called the police.

Instead, all I had done was jump in the Jeep and speed out of town. Why did the logical ideas always occur so long after the fact?

When I reached the drive and got out of the Jeep, I made sure to click the lock button on the fob twice so I could hear the car alarm engage. Which was essentially stupid and unnecessary because I was out here in the middle of nowhere now. Still, I practically ran into the house, and when I had the heavy front door closed behind me, I locked it and set the house alarm.

Jesus, the guy had really rattled me. What was I so afraid of now? He clearly didn't have a second set of clothes to change into, did I honestly think he had access to a vehicle that could carry him forty-five minutes out of town and here to the house.

Plus, it wasn't even about me. At least, it probably wasn't about me. He was either trying to steal something from the Jeep or steal the Jeep altogether. Or… my first hunch about him was correct, and he thought the Jeep still belonged to Jessica.

I pushed myself away from the door and headed toward the kitchen to get a glass of water and calm myself down. Maybe I should still call the cops? At least file a report so that they had a history should something happen in the future. Although I did wonder what, if anything, they would do about it. Especially given the fact that, because I had interrupted him, the guy hadn't actually done anything. Maybe I should've let him break the window?

I pulled a glass from the cupboard, opened the fridge, and took out the pitcher of chilled filtered water.

What was it Kyra told me on the first day we met? It was something about how Jessica used to volunteer at the local homeless shelter. And that maybe the guy recognized her Jeep and was looking for her.

The more I thought about it, the more I realized it was unlikely the police would do anything since nothing had happened. But now I wondered, as I was coming down and feeling more confident, if maybe I should.

I took a drink of my water and used my free hand to press at the stressed and tight muscles at the back of my neck.

The guy certainly looked homeless. And if that was true, chances were someone at the local shelter would know who he was. Maybe this could all be resolved without making a giant federal case of it. Maybe somebody who knew him could simply talk to him. Explain to him that if it was Jessica he was looking for, she was no longer here.

The more I thought about it, and the more water I drank, the more I realized this was actually a very rational plan with a good chance of producing a positive result.

He was probably confused. And maybe even had a mental health problem? Drug abuse concerns? Instead of just running to the cops, wouldn't it be more socially responsible and kind to try to talk to the people who probably knew him and his situation?

I put the glass down on the counter in front of me and already felt better about coming up with a possible solution.

I let out a deep sigh. Tomorrow, after I dropped the kids off and had coffee with Kyra to discuss my plan, I would head to the homeless shelter to see if I could find somebody to help me.

A loud thump reverberated through the ceiling above me.

My gaze shot upward. "What the hell?" I whispered. I'd only just gotten my nervous system under control. Now, adrenaline was again pumping through my system, making my heart beat fast. A fresh bead of sweat ran down my spine.

I gripped the marble counter edge and listened, waiting to hear the sound again. The kids were at school, and Jacob was at work. Who or what could possibly have made that noise upstairs?

My mind bounced back and forth between imagining an intruder upstairs, ready to attack and kill me the moment he saw me, and more benign thoughts, like a door blowing closed or books falling from shelves.

That was when I remembered...I had heard something very

similar to that sound before. I looked up at the ceiling and thought about this house's strange and confusing layout. What was the space directly above the kitchen?

I realized it was the same room where I had heard a loud thump before.

Alexi's office.

CHAPTER 26

I stood at the end of the hall, staring at the closed door to her office.

My mind ping-ponged between calling Jacob to let him know what had happened this morning and just handling it all myself.

Including the weird noise.

I felt scared and panicky, and part of me wondered about the possibility of the guy from the street somehow being inside Alexi's office. Which was ridiculous—I knew.

He had caught me off guard, frightened me by trying to break into the Jeep, and got me all riled up on adrenaline and fear. Now, probably some object had just fallen in Alexi's office, a total coincidence, and the unexpected noise had freaked me out all over again.

I took a deep breath, held it for a few seconds, and let it go. I didn't need to call Jacob. I would tell him about the guy and the Jeep, but that could wait until he got home tonight. As for the sound, well I was going to see if I could figure that out right now.

I strode down the hall, determined not to feel afraid but with my cell phone ready in my hand—just in case. I knew the door was locked, so I placed my ear again to the warm wood and tried to listen for any sounds coming from the other side. Maybe the Norths had forgotten to close a window in there.

Like the last time, I didn't hear any loud or strange sounds—just the soft electrical hum that made me wonder if there was some sort of machine on in there.

I pressed my ear against the door a little harder, closed my eyes, and tried to focus on the sound to see if I could imagine what it might be. As I did, my left hand drifted from the space beside my face and came to rest on the door handle.

Under the weight of my palm, the handle moved slightly. More than I remembered from the last time I tried opening the door.

Surprised, I pulled away from the door and stared at the handle. I had assumed the door would still be locked. Without thinking it through, I grasped the handle, turned it, and watched as the door to Alexi's office swung open, slow and silent.

I stepped back and stared at the crack in the door.

I couldn't see much, just the wood floor on the other side and a dim light. I took a step forward and leaned into the opening. The air from the room streamed over my face. It felt much warmer than the rest of the house and smelled strange. It reminded me of something, but I couldn't think what.

I should close the door and leave. After all, this door was

locked before, presumably because Alexi had locked it. It was obvious that she didn't want anyone inside her office.

Then again, why was it unlocked now? It was unlikely Daniel had done it. It might have been Garrett, but it seemed more likely to have been Jacob. Obviously, there was a key to this room that was kept somewhere.

My mind returned to the noises I'd heard.

What if something was wrong? What if a window had been left open? What if rain got in? Or heated air was streaming out? What if, somehow, an animal had gotten inside? Like a squirrel? A bird? It could happen, especially if the window was open. Or through the venting from the attic? I had heard of things like that happening.

Would Alexi really want the rain or feral wild animals ruining her office?

No, obviously not.

So, I pushed the door open further and went inside—not because I was curious, not to snoop, but to investigate a potential problem. Besides, it's not like I wouldn't report all of this to Jacob as soon as he got home.

The strange smell was stronger now that I was inside the room. It was so familiar, but I still couldn't place it, like a memory or a dream, just beyond my conscious thinking. It was irritating that I couldn't place it.

The room was so much smaller than I thought it would be. Given the size of all the bedrooms and the vast grandeur of Jacob's library office, I was shocked to see that Alexi's office was about the same size as the walk-in closet in my bedroom.

Even more stunning—it was packed. Completely jammed, utterly overflowing with what at first looked like piles and piles of crap. There was paper everywhere. Covering every surface. Even the walls had hundreds of pages tacked up from the floor to near the ceiling.

A small desk was pushed against the far wall in front of a window that overlooked the forest on this side of the house. Just as I had guessed, the window was cracked open several inches. Maybe that could somehow explain everything I'd heard?

Unlike the view from my balcony, this side of the house was right against the tree line. There was no view of the grounds below, just the dense, dark green pine trees.

I wondered about the electric hum. I couldn't figure out what it could be, but then I realized what the smell in here reminded me of.

My high school. Specifically, the technology lab that held all the audio-video equipment and rows of computers for the technology classes. Since my high school was so tiny, there were only thirty kids in my graduating class, and many classrooms and teachers had to do double duty across subjects. The tech room where I'd taken a coding class my freshman year—a subject that had bored me to tears and which I'd barely passed with a D--was also where the film and video class stored their equipment.

This room smelled exactly like that classroom—warm plastics, dusty computer fans, and electricity. The weird thing was Alexi's office had zero technology in it.

Paper, pens, a wood desk, a leather chair, and a worn-out rug on the wood floor. Books on shelves, a dead plant on the windowsill, and thin, gauzy curtains that could, as best, only hope to diffuse the light from the window. Not that it would get direct sunlight anyway. And there was certainly no worry about privacy since the house was surrounded by trees and was in the middle of nowhere.

Still, I could hear the electric hum coming from somewhere. Not from any singular direction, I realized. It was more like the sound emanated from all four walls around me.

"Weird," I said. I looked closer at Alexi's desk, all the papers strewn across it and the ones pinned to the walls.

It was research. Cut-out newspaper articles, printouts from the internet, handwritten notes—and all of it was about serial killers, murders, unsolved cases, victims, locations, psychological profiles, hypotheses, explanations…mountains and mountains of information.

I touched Alexi's small leather office chair and imagined her sitting here. Poring over the details of some of the most heinous acts of torture and killings that occurred in the world. Organizing the facts and speculations, made by herself and others in the field, into some sort of narrative that translated into a visual account suitable for public consumption.

On the shelf to the left of her desk, shoved between several ratty paperback books, her academy award stood gathering dust like it was a trinket she had long forgotten.

I was actually looking at a real-life Academy Award—just like the ones I'd seen on TV. Here it was, right in front of me. I reached out my hand and ran my thumb across the inscribed plate, leaving a clean trail in the dust.

ACADEMY AWARD

TO

"IT HAPPENED TWELVE TIMES"

BEST DOCUMENTARY FEATURE

ALEXI NORTH

What was it like, I wondered, to have earned something as prestigious as this? To be this driven, focused, and successful?

"Libby?"

I gasped and turned around fast. Jacob stood in the open doorway, staring at me, his expression a mixture of confusion and annoyance. "What are you doing in here?"

CHAPTER 27

"Jacob," I said as my mind raced to find an answer. I knew I shouldn't be in here, but....

"There was a noise," I blurted. "I was in the kitchen and heard a loud sound coming from this room. And I wasn't trying to invade Alexi's space, but I guess I was pretty freaked out because in town there was this guy who tried breaking into the Jeep and when I heard the sound up here and being all alone, well I figured I was probably being irrational, but I didn't want to bother you—"

"Libby, slow down," Jacob said. He came into the room and took both my hands in his. It wasn't until he held them that I realized I was shaking. "It's okay." He gave my hands a gentle squeeze. "But I need you to tell me again, slowly, what happened. Someone broke into the Jeep?"

I stared at our clasped hands, suddenly conscious of how close we were. When I looked up into Jacob's eyes, I saw his worry, the genuine concern he had for my distress. His sudden appearance had rattled me. After all, it was the middle of the day, and I certainly didn't expect him to be home. But what I felt at this moment was far more than just confusion over seeing him. Standing so near to him, his large, warm hands holding mine, it was impossible to deny how much I would have loved for him to also pull me into his arms.

It had been so long since I'd had any physical contact with another human. The last hug I'd been given was from my father, one-armed and weakened by his stroke, when I was saying goodbye to him as I left for New York.

It had been years and years since a guy had touched me with any interest. And Jacob was certainly not just some guy.

"Libby?" Jacob asked. "Are you okay?" One of his hands left mine and came to rest on my face. It was a simple gesture, one born from a genuine worry about my safety, yet the feeling of his hand on my cheek burned and ignited a fire that ran through my body.

It was so wrong that I was feeling this right now.

"Yes, I'm sorry. I am fine. The Jeep's fine. Yes, someone did try to break into it, but I turned on the alarm and he ran away."

A look of relief swept across his features. He lowered his hand from my face and let go of my hand. "Thank God. I'm so sorry that happened, and it's so weird. Our little town is generally so safe. Did you get a good look at the guy? Would you be able to describe him to the police?"

"Not really," I lied and couldn't help averting my eyes because of it. I could describe the guy; I had seen him clearly both on my first day in town outside the coffee shop and today as he tried to bash into the Jeep with a rock. So why was I lying to Jacob about it? "It all happened so fast, and he had a hoodie pulled up over his head...it was impossible to get a good look at him." I shook my head for dramatic effect.

It was ridiculous, but a part of me felt sure that this guy had known Jessica or, at least, was looking for Jessica. And I didn't want to sick both Jacob and the police force onto him before I had a chance to do a little more digging.

"Honestly, he looked like he maybe had a drug or alcohol problem. I was stupid and had left my wallet on the Jeep's passenger seat. He was probably trying to get some cash." This was also a lie. I'd had my wallet with me the entire time I shopped in the store.

"Wow," Jacob said. "I kind of can't believe this happened to you." He ran his hands through his hair, a gesture I now realized was his tell for when he was nervous or upset about something. "But now, what were you saying about hearing a sound up here?" Jacob was gazing around at Alexis's office. I couldn't tell, but it looked like he was checking to see if anything was missing or out of place. Although, honestly, I had no idea how he'd be able to figure it out. The small space was such a catastrophe of loose paper and debris.

"I'm sure it was nothing," I said. "Although I did see that the window was open, maybe whatever I heard was from outside. Maybe an animal was in here."

Jacob stared hard into my eyes like he was searching for something. But then he nodded, and his expression relaxed. "Yeah, that's my fault. The last time I spoke with Alexi, she asked me to look for something in here. I thought it was kind of stuffy, so I opened the window. I must've forgotten about it." He ran his hand through his hair again. "But I'll take care of it. Thanks for noticing. It would've been terrible if we had a rainstorm come through. I can't imagine how mad Alexi would've been to come home and find her work soaking wet."

I nodded. "You're home so early. I wasn't expecting you, it scared me."

"Yes.... There's a guest speaker in my department today. My last two classes were canceled. I probably should've stayed and attended the lecture myself," he said as a sheepish, embarrassed look came over his face. "I guess I saw my chance to play hooky for the rest of the day and took it." His embarrassed smile was warm and infectious, and I couldn't help smiling back. "And now I'm glad that I did," he said. "You've had quite the day. Why don't you come downstairs and let me make you some lunch. You've been working so much with hardly any time off at all. It's the least I could do."

I shook my head and was about to object, but Jacob cut me off.

"I insist, Libby. Let me do this small thing for you."

I looked up into his pleading expression. His eyes were so kind, and his concern felt so genuine that it felt impossible to refuse him anything right now. "Okay," I agreed. "But you should know, I'm not used to having people do things for me. I'm usually the one taking care of people."

Jacob smiled at me again and raised his eyebrows. "Well, that doesn't seem right. Someone as beautiful and kind as you should be cared for sometimes. Maybe we should work on that."

Jacob North had just called me beautiful. And because of that, it was impossible to stop the warm blush I felt spreading up my neck and across my cheeks.

"You head downstairs," he said. "I'll take care of this window and be down in a second."

Without needing further coaxing, I turned around and did as I was told. As I headed down the stairs, I wondered exactly what Jacob might do to take care of me, and any worries I'd had about strange sounds and homeless men were practically forgotten.

For now.

CHAPTER 28

"There you go," Jacob said as he slid a thin wooden platter across the marble countertop to where I sat perched in one of the counter height chairs. On the platter was the most delicious looking sandwich and bowl of butter squash soup I had ever seen. The wheat bread was soft and from a local bakery in town where Jacob liked to shop on the weekends. He had somehow constructed the sandwich with perfect proportions of Dijon mustard and mayonnaise, also from the bakery, organic lettuce and tomato from the farmers market, and Havarti cheese that he'd bought at the deli along with the fresh sliced turkey.

"The soup is from one of my co-workers." Jacob shrugged. "She has a huge garden in her backyard and is always pawning off vegetables or the soups she's made from them. She lives alone and grows more than she could ever eat herself. Alexi always joked..." He didn't finish his sentence.

I met Jacob's gaze as I swallowed a spoonful of the gorgeous and aromatic soup. It was obvious that he had, in the moment, completely forgotten that he and Alexi were heading for a divorce.

"I'm sorry," I whispered. "About you and Alexi. It must be difficult."

Jacob took a deep breath and let it out. "Yes...and also no, to be honest. The hardest part was living together and pretending for the last five years. Making the decision to divorce? It was actually a relief in the end. For both of us, I'm sure." He gave me a half smile that showed his resignation on the topic.

As I took another spoonful of my soup, I had the urge to press him a little further on the topic of Alexi. After all, I was living in her home, taking care of her kids, and I had never even met her. I was curious as to whether I ever would now.

"So, will she come back here after she's done with her project?" I tried to keep my tone light like we were talking about a friend who might come for a visit, not his wife, and the end of his marriage.

"At first, I thought so. But after our conversation the other night...honestly, I'm not so sure." Jacob lifted his sandwich to his mouth, but just before he was about to take a bite, he placed it back onto his plate. Instead, he took a long swallow from his glass of water and looked at me.

There was something else he wanted to tell me; I just knew it.

"I'm sorry, Libby. Truly, about all of this. And I guess, well, I hope you don't feel too weird about the fact it will just be me here...and the boys, obviously. But the truth is..." He started to shake his head slowly as if he couldn't quite believe he was going to say what he was about to say. "Alexi, well, she's actually with someone else. Like, romantically. She has been for years."

I was about to take a bite of my sandwich, but his words stopped my hands halfway to my mouth. I had no idea what to say to this.

"I can't imagine what you must think. But you should know that I always knew. Like I said before, Alexi has always been both very direct and very honest." Jacob may have always known about the affair, but he still let out a long sigh before continuing. "His name is Chad. He came to work for her on one of her films four years ago. The way she tells it, they fell instantly in love. So much so that after only two weeks of working together, Chad flew back to Los Angeles, told his wife about his feelings for Alexi, and left her."

"That's terrible," I blurted, but then regretted it and put my hand over my mouth.

Jacob shrugged and nodded once. "Thankfully, I suppose, Chad and his wife didn't yet have any kids."

"But you did," I whispered.

"Yes," Jacob confirmed. "Garrett was eight, and Daniel was only a year old." Jacob shook his head. "I didn't want to believe it. I kept trying to convince her that it was just a fling. That it was all the big changes in our lives. Daniel had just been born. Her career was taking off. I was sure that once she moved past the shock of it all, she would see that Chad was just a band-aid and she would eventually come home to us and our life and finally settle down."

"But she didn't?" I asked.

"She. Did. Not," Jacob enunciated each word. "And I was basically a delusional idiot for ever thinking that the most independent, beautiful, forward-thinking, successful woman I had ever met somehow didn't know herself as well as I believed I did."

"Are they together right now?"

"As far as I know, they are only ever apart when she is here with us. Which has been less and less over the years."

"But," I reasoned. "The boys? She must…I don't know. Care?"

Jacob nodded. "Yes. But I think her feelings about them and motherhood in general are far more complex than I can even begin to fathom." He let out another sigh. "Anyway." He picked his sandwich back up. "That's it. All of it. And I'm sorry I couldn't tell you during the interview or before you came all the way out here. I was desperate. I needed you to say yes and take this job. And I will get on my hands and knees and beg you to not quit and leave us if that's what I have to do."

I smiled and couldn't help but laugh a little despite everything Jacob had just shared. "I'm not quitting," I said. "But I may force you to give me the secrets of this sandwich. It's delicious."

"Oh no. I'm not telling you that. Why, so you can leave and make delicious sandwiches all for yourself? I think it's much better for me if I get you hooked on them and keep my sandwich secrets to myself. That way, you'll be forced to stay with me."

I smiled and shook my head, unable to help the way my gaze dropped shyly away from his.

It had been a long time, and I was certainly no expert on men, but I was almost one hundred percent certain that Jacob North was flirting with me.

And I liked it.

CHAPTER 29

After I had picked up the boys from school and returned to the house, I was surprised to find that Jacob had already prepared dinner.

"Given everything that's happened today, why don't you take the evening off," he suggested as he spooned sautéed broccoli onto Daniel's plate. "I'll spend the evening with the boys," he said as he reached out and tousled their hair. Daniel smiled up at his father. Garrett yanked his head away and shot his father a withering glare. "That way, you can do whatever you like."

I had opened my mouth to protest, after all, he had already made me lunch and been so kind all afternoon.

"I insist, Libby. Really. Besides, we haven't spent any guy time together since you arrived."

And with his final statement, my shoulders sagged, and I gave up. How could I possibly argue with dad-son bonding time?

However, when I glanced at Garrett, he had a look of disgust mixed with disbelief. It made me wonder if Jacob ever really spent "guy time" with his sons or was maybe putting on a bit of a show for my benefit. When Garrett noticed me staring, he rearranged his face into a more neutral expression and shoveled a large bite of mashed potatoes into his mouth.

Jacob and Daniel, not paying Garrett any attention, both gave me triumphant grins, and I knew I was outnumbered. "Fine. I guess I'll go relax or something."

"Yes, that's a perfect idea," Jacob said as he pulled out the counter chair next to Daniel. "And make yourself completely at home. Seriously. Go anywhere, use anything. Make free use of any book you like in the library. There's the TV room, the pool—"

"She can't go swimming at night," Garrett suddenly protested.

Clearly, this was a rule I hadn't yet heard.

"You can't go swimming at night," Jacob clarified. "Libby is a grownup and can do whatever she likes."

Garrett gave his dad a brief scowl but didn't argue with the logic. By the time he had shoveled another scoop of mashed potatoes into his mouth, he had let it go.

"That does sound good," I said. "But unfortunately, I don't have a bathing suit." I had been slowly working to replace the wardrobe that, as far as I knew, was still piled in the backseat of my crappy car at Izzard's Impound lot in New York. Buying a bathing suit just hadn't been a priority when I still needed more than one pair of jeans.

Jacob waved his hand. "There are loads of spare suits out in the pool house. Help yourself to any of them. Plus, I will have to close the pool for the winter pretty soon... I'd enjoy it while you can."

So, while they finished dinner, I ventured out to the backyard for the first time since I'd moved in.

Jacob had explained that there was a panel on the wall beside the backdoor that had all the switches to the yard lights. As I examined it, I could see that each switch was carefully labeled: Flood, String, Pool, Gazebo—there were ten switches in all. I flipped the ones labeled String, Pool, and Path. When I turned around, I saw the yard now beautifully illuminated in a warm yellow glow.

String lights hung in a swag above the covered seating area to my left, soft white lights embedded into the walkways illuminated the paths to the pool house and the gazebo, and the water in the pool glowed with a soft blue hue.

I had stood on my balcony every morning for weeks now. Watching Jacob swim laps below me as my mind wandered again and again to thoughts it shouldn't. I only ever saw this view during the early morning light as the sun rose behind the trees. Now, at night, I felt like I was visiting an expensive resort. I imagined the Norths hosting pool parties here for all their influential friends and colleagues. Who wouldn't want to hang out here every chance they could?

Then again, considering how Jacob had described his and Alexi's relationship over the past few years, maybe there hadn't been much partying going on.

In the pool house, I opened the cupboard where Jacob said I'd find some suits. They kept several on hand in case a guest needed one. There were three baskets on the shelf, carefully labeled for men, women, and children. I pulled out the women's basket and found four choices.

Apparently, any female friends Alexi might invite over would only be wearing absolutely tiny bikinis. I double-checked the other two baskets. Maybe I had accidentally pulled out the one with the children's suits, or perhaps there were more and larger women's suits mixed in with the men's.

No such luck.

The biggest one I could find was a size six. It had a bright red triangle top and what was clearly, at best, a Brazilian-cut bottom.

I had always felt self-conscious about my body in a bathing suit. From the time I first got boobs at twelve years old, I'd been painfully aware of the eyes that followed my body if it wasn't draped in oversized fabrics designed to hide the curves I didn't know how to manage.

It was better now—or I was better about dealing with it. I wasn't a child anymore, and I realized that men, and women quite frankly, would always stare at me—especially in a bathing suit. I wasn't stupid or naïve. I knew I had what other people wanted. Some women worked hard or paid a lot of money to look the way I did. But it was simply my happenstance in the genetic lottery. I often thought about how, had she lived and been able to raise me, my mother would have taught me how to handle becoming a woman in this world. As it was, I'd been left to figure everything out on my own and the hard way.

I supposed most people would consider the way I usually covered myself up a waste. But in my experiences thus far, the way I looked and the attention it brought me generally caused me more trouble than anything else.

The way I looked was the number one reason Nicola had fired me. Looking back, it was also probably the main reason Damion had hired me.

Maybe some women knew how to use gifts like mine to their advantage. I, for one, had never figured it out. If my body could be used as a tool or a weapon in this world, I suspected you also needed a commensurate amount of self-confidence to wield it.

This, I did not have.

So, I mostly hid my looks and body as much as possible. But in the red bikini, in the privacy of the Norths' beautiful pool house, I allowed myself to consider the reflection in the full-length mirror and appreciate the fact that I looked great in this bathing suit.

Thankfully, I would be the only one to see it.

Or so I thought.

CHAPTER 30

In the pool, I floated on my back and watched as the stars and planets began to appear in the darkening sky above. The water temperature was perfect, neither cold nor too warm. It surrounded my body and filled my ears, so I felt suspended in space and perfect silence.

The moon, which wasn't quite full, was just cresting over the tree line when I heard movement in the water. It startled me, and I quickly shifted my body so that my feet were again firmly planted on the concrete below me. Water ran from my ears.

When he saw my surprised expression, he stopped. "I'm sorry to disturb you," Jacob apologized. He was standing on the steps. It was his entrance into the pool that I'd heard underwater. "I wasn't able to get my usual swim in this morning. And well, I saw you out here, and it looked like such a perfect evening." He held up both his palms to me. "But if you'd rather be alone..."

He was wearing a pair of the swim trunks I'd seen him in before. Black boardshorts that sat just below his hips and showed off his muscled abs. As I stared, he ran his fingers through his messy brown hair.

He was waiting for an answer, and my silent staring was making him nervous.

I forced myself to look away from him. "Of course," I said, finally finding my voice. "I mean." I smiled and tried my best to act casual and not like his gorgeous, half-naked presence was having a disturbingly profound impact on my ability to form sentences. "It is your pool."

He smiled and moved further down the stairs until he was standing in the shallow end, and the water lapped against his waist. "Yes. But this is your time. Maybe you wanted to be alone?"

I lifted one shoulder in a half-shrug. "I spend a lot of time alone."

I hadn't intended it, but my statement made him suddenly look at me with concern. He moved closer to me. "I'm an idiot," he said. "I'm sorry, Libby. I hadn't thought about that at all." When he stopped, he was less than a foot away from me. "I've been so consumed with all my own crap. Alexi leaving us, Jessica quitting,…work. I never even stopped to consider what all this must be like for you. Moving here, so far away from everything…and you don't even know anyone."

With him so close, and the way his proximity made me feel, I found it difficult to look him in the eye. I forced myself to do it. "Well, I do know Garrett and Daniel," I tried to joke. Only I was so nervous, my voice came out in a whisper. I cleared my throat. "And you," I managed a little louder.

All I could think about was what it would feel like for him to reach out, take me in his arms, and hold me against his bare chest.

"We don't count," Jacob smiled.

"You count to me."

At that, we both fell silent for several awkward seconds.

"You know, I was thinking I'd come out here and get my swim in before bed. But honestly, it's so beautiful out, I don't really feel like exercising right now."

I nodded.

"Maybe it would be nice to have a glass of wine? Would you like one? There's a wine fridge by the grill, and I keep a few really good bottles in there."

Still unable to form a complete sentence, I swallowed and nodded.

"Great," he smiled and looked genuinely happy to share a drink with me under the stars. "Is cabernet okay with you? The one I'm thinking of is delicious, but I have some whites in the colder fridge if you'd prefer."

"Cab is fine," I said.

"Perfect," he said as he walked backward toward the stairs. "I'll be right back. Oh, and there's also the spa." He pointed to the far end of the pool. "If you feel like having a soak, I can turn the jets on."

While Jacob got the wine, pulled the cork, and found two wine glasses in the outdoor kitchen, I treaded water in the deep end and tried to look casual. Like this was no big deal. Of course, because I usually hung around in sexy red bikinis in heated pools attached to multimillion-dollar homes with a man so handsome it nearly made my heart stop.

God, this was so stupid. Wasn't it? I had the distinct impression that Jacob was flirting with me. Or, at the very least, he was skating a very thin line between appropriate employer-employee interactions. And quite frankly, so was I, and I knew it. Wine? In a hot tub? While barely dressed? Come on, Libby. I was twenty-six, not sixteen. I knew exactly what could happen.

Especially once we started drinking that wine.

As Jacob made his way back across the pool deck, holding the bottle by the neck in one hand and the two glasses in the other, I took a very deep breath and let it out.

The truth was, a big part of me wanted something to happen—something irrevocable, something irresponsible, something that involved the feel of his hands running over my body and the taste of his mouth against mine.

It had been so long since I'd had that.

CHAPTER 31

We decided to sit in the hot tub. All it took to convince me was Jacob's questioning look and a suggestive nod toward the bubbling spa at the end of the pool.

As I lowered myself into the roiling waters, it was impossible not to notice the nervous flutter of anticipation in my stomach. The hot water burned my skin at first, but after several seconds, I became used to it and enjoyed the heat as it penetrated muscles I didn't know needed to relax. I knew the last several weeks had been stressful, but maybe it had been more traumatic than I'd given myself credit for. I eased myself back up into the seat and positioned my spine between two intense rows of jets.

I should've taken advantage of this earlier.

I watched Jacob enter the hot tub, still carrying the bottle and two glasses. I was only slightly disappointed when he chose to sit a respectable distance away from me on the opposite side of the tub. He set the glasses on the tile behind him and filled them with rich red wine. With one glass in hand, he turned to me and reached across the sizzling waters between us. When I took it from him, his fingers brushed against mine.

Was it completely my imagination, or was the way his eyes met mine slightly suggestive?

I was suddenly very worried that I was completely off base and in danger of making a fool of myself. Was my boss was flirting with me? Or was it just wishful thinking?

"Thank you," I said, feeling like I should probably steer my thoughts back to safer territory, I asked him, “So. Did you and Alexi buy the house, or build it?”

Jacob returned to his seat, picked up his glass of wine, and then turned his gaze on me. “Built it. From the ground up. Both my parents…they were in a car accident. I used the money I inherited from them to buy this land and build us this house. I had imagined it as a sanctuary for our family. Unfortunately, I think Alexi only ever saw it as an isolated prison.”

“I'm sorry about your parents,” I whispered.

He nodded. “Thank you. It was a long time ago.”

“How did you and Alexi meet?”

Jacob took a sip from his wine and placed the glass on the tile ledge behind him. “At a lecture,” he said. “She had released her second film and was becoming known as an expert in her field. I was doing some research for a book I wanted to write… which I never did, actually.

“You write books?”

Jacob smiled. “As a professor of literature at a university? Yes. At least, I'm supposed to. I should publish work regularly. But to date, the only thing I've ever managed to get to print was my original project for my Ph.D. Back then, I'd been feeling stuck, and pigeonholed, and I imagined I might find some creative liberation in a pseudonym and trying my hand at popular fiction. Alexi, who I had never met, was a guest lecturer at NYU. I signed up thinking I was doing research for my new writing career. To my surprise, when I approached her after and asked if we could speak more over dinner, she said yes."

I nodded. It was easy to imagine the two of them meeting for the first time. Falling in love over drinks, a delicious meal, and inside a perfectly lit expensive New York restaurant. "What was her lecture about?" I asked.

"What else other than serial killers?" He smiled.

"So, you were going to write a book about…"

"Yes." He nodded. "A serial killer. One who got away with it. I imagined it from his, or her, perspective. I was tired of being an unsuccessful, unread, underpaid writer. I imagined I could milk an entire series out of one killer's crimes before he, or she, was finally caught or killed."

"So, like it'd be from the bad guy's perspective?"

Jacob broke into a wide grin and raise his finger. "Ah, but no one is ever the bad guy in their own story. I imagined my protagonist as more of an antihero, I guess." He reached for his wine and took another long swallow. "Although, I never did scratch out more than a few pages. So much for bright ideas. Anyway, that's enough about me and my tragic beginnings. Let's hear about you."

This surprised me, and I fell into an awkward silence as I tried to figure out what he meant. "Me?"

Jacob finished a big swallow from his glass and smiled. "Yes, you. It occurs to me that, for weeks now, this has been a pretty one-sided conversation between us. You listening to and learning about every aspect of our lives. Taking it all on without question. Which, believe me, I am more than grateful for. I would never have survived these huge transitions without you. Seriously, Libby, you've been a lifesaver."

It made me blush and look away. I hated to admit how good it felt to be complimented for a job well done. To be recognized and appreciated. With Nicola, it had been nothing but insults, accusations, and a constant barrage of micromanaging that she seemed to relish. Here, Jacob had pretty much given me full rein. It was nice to know he noticed I was doing a good job.

"I guess I don't really know what to say. What would you like to know?"

"Start by telling me a little more about yourself. I mean, obviously, I know you're from Nebraska. You're a hard worker. Incredibly reliable. And my sons, despite being sometimes difficult, seem to be warming up to you. So, you must also be some sort of a magician."

I felt my eyebrows raise. Daniel was coming around, sure. But Garrett barely spoke to me and basically lived in his room playing video games non-stop—I would hardly consider this warming up. Did Jacob really not see that his oldest son acted like he hated my guts?

Jacob smiled at me again, and maybe it was just the way the light from the hot tub was illuminating his features, but his grin was decidedly more wicked.

I took a drink of my wine, which was strong but smooth. Rich and oaky, with an aftertaste that reminded me of cherries. I didn't really like red wine, but maybe I just never had one as good as this one. Something told me Jacob was the kind of man with a wine cellar meant to impress.

"Well... I work as a nanny."

Jacob rolled his eyes at me.

"Okay. I went to a small high school. And I mean really small. There were less than a hundred kids in the whole thing. I had originally planned on moving down to Colorado to go to college. But when my dad got sick...." I shrugged. "Things change, I guess. My life carried me in a very different direction from the one I had imagined."

"So, you never finished college?" Jacob asked.

"I never even started college. My dad had a stroke, a bad one, the summer after my senior year. First, we were thinking I could just delay my admission that first semester while we figured out what his prognosis would be. But then a semester turned into a year, one year into two." I shrugged. "For a long time, I stayed in town and was able to manage caring for him while working at one of the local restaurants. But it got more serious, he needed professional care, and I wasn't equipped or qualified to handle that. So that's when I started to nanny. I figured out fairly soon that if I could nanny for a family in a big city, they would pay more money. What I send home, coupled with his Medicare, affords better help to take care of him. I don't want him in a state-run home. At least not any of the ones in our state."

Jacob's expression turned serious. "That was a lot for somebody to take on at your age."

"I guess. But I never really thought of it that way. It was just one of those things that had to be done. And as the things that needed taking care of kept cropping up, I just kept taking care of them."

Because what choice did I have, really?

Jacob reached for the wine bottle on the tile behind him and held it out to me. "Would you like another glass?"

I looked at my glass and was surprised to find it already empty. "Wow," I said, a little embarrassed. "That went down fast."

Jacob crossed the distance between us and poured more wine into my glass. "It's really smooth. One of my favorites." He then topped off his own glass, and instead of making his way back across the spa, he placed the nearly empty bottle on the tile behind me and then sat next to me. "Is this okay?" he asked. "You're so soft-spoken. It's hard to hear you over the jets." He smiled. "But I don't want to make you uncomfortable."

I shook my head even though, with him this close, I was uncomfortable. Very uncomfortable. But not in the way he was suggesting. Fireworks exploded across my nervous system and awakened a desire in me. It was unlike anything I had ever experienced. Only a few inches separated his body from mine. Certainly, it could only be a matter of time before we accidentally brushed against each other. "It's fine," I said. "I do speak too quietly. In school, my teachers always tried to get me to speak up."

Jacob turned in his seat so that his body faced mine. "Their coaching never stuck?"

I smiled, closed my eyes, and shook my head. "I guess not."

"Well, I happen to think it's a charming quality. And perfectly matches all your other wonderful characteristics." He raised his wine glass to mine. Picking up on his cue, I raised mine, too, and we toasted. "Libby Luck, I don't think you should change a thing."

CHAPTER 32

The bottle was gone. I had no idea how long Jacob and I had been sitting in the hot tub, but the moon was now high and directly over our heads, and the tips of my fingers had turned into deeply wrinkled prunes.

He had listened intently, and it seemed like he actually cared about my father's illness, my mother's death when I was eight, and the seemingly small and insignificant things I had been doing with my life since I left high school.

Laying it all out like this, for the first time ever, made me realize exactly how much I had not done with my life in the last eight years.

It wasn't like he brought it up as a comparison or a dig at me in any way, but when I asked Jacob how old he had been when he finished his PhD, he shared that he'd been twenty-seven years old.

Only one year older than I was right now.

Thinking about it made me feel panicky. Like my life had

been slipping away from me. Faster and faster, day after day, week after week, and now years had gone by. What could I say I had accomplished?

"I should go back to school," I blurted. My sudden admission surprised me, and I felt the heat of my own embarrassment rush to my cheeks.

But Jacob didn't miss a beat or even seem surprised that I said such a thing. "You're obviously very smart, Libby. You absolutely should go back to school." Then he finished off the last swallow of his wine and placed his glass on the spa's edge behind us. "I know it can be hard to go back. Doing what I do... Well, let's just say I have seen people of all ages come and go for a variety of life circumstances. But if you ever need anything from me, a letter of recommendation, or even just some guidance on how to get it done, I hope you know I would be happy to do it."

I looked up at him, his complexion ruddy from the heat, his thick hair now wet and slicked back from his face; it was difficult to understand how Alexi North could choose to leave a man like this.

“I know it can be difficult. Choosing what's best for you instead of what is expected by everyone else. My parents...they owned a trucking business. I was their only child and was left alone a lot as a kid. Which is probably why I ended up loving books and literature as much as I do. But once I finished college, they fully intended for me to step into the lives they had built and take over their business so they could retire.”

“Obviously that didn't happen,” I said.

“No. I worked as a student teacher while I waited to hear back from the schools I'd applied to for graduate school. *A complete waste of time and money.* That's what my parents thought and said. They never understood me. Not as a child, and definitely not when I became an adult unwilling to mold my life to their wishes." Jacob shook his head and took a long drink. "So, while it may not be obvious to you given how far I've come, I want you to know that I know what it's like to go it alone in this world. If you ever decide you want some help, or even just some advice, please know I'm available and happy to provide it."

I couldn't remember the last time someone had offered to help me—with anything. His generosity, coupled with his good looks and general proximity to me at the moment, was an intoxicating combination. The fact that I actually was intoxicated and likely had seriously impaired judgment wasn't helping.

"Thank you," was all I managed to say. Because my mind was thoroughly occupied with running through what-if scenarios. What if I reached out and touched his arm? What if I leaned in just a couple inches closer to him? What if my hand slid across the bench between us and came to rest on his thigh?

"Well," Jacob suddenly said and stood up. "I don't think we should probably boil ourselves too much longer in this hot pot. Especially after finishing a whole bottle of wine. The next thing you know, one of us will be passing out, probably me, and after all you've already done, I certainly couldn't ask you to drag my drunk ass out of the hot tub as well."

His sudden declaration--he was clearly ready for the night to end--took me by surprise. It also made me feel incredibly stupid for absolutely everything I'd been thinking and fantasizing about since we'd gotten into the hot tub. Jacob made his way to the steps with more force and less grace than when he'd gotten in. With his hasty exit, water sloshed around his body and churned up from his legs.

I swallowed my embarrassment, hoping against hope that my body language hadn't given away the highly inappropriate thoughts I'd just been having. It certainly seemed like something I had done suddenly spooked Jacob and scared him away. I grabbed the bottle he left behind and my own empty glass and followed him to the stairs. Maybe if I didn't say anything, just acted like nothing was weird, and like I hadn't just been having crazy thoughts, everything would be fine.

Because the truth was, I reminded myself, nothing had happened. I hadn't actually done any of the things I had imagined. I hadn't made a move or touched him in any way. There was nothing for me to feel ashamed about.

And yet, when I reached the stairs, and Jacob reached out his hand for me to take, I did feel ashamed when his eyes traveled the length of my wet, mostly naked body.

Because what I wanted, more than anything right now, was for him to take me in his arms, hold me close, and kiss me.

Could he sense this, somehow? Was there a look on my face that gave it all away?

It seemed like Jacob dragged his gaze away from me as he turned toward the house. "Stupid me," he said. "I should've thought to grab us some towels. I'm sorry, Libby, I don't know what I was thinking." He walked away so quickly, it was impossible to not see he was trying to escape.

I crossed my arms over my breasts and followed him, walking slow through the slick, wet puddles he left in his wake, careful not to slip and fall. Before I even reached the house,

Jacob was already re-emerging from it with two oversized, blue and white striped, fluffy pool towels. He slung one over his own shoulders and unfolded the second one. To my surprise, he held it out for me, and when I reached him, he swung it behind my shoulders and wrapped it around my wet body.

He held the towel closed in front of me for several seconds, and even though I wasn't brave enough to look up, I could feel his eyes gazing down at me.

He dropped his hands and turned away in one swift movement. "Well, it was good hanging out with you, Libby. I should probably get to bed, or I'll never wake up tomorrow morning." He stood by and held the back door open as I passed in front of him.

The house was dark. The only illumination was from the outdoor lights streaming through the back windows.

Jacob looked outside, seeming to realize we left all the lights on out there. "I'm just going to go shut everything down outside."

"OK," I said. "Good night."

"Good night, Libby."

CHAPTER 33

Lying in my bed, with my wet hair now twisted into the enormous pool towel, I stared at the ceiling above me, thinking of Jacob and the evening we'd just shared.

He had looked at me. Really looked. I wasn't crazy. The more I thought about it and the expression on his face when I stepped out of the spa, the more certain I was. It didn't last long; he'd turned away so fast…but not before I saw it.

The hunger in his eyes.

I flung my arm above my head, closed my eyes, and allowed myself to imagine what might have happened if either of us had leaned even a fraction of an inch into the other. It was probably just the wine still creating havoc in my body and mind, but when I thought about Jacob's hand touching mine, it was like I could feel it. When I imagined him pulling me into his arms, it was like I knew the heat of his chest against mine and the weight of his arms across my back.

When he lowered his head, and I tilted mine up, the brush of his lips—

Stop. I opened my eyes and rolled onto my side. I needed to stop right now. Yes, I had been drinking, but letting my fantasy run away with my reality was a huge mistake. I didn't need this depth and degree of confusion in my life.

Outside, the moon now hung high in the sky. When I came into my room, I hadn't bothered to pull the drapes. Now, as I lay on my side trying to not think about Jacob, the blue light flooded in through both the windows in my bedroom and the attached sitting room next door. The view was too bright, too beautiful, too distracting for me to fall asleep. I would either need to get up and shut the drapes or throw a pillow over my head and wait until my body and mind wound down.

As things stood, I didn't feel like I would be able to get to sleep for hours.

I took a breath and pushed myself up from the bed. My head spun slightly from the sudden movement, and I realized I should probably drink some water before bed anyway; otherwise, I would likely wake up with a hangover.

Still only wearing the damp red bikini, I grabbed the white bathrobe from the hook on the back of the door in my bathroom. As I walked toward the bedroom door, I pushed my arms through the oversized sleeves and cinched the thick tie around my waist. I would head downstairs, get myself the largest glass I could find, and fill it with water to keep on my bedside table for the night. It might be a good idea to find some ibuprofen as well.

I pulled the door open, then fell back a step in shock. "My god!" I said as my hands flew to my chest. Adrenaline shot through my nervous system and made my hands and feet tingle. A second later, my mind processed what I was seeing, and a nervous laugh flew from my mouth.

"I'm so sorry," Jacob said. He held up both his hands, his expression wide-eyed and surprised. "I didn't mean to scare you, Libby. I'm such an idiot."

"No," I said, still laughing at myself. "I just wasn't expecting...." I shook my head. "It's fine." I lowered my hands and stuffed them into the robe's deep pockets.

Jacob North was standing outside my bedroom door in the middle of the night.

"Is everything okay?" I asked. Maybe there was something wrong with Daniel, I thought.

Jacob nodded. "Yes. Everything is fine," he said.

But he was having a hard time making eye contact with me.

"I just..." he started but struggled to finish his sentence. "Wanted to check on you," he said. "Make sure you were okay." His eyes found mine and held my gaze. "We were in the spa for a long time...plus the wine...maybe you didn't feel...." He trailed off, and it didn't seem like he was going to find his way back to his sentence.

"I'm okay," I whispered. "Thank you for checking on me."

Jacob nodded. Even in the dark, I saw the lost expression on his face. I knew, instinctually, that this man was not only here to check on me. The problem was--who could and would cross the uncrossable line between us first.

He wanted it. I could feel the need radiating off him.

I wanted it. My own body felt like an inferno that would spontaneously combust at any moment.

"Good," he breathed. "That's good." But he just stood there, waiting, watching, hoping.

He wouldn't make a move. I knew it. He was in a position of power. He was the one probably most in the wrong.

And everything about this was wrong.

I didn't think, I reached for his hand. Took it into my own. It was a simple gesture. Common. Innocent. A little act that allowed us to back away from it without another thought or feeling about anything inappropriate transpiring.

I pressed my thumb into the center of his palm. "I was just going to get some water," I said.

Jacob stared down at our joined hands. Seconds passed. When I didn't pull my hand from his, and he didn't either, he exhaled and raised his eyes to mine. "I'll get it for you."

I met his gaze and knew…we'd already gone too far to turn back. "Yes. Please."

Jacob closed his eyes and pulled my hand until my body fell into his. He pulled my body close to his and lowered his mouth to my ear. "Tell me to leave, Libby. Right now. Tell me to go away, and I'll do it."

My hands ran up his back, and I pulled him closer. "Stay," I whispered back.

Things moved fast after that.

His mouth was on my neck in an instant. I felt his tongue, his hot breath, and then his hand pulling at the robe's tie around my waist as he swept me backward and into the room.

He must have used his foot to slam the door shut behind us because his hands—they never left my body.

CHAPTER 34

Lying in my bed, with my disheveled hair spilled across the white pillow beneath me, I stared at the ceiling and thought about what I'd done. What Jacob and I had done.

Next to me, he was still asleep. His hand rested like a heavy weight on my hip. I could hear his deep and rhythmic breaths; he was sated and sound asleep.

Out of the corner of my eye, the red bikini sat, discarded and accusing, on the floor beside the bed. Jacob had removed the garment quickly but then taken his time with absolutely everything that came after. I had never before experienced anything exactly like what had happened between us, and it occurred to me that I had never before truly made love with a man.

I'd had sex before, yes. With those other men, boys really, my body had been felt up, fondled…fucked. It had been used as a vehicle mainly for someone else's pleasure.

But tonight, with Jacob, everything I thought I knew about sex was rewired. At first, when he'd basically ripped the bathing suit from me, I had assumed it would end up just like every other time for me. A man panting and thrusting on top of me while I lay there waiting for them to finish.

But that wasn't even close to what had happened last night. Once the initial flurry of getting into the room and getting naked had passed, Jacob paused, took a step back, and just looked at me.

"My God, Libby. Do you have any idea how wonderful you are?"

Overwhelmed by both his stare and frank appraisal, I found I couldn't do anything other than close my eyes and shake my head twice as a deep blush spread throughout my entire body.

Then he swept me into his arms again and kissed my lips, my ear, my neck, and whispered in my ear, "You are so beautiful, Libby. And if you don't know that, then I can only assume someone hasn't been treating you right."

And that was probably true, but there was little time for me to worry about or dissect this factoid from my past because that was when Jacob lifted me into his arms, carried me to my bed, and proceeded to spend the next hour, kissing, caressing, and coaxing my body to life in a way no one ever had before.

And when I came and cried out from the sheer pleasure and joy of finally, finally understanding what it meant to be made love to, only then did Jacob seem to shift his focus from my enjoyment to his own, allowing himself to thrust deeper and harder into me until he also cried out and came to rest on top of me.

His body was heavy, and it pressed mine into the bed

beneath us, but it felt good, solid, like an anchor keeping me connected to a safe space. I wrapped my arms and legs around him and held on. Willing myself to be present and enjoy this moment and not worry about what might happen when we were both sober and facing the light of day tomorrow.

And now, as the light of day flooded through my still-open bedroom windows and the beginning of a headache started to take shape at the base of my skull, the worry did come.

What the hell had I been thinking? Once again, Nicola Drake's prediction, which now felt like a curse, wormed through my mind.

It was easy to imagine her smug and satisfied expression should she ever discover how right she had been. Here I was, landed on my back, naked next to my boss.

What if, by the end of the day, I found myself once again unemployed and with nowhere to go? I didn't even have a car I could live in anymore.

"What are you thinking about?" Jacob suddenly whispered from his pillow beside me.

I turned my head and saw his eyes were now open and gazing at me. Two lines of worry had formed between his eyebrows.

"Nothing," I lied.

"Why don't I think that's true?" He said, lifting himself up on one elbow so that he could look down at me. "I'm afraid to ask this, but do you regret what we did? Because that's the first thing I thought when I looked at your face, the expression you had... It made me afraid that you wished I wasn't here, that it never happened, like, maybe you needed to plan an escape."

This surprised me. It was not at all what I expected he'd say.

I looked into his eyes and blurted out the truth, "I'm scared, Jacob. I'm scared that we'd been drinking, got caught up in a moment, and that you're the one who would have regrets this morning. I need this job. I mean, I really, really need this job. And I'm lying here absolutely terrified that I have completely messed up."

The worry on his face melted away, and he smiled before he leaned down and kissed my lips once. "I don't regret anything. And I hope you don't either because this, you, Libby, are the best thing that has happened to my life in years." He moved closer until his naked body was pressed next to mine. He pulled me tight into his arms until my back was spooned perfectly against his chest. He brushed my hair from my neck, and I felt his lips below my ear, hot and soft for a moment before he whispered, "I don't want you to worry anymore. I don't want you to worry about where you'll go or how you'll live. This is your home now, Libby. You live here. And I'm going to take care of you. I promise."

I closed my eyes, surprised by the tightness in my throat and the sudden urge to cry. I hadn't realized how much I needed to hear that. How desperate I was to feel safe, like everything would be okay. The relief of knowing that someone else, for once, would protect me.

I had been doing that for myself and others for so long...I was tired. So very tired of trying to keep it all together. As Jacob's hand ran down my side and over my belly. I let out a breath and felt something inside me release. Like a tightly wound tendon of dread and worry that had been strung inside me since childhood. Since my mother's death, since my father fell apart, since my whole identity has been shaped and crafted by dread and responsibility and never, ever being able to let go.

So as Jacob kissed my neck, touched my body, held me close, and promised I would be okay, I felt that tightness I'd been hanging onto let go. I rolled towards him. I gently pushed him onto his back so I could straddle him. "I don't regret this," I whispered as I reached down and put him inside me, wanting him in a way I had never wanted anyone before.

Jacob closed his eyes and pulled me down on top of him. He kissed me again as he thrust up into me.

"I'll take care of you, Libby. I'll take care of everything if you let me. I will be perfect for you. I will make everything perfect for you. Everything. I promise."

And when he pressed himself once more, deep and hard inside me, I arched my back, and believed every word he said.

CHAPTER 35

On the drive into school, my eyes kept wandering to the rearview mirror and the reflection of Daniel in the backseat. Next to me, Garrett sat in his usual stony silence with one exception. Instead of having his face glued to his phone for the entire drive, he stared out the passenger window.

Once Jacob and I had pulled ourselves out of my bed, we went downstairs to the kitchen and found Daniel already sitting at the counter with a bowl of cereal in front of him. I had assumed Garrett wasn't up yet until I heard the back door open and shut. A second later, he walked into the kitchen.

"Hey there!" Jacob said with obviously forced enthusiasm. "You're up bright and early," he said, and reached to tousle Garrett's hair. But Garrett was faster and dodged his dad's attempt at awkward affection. "What were you doing out so early?"

"Walking," Garrett said flatly.

"Aren't you hungry?" Jacob asked. "I can make—"

"Not hungry," he said, then headed up the stairs to his room.

Jacob was jovial and acting like nothing was wrong, but I was immediately worried that Garrett somehow knew what his father and I had done.

At the counter, Daniel appeared oblivious and his usual self as he scooped sugary cereal into his mouth while watching a cartoon on his iPad.

I was probably being paranoid. When I saw that Jacob was going about his morning as usual, making coffee and putting his bagel into the toaster, I decided to pull myself together, follow his lead, and try my best to pretend nothing weird had happened or changed.

When it was time for him to go, Garrett was still nowhere to be seen, but Jacob kissed Daniel on top of his head and gave my hand a private squeeze. When I looked into his eyes, he gave me a knowing look and a smile, but all he said was, "I'll see you guys later. Have a good day…. All of you." And then he headed out the door.

I returned my eyes to the road in front of me, determined to not worry, at least not right now, about how Garrett would react when he found out things had changed between his dad and me.

Not good was my first guess. Horribly was my second.

Instead, I let myself think of other things. My heart and mind both started to consider, in a real way, what Jacob was promising me. My hand squeezed the steering wheel. If things worked out, and I really wanted them to, this could become my actual life. Not just somewhere I worked.

"This is your home now, Libby," Jacob had said in bed this morning. I didn't think he only meant I should make myself really comfortable. Somehow, his tone had conveyed more gravity and weight. And while it felt slightly ridiculous to imagine, I had only slept with this man one time, twice if you counted this morning. It wasn't like I was going to start picking out a wedding dress, but I got the impression Jacob wasn't just thinking of me and my place in his life as a temporary pleasure.

My eyes again pulled to the rearview mirror, but this time, Daniel was no longer staring at his iPad. He was staring back, directly at me, as if he could read my every illicit thought.

It was ridiculous, but I couldn't help but feel like the kid just caught me doing something I shouldn't. Imagining myself in his mother's place before the divorce papers were even drawn up. Guilty, I looked away and returned my eyes to the road as my hand adjusted the mirror.

When we reached the school and pulled into the drop-off lane, Garrett and Daniel were unbuckled and out their doors before I could even turn around in my seat. "Have a good—"

Garrett slammed the door shut, cutting off my sentence.

"Day," I finished as he strode up the sidewalk. Daniel ran beside him, trying to keep up, his bag bouncing on his back.

Did Garrett know? Did he see something? Hear something? I suddenly felt sick. What if Daniel had gotten up in the middle of the night, looking for either Jacob or me, and had stumbled into my room and seen us? Sweaty, naked, entangled, and passed out in my bed. Just the thought of it made me panic. Because whatever Jacob and I were going to be, I didn't want the boys to get hurt. Jessica had already left them. Their mother had up and disappeared and was barely in communication with them as far as I knew. The last thing those kids needed was more upheaval.

I would talk to Jacob about it tonight when he got home. I pulled the Jeep into a parking spot on the street outside the Coffee Klatch and switched off the engine.

Through the window, I could see Kyra behind the counter making drinks for the three women who were standing and talking to each other near the register. There was another woman behind the counter. She was older, with pixie-cut brown hair and a slight rounding of her neck and shoulders, like she'd spent years hunched over a desk staring at computer work that had taken an irreversible toll on her. When the woman moved to the register and began ringing the customers up, I realized this must be Trisha, the owner of the Coffee Klatch. The jealous wife who hated Jessica for the rumors, valid or not, that she'd slept with Trisha's husband.

I sat back in the driver's seat and wondered if I should go inside. I had rushed over here, nervous and excited to tell Kyra about what had happened last night with Jacob. But now, seeing the busy shop and the presence of Trisha, I was having second thoughts.

Kyra was my friend, the first real friend I'd had in years. I wanted to trust her and tell her how amazing last night had been—but what if she thought of me like Nicola? Just another stupid girl who had landed on her back. Another Jessica who had slept with another married man?

Because I knew that was precisely what Trisha would think of me if she found out.

And there was also that—the finding out. The opening myself, Jacob, and the kids up to town gossip and speculation—just like Jessica had.

Alexi had left Jacob. She was seeing another man and had

been for years. She was the one who wanted the divorce—that was the truth. But I knew as well as anyone that when it came to salacious gossip, the actual truth didn't matter at all. All people would see is that a new nanny had come to work and live with the North family, and now she was fucking the father.

They would assume I was the reason Alexi and Jacob broke up.

I took a breath and blew it out. No, I wouldn't tell Kyra about what had happened, at least not yet. I would act like nothing at all had changed.

I grabbed my wallet from my backpack, got out of the Jeep, and closed the door behind me. I headed into the shop just as the three women were leaving with their brown paper to-go cups. As I approached the counter, Kyra looked up and smiled at me. "Hey there," she said, but then her sight line slid over my shoulder, and her mouth dropped open in surprise. She pointed out the window behind me. "Libby! Your car!"

CHAPTER 36

Confused, I turned around and saw that the backdoor of the Jeep was wide open. Someone, a man, was leaning into the backseat.

I froze. Speechless, all I could do was watch as my brain worked to figure out what was happening. The man stood up straight for a second before diving back into the car. I recognized him immediately. It was the guy, the same one who tried to break into the Jeep yesterday.

My hand moved to the front pocket of my jeans, and I felt the key fob still there—I hadn't locked the doors. Distracted by my thoughts about Jacob and last night and whether or not I'd tell Kyra, I'd never reached into my pocket and locked the doors.

How could I be so stupid?

The guy stood back up, and all I could do was watch while he slammed the door and turned away.

"Hey!" Kyra shouted. She ran past me and barreled through

the coffee shop's glass door. "Stop!" she screamed at the guy. Kyra was holding a wooden baseball bat. I stood, stunned and speechless, as she raised it over her head and ran toward the guy.

"Kyra," I said, but my voice came out in a whisper and held no power to stop whatever horrible thing was about to happen.

Seeing Kyra and the bat coming for him, the guy looked scared and backpedaled away from the Jeep and into the street.

Kyra swung the bat in front of her twice, then used it to point at the guy. "Next one is going to take your head off," she screamed.

I couldn't believe what I was watching. I turned around and looked at Trisha, whose expression was just as shocked as I felt. I had to stop this before Kyra or someone else got really hurt. There wasn't even anything in the Jeep for the guy to steal.

Do something, Libby. Move. Now

I forced myself to take a step, then another, and before I knew it, I was pushing through the door just as Kyra was taking another swing at the guy. Several onlookers had emerged from the shops lining the street, watching it all go down. Several people had their phones out, recording, but no one seemed to be doing anything to help the situation.

"Kyra!" I shouted. "Stop!"

She didn't stop or even turn around, but the guy glanced at me as he backed into the middle of the street.

"Drop it!" Kyra shouted as she made another charge at the guy.

He glanced around him, looking panicked, and took several more clumsy steps backward before he stumbled and fell in the street—something flew out of his hand and landed several feet away from him.

A vehicle was barreling down the street. It didn't stop or even slow down—the driver didn't see the guy.

No.

The guy lunged to grab what he'd dropped right as the driver slammed on the brakes. The sound of screeching tires filled the chilled autumn air, and the truck stopped inches from the man who was now staring down the chrome grill of the pickup that had almost ended his life.

Kyra ran for the object the guy had dropped and swooped it up as the guy rolled over, got to his feet, and started running. He sprinted to the other side of the street, and weaved between shocked pedestrians who yelled at him to, "Stop!" and, "Watch it!"

On the next block, he took a left down an alley next to the deli.

I stood, shocked and staring after him as the chaos from the truck driver and all the witnesses continued to play out around me.

"I got it!" Kyra said.

She was now right next to me. I turned and looked into her triumphantly smiling face as she held out her hand to me. She was holding a cell phone. I stared at it and tried to make sense of it.

Tired of waiting for me to catch up, Kyra shook her head, grabbed my hand, and placed the phone in it. "Good thing I stopped that guy. It would have totally sucked for you if he'd gotten away with your phone." She was panting hard as she came down from her adrenaline rush. "I had my phone stolen in Rio two years ago. What a pain in the ass that was."

People were starting to crowd around us. A few were asking Kyra if she was okay. The guy driving the truck was standing in front of his vehicle, shaking his head and staring down at the place where he'd almost killed another man. One woman suggested that the police should be called. Several people shared that they had the whole thing on video in case they needed the evidence or a description of the guy.

It was a circus of activity on the normally sleepy street.

But all I could do was stare at the cell phone in my hand. The phone the guy had tried to steal from the backseat of the Jeep. The phone Kyra assumed was mine, but that was, in fact, not mine.

My phone was in my back pocket.

I turned it over twice in my hand, trying to think. It wasn't Daniel's or Garrett's. They both had the latest model.

It wasn't Jacob's. His had a blue case.

This phone was small and old. The screen was cracked.

And while I'd been driving the Jeep for over a month now, I'd had no idea this was anywhere inside it.

But that guy? He knew this phone was in the car.

And exactly where to find it.

CHAPTER 37

Back at the house, I stared at the cracked phone on the kitchen counter. Several logical explanations had occurred to me on the drive home. The most obvious was that it was a phone that either Daniel, Jacob, or Alexi had lost at some point. When they were unable to find it, they simply replaced it with a new phone.

I picked it up and held its dead weight in my palm.

I realized it could also have been a phone that once belonged to Jessica. And, given the fact it was found in the vehicle she used to drive, it was highly likely.

It was also clear that *the guy* had been after this phone all along. Which meant he knew it was there and who it belonged to.

It could be his phone. Maybe he had been inside the Jeep at some point, for whatever reason, and left his phone?

But then why not just say that? Instead of skulking around and acting shady, he probably would have just explained the situation to me. If it was his, it would be easy enough to prove by just turning the thing on.

And why would that guy have wanted an old, lost phone that belonged to one of the Norths?

I took a breath and blew it out—it had to be Jessica's. And there had to be a reason that guy had been trying so hard to get his hands on it.

I flipped it on end and looked at the charging port—the thing wasn't just old; it was ancient. Nothing at all like the small charging hole on more modern phones. This one was like the first phone my dad had given me when I was twelve, his ancient hand-me-down. I didn't have any way to charge this thing.

Unless.

I pushed myself away from the counter and headed up the nearest set of stairs with the phone. If the Norths were like every other family on the planet, there was a good chance I would find a cupboard, drawer, or storage box with a collection of charging cables, both old and new, for a variety of devices. If they'd never sorted through it, I would probably find what I needed to bring this tiny dinosaur to life.

I turned down the hall that led to Alexi's office. It was such a collection of odds and ends, I felt sure that among Alexi's detritus there would be a box of cables and chargers. Probably a whole closet filled with an enormous tangle of cords.

I reached for the doorknob and turned, but it didn't budge.

I tried the other direction…it was locked again. I dropped my hand and stared at the closed door. Obviously, Jacob had relocked the door after he'd found me in here yesterday afternoon. I stepped backward and tried to push down the uncomfortable feeling taking shape in my stomach.

This was Alexi's office. Her private space. Jacob had every right to protect her privacy.

But, given what had happened between us last night and again this morning…something about this also bothered me. It wasn't like I thought having sex with Jacob entitled me to access every square inch of his house.

But relocking the door? It made me feel like, despite having confided in me about his marriage ending and having sex with me, he didn't trust me.

Or he's hiding something from you.

I closed my eyes and shook that last thought away. I didn't really believe that. Jacob had been nothing but kind, supportive, and demonstratively grateful for me being here. And now, right when our relationship was becoming more, wasn't the time to poison the well by entertaining unhelpful and suspicious thoughts.

I reached out and ran my thumb over the keyhole in the knob.

It was probably a force of habit, just muscle memory. When Jacob left this room, he was used to locking it for whatever reason. Maybe it was something Alexi insisted on. After all, her work and research were in there. She was artistic and famous; maybe she was a little weird about her space.

Then again, given Alexi's grim documentary subject, maybe they kept this room locked to keep the boys out. It was their attempt to shield and protect their sons from the horrors of Alexi's work for as long as possible.

I took a deep breath and a step back. That was the most obvious answer. Alexi's walls and desk were littered with notes detailing the disturbing crimes and criminals central to her films. But far worse were the photographs paper clipped to those pages and pinned to the walls.

I may have been inside the room for only a few moments, but it was enough to notice the tragic and violent imagery all around me. Alexi had photographs of the serial killers she studied, but also their victims. The photos were the ones used in the missing-person flyers and news articles. The victims were primarily women, but not all, and the before photos were taken from school pictures and driver's licenses or were candid shots snapped by family and friends during smiling happy times. Those were the before photos, and there were only a few.

If this had been all there was to see, there wouldn't have been much reason to keep the door locked. However, Alexi had far more photos detailing the gruesome aftermath of the crimes. These photos were taken by the investigators and were documents of the unimaginable horrors that were inflicted on the victims.

I hadn't looked closely, but it was enough to see the flayed flesh, dead eyes, missing limbs, and more blood than I could stomach.

It was terrible to imagine what impact those sights could have on a child who was simply stumbling into his mother's workspace.

I backed away from the door and headed downstairs. There was somewhere else I might find what I needed to charge the phone.

Jacob's library.

CHAPTER 38

Unlike Alexi's office, the double doors to Jacob's library swung open with ease. I stepped into the space. Here, I felt welcomed and at home, not like an interloping spy. This was probably because Jacob had invited me in the first day I had arrived. He encouraged me to use the space and read any of his books anytime I liked.

If he came home at this very minute and found me here, I was certain there wouldn't be anything awkward about it. He'd probably love to see me lounging in one of the plush, cushioned armchairs, reading a book I'd selected from his shelves.

But today, I wasn't here to read.

I headed straight for his enormous desk near the fireplace. I pushed his chair out of the way so I could access the drawers. I pulled them open, one after another, and found that Jacob, unlike his soon-to-be ex-wife, was very organized and meticulous in his office space. The thin center drawer had two sectioned trays. The items Jacob kept here, pens, pencils, sticky notes, tape, and a stapler, were kept separated and tidy.

I was about to close the drawer and move on to the next one when I noticed something else and stopped. Everything was also precisely aligned. The sticky notes, all yellow, were perfectly stacked. The pens, all black and the same type, were laid side by side like writing soldiers, ready and reporting for duty. The stapler was perfectly even with the tape dispenser, which was equidistant from the scissors—everything was arranged in a perfect grid. I reached out and touched a pen, rolled it over to its opposite side to disrupt the perfection a little bit.

Clearly, Jacob had set up and supplied this space at some point and then never used any of these things. I shut the drawer and moved on. All the other drawers were either equally tidy or unused. I had been hoping to open one and discover a tangle of cords—no such luck.

I closed the last drawer, stood up, and stared at the shelves around me. I could try Garrett's room. Although, if he ever found out I had stepped foot in his bedroom without his permission, especially when he wasn't even here, it would probably make him hate me even more. And it seemed unlikely that a kid his age would ever have had a device that needed such an old charger.

I was wondering if my only solution would be to order one online when it occurred to me to check the kitchen. Every family I'd ever worked for had at least one junk drawer in the kitchen. I pulled every one open, even the ones I knew only held utensils and silverware—the Norths must be the only family on the planet with no junk.

I sighed and was on my way to my room to open my computer and order what I needed when I stopped.

Maybe the garage?

Jacob kept his spaces exceedingly well organized and clean, and the garage was no exception. It was an enormous and well-lit space, with painted concrete floors and a high-end cabinet and shelving system that stretched along one entire wall from floor to ceiling.

A car wouldn't dream of even having an oil drip in this place.

Jacob had a collection of high-end power tools, hand tools, and workbenches, which was interesting since I'd never once seen him use any of them. Maybe he was one of those guys who enjoyed having all the guy stuff--and clearly the best of it--but didn't really have any cause or desire to get his hands dirty.

It was easy to imagine how envious my father would be if he saw all this. If he could register any of it, that was.

I tried several of the metal drawers and was disappointed to find the first several of them locked. Why, I had no idea. The house was out in the middle of nowhere. Was Jacob actually worried someone would come all the way out here to steal tools?

I was about to give up hope, but once I moved past the first two cabinets, the drawers opened right up. They were filled with small jars of drill bits, screws, and nails—all organized by size, I noticed. When I pulled open the very bottom drawer under the wooden worktable, I smiled.

"Bingo."

I reached in and began sifting through various black and white charging cables. Thankfully, each and every one, and there had to be over a hundred in here, was carefully coiled and secured with a tiny strip of Velcro. It took me less than a minute to find exactly what I would need to get the mystery phone charged and turned on.

As I closed the drawer and stood up, my own phone pinged and vibrated in my back pocket. I slid it out and saw a text message from Kyra.

One of the customers sent me this.

Attached was a video. I pressed play and after a few seconds, realized it was footage of Kyra and the guy. I watched as she swung her bat, and he backed into the street.

Another message came through before I'd finished.

Also, the cops came by the shop and asked for your number. They need a statement. Please tell them I'm not as psycho as I look in the video.

Two seconds later, my phone rang.

The caller ID read Gillam County Police.

"Crap," I whispered.

CHAPTER 39

"Hello?"

"Is this Libby Luck?"

"Yes," I said, but the word caught in my throat. "Yes," I repeated. "This is Libby." Police made me nervous. Ever since I was a kid, and they had shown up and swarmed all over our house after my mother's death.

"Libby, this is Officer Dean Riteman with Gillam County Police. I'm calling about the incident that happened today outside the Coffee Klatch."

"Yes," I said, walking back through the garage and toward the house.

"We'd like you to come down to the station at your earliest convenience to provide a statement."

"Okay," I said as I opened the heavy exterior door that led to the mudroom.

"Is there a day and time that work best for you?"

"Um." My mind raced. I could technically come in right now

and get it done before picking the kids up at school this afternoon. But there was something I wanted to do before getting the police involved further. "Is tomorrow okay? At ten?"

"That works. When you arrive, check in with the clerk at the front desk and let them know you have an appointment with Officer Riteman."

We said our goodbyes, hung up, and I checked my phone. I didn't have much time, but I still thought I could get it done before picking the boys up. I grabbed my bag from the kitchen and headed for the Jeep.

I PARALLEL PARKED on the street outside the Gillam County Shelter and checked the status of the mystery phone. There wasn't any time to sit around waiting for it to come to life at the house, so I'd been letting it charge for the whole drive into town. It was only at fifteen percent, but it was enough to turn it on and be disappointed to see that, yes, even this dinosaur required a passcode to get in.

It was only four digits, but after trying 1234, which didn't work, I knew there was no point in me guessing—I'd just end up locking the phone. I'd have to try and figure something else out. I slipped it into the side pocket of my backpack and headed inside. The building was old. It looked like it had once been a government facility that was built sometime during the nineteen-fifties. I didn't get the impression it had ever been renovated. The linoleum tiles on the floor were pulling and peeling away from each other, and the cinderblock walls needed a fresh coat of white paint, but it was clean and smelled like disinfectant. Just past the entrance, the front office was visible behind protective plexiglass. The woman at the desk glanced up when I entered and stood.

"Hello. Can I help you?" She asked as she grabbed a clipboard that had a pen attached to it with a string. It looked like a sign-in sheet.

Now that I was here, I wasn't entirely sure how to ask my questions. In my imagination, I just walked into this place and started talking to a super friendly worker who absolutely told me everything I needed to know about the strange guy following me around town.

"Um, hi," I said, moving closer to the glass. "I'm not sure if you can help me…I'm looking for someone. Or wondering if there's someone here that maybe knows the person or has seen him."

The woman focused her eyes on me and sighed. "Are you a family member?"

For half a second, I considered lying and saying yes. I worried that if I said no, this woman would shut me down and stop me from investigating this guy any further. My gut told me this was a bad idea. She didn't strike me as the kind of person that easily fell for other people's bullshit.

"No," I confessed. "But I think he's looking for someone, and I really just want to help him out by letting him know she's left town." This was at least somewhat true.

She narrowed her eyes at me, and I worried she was about to tell me to take a hike when an idea hit me. "Hang on," I said as I pulled out my phone and found my text messages from Kyra. I clicked on the video she had sent me this afternoon and turned the screen so the woman could see it.

"This guy. He's been following me all around town. Today, he broke into my car." I held up my free hand and shook my head. "And I'm not trying to get him into trouble or anything. I'm not even sure he's homeless, but I think he may be very confused. I was hoping if someone here knew who he was or his situation, then maybe they could help explain to him that the person he's looking for—"

"Jessica," the woman suddenly blurted.

I was stunned. "What?"

"Jessica," she repeated. "The man in your video? That's Crawford, and he's looking for someone named Jessica."

Speechless, I pulled my phone back and looked at the screen myself.

"So…I take it you're *not* Jessica." the woman said.

CHAPTER 40

I slid my phone into my back pocket. "No." I shook my head. "I'm not Jessica, but I am the person who has her old job and drives her old car."

The woman raised one eyebrow and looked skeptical.

"Jessica was the nanny for Jacob and Alexi North. She quit a little over a month ago and moved away. This guy…Crawford?"

The woman nodded.

"Well, he's been following me all over town. Actually, I don't even think it's me he's following. He's following the Jeep, which is the same car Jessica drove when she worked for the Norths. This morning, he broke in and took this from the backseat." I pulled out the mystery phone and showed it to her like it was evidence. "I didn't even know it was there, but he obviously did. I have no idea if it's his, or Jessica's, or someone else's, and I'm not trying to get him in trouble. I just wanted a chance to speak to him."

The woman shook her head. "Well, I haven't seen him here

for a few days. He's not a regular. Drops in on occasion when he needs somewhere to sleep."

"Has he been coming here long?"

"No. The first time I remember him checking in was a few weeks ago."

After Jessica had left, I realized.

"I remember him apologizing to me. Like he felt bad for being here. I got the impression that he maybe hadn't stayed in a shelter before, not that you'd know it from the shape he was in."

My mind was spinning. Maybe Jessica used to help him out? Then, once she'd left, he needed to come here?

"And the reason I know who he was looking for was because it was practically all he ever talked about." She again raised one eyebrow and gave me a knowing look that left me with the impression that she thought something was more than a little off with Crawford. She seemed to have warmed up to me; it made me bold enough to ask my next question.

"Do you think there was something, I don't know... Obsessive about it?"

"Oh, honey, that man was clearly obsessed with that girl. So, if you're looking for him, and you're determined to find him, well, I feel it's my obligation, and duty, to tell you to be careful. Because, based on what I saw, and I'm certainly no expert, that man is clearly not altogether right in his head." She touched her temple with her long red fingernail and tapped it twice. "And that video you've got there on your phone should be evidence enough of that."

"You think he's dangerous?"

The woman shrugged and sat back down in her chair. "Like

I said, I'm no expert. Let's just say he's one of those fellas that leaves you feeling uncomfortable. I wouldn't want to be walking to my car alone at night and find him standing behind me, if you know what I mean."

I did think I knew exactly what she meant. "Did he ever say why he was looking for Jessica?"

The woman shook her head.

"Did you get the impression he wanted to… I don't know, hurt her?"

The woman shifted her mouth to one side like she needed to chew on her response for a minute before she answered. "Honestly honey, it's impossible for me to answer that. I mean, on the one hand, you don't want to go around throwing a man so far down on his luck under a bus with absolutely no evidence at all. Then again, in this day and age, and the things that people do to each other… Well, if you have a chance to warn a woman who may be in danger, even if you're wrong, seems like that would be the right thing to do. So, did he want to hurt her? I have no idea, and no evidence to suggest he did. All I can say is the way he incessantly spoke about her, and seemed to be looking everywhere for her, made me feel uncomfortable. And if this Jessica girl had been my daughter?" She shook her head twice. "There isn't any way I would've allowed that man within one hundred miles of her."

CHAPTER 41

Despite the woman's misgivings about the guy, I asked her anyway. "If you see him, can you ask him to contact me at this number?" I scribbled my name and cell number onto one of their trifold pamphlets.

She took the paper from me but looked surprised. "You sure you wanna do that?"

I nodded. "If you could tell him I would like to speak with him about Jessica, I would really appreciate it."

"Okay. If I see him, I'll do it. But, like I said, I hope you know what you're getting yourself into here. Crawford isn't right. Like in the *head*. You can just tell. You're obviously a grown woman and can do what you like, but I hope you have enough sense to not meet a man like this anywhere but broad daylight on a crowded street, if you know what I mean."

I assured her I knew exactly what she meant. "I'll be careful. And thank you for your help," I said.

On my way out to my car, my phone rang. The caller ID read: Westbrook Academy.

I stopped in the dead and overgrown grass that lined the sidewalk next to where I was parked. What now? I swiped to answer. "Hello?"

"Ms. Luck?" a woman asked.

"Yes."

"This is Principal Adams from Westbrook Academy. I'm afraid there's been an incident involving Garrett. Neither of his parents is answering my calls, but it seems Mr. North recently added you to the emergency contact list."

Oh God.

"Yes," I stammered. "I'm their new nanny. What happened?" I asked as my mind ran through a multitude of accidents that may have occurred.

On the other end of the line, Ms. Adams took a moment to respond, and her silence made me wonder if it was something far more significant than a broken bone. "We are still investigating the specifics. And I'm afraid since you're not a legal guardian, I'm unable to divulge the details to you at this time. But Garrett is in my office under direct supervision. I am unable to release him from the building unsupervised. Will you be picking Garrett and his brother up from school today?"

"Yes," I said, trying to make sense of what was happening while I hurried around the Jeep to the driver's side door. "I'm on my way now."

"Good. They won't be in the pick-up line. You'll need to park, come inside, and sign a document releasing Garrett into your custody."

I slid into the driver's seat and stared at the cracked and uneven street in front of me. "What happened?" I asked.

"Like I said, I'm unable to share the details with anyone other than a parent or legal guardian. Do you know if there is another way I can contact either Mr. or Mrs. North? I've tried both their cell phones on file...several times. And I've left messages, but no one has replied."

"I'll try them on my way there," I said, starting the Jeep.

"Thank you, Ms. Luck. We'll be in my office."

When I arrived at the school, the woman in the front office buzzed me through the front door. Outside, other kids were laughing, talking, texting, and walking toward the line of cars waiting to carry them home. Inside Principal Adam's office, Daniel sat at a conference table coloring a printout picture of Spiderman with markers and Garrett sat slumped and looking pissed off across the table. When I walked in, he glanced up briefly and made eye contact from behind his sheet of greasy brown hair, then immediately averted his eyes to some invisible spot on the table before him.

"Ms. Luck," Principal Adams rose from her desk chair where she'd been working on her computer and came to greet me with her hand outstretched. "It's a pleasure to meet you." We shook hands, and she gestured for me to take a seat at the table. I sat down next to Daniel, but he didn't even glance my way or stop his laser-focused coloring. I noticed that his every mark was measured and neat. Not a single stroke ran outside the lines of the picture.

Principal Adams took a seat at the head of the table and placed a large file folder on the table. It was worn around the edges and overstuffed with pages and pages of documents. From where I sat, I could see the label: North, Garrett. She rested her hand on top of the file and smiled at me.

"I'm sorry we haven't had a chance to meet yet. Jessica York, your predecessor." She smiled at me. "She and I were well acquainted."

Beside me, Daniel stopped coloring. He sat frozen, his green marker hovered over the page but he did not look up. I assumed it was the mention of Jessica that had him transfixed. Across the table, Garrett shifted uncomfortably in his seat but kept his eyes down.

"The Norths had signed permissions on file. So that if and when incidents like today occurred, I could share the details with Ms. York. It allowed us to work together, problem solve, and come up with solutions since the Norths...well, since they are so very busy. And, of course, this is why they hire such exceptional childcare support." She gestured to me and bowed her head slightly. "But, seeing as we don't have something similar on file for you, I'm just asking you to sign a release of responsibility today." She opened the file in front of her and slipped out the top sheet. She handed it to me along with a pen. "It basically states that you are accepting supervision responsibility for Garrett and that you will ensure he does not pose any physical threat to others or himself while under your care. Additionally, if you feel that Garrett does become a danger to others or himself, you agree to seek medical help immediately."

Physical threat? Danger? I stared at the page and the words swimming up at me. I had no idea what was going on, but I picked up the pen and signed on the line marked for me with a bright red sticky tab.

Principal Adams held out her hand for the page, which I handed her, and then placed it back onto the huge stack of papers already in Garrett's file. "Okay then. He's free to leave with you now. I would like to reiterate how important I feel it would be for us to communicate openly about the boys considering that, and I assume this is still the case, you'll be the one handling the bulk of their needs now."

I nodded even though I wasn't exactly sure what I was agreeing to. What was Principal Adams implying, exactly? I wasn't sure, but I got the impression she thought the Norths were uninvolved at best—negligent at worst. And maybe Alexi was. According to Jacob, she'd never really wanted to have kids in the first place. The woman had never even spoken to me, and I'd been taking care of her kids for over a month now. But, Alexi aside, I wanted to point out to Ms. Adams all the time that Jacob did spend with his boys when he was home.

Well, at least all the time he spent with Daniel. But it wasn't like it was Jacob's fault that Garrett was moody and withdrawn. It wasn't like Jacob wouldn't spend more time with his oldest son if Garrett would ever unglue himself from his computer monitor.

Ms. Adams stood, clearly dismissing us all from her presence. I followed her lead and said, "I'll be sure to speak with Mr. North about the paperwork this evening."

Ms. Adams nodded. "Thank you. Additionally, in case either he or Mrs. North don't get around to listening to the many voicemails I've left them today, please also let them know that Garrett is suspended and will be out of school for the remainder of the week. We will need to hold a reentry meeting prior to his return next Monday."

"Wait." My hand flew to my forehead. "He's suspended?"

Principal Adams gave me a sympathetic look and a single nod.

CHAPTER 42

When we reached the Jeep in the parking lot, Garrett—I assumed because he felt guilty about whatever had happened today—sat in the backseat with his little brother instead of the front seat. I didn't mention it. Or even question him about what had happened. I just drove all the way back to the house with my eyes constantly shifting between Garrett's sullen expression in my rearview mirror, my phone resting on the console next to me, and the road ahead. I tried to imagine what it was he had done to get suspended for practically a whole week and how I could get him to tell me. Under the best of circumstances, Garrett largely ignored me or pretended like he had no idea why I was even around. Now that he was clearly mad, and maybe even a little upset, it was impossible to predict how he would react to me questioning him.

I realized, I was a little afraid of Garrett.

Halfway to the house, a text message came through, and I snatched the phone up to check and see if it was from Crawford. Despite all the drama with Garrett this afternoon, I was still hoping that Crawford would show up to the shelter today and that the woman behind the counter would be true to her word and give him my message.

But it wasn't Crawford. It was Jacob.

I came home a little early. I'll get dinner started.

I was about to use my thumb to reply, but Garrett's voice cut through the silence from the backseat.

"So, you really don't care if you run us off the road and into a tree," he said.

I glanced at my rearview mirror and saw he hadn't bothered to lift his eyes from his own phone. "Jessica had the same problem. That's why she kept her phone in the pocket of the backseat, so she wouldn't be tempted. If you also have a problem with temptation, maybe you should put your phone somewhere you can't reach it so we don't all die," he spat.

I placed my phone face down on the console, moved my hand back to the steering wheel before me, and gripped it until my knuckles turned white. Garrett's admonishment and blatant disrespect made my blood boil. I should say something. I shouldn't let him get away with treating me the way he did.

But there was something in the way he used the words. Tempted. Temptation. It immediately made me think of Jacob in my bed last night and waking up to him this morning. Is that what Garrett is hinting at here? *Does he know I slept with his father? Did he somehow see us?* And is that, quite possibly and understandably, why he got into trouble at school today? Trouble that was so bad he managed to get himself suspended for a whole week. Was he acting out?

Of course, it was impossible for me to tell because, to me,

Garrett was always acting out. Even if that meant he was withdrawn, reclusive, and uncommunicative. But if Garrett had seen Jacob and me that would be, well...confusing at best. And given he didn't know about Jacob and Alexi's imminent divorce? It would be a life-shattering heartbreak at worst.

I was the adult here, I reminded myself. I was the nanny. And while I neither liked nor condoned Garrett's treatment of me, maybe I should try to be a little more understanding.

Especially because I was now involved with his father.

I took a deep breath, let it out, and gave it a shot. "Do you want to talk about what happened at school today?"

Garrett didn't respond, and when I glanced in my rearview mirror, I saw that he was no longer staring at his phone but out his window instead.

"Because, you know, if you want to talk about it...or anything, it's what I'm here for."

Garrett turned away from the window and stared back, directly meeting my gaze in the mirror.

"Is that what you told my dad? That you'd do anything?"

I held his gaze for a second longer, then shifted my eyes back to the road.

Well, that answered my question. Clearly, Garrett knew.

CHAPTER 43

When we pulled up to the house, I could see Jacob's black pickup parked inside the open garage. I pulled the Jeep into the space next to his and cut the engine. I let my head fall back against the headrest as I listened to Garrett and Daniel open their doors and gather their things behind me. After they both slammed their doors, I watched them walk to the mudroom door.

I was surprised when Garrett stopped, turned, and made eye contact with me through the windshield. His expression was a question, like he was wondering why I was just sitting here and not getting out of the car.

It only lasted a moment, but Garrett usually didn't pay attention to anything I did. The fact that he'd even noticed and then acknowledged me with an actual look felt like a miracle. But it was a mistake to think he cared about how I was feeling —that, I knew, would be reading way too much into his attention.

When the door closed behind him, I imagined him turning the deadbolt to lock me out of the house. Now *that* would seem more in line with behavior I'd come to expect from Garrett. And thinking about his behavior—what the hell was in that giant file of his at school?

That principal, Ms. Adams, she had been professional with me. Ultra professional. Maybe even standoffish. But there was also a bone-weary exhaustion about her as well. Watching her sit there, with both hands resting on Garrett's huge file like she herself had constructed and dealt with the entirety of its contents—it wasn't hard to feel some empathy, maybe even camaraderie with the woman. Was this how Jessica had felt?

What was it the principal had said? Your predecessor. She and I were well acquainted.

And it occurred to me that the only reason that would have been necessary was because Garrett had significant behavior problems at school. Yes, Garrett had serious issues, and Jessica had been the one to deal with them.

Which led me to a question that had been nagging at the back of my mind the whole drive home. A question I didn't really want to ask because maybe I wouldn't like the answer.

Why on earth didn't Jacob ever mention any of this to me? Not during the interview. Not after I arrived. Not in the entire month I'd been taking care of the boys.

And not just Jacob, I reminded myself. It was easy to forget Garrett and Daniel actually had two parents because I'd never yet even spoken to their mother. I could see that Alexi North was very talented and successful. I could easily imagine her being career-obsessed and self-absorbed. And Jacob had said she never wanted to be a mother in the first place.

But did she really care so little about her sons? Especially one who had a towering stack of pages, presumably for bad behavior, in his academic file. Had she simply had enough? Fled? Was she busy starting a whole new life? One that didn't involve being a mother to a difficult child?

And had Jessica also felt the same and finally given up?

Which only brought me back to my original question. Why hadn't Jacob talked to me about any of this?

I grabbed my backpack off the passenger seat beside me and opened my door. I didn't know why Jacob hadn't said anything, but I, for one, would be saying many things and asking many questions right now.

CHAPTER 44

What had I expected to see when I walked into the kitchen? Well, for starters, I imagined Jacob had, by now, listened to the many messages Principal Adams had left for him. And, like most parents, Jacob would be upset, perhaps stern-looking. He might even be angry. Garrett would be standing before him, looking either sullen or pissed—it could go either way—while he listened to his father rail on and on about whatever it was that had happened at school today.

That was what I expected to find.

Which was nothing even remotely like what was actually going on.

First of all, both kids were nowhere to be seen. It was dark. The blue light from the refrigerator door was the only light in the kitchen. Jacob stood, waiting for me, next to the island. I couldn't see his face and didn't know what was happening.

A chill ran down my spine. I stopped, dead in the doorway, stock still.

"What's going on?" I asked.

"I could ask you the same thing," he said. I still couldn't see his face. Was he angry at *me*? Was he, somehow, going to try and blame me for Garrett getting into trouble today.

"Where are the kids?" I asked.

"In the family room. I picked up a pizza and some Cokes and told them they could eat while watching a movie on the big screen tonight." He stepped closer, and I could just make out the curl of his lips.

He was smiling at me. Practically beaming, in fact. "What on earth took you so long to come inside?" he asked. "I've been standing here waiting for you." He moved toward me, closing the last few feet of distance that separated us, and pulled me into his arms. I felt his lips near my ear. "I've been thinking about you all day," he whispered.

I stood there, arms hanging limp at my side, too stunned to move as Jacob squeezed me tight. A second later, he let me go and took a step back. His expression was quizzical, and the space between his eyebrows creased with concern. "What's wrong?" he asked.

I stared up at him in disbelief. Did he really not know? "Have you listened to your voicemails?" I asked. "The principal at the school has been calling you and Alexi all day."

Jacob just looked at me. Several seconds passed, and I couldn't help but wonder if he hadn't heard me correctly. "Jacob—"

"What?" he interrupted me, and pulled his phone from his back pocket. "I didn't get..." he stared at his phone like he couldn't understand what was happening. His shoulders sagged, and he looked back at me with a sheepish expression.

"I've had it on do not disturb all day." He shook his head at his mistake and then scrolled to what I assumed were his messages. "I'm so sorry. I had a faculty meeting this morning…I usually remember to turn the ringer back on." He tapped something on his phone and then held it to his ear. "I'm so sorry."

He turned away from me and placed one hand on the kitchen counter while he listened. A moment later, I watched as he pulled the phone away from his ear, sighed deeply, and nodded. "Well, this changes what I had planned for us this evening." He turned back toward me with a sorry expression. "Looks like instead of enjoying a gourmet, candlelit dinner with you alone in the dining room, I'll be playing the role of pissed-off and disappointed dad for at least the next hour."

Confused, I shook my head. He took my hand, led me out of the kitchen, and down the hall. When we neared the doorway to the dining room, I could see faint yellow lights flickering and illuminating the dark. Once we rounded the corner, Jacob stood next to me, my hand still in his, as I took in the sight before me.

CHAPTER 45

"Oh, Jacob," I said.

"Yeah," he said, sweeping his free hand through his hair. "I wanted it to be a special night. Just you and me and an amazing meal."

On the long, roughhewn table before us, Jacob had orchestrated the most beautiful, romantic, and delicious looking dinner I had ever seen. It was like a scene in a movie.

There was a cream-colored, damask table runner dividing the table lengthwise. It was decorated with four cast-iron candle sticks that held cream-colored tapered candles, their flames flickering and casting warm and romantic light. A porcelain vase was filled with dozens of long-stemmed white roses at the center of the table. The table, set for two, was expertly laid, complete with white china plates centered on top of brass chargers. I could see the opened bottle of red wine, waiting and ready to be poured into the large crystal wine glasses. He even had linen napkins folded into a tent at the center of each plate.

The food was being kept warm in covered ceramic dishes suspended over small blue flames on the sideboard.

I turned my head and looked up into his eyes. "You did all this? For me?"

He nodded. "Well...sort of. The food is from Roman's Steakhouse near campus. But this perfectly romantic setup?" He held up both hands like he was framing a photo shot. "That's all me." He turned toward me and took both my hands in his. "Me and Pinterest."

Despite the crazy and stressful day I'd had, I smiled.

Jacob bent down and kissed me gently on the lips. "You're special, Libby. I just wanted to do one small thing to let you know that. I'm sorry about what happened today with Garrett at school. I'm going to have to deal with that first. But..."

He led me to the table, pulled out a chair, and gestured for me to take a seat. "I swear I won't take long." He picked up the bottle of wine and poured it into my empty glass. "You sit, relax, have a drink, and I'll be back to join you for what I can guarantee will be the most delicious meal you've ever had before you even realize I'm gone. Sound good?" he asked and handed me my glass.

I nodded. "Sounds great."

He smiled and leaned down to kiss me again. This time, it was deeper, slower, and hinted at the possibility of him coming again to my room tonight. When he pulled away, I found I was a bit breathless.

"I'll be right back."

I nodded and watched him leave as I took a sip of red wine

from my glass. It was a relief to see that Jacob was taking whatever had happened with Garrett at school today seriously. He wasn't a bad or neglectful father. He clearly loved both his boys and wanted to do the right thing.

Which certainly didn't appear to be the case with their mother. When Jacob came back, I'd be sure to ask him if he'd received any word from her lately. At least Jacob had a reasonable excuse for missing all those calls from the school today.

Was Alexi too busy building her new life with her new man to take ten minutes to talk with the principal about her own son?

What had happened today at school? The principal wouldn't tell me, and Jacob hadn't said after listening to the message. I thought about asking him when he came back...but then again, I didn't want to further spoil the romantic evening he'd obviously worked so hard for us to share. Letting the Garrett topic rest for tonight was probably best—I'd talk with Jacob about it in the morning.

I took another sip of my wine and felt my phone buzz in my pocket. My heart sank a little. I hoped it wasn't Jacob calling me from the other room to say he couldn't join me after all. Maybe his conversation with Garrett wasn't going as he'd hoped?

When I looked at the screen, I was relieved to see that it wasn't him, but it wasn't anyone from my short list of contacts either. I swiped to answer the call. "Hello?"

"Is this Libby?" a man's voice asked.

"Yes. Who's calling?"

"You have something that belongs to me, and I want it back now."

CHAPTER 46

A trickle of fear ran through my chest, and I placed my wine glasses back on the table. "Is this Crawford?"

On the other end of the line, he hesitated. Maybe he hadn't expected me to know or use his name? "It is. And that phone you have, it doesn't belong to you."

I stood up from my chair and glanced down the hallway toward the family room. There was no sign of Jacob or Garrett; it was safe to assume the lecture and doling out of some discipline was still in progress. It wasn't that I wanted to hide or lie to Jacob about finding the phone and tracking down Crawford, but neither did I feel ready to fully involve him. "And how do I know it belongs to you?"

"It belonged to Jessica!" he yelled. "And you're going to fucking give it to me!"

His anger made the small seed of fear I'd been feeling bloom into a terror that flooded my body and made my legs weak. With my phone pressed to my ear, I walked to the dining room window and pushed aside the heavy drape. The view from here was of the front drive and road leading to the house. I suddenly wondered if, by telling the woman at the shelter to have Crawford call me, I'd made a huge error in judgment and just led him directly to the house. Was he here? Standing somewhere out there in the dark? Hidden in the trees?

"Did you hear me?" he shouted. "I want that phone back. Bring it to me by tomorrow, or I swear, I'm going to make your life a living hell."

I let the curtain drop back into place. If he wanted me to bring it tomorrow, he wasn't at the house tonight. "And how do I know Jessica would want you to have it?"

"Are you fucking kidding me? I'm the only person who should have it. You don't even know her! And the fucking Norths shouldn't have it either."

"Why?" I asked. "She worked for them, after all. It seems like maybe they would be the best people to—"

"I'm the best person to worry about Jessica and what she needs! So, bring her fucking phone to me tomorrow or...you'll be sorry, Libby."

It was a threat, no doubt. But something about how his voice trailed off at the end made me wonder if he really meant it or was just trying to scare me into doing what he wanted.

"Think about it from my perspective? What proof do I have that Jessica would want me to give you her lost phone? You could be anybody."

The line was quiet for several seconds, then he said. "Zero, four, two, seven."

"What?"

"Zero, four, two, seven! It's the code to the fucking phone.

Log in, look at her socials. See for yourself that I'm the one, the only one, who should have anything that ever belonged to her. Tomorrow, meet me on the corner of Seventh and Grant Street at twelve with the phone. If you're not there, you should know, I'll find you. One way or the hard way, I'm getting what I want," he said and hung up.

"Who was that?" Jacob asked.

Startled, I turned away from the window. He was standing in the doorway to the dining room. I had no idea how long he'd been there. "Wrong number," I blurted and averted my eyes, knowing my lie was obvious.

But Jacob didn't question me. He smiled, big and beautiful, clapped his hands, and said, "Ready to eat? I'm starving."

CHAPTER 47

Jacob spent the night with me again. I lay beside him, naked and spent, listening to his breathing as it slowed, deepened, and eventually led me to believe he was asleep. I rolled away onto my side and stared at my bag illuminated in the moonlight streaming through the open window. I could see the outline of Jessica's phone inside the bag's side pocket. I should wait until morning. Once Jacob left for work, and I'd dropped Daniel at school, I could find some time to myself to unlock it and look through it.

All night, throughout the entirety of my candlelit dinner with Jacob, as we cleared the table, washed the dishes, kissed in the darkened kitchen, walked up the stairs holding hands, got Daniel ready for bed, and eventually fell into my bed together, my mind kept pulling to the found phone in my backpack and the code Crawford had given me.

Zero, four, two, seven.

Zero, four, two, seven.

It would probably take me less than five minutes to get into it, pull up her social media, do some light investigation, and look for evidence to support Crawford's claim that he was the only person who should have Jessica's phone.

Which, of course, begged the question: Why wouldn't the only person who should have her phone be Jessica herself? Did he mean he was the only one who could return Jessica's phone to her? Or was Crawford inadvertently implying something else with his statement? Did he know something, maybe something terrible, about Jessica that everyone else didn't?

And was he maybe responsible for whatever that something was?

I thought about the desk clerk at the shelter and her warning to me. I had agreed to meet with Crawford tomorrow, but would I be stumbling into a huge mistake I would regret.

Or was regret the last thing I should worry about because meeting Crawford alone, without telling anyone else my plan, might actually be the last thing I ever do?

I suddenly felt like I was probably being really stupid. I should have told Jacob about the phone as soon as I found it. I should have given it to him so he could make sure it was returned to Jessica.

Assuming he knew where she was.

I rolled onto my back and stared at the ceiling above me—of course Jacob would know where she was. He almost never spoke of Jessica, and he never mentioned where she had gone after quitting but surely, if I'd given him the phone, he would have known exactly where to send it.

I turned my head and looked at his slack, sleeping expression. So why was I keeping this from him? Why not just wake him up right now and tell him about the phone and Crawford stealing it from the Jeep, how I went to the shelter to try and find Crawford, and how I was meeting Officer Riteman tomorrow? I had so many secrets from this man. This man who was amazing, and sexy, and seemed to relish taking care of me. Why was I hiding all this?

I turned my gaze back to the ceiling above—it was simple. Since Kyra told me what she knew about Jessica, about the speculation and rumors, and her unexpected departure from town, my curiosity about Jessica had grown insatiable. The fact that I now had her personal phone and the code to access it was irresistible. I wanted to see for myself. Her pictures, her socials, her messages. Was it true, the rumors and gossip? Was she unjustly branded, or was the truth actually worse than anyone in this town had been capable of imagining?

If I gave the phone to Jacob, I would never know anything more about Jessica than I already did.

It would take me less than five minutes to take a cursory look.

Beside me, Jacob took a deep breath and blew it out through parted lips. He'd had most of the bottle of wine we'd shared at dinner—he wouldn't be waking up anytime soon.

Careful not to disturb the mattress, I slipped my legs over the side of the bed and got up.

CHAPTER 48

I was naked, so I grabbed my robe off the floor and then my bag from the chair. At the double doors that separated my bedroom from the sitting area, I stopped to look back at Jacob, still sound asleep, before I pulled the doors close.

I cinched the robe's belt around my waist and pulled out the phone. As I nestled into the corner of the couch, I considered turning on the table lamp beside me. I had been afraid the sound of the doors closing completely might wake Jacob, so I'd left a thin crack. I worried any more light than the phone's screen might also wake him, so I left the lamp off.

In the dark, I found the phone's power button and turned it on. My hands were sweaty, trembling as I waited for the keypad to appear. When it did, I typed the code. I half expected it to not open. I mostly thought Crawford was probably full of it and a complete psycho who was obsessed with Jessica. But as I hit the last digit and watched the phone screen switch to a display of all the available icons, I knew, whatever the reason, Crawford was right.

He knew Jessica well enough to know the passcode to her phone.

I pulled my bare feet onto the couch and my knees close to my chest as I scanned her home screen and considered where to start. I had looked for Jessica on social media several times without any luck. But as I swiped to the next page, I saw she had an account. I clicked on the icon and watched as it opened up to the stream of people she followed. I scrolled past a few videos and posts, thinking that maybe some of these people were Jessica's actual friends. People who would not only know who she really was, but where she was.

All the top posts were celebrities and big influencers. I clicked on her profile picture. It was a woman standing in the woods with a rough path before her. Her back was to the camera, so her only discernible feature was her long brown hair, which fell halfway down her back. I scrolled through her posts; there were only nine. The most recent was three years old—a photo collage of a hiking trail and views from the top of a small mountain. The next most recent posts were similar: trails, woods, views. The posts were old, with months or years between them. I scrolled to the very bottom, the oldest post, and clicked on it. It was a grainy photo of two kids. They sat on a picnic bench outside, their arms around each other's shoulders as they smiled for the camera. In the background, I could see a banner hanging across the entrance to a gazebo with peeling white paint.

McFadden Middle School
Class of 2010

Commencement

The picture wasn't great. Taken on older technology and in terrible lighting, I used my thumbs to enlarge it and get a better look. The girl in the picture had cropped brown hair, brown eyes, and a wide smile that revealed her crooked teeth. The boy next to her had the same color hair. It was shaggy, overgrown, and falling into his face. He also wore a smile for the picture, but he had kept his closed and tightlipped. They both had a reedy, desperate look about them. Their clothes were faded and threadbare, hand-me-downs that had been handed down before. The boy's black T-shirt collar was stretched and hung loose below his jutting collarbone. The girl's sweatshirt had raggedy, torn cuffs. Some kids wore intentionally distressed clothes on purpose—these kids looked like they lived in distress.

Their heads tilted ever so slightly toward each other—they were close.

I assumed the girl was a young Jessica. I clicked on the picture and read the caption.

I love you Crawford. Today and forever. And ever. And ever…no you shut the fuck up! Was followed by three laughing face emojis.

I looked back at the photo. And this was Crawford. A boy before he became a homeless drug addict living on the streets in New Hampshire. He had known Jessica. He had a history with her. It was true.

But that didn't mean Jessica still had, or wanted, a relationship with him now. A lot had changed in the fourteen years since this photo was taken. Just because Crawford had known Jessica and was searching for her didn't mean he necessarily had her best interests in mind. He could be stalking her. He could be the reason she left.

In fact, given the state he was in and his temperament, it seemed likely she would be trying to get away and stay away from Crawford.

"Libby?" Jacob called from the bedroom.

My eyes darted to the cracked door. His voice sounded groggy. Like he'd just woken up and found I wasn't beside him. "Yes," I said, slipping Jessica's phone into my robe pocket. "I'm coming." I opened the door, took off my robe, and placed it on top of my backpack on the chair. In bed, Jacob held the sheet and blanket up for me, and I slid onto the mattress and into his arms.

He pulled my naked body close to his, and I rolled onto my side so he could spoon against my back.

"Where were you?" he whispered before kissing my neck.

"I couldn't sleep." Which was true. "So, I got up to read in the other room." Which was a lie.

His hand moved to my breast, and he cupped it in his large, warm palm. "I don't like it when I don't know where you are," he whispered. I felt his mouth hot against my skin as he kissed my neck again, and then the muscles in his arm flexed as he tightened his grip.

CHAPTER 49

The next morning, Jacob kissed me goodbye, got in his truck, and left for work without a single word of instruction about what to do about Garrett. Because of the out-of-school suspension, he would be home with me all week. Of course, I wasn't a parent myself, but it seemed like there should be some discussion about consequences, reparations, maybe some manual labor Garrett should or would be expected to accomplish during the days he wouldn't be spending at school.

As it stood, Jacob had said nothing and Garrett had, I assumed, slept in while I got Daniel ready for school and Jacob got ready for work.

Daniel sat at the counter eating his cereal while I, out of eyesight, kissed his dad goodbye at the door to the garage. In that moment, I nearly said something. The questions were right there, on the tip of my tongue. What about Garrett? Is he grounded? Is there anything he shouldn't do? TV? Video games?

Anything? Under normal circumstances, on any other day, I'm certain I would have asked these questions and more.

I still had no idea what had happened at school yesterday. Or anything about what might be in Garrett's enormous file at school.

When Jacob's lips left mine with a smile and the words, "I can't wait to see you tonight." All I said was, "Bye. Have a good day." Because the truth was, today, all I wanted was for Jacob to get out of the house as soon as possible so I could get into town and deal with what was actually at the forefront of my mind.

My meetings with both Officer Riteman and Crawford.

I SAT IN THE JEEP, parked outside the Gilpin County Police Department, and scrolled through Jessica's phone. There were no text messages, call history, voicemails, or contacts listed. Her camera app held no photos. I would think this was a burner phone if it weren't for a few nonstandard apps.

Or a phone that had been wiped and reset.

The single distinguishable item was her social media app, which provided practically no information about Jessica or the life she had lived. Aside from the fact that she had enjoyed hiking and that she and Crawford had gone to middle school together, there was nothing.

I opened her social media again and revisited her infrequent posts. It seemed weird that her first post was from 2010, and her last was three years ago, and there were only nine posts. She only followed a handful of celebrities and influencers and had zero followers. Her account was set to private.

So, assuming she'd always kept it private, no one would have ever seen her infrequent smattering of photos anyway.

Why bother, I wondered.

Unless…I clicked on the most recent post from three years ago. There were no comments, but it had been liked by over three hundred people. The next post, which was four years old, had been liked six hundred and fifty-two times—zero comments.

Jessica's account hadn't always been private; it had once had followers, and I suspected there had at one time been many, many more posts. Like the phone, it felt like her social media account had been wiped.

Sort of.

With that many likes on her photos, there must have been comments. Jessica, or someone else, had deleted them along with all the posts that probably once existed between the few that remained.

But why delete most everything but not actually everything? What was the point of leaving these few old posts, scrubbing all your followers, deleting all the comments, and making your account private? Why wouldn't she just delete the whole account if she didn't want to be on social media anymore?

I had no idea.

I glanced at the time in the upper right-hand corner of the phone, 9:58. I dropped her phone into the side pocket of my backpack, got out of the Jeep, and headed inside to meet with Officer Riteman.

CHAPTER 50

The police station reminded me of the homeless shelter. It had been updated more recently and had a fresh coat of paint on the outside. Still, the buildings were both low-slung, brick government buildings constructed sometime in the nineteen fifties. I walked up the concrete steps that led to the double glass doors of the front entrance and went inside.

The officer at the front desk was young, rail thin, and looked like he might have only just graduated from high school. He greeted me with a serious expression and a hint of suspicion in his eyes. I got the impression that this was a persona he had adopted after realizing that most people, despite his perfectly pressed uniform and the gun holstered at his hip, didn't take him very seriously,

"Name and business?" he asked, keeping his eyes on his computer screen.

"Libby Luck. I have an appointment with Officer Riteman,"

He made a few clicks with his mouse, scanned his screen,

then nodded once. "Down the hall, first right, office number thirty-two."

"Thanks," I said, letting the word fall between us without a hint of sincerity. It occurred to me that he was trying and failing to appear powerful by being rude.

He reminded me of Garrett.

I turned and followed his directions until I found myself standing in front of Officer Riteman's open office door. He was sitting behind his desk, typing on a laptop in front of him. Unlike the guy up front, Riteman looked up when he sensed my presence and even smiled when he saw me. "Libby Luck?" he asked.

I nodded.

He stood up and gestured to the seats in front of him. "Please take a seat. Thank you for coming."

I pulled out the chair to my right and sat down. The center of the cushion beneath me gave away immediately. It made me feel like I was sitting in a hole. The chair's wooden arms were worn and shiny. These chairs had seen a lot of use over the years. They may be as old as the building itself.

Officer Reitman took his seat and returned his eyes to his computer. "I wanted to meet with you because I received a report about a disturbance in town yesterday outside the Coffee Klatch involving a vehicle break-in and an attempted theft. An employee from the coffee shop and four other people sent in video footage of the event. No one got a look at the license plate on the vehicle, a white Jeep, but it was reported that it belonged to you." He lifted his eyes from his computer and met my gaze. "Is that true, Ms. Luck?"

I was digesting all he had just said while also realizing that either Kyra or Trisha had pointed him my way. "Yes. Well, it's not mine, but I do drive it. It's for my job. I nanny for the family that owns it."

He folded his hands on his desk and nodded once. "Yes. So the Jeep belongs to Jacob and Alexi North?"

"Yes." He knew more about me than he was letting on. What I didn't know was why.

"How long have you been working for the Norths?"

"Just over a month."

Officer Reitman nodded once, picked up a pencil, and jotted a note onto his yellow legal pad. He smiled before asking his next question. "You're not from around these parts. Have you been enjoying the town? Settling in, okay?"

I shrugged. "Yes. I guess so."

"I've lived here my whole life. But I imagine it must be tough to uproot yourself and start all over in a brand-new place. Where is it that you're from?"

He held his pencil, poised and ready over his yellow pad, but for some reason, I had the impression he already knew the answer to this question. "Hallsworth, Nebraska."

"Hallsworth?" He used the eraser end of the pencil to scratch an itch just above his temple. "Can't say I've heard of it. Then again, I never was that great with geography."

"It's a pretty tiny town."

Officer Reitman nodded again and made another quick note on his page. "Have you had a chance to meet many folks since moving to Walford?"

"Not really. I sometimes chat with Kyra at the Coffee Klatch."

"I imagine it can be tough. What with the Norths living so far out of town, in the middle of nowhere like that?"

"I guess so."

It was clear that Officer Reitman was interested in having this chat and learning more about me. What was less obvious was what any of this had to do with the Jeep break-in. Reading my mind, he switched gears and got to the point. "So, this fella that broke into the Jeep… is this someone you know?" I didn't answer right away. What exactly constituted knowing somebody in this context? "No, I don't know him. I have seen him a few times around town."

I decided to leave out that I had tracked him down to the homeless shelter and had, in fact, had a phone conversation with Crawford. Officer Reitman shifted his tongue to the right side of his mouth and probed at a tooth before continuing. "Well, *I do* happen to know him. His name is Crawford Allen. He's a homeless man who seems pretty down on his luck. I have it from fairly reliable sources that he's a customer of one of our local drug dealers. He showed up in town several years ago, seems to come and go, and will check himself into the Gilpin County Shelter on colder nights."

I nodded but focused on the yellow pad in front of Officer Reitman. I had a hard time keeping eye contact with him, and it was impossible to not feel like I was somehow being accused of something. "So, what? Do you think he was just looking for money?"

It was Officer Reitman's turn to shrug. "Under other circumstances? Yes, probably. Except our friend Crawford Allen has a little bit more of a history than just his drug use and homeless lifestyle. How much do you know about the North's last nanny, Jessica York?"

"I mean... Nothing really."

Was it my imagination, or had Officer Reitman's tone shifted from conversational to interrogational?

"You say you've been there just over a month; in that time, the Norths haven't spoken to you about Jessica? Told you a little bit about her or her history with them?"

I swallowed and shifted in my seat. "No. I know it seems weird, but it's true. The boys... well, the youngest, was really attached to Jessica. I think he took her quitting really hard. I think the whole family has taken her leaving hard. I assumed it was difficult for them to talk about, so I haven't really brought it up or asked too many questions. All I know is that she was with them for a long time and that the boys, at least the youngest, loved her a lot." I considered for half a second sharing what Jacob had told me about how much they had come to rely on Jessica over the years but decided that was probably too personal and not really relevant. After all, Officer Reitman hadn't told me why he was asking about Jessica. I figured it was because he knew Crawford was looking for her.

"You keep saying Daniel was close to Jessica. You don't think the older boy, Garrett, was?"

I hadn't mentioned any of their names, not Daniel or Garrett, so clearly, he had researched the whole family. I hesitated before answering his question. "Honestly, I don't know Garrett that well."

"You don't know him? But you've been his nanny for over a month now. Presumably, you spend a lot of time with both of them."

His questions were making me increasingly uncomfortable. Mostly because I had no idea where any of this was going.

"Can I ask what this has to do with the Jeep break-in?"

Officer Riteman sat back in his seat and put his pencil down. "I'm in the middle of an open investigation. And so I can't share all the details. But I can tell you that for the last six weeks, Crawford Allen has been calling or coming into our station daily. At first, he was only concerned that Jessica York had left and apparently quit her job with the Norths. He claims that they had such a close relationship that she would never do such a thing. He has recently concluded that something has happened to her. So, when I see that Crawford Allen has broken into your vehicle, the vehicle that Jessica York used to drive, it is making me more concerned. And also more curious, to be quite honest, about what his intentions are now and what he imagines has happened. I have it on good report that Crawford Allen is a highly unstable individual. When I spoke with Jacob North, after the first time Crawford contacted us, he assured me that while it had taken the family by surprise, she had left of her own volition and stated that she would be moving to California."

"Did you share this with Crawford?"

"Yes, and no. Given the very real possibility that Crawford might be somebody she was trying to get away from, provided she knew him at all, I didn't think it was in her best interest to give him too much detail. I assured him that, while it may be surprising, it did indeed look like Jessica had decided to leave Walford and move away."

"But he doesn't believe this?"

"It would appear not."

"You say you're working on an open investigation? Can you tell me what it is?"

Officer Riteman leaned forward in his chair and folded his hands on the desk. "I cannot. But what I can tell you is this, if you cross paths with Crawford Allen again, if he harasses you, bothers you, or tries to break into your vehicle again, I want you to call 911 immediately. You should consider him not only highly unstable but probably dangerous. He obviously was, and still is, obsessed with Jessica York. I have no reason to believe that obsession would or should have anything to do with you. But in light of what happened yesterday, I don't think we could or should rule out the possibility that, for whatever reason, Crawford Allen may be experiencing some transference to you. Until I have more information, I'll ask that you be extra vigilant when you're in town and keep an eye out for him. If he bothers you in any way, I want to hear about it."

He plucked a business card from the acrylic holder at the front of his desk and handed it to me. If you are in real danger, call 911, but if Crawford Allen so much as looks in your direction, I want you to contact me immediately."

"Okay," I said, took the card from him and stood up. I was about to leave when a question occurred to me. I thought about the picture on Jessica's social media account. The young Jessica and Crawford, heads bent together, and her words captioned underneath. "I love you, Crawford. Today and forever." "What makes you think that he is dangerous and that Jessica was moving to get away from him?"

Officer Riteman held his pencil between both his hands as he met my gaze. He looked like he was deciding exactly how much he would tell me. A moment later, he let out a sigh. "You didn't hear this from me..." He tilted his head and raised his eyebrows while he waited for me to respond.

"Okay," I agreed. This would be our secret.

He took a big breath, let out another large sigh, and nodded once as if resigning himself to whatever he was about to reveal. "Two weeks before Jessica quit the Norths and left town, she came in here."

I stood still and listened, afraid that if I asked any questions or even shifted my weight, Officer Riteman would change his mind and realize he was about to share something with me that he probably shouldn't.

"She wanted to know what she needed to do to file a restraining order."

"Against Crawford?" I whispered.

"She didn't say. But given what I've seen of his behavior since she's left? I'd say most likely yes, against Crawford Allen."

CHAPTER 51

I sat in my car two blocks from where I was supposed to meet Crawford in fifteen minutes, holding Jessica's phone. I willed my brain to think clearly and make a smart decision.

Should I keep my promise to meet with Crawford and give him Jessica's phone?

Should I take Officer Riteman's warning seriously and stay as far away from Crawford as possible?

And why was any of this even a question in my mind in the first place? I had withheld information from the police. I hadn't lied, but I'd also not been exactly forthcoming.

I closed my eyes. At my core, I didn't trust the police. I knew it was an irrational feeling. A prejudice planted in my childhood. Born from the terror I'd experienced when the Hallsworth police burst into our tiny apartment, grabbed my father, and announced he was being arrested for my mother's murder. I had watched, frozen, confused, and more afraid than

I had ever felt in my life as they handcuffed him and led him out the door.

I had screamed, cried, and tried to follow him while two social workers held me in place.

I opened my eyes and forced the memory from my mind. It wasn't something I allowed myself to think about. That was in the past, and right now, I had more immediate concerns to consider.

I glanced at the clock on the dash. It was 11:55, five minutes before I was scheduled to meet Crawford and give him Jessica's phone. I had been advised to watch out for and stay away from Crawford by not one but two people now. People who, presumably, knew him and his history. What I needed to decide within the next five minutes was whether I should heed their advice and stay away from him or do what I told him I would.

Part of me believed that if I didn't give him Jessica's phone like I said I would, my Crawford problem would only get worse. I didn't think Officer Reitman was correct. Crawford's only interest in me was this phone. His only concern was Jessica, and I doubted with every fiber of my being that Crawford would want anything more to do with me once I gave it to him.

I shifted the Jeep into drive, glanced over my shoulder, and pulled away from the curb.

As soon as I pulled the Jeep up to the intersection where Crawford had told me to meet him, I saw him materialize, seemingly from nowhere. Had he been waiting, crouched and hidden, in the tangle of overgrown bushes that skirted the rundown apartment building?

Had he been hidden behind the large pine tree whose

shallow roots had pushed up and cracked the concrete sidewalk?

Or had he simply been standing there all along? A man so accustomed to being routinely overlooked and forgotten that he simply blended into any environment?

As I pulled up to the sidewalk and shifted into park, Crawford crossed the dead grass to meet me. When he was outside the door, I rolled down the passenger window and leaned across the seat to hand him the phone.

Without making eye contact or uttering a word, Crawford reached through the window, pushed the button to unlock the door, and opened it.

I sat back, recoiling against the driver's seat. Fear swept through my body as he slid onto the passenger seat and closed the door behind him. I knew immediately I had seriously miscalculated the situation and made a huge mistake.

My mind raced as I fumbled for my door handle, forgetting that I was still strapped into my seat.

Crawford dropped a ripped and dirty backpack on the floor between his feet, then turned his attention to me. He leaned across the console between us and plucked Jessica's phone from my hand. He seemed to consider me for half a second before sitting back.

"Will you fucking relax already? I'm freezing my balls off out there. I'm just sitting in here to warm up for a minute." I took a second to catch my breath as I processed his words and body language. He had surprised me by just getting into the car. Given all the warnings I'd received about him and his general demeanor, I had assumed the worst and, of course, panicked. It was hardly a stretch to imagine him pulling a knife or a gun from his crappy backpack and threatening my life while telling me to drive the car to some remote location where he'd leave me for dead, or worse, before making his escape.

But he wasn't reaching for anything. In fact, his head had fallen back against the passenger headrest, his eyes were closed, and his throat exposed. If anything, Crawford looked absolutely exhausted, like a man at the end of his rope.

I let the tension in my shoulders release a fraction of an inch and allowed my body to relax away from the door. I watched Crawford take a deep breath, then reach up with his left hand to rub his eyes. On the dash next to the digital clock, the temperature gauge said it was sixteen degrees outside. Without asking if he wanted me to, I used the button on my door handle to roll up the passenger window and turned up the heat in the car.

"Do you have... anywhere you can go? Somewhere inside, maybe the shelter?"

Crawford sat up straighter, turned his head to face me, and gave me an angry glare. "What I do and where I go is none of your fucking business." He snatched his backpack off the floor, opened the car door, got out, and slammed the door behind him so hard it made the car rock. I watched as he shoved Jessica's phone into his backpack and slipped his arm through one of the straps. He took several angry steps back into the cold before he stopped. His arms hung straight at his side, rigid with the anger that seemed ever ready to explode from within him. He clenched and unclenched his hands several times, then tilted his head back and screamed at the sky.

He turned around and stormed back toward the Jeep. I reached for the button and locked the doors. When he reached the passenger side door again, he glared at me, lifted his fist, and banged on the window three times. "Roll down the window," he commanded.

When I didn't do what he asked, Crawford looked ready to bang on the window again, but whatever the expression on my face was, it must've made him rethink his current tactic.

He squeezed both his eyes shut and seemed to take a breath. When he spoke again, his voice was calmer, but I could tell he was barely constraining the rage he felt. "I have to tell you something. I swear, one thing, and you're never gonna see me again." When he opened his eyes again, I saw that he meant it. Crawford wasn't coming through the window to grab me by the neck. But he did have something to say.

Without taking my eyes off him, I reached for the passenger window button and lowered the glass three inches.

"You should leave, he said. "Leave the Norths, leave their house, leave this town, get the hell away from here. As far as you can, as fast as you can."

"Why? What do you know? Why did Jessica leave?"

Crawford stared at me for several seconds, then turned his head away. "They're not who you think. They're not what they say. Jessica went into that house, got mixed up with that fucking family, and she was never the same. They changed her, stole her. None of it is what anybody thinks. I tried telling the police, but what the fuck do I know? I'm just a homeless, drug-addicted dirtbag. I don't live in a fucking mansion in the middle of acres and acres of forest making millions of dollars every year." He threaded his arm through the other backpack strap and banged on the jeep door with his fist before turning away. He took several steps before shouting over his shoulder, "But if I were you, Libby Luck, I'd get the fuck out while you still can!"

CHAPTER 52

Because my meeting with Officer Riteman and my encounter with Crawford had taken so long, I didn't see the point in driving to the house now only to turn right back around to pick up Daniel from school. I waited out the couple hours I had to spare at the Coffee Klatch sipping down two white chocolate mochas, an extravagance I could now easily afford on my generous salary from the Norths, and chatting with Kyra between customers.

I had come here intending to get a few things off my chest and listen to what she would say about it. Any of it. But every time a customer left the shop and she'd sit down at the table across from me, I couldn't quite find a way to bring up the fact that I'd slept with my boss. Or that Alexi had left him, and they were getting a divorce.

I wanted to ask her what she thought about the fact that Garrett had a school file that was a mile high. Or that he seemed to still hate me and now probably more so because I was pretty sure he knew I was sleeping with his dad—while also not yet knowing about the divorce.

I wanted to hear what she had to say about my visit with Officer Riteman. My run-in with Crawford. That I'd been in possession of Jessica's phone and what I'd found, and not found, on it. I wanted to reach out to her, ask her advice, listen to her recommendations, and find out if she thought I was being completely crazy or just stupid.

I wanted a friend and a confidant who could help me make sense of everything that was happening. Someone who could let me know if I was flying off the rails. I didn't have anyone like that in my life.

I'd never, not since my mother's death, had anyone like that in my life.

Was it any surprise that I had no idea how to start a conversation about any of these topics with Kyra? Every time she came and sat down, I would start to form a confession, but the words would freeze in my throat. It was, in part, the vulnerability. I liked Kyra. I thought of her as a friend. One of the first real friends I'd ever had. What if I told her any of this and it made her think and feel differently about me?

It was quite possible that she wouldn't understand how I could allow myself to become romantically involved with Jacob North—imminent divorce or not. There was also the matter of trust. I thought I could probably rely on Kyra to keep my confidence, but what if I was wrong? What if she told Trisha, the last woman on the planet who would ever understand my particular situation. And then, what if Trisha told even one other person in her vast, gossiping network?

Like Jessica, I'd become the center of town attention—for the most horrible reasons.

So, for two hours we chatted about her last blind date, the other customers, and Trisha who was again paranoid that her husband was cheating on her. Despite the fact she had zero proof.

"She's soooo insecure," Kyra said before sipping the caramel latte she'd made for herself. "I don't know who, but someone did that woman wrong and messed her up for life. She does not trust Rich at all. Not with anything."

"Maybe it was Rich who messed her up," I suggested.

Kyra thought about this for half a second, then pointed at me like I was onto something. "Yes. And she didn't leave him because of the kids...and the business." She took another sip and nodded like we'd arrived at the obvious answer to Trisha's paranoia. "It would explain a lot. She's now completely out of her mind imagining that guy from yesterday will come back and break into the shop."

I lowered my cup to the table. "Why would she think that?"

"Because I stopped him and went after him with the bat. She's sure he's going come back and exact revenge by breaking a window or robbing us." Kyra shook her head. "Can you imagine being that paranoid? That guy probably had no idea where he was, let alone remember what happened yesterday."

This was it. My perfect opening to tell her about finding Jessica's phone and my own minor investigation into who Crawford was and why he kept following me, or rather, the Jeep, all over town.

But the seconds of silence kept stretching between us. I wasn't saying anything, and I felt the moment slipping away.

Part of me was terrified that even if I only shared this minor detail, I'd soon be spilling my guts about absolutely everything.

Kyra's phone buzzed on the table. She picked it up and rolled her eyes. "Jesus," she said. "He wants to go out again... tonight. Ugh." She looked at me. "Should I go?"

And just like that, my opportunity to tell Kyra the truth evaporated. I shrugged. "You did say there were some good moments."

Ten minutes later, I left the shop to pick Daniel up from school and return to the house.

As I started the Jeep, I thought about how I had been gone all day.

Which meant Garrett had been home alone all day.

CHAPTER 53

When we got home, the house was dark and silent. Even though the sun had fallen below the tree line, no lights had been turned on. There were no dishes in the sink, no crumbs on the counters, and the television was not playing in the family room. There was absolutely no sign that Garrett had even left his room.

The house was so still, so quiet, a feeling of dread bloomed in my chest.

Garrett was in middle school, and Jacob had not mentioned the need for Garrett to be supervised at all times. Then again, Jacob hadn't given any instruction about how Garrett's suspension should be handled. But I probably shouldn't have left him at home all alone for the entire day.

I started flipping on lights as I moved through the house to fill the empty spaces with some energy, some life. I got Daniel settled on a stool at the kitchen island with a snack and a drink, then headed toward the stairs.

"I'll be right back. I'm just going to go find your brother."

Daniel kept his eyes focused on his plate of goldfish crackers and apple slices and didn't say a word. His silence stopped me. Since the meeting in the principal's office yesterday, Daniel had barely uttered a handful of words. "Everything okay?" I asked.

He didn't look at me right away, and for half a second, I thought he might continue to ignore me. I suddenly had a horrible thought. What if Garrett, with his anger and spite, had told his little brother about Jacob and me?

My hands clenched at my sides. I tried to imagine any way I could explain to a six-year-old what was going on, especially since I had no idea, although I could easily imagine, how Garrett might have put it.

But then Daniel turned to me, and his expression wasn't confused or angry. No. If anything, Daniel looked scared. "You should stay away from Garrett," he whispered, returning his gaze to the plate in front of him.

I opened my mouth to ask what he meant, but a loud thump from upstairs interrupted me. I turned my attention to the ceiling above me. I recognized the sound. It was the same thump I'd heard before coming from Alexi's office.

I would go up and see if I could figure out where the sound was coming from, but first, I wanted to know why Daniel had said I should stay away from his brother. When I turned back, I saw Daniel looking at the ceiling above us. He had also heard the sound.

"Do you know what that is?"

"What?" Daniel asked before returning his eyes to his plate.

"That sound, from upstairs. That thump. I've heard it before."

Daniel hunched further over his plate and shrugged. "I didn't hear it."

I narrowed my eyes. "What? How could you not hear that, Daniel? It was so loud."

He shrugged and wouldn't look at me.

I took a breath and let it out. What the hell was going on with him? I didn't know, but right now, I wanted to find Garrett. I imagined he'd be in his room gaming. It was probably where he'd been all day long. Still, I was nervous about leaving him home alone for so long and wanted to put my mind at ease by seeing him with my own eyes. "I'm going to find your brother and see what that noise was. I'll be back in a minute."

I was about to head up the stairs when I heard the door to the garage open and close. A second later, Garrett walked into the kitchen.

He was covered in mud.

CHAPTER 54

Speechless, all I could do was stare at him. It wasn't only his hands. Mud was smeared across his left cheek and up his right arm. His shirt was covered in it. His shoes were caked in it. He stood in the doorway between the kitchen and mud room, with his arms hanging limp at his sides and his eyes staring straight into mine.

"Garrett?" I finally managed to ask. "Are you okay? What happened to you?"

He didn't answer me. He stood, stock still and staring at me so intently I found I couldn't continue to bear the weight of his unwavering gaze. My skin crawled. Something felt very wrong. I broke eye contact but managed to make myself move closer to him. I walked slow. Approached him like a wild animal. Garrett and I had no relationship, no foundation, and I had absolutely no idea what I could expect from him in this condition.

He looked like he was in shock. Like he could fight, flee, or break into sobs any moment. When I was about five feet from him, my body refused to let me get any closer. Garrett was still only a boy, but he was big for his age—he could hurt me if he wanted to.

And that huge behavior file at school made me think that Garrett was no stranger to violence.

"Garrett," I whispered.

He blinked. His expression seemed to clear. Whatever had frozen his mind was beginning to thaw. He seemed to not only be staring at me but seeing me now as well.

"Garrett," I tried again. "Are you okay?"

He swallowed and looked like he was processing this question. A moment later, he shook his head.

"Are you hurt?" I asked.

He looked at his hands, then back at me, and shook his head again.

I took a breath and let it out slow. "Okay, good. But you look pretty upset. And clearly, something has happened. I'm going to call your dad and—"

"No," he said and shook his head repeatedly. "I…I have to show you." He stared at his hands. "You have to come and see. Don't call my dad."

I felt sick. Weirdly trapped between wanting to help Garrett and get away from him. On a good day, he made me feel uncomfortable. Right now, a terror had taken root at my core and was spreading throughout my body. "I don't think—"

"Please, Libby," Garrett said, and I watched in disbelief as tears welled up in his eyes and one rolled down his cheek. "Please come and see."

My shoulders dropped, and I glanced at Daniel. He was still sitting at the counter, now staring at his brother, and all the color had drained from his face. I thought about what he had said to me not more than five minutes ago, "You should stay away from Garrett."

Why had he said that about his own brother?

I held my neck between my palms as I tried to think logically about what to do, what to say, next. "Can you just tell me what it is?"

Garrett shook his head, and more tears streamed down his face.

"You're scaring me, Garrett. I really think we should call your father. Or even your mother," I tried.

"You can't. Please." He stepped toward me, reached for my left hand, and held it between his hands. I could feel the dirt and mud transferring from his skin onto mine. "It's not far. But we have to go now before it gets dark. I don't know what to do. Libby, please…I need help."

CHAPTER 55

Garrett had insisted that we leave Daniel at the house, but on this, at least, I would not budge.

"You can't expect me to leave your little brother home alone."

"He shouldn't come."

"Well, if you insist on showing me whatever it is right now, he will have to because I'm not leaving him here alone."

Garrett considered his little brother, who stared blankly back at him. "Fine. But when we get there, he has to stay back."

I nodded and went to get our coats and boots from the closet. Once I rounded the corner to the hall and was out of Garrett's sight, I quickly texted Jacob.

Something is going on with Garrett. He's really freaked out, covered in mud from the woods, and wants to show me something. Please call.

I hit send and hoped my phone would ring before we even

got beyond the garage door. Garrett didn't want me to call his dad, and I wanted to give him a chance to show and explain to me why that was—but what could I do if Jacob called me?

Once Daniel and I were bundled up, we followed Garrett through the garage. He was still only wearing his muddy clothes and sneakers, and the temperature was dropping with the sun. "Don't you want some warmer clothes?" I asked him, hoping he would decide yes and that changing would delay this excursion long enough for Jacob to either call or get home.

But Garrett just shook his head and kept walking. "It won't take long. It's not that far."

I sighed and reached for Daniel's hand as we stepped out of the brightly lit garage and into the cold, darkening evening.

"I don't want to go," Daniel said, his voice so quiet only I could hear him.

"It's okay," I whispered. "We'll only be a few minutes."

At least, that was what I had hoped. But when Garrett led us into the woods onto a rocky trail, and we were still walking ten minutes later with no sign of slowing down, fear flared at my core. As Garrett marched on with a brisk purpose several yards ahead of us, I pulled my phone from my pocket to check if I had somehow missed a message from Jacob.

There was nothing.

"It's getting really dark, Garrett. I thought you said it wasn't far. We should turn back. We don't have flashlights."

Ahead of me, I watched as Garrett reached into the pocket of his pants, and a second later, a bright light illuminated him in the darkness. Of course, we had the lights on our phones. I swiped down on my screen and hit the flashlight icon.

"Libby?" Daniel said.

"Yes?"

"I'm scared," he said, and I felt his small hand tighten its grip on mine.

"It's okay. Nothing to be scared of," I said, even though I didn't feel that way at all. It was dark out now. Pitch black, and we were surrounded by dense woods. My fear grew exponentially with every step that took us farther away from the house and deeper into the forest. It wasn't only the psychological fear, the unseeing, unknowing of what or who might be out here. There was also the very real danger of wild animals in this area. Jacob had warned me multiple times about walking or hiking in the woods. The land around the North's home was teeming with coyotes, bobcats, and even bears.

I stared into the dense forest beside us, nearly blind because of the bright light from my phone. I couldn't help but imagine all the dangerous things that could so easily be stalking us. We had been walking for over twenty minutes and had to be at least a mile from the house. When Garrett said it was close, I assumed he meant much closer than this. I never would have agreed to come if I'd known it was this far.

"Garrett," I called. "This is enough," I couldn't help the hysterical edge that had crept into my voice. I was scared and no longer had any emotional resources to hide it. "I'm taking Daniel back to the house now. You can tell me where we're going or show me in the morning."

For the first time since we started on the trail, Garrett stopped and turned around. His face was illuminated by the light from my phone, and I could see that he'd been crying this whole time. Wet streaks had left tracks on his dirt-smeared face.

"Please, Libby, I swear we're almost there. It only a little farther," he sobbed outright.

I had never seen Garrett like this. He was always defensive, distant, and quick with a rude comment aimed at me. I didn't recognize this vulnerable and scared boy before me.

For the first time since I'd come to work here, I could see what a child Garrett still was. He tried to hide it, tried to be bigger and meaner than he really felt. But he was just a kid.

For the first time, I wondered why Garrett acted the way he did.

I took a deep breath. "How much farther? Exactly? It's cold, and it's dark."

Garrett nodded. "I don't know exactly. It has to be close. I left a piece of my shirt tied to a pine tree to mark where to turn."

I noticed he'd ripped off the hem of his t-shirt. "Turn?" I asked. "What you're showing us isn't on the trail?"

Garrett shook his head and started to cry again. I watched his shoulders shake as whatever he was carrying overwhelmed him. Even though he had been absolutely miserable to me every second since I'd arrived, I couldn't help feeling sorry for him. On instinct, I went to him and pulled him into a hug.

He felt stiff at first like he might try and push me away, but a second later, he dissolved. Both his arms wrapped tight around my waist, and he buried his tear-soaked, muddy face into my shirt.

"Garrett," I whispered as he cried. "Just tell me what you saw."

He cried for a few more seconds and then whispered something into my shoulder, too soft for me to hear.

"What?" I asked and pulled away to hear him better.

He looked into my eyes and said it again.

"A body."

CHAPTER 56

Garrett was right. We were nearly there. The pine tree with the piece of Garrett's ripped shirt was another ten yards from where I'd threatened to turn back. Daniel saw it first.

"There it is!" he said triumphantly as he yanked his hand from my grasp and ran to touch the thin strip of cloth tied to a low branch. Daniel beamed like he'd won a game. He hadn't heard his brother say what we were about to see.

I stood with the boys on each side of me and stared into the dark forest before us. We were deep into the woods, at least a mile from the house, with only two cell phone flashlights illuminating our way through the pitch dark. I checked my phone, hoping I'd somehow missed a call or a text from Jacob, knowing full well that I had not. As I stared into the dense trees before us, I opened my phone app to call Jacob. At this point, I didn't care what Garrett felt about telling his dad or why. I was so alone and scared right now. I needed to hear another adult's voice.

I wanted to let him know where we were. Tell him what Garrett thought he'd seen and ask for help. I needed to hear his reassuring voice telling me this was crazy. Of course, there wasn't a body buried in the woods. I wanted Jacob to tell me either to bring the boys back to the house or to wait just a few more minutes while he sprinted down the path toward us to help.

But I wouldn't be getting any of that because I had zero signal out here.

"Shit," I breathed.

I felt Daniel's eyes glance up at me, but he didn't say a word.

"It's probably not what you thought," I told Garrett.

"I know what I saw," he said, a little of his usual defenses bolstering him.

"I could just be an animal. A big one. There're all sorts of animals that live out here."

Garrett didn't say anything, but he at least appeared to be considering the possibility.

"How far in is it?"

Garrett shrugged, never taking his eyes off the forest before us like he was watching and dreading an attack. "Not too far. Maybe a minute walk."

I turned to look at him. "How did you even find it? It's off the trail."

"I heard something. I left the trail to go see what it was. It was a coyote…digging."

"Digging?"

Garrett took a second to respond, and I wondered if I'd lost him again. "It was digging it up." Then he turned his head to meet my gaze. "It was eating it."

I held his gaze for a second. My lips rolled between my teeth, and I was unable to keep the horrific image from my mind. "It might still have only been an animal," I whispered.

"Buried?" Garrett asked.

He was right. At least his memory of what he thought he saw was right. "Less than a minute?" I asked.

He nodded.

I took a deep breath and tried to gather every ounce of courage I had. "Let's just get this over with," I declared, taking the first step off the path. One way or the other, I would get to the bottom of this. Either I'd take a look, laugh with relief, and head us all back to the house with a story to tell Jacob about the wild imaginations of children.

Or I'd be calling the police the moment we were back in range of a cell signal.

CHAPTER 57

Garrett must have been distraught, confused, or most likely both when he was out here earlier because what he'd found was nowhere near a one-minute walk from the trail.

It was less than twenty feet, and we reached the spot in less than ten seconds. We reached the spot so fast there wasn't any time to tell Daniel to hang back, don't look, or shield your eyes. The site was so near the trail that, in the dark, we practically stumbled into the middle of it. I hadn't been expecting it, I had the light from my phone aimed far into the forest ahead of us, not at the ground right in front of us. When I took a step and felt the uneven softness of disturbed, dug-up earth, I swung my light down quickly and grabbed for Daniel's hand.

Garrett would have been in shock, I realized. After working with his bare hands to dig and confirm what was here, his mind had probably shifted, slowed down, and tried very hard to protect him from what he found. It was why he thought the walk along the path was much closer than it was and the position off the path was farther away.

His mental guidance, clarity of thought, and reason were completely out of wack and playing tricks on him. His mind needed to do whatever it could to cocoon him and keep him safe. Because what it absolutely could not do was lie to him.

The three of us stood, still as stone, at the edge of this turned-over shallow grave, staring at the remains illuminated in my light.

It was no wild animal.

This was a human.

Before I could manage any rational action, my mind registered several things.

This was a woman.

She had long hair.

Due to decay, exposure, and animal interference, the corpse was unrecognizable.

Despite that, my mind immediately realized this woman was Jessica York.

Daniel screamed.

Somehow, I had a sliver of rational thought available to take a picture of what we'd found before grabbing the hands of both kids and dragging them back to the path. "Do you think you can run?" I asked, and they both nodded.

"Good, we are running back to the house as fast as we can, and I'll call the police the second I have a signal."

They both nodded again, in unison, like I was their commander, giving a simple order they could both comprehend and focus on. We would run. We would call the police. We had a plan.

Without another word, Garrett took off at a pace I would not have thought him capable of. He quickly outpaced his little brother's legs, but I did not stop him or tell him to slow down. Let him run, as fast as he could, back to the light and safety of the house.

I stayed by Daniel's side, keeping his pace once his initial sprint petered out. I checked my phone incessantly for the barest breath of signal. I knew Daniel was terrified and was running as fast as his little legs could manage, so I resisted the urge to tell him to Hurry up! Run faster! But the woods' impenetrable darkness pressed on me from all sides. I felt its cold breath on my neck, its skeletal finger run down my spine. I glanced over my shoulder every few minutes, convinced and afraid I'd see we were being followed.

It was taking so long to get back to the house—I wished I'd made Garrett stay with us. Even though the path we'd taken was a straight shot through the woods, I started to wonder if, in our hysteria, Daniel and I had managed to take a wrong turn. The thought of being stuck out here, lost in the dark, in the middle of the woods, with only my phone's flashlight, made my throat tighten and panicked tears rise.

I clenched my fists and shook my head hard. Pull it together!

Beside me, I could hear the sound of Daniel's shoes rhythmically hitting the dirt, interlaced with the hiccups of his sobs.

CHAPTER 58

I grabbed Daniel's hand when I saw the lights from the house emerging through the trees ahead. "We're almost there," I said, urging him to go faster. I knew he must be practically sprinting, but he didn't complain and I needed to get as much distance as possible, as fast as possible, between us and the darkness that held Jessica's body.

When we finally broke free of the woods, and I felt the North's manicured, even lawn beneath my shoes, I couldn't stop the tears of relief that ran down my face. When I saw Jacob's truck parked in the drive, a flood of relief washed over the grip of fear that had held me.

As we approached the house, our pace slowed, and I glanced over my shoulder one last time. Daniel continued toward the safety of the house and his father's arms, but I stopped dead in my tracks, frozen in fear. I wiped tears from my eyes as I tried to make sense of what I had just seen.

It was a person. I would have sworn to it. Disappearing back into the woods just beyond the path we had left.

I could barely breathe because of the running. Hardly see because of my tears. And felt hysterical from fear.

I walked backward toward the house, keeping my eyes trained on the exact spot where I'd seen someone evaporate into the trees.

I wasn't thinking straight, I reasoned. I was overwhelmed, confused, exhausted... It was nothing. A figment of my imagination.

Still, every cell in my body felt the presence of danger. Like I was being watched. Hunted. Like I was prey and a predator was close.

"Libby!" Jacob's voice cut through the air behind me.

Only then, with the certainty of his presence and security within reach, did I dare to turn away from the woods. When I saw him striding across the lawn toward me, I ran to him. Without considering what either of the boys would think if they saw us, I flung myself into his arms and buried my face against his chest. When my legs gave out beneath me, Jacob held me tighter, so I didn't fall to the ground.

"Libby?" he said as his hand cradled the back of my head. "What on earth? What is going on? The boys said..."

I shook my head. I didn't want to say it. I didn't want to think it.

"Libby?" Jacob said, his voice firmer now. He grasped my arms, pulled me away from his chest, and looked into my face. "What the hell is going on? The boys said...they..."

He wanted me to explain, but I could see that even he was at a loss trying to wrap his head around whatever he had already been told. I shook my head as more tears streamed down my face. "There's a body," my voice came out in a whisper.

"What?"

"A body. In the woods. It's... it's Jessica." Saying it out loud helped me to find some strength, find some objectivity, and quell the raging fears that had hounded me in the forest. I managed to stand on my legs without falling into Jacob. I took a breath and found a clear thought. "We need to call the police."

Jacob stared over my head into the trees beyond me. He looked like he was trying to imagine how anything I said could be possible. He shook his head, and a second later, I saw the confusion and worry drop from his expression. It was replaced by a look of incredulity. "Libby. We're not calling the police." His tone was sympathetic like he was speaking to a small, distraught child. "You're confused."

His words stunned me.

He reached for my shoulders and pulled me into an embrace. "Look, these woods are full of animals. If you and the boys did see bones, I can promise you it's just a deer or something."

I pulled away from him and looked him in the eye. "I know exactly what I saw out there." I pointed to the path behind me. "That wasn't a deer, or a dog, or anything other than a human body. A female human body. We need to call the police right now."

"Libby, don't be ridiculous. I'm not calling the police out here this late at night for a wild goose chase. Now, come on, let's go inside and calm the boys down." He reached for my hand, presumably to pull me back to his way of thinking and into the house. "In the morning, when it's light, I'll head out there...hell, we can all head out there, and I'll show you. You've all gotten each other worked up over nothing."

I pulled my hand from his grip and held up my phone. "The last time I checked, dead animals aren't usually found wearing gold necklaces," I said and dialed 911.

CHAPTER 59

An hour later, I was walking back along the same path flanked by those same dark woods I'd been so desperate to put behind me. Only this time, I was accompanied by eight police officers, two K9 shepherds, and Jacob, who was still in disbelief that a 'mistake' was being taken so far.

When Officer Riteman arrived, Jacob greeted him and his team with a handshake and an apology. "Honestly, I'm quite certain this will be a waste of your time." He ran his fingers through his hair. "My nanny and my sons have probably made a huge mistake."

I stood behind and to the side of Jacob, silently seething that he'd refer to me and my judgment this way. Not only was I not a child, but we were in a relationship that had far surpassed the title of his *nanny*. I didn't say a word, but Officer Riteman caught my gaze over Jacob's shoulder—he didn't think I was wasting his time.

"Well," Riteman said. "We'll get out there and have a look."

He turned on his flashlight and signaled to his team. "About how far would you say the body was, Ms. Luck?"

"About a mile? Maybe less."

Riteman nodded his head and returned his penetrating gaze to Jacob. "So, twenty minutes, and we'll all know if I dragged these folks away from their dinner tables for nothing or a very big something." He tilted his head and nodded at me. "Think you're up to leading us back to the spot?"

I considered his request for only a moment before realizing that 'no' wasn't really an option. It's not like I could expect Garrett or Daniel to lead the police to the dead body of their beloved ex-nanny. "Yes," I said.

Riteman gave me an encouraging smile. "We'll be right beside you and behind you the whole way. After you, Ms. Luck."

We were halfway across the lawn when Jacob called out. "Wait!" I stopped, and so did all eight police officers and the two dogs. Four flashlights swung around and lit up Jacob's face. He lifted his hand to block the intense lights from his eyes. "I think I should come too...I mean, if that's okay." He jogged to close the distance between us. "If it is Jessica, and I'm sure it isn't, but if... I'm the only one here who really knew her."

Beside me, Riteman nodded his head. "The boys will be okay alone in the house?" he asked.

Jacob turned his head and glanced back at the house as if just now thinking about the fact he'd be leaving them alone after the trauma they'd endured. "Yes." He nodded. "They're watching television...this should take less than an hour to get there and back. Plus, I'll be able to confirm for them that everything is okay."

The other officers turned their lights back toward the

woods and the trail, but Riteman kept his eyes trained on Jacob for several seconds longer before he said. "All right then, Mr. North. Let's get moving."

Surrounded by eight armed police and two specially trained dogs, the walk back through the woods felt infinitely less terrifying than the one before. The pace was brisk, and the officers kept a few lights on the path ahead while others swept through and cut the darkness of the trees around us.

Once, I saw two eyes shining red and staring back at us. Startled, I gasped out loud and thought again of what I thought I'd seen when I first left the woods—a person disappearing back into the trees.

"Just a coyote," Riteman said beside me. "These woods are full of them."

I nodded and glanced back at Jacob, who was bringing up the rear of our group several feet back. I couldn't help but wonder if he was now having doubts about what we would find out here.

When we reached the branch with the torn hem of Garrett's shirt marking the spot, I pointed it out. "It's here. Only a few feet off the path."

I stood back and let the officers and Jacob pass me by. I had no desire to see Jessica's mangled remains ever again.

It only took a few seconds before I heard Jacob's voice. "Oh my God. Oh my God. What...how is this...why?" A moment later, Riteman and a younger female officer escorted him out of the trees and back to the path.

"Libby, I know this was difficult. Thank you for your help this evening. Officer Carter will escort you and Mr. North back to the house. I'm going to ask both of you and the boys to remain inside until further notice. Additionally, as this is now an investigation, I will need you all to keep the details about this evening to yourselves. As you may imagine, finding a body is a sensitive issue and needs to be handled with great care."

"Of course," I said.

Jacob, who stood further down the path and was facing away from us, said nothing at all. I wasn't even sure he had heard Riteman's request.

"And Mr. North."

At the sound of his name, Jacob turned his head so that his face was in profile for us.

"Two things. I understand Mrs. North has been out of town for some time. I'm going to need to speak with her as soon as possible. Additionally, I'd like you to come to the station tomorrow to give a statement."

Jacob nodded once, then started walking back toward the house.

Riteman and I watched him for several seconds before he turned to me. "Shock is an odd thing," he explained. "Makes people act in all sorts of ways you wouldn't necessarily expect. I'm afraid I'll also need you to come back in for a statement," he said.

I nodded and turned to leave when a sudden thought stopped me in my tracks.

"Officer Riteman?"

"Hmm?" he said and turned back to me.

"One thing you should probably know. Crawford Allen, the man you warned be about."

Riteman had me locked in his gaze now as he nodded.

"I'm sorry. I didn't listen to you. I had Jessica's old cell phone, and Crawford wanted it. He said, because of his history with Jessica, he was the only one who should have it." I shook my head now and looked at the dirt under my feet.

"When was this?" he asked.

"This afternoon."

"After we met, I presume?"

I nodded.

Riteman lifted his gaze to the path behind me. "Carter!" he called out.

"Yes, sir?" she yelled back.

"Once you get them settled, I want you to call in an APB for Crawford Allen! Have them check the shelter first!"

"Will do!" she shouted.

"Anything else you think I should know about?" Riteman asked me.

I shook my head.

He kept me pinned under his stare for a few seconds, then added. "Okay. Just remember, your life over the next several days will be infinitely easier if you cooperate and are level with me. Understand?"

I nodded and turned to catch up with Jacob and Officer Carter.

The last thing I wanted tonight was to get left alone in these dark woods again.

CHAPTER 60

As soon as Jacob and I returned to the house, he disappeared into his office and closed the door.

"I need to call Alexi," he said as he walked away from me without even a glance in my direction.

I stood staring at his closed door, trying to imagine what could possibly be going through his mind. Was he sad? Angry? Grief-stricken that the woman who had lived in his home and cared for his children for so many years was lying dead in a shallow grave just minutes from their house?

Was he upset that it happened in such proximity?

Was he devastated that he didn't even know and hadn't been able to help or stop it from happening?

I had no idea because Jacob was barely speaking and looked like every ounce of blood had drained from his body. I remembered Officer Riteman's word—Shock. Jacob was in shock, and this is what shock looked like on him.

I found both boys in the family room. Daniel was asleep on

the couch. Garrett was staring at the TV—it wasn't turned on. How long had he been like this?

All afternoon, I realized. Ever since he'd first seen that body and used his bare hands to dig it up—Garrett's mind had shut down and remained that way.

Everyone handles shock differently.

When I lifted Daniel up off the couch, he woke up immediately. With his eyes wide open and his body rigid, he looked ready to fight. "It's me," I whispered. "I was just going to carry you to bed."

Daniel squirmed out of my arms until his feet were on the floor. He wanted to walk on his own.

When we were upstairs and halfway down the hall to their bedrooms, Daniel asked Garrett if he could sleep with him in his room. To my surprise, Garrett said yes. Garrett put his hand on his little brother's shoulder and guided him into his usually forbidden domain. I watched from the hall as they disappeared into the dark room—Garrett didn't slam the door shut like he usually did at night.

He didn't even close it.

He turned on his bedside lamp, pulled back the blankets on his double bed, and helped his little brother climb in. Garrett looked at me and held my gaze for several seconds before he, too, got into bed.

His usual hostility that seemed ever ready to boil up was completely gone.

In that instant, I knew...Garrett wanted me to help him.

He lay flat on his back, both hands on his chest, eyes closed.

He had left the light on.

I took a breath, let it out, and decided to not think about it too much. Garrett was a child, I reminded myself. I crossed the threshold of his room, pulled his gaming chair away from his desk, and rolled it to the side of his bed. I didn't say a word, but Garrett was awake and knew I was there. I sat back and watched over them for several minutes until Daniel's breath shifted to a deep and even rhythm.

I thought Garrett may have also fallen asleep.

I switched off the lamp and shifted in the chair to stand up, then felt a hand land on top of mine.

Garrett, still on his back, still with closed eyes, had reached out. I stared at his hand resting on top of mine on the arm of the chair. I didn't move.

"Libby?" he asked.

"Yes?" I whispered.

"Is she really dead?" his voice broke on the words, and I knew Garrett was crying in the dark.

I placed my other hand on top of his and gave it a slight squeeze. "Yes. I'm so sorry, Garrett."

I heard him sniffle in the dark. We sat that way, his hand in mine, for another minute until he gently pulled away and rolled onto his side.

"Good night," I whispered. He didn't say anything back.

I left the door open and the hall lights on for them.

In my own rooms, I left the lights off, drew back the heavy silk drapes in the sitting room, and pulled open the sliding glass door. The cold night air rushed into the room and through my clothes. I crossed my bare arms over my chest and stepped out into the night. Off to the right and in the distance, I could see the police's bright lights illuminating up through the trees as they worked to recover Jessica's body and look for evidence.

Officer Carter had shared that they would likely be out there all night and well into the morning. The trail and all the surrounding areas would be cordoned off for a very long time.

The wind picked up and blasted a freezing stream of air over me, whipping my hair into a frenzy around my head. I was covered in goosebumps and shivering so hard it made my muscles ache. I moved farther out onto the balcony and welcomed the pain. Feeling it meant I was alive. I was still here, capable of experiencing the multitude of sensations, good and bad, that life had in store for me. I was breathing, feeling, and existing in a world that had taken the short life of the woman they were now digging out of the ground. The woman who had once lived a life within this house. Slept in this very room. Stood on the balcony now beneath my own feet.

In that moment, I was overcome with a relief so acute—I was Libby Luck, not Jessica York--it made me weep for the joy of my own life.

And the horror of her death.

CHAPTER 61

The next morning, the boys and I waited in the Jeep for Jacob to join us. When he still hadn't materialized from his office by nine, I knocked at his door. When he didn't answer, I let myself in.

Jacob was a neat and meticulous person, so it was bizarre to find him passed out on his couch, stinking and still drunk beside an empty bottle of Jack Daniels. When I shook his shoulder, he didn't respond. He was so passed out I worried at first if he was even still breathing.

"Jacob," I said, shaking first his arm and then his whole face.

"Jacob!" I yelled right next to his ear.

This, at least, interrupted his drunken stupor enough for him to open his eyes. When he looked up at me, it was as if he had no idea who I was. I would have been offended, except I suspected that Jacob would likely have had difficulty remembering who he was should I ask him.

I let out a loud and very annoyed sigh. I could understand

the family was dealing with a crisis, but to say that Jacob was complicating the matter with this behavior would be an understatement. "Officer Riteman wants you at the station by ten," I reminded him despite the fact there was absolutely no way we could possibly get there in time, given these conditions.

Jacob managed to sit upright, but his head hung between his knees. I had no idea how full the bottle of Jack had been before he started in on it last night, but my first guess was that it had been full. "Should I call and tell him you need to reschedule?"

Jacob lifted his head and looked at me. His eyes were bloodshot, and his expression looked confused, but he was cogent enough to answer my question. "No," he said. "Just call and tell him I'll be a little late."

I let out another sigh. "Fine. Do you need help—"

"I've got it, Libby," he cut me off, and his tone suggested he thought I was somehow the problem here. "I'll be ready and out the door in fifteen minutes."

"You're not driving yourself," I said.

For a second, Jacob looked like he would try to argue the fact. But he must have realized it would be insanity for him to try and operate a vehicle under his present condition. He nodded. "You'll have to drive me."

"Yes. And the boys will have to come too. I can't...we can't leave them alone after what happened yesterday."

Jacob nodded again, and I left him to pull himself together.

Fifteen minutes later, I sat with both boys in the Jeep and watched as their father struggled to navigate the four stairs from the mudroom door to the garage. Jesus, how the hell was he supposed to answer questions about Jessica's death?

When Jacob slid onto the passenger seat beside me, I handed him the tumbler of hot coffee I'd made for him.

"Thank you," he said.

"Hopefully, it helps," I said and shifted the Jeep into reverse.

CHAPTER 62

Officer Riteman thought he would likely need to speak with Jacob for quite a while.

"Why don't you take the boys into town," Jacob suggested. "I don't really want them hanging around here," he whispered. The coffee had helped, but his words still had a hint of slur about them.

"Okay. Call me when you're done."

Other couples, normal couples, would have kissed goodbye. Given each other a reassuring hug. Jacob and I were not a normal couple. We were a secret couple. So, instead of a kiss, Jacob patted my arm. "Thank you, Libby."

"Sure thing, Jacob," I said, finding it impossible to keep the edge out of my voice.

But Jacob was both still drunk and reeling about yesterday—my tone of voice was not an issue pressing enough to breech his awareness.

I was being ridiculous, I told myself as I left the station and returned to the parked Jeep. Yes, Jacob had been distant since last night, and it could be easily argued that he was shutting me out, both emotionally and physically. But could I really blame him or even be upset about that right now?

The man was clearly drowning. He probably didn't have a clue about how he was behaving toward me.

He wasn't even thinking about me, I realized. And honestly, could I expect him to be worried about my feelings when his mind was utterly consumed with the fact that Jessica was found dead in his own backyard?

Of course not.

By the time I got back in the Jeep, I had decided to let all my silly, girlish, hurt feelings fall away. There were much, much bigger problems to be managed right now.

I started the Jeep and shifted into reverse.

"Where are we going?" Daniel asked.

"To get some coffee," I said.

Despite yesterday's tragic events and discoveries, today, the sun was bright, cheery, and brought an unseasonable warmth to Walford. At the Coffee Klatch, Garrett and Daniel sat at the bistro tables outside eating ice cream while I sat with Kyra inside and relayed every single thing that had happened. The secrets I'd kept from her and the truth about what had become of Jessica York.

The minute I walked through the door, both she and Trisha took one look at me and realized I needed help.

"You get her something to drink and sit her at the back table," Trisha said. "I'll manage the shop and the boys."

I looked into Trisha's eyes and hoped she could sense how grateful I felt for her right now. She may be an insecure town gossip, but Trisha was incredibly astute at realizing what was going on with people.

When I had finished spilling absolutely everything to Kyra, she sat in her chair across from me, looking stunned. I had no idea what she was thinking or feeling. If she was judging me or feeling sorry for me. All I knew was the relief I felt after confessing everything out loud to her.

I wish I'd been brave enough to do it sooner.

"I can't believe it," she finally said.

"Which part?" I asked.

"Literally, any of it." Kyra leaned forward across the table and lowered her voice. "How could you not tell me?"

My shoulders sagged. "Which part?"

"Literally, like, any of it, Libby. I can't believe you've been sleeping with Jacob North for weeks, and you've never breathed a single word to me about it."

I glanced at Trisha behind the counter, making an espresso for a customer. "I didn't want…I don't know. I guess I didn't want you, and especially not Trisha, to think I was like her."

"Like who?"

"Jessica," I said. "You both told me how the whole town talked and gossiped about her. I was afraid."

Kyra reached across the table and took my hand in hers. "How could you even think that? I mean, yeah, you were absolutely right to not tell Trisha. And you never should let her find out. God, she'd have a fucking field day. But me? Libby, I'm your friend. That means I'm on your side. Even when I also think you're doing something fucking crazy like sleeping with Jacob North. Although, don't get me wrong. I totally get why you would. He's so fucking hot, right? But to ever imagine I would think you were anything like Jessica York? No way."

"You hardly knew her," I said and sipped my coffee.

"I knew enough."

"Knew enough about what," Trisha asked. She had finished with the last customer and was pulling up a chair to our table.

"Jessica York," Kyra blurted out before I could even think to try and stop her.

"Oh, that bitch," Trisha said and sat down. "What's she done now? Run off with someone else's husband?"

"No. She's dead," Kyra blurted.

This stopped Trisha in her gossip tracks, but only for a moment. "No! You're not serious?"

"Dead serious," Kyra said, then glanced at the ceiling. "Sorry for the joke," she added and crossed herself.

"Actually," I interjected as Officer Riteman's request to keep this information confidential came rushing back to me. "The police are investigating it right now. I wasn't supposed to say anything." It was one thing to lean on a friend in my time of need. Sitting here chatting with the town's biggest gossip was another thing entirely. A woman who had openly hated Jessica and probably didn't feel much genuine sorrow about her tragedy.

But it was like I hadn't said anything at all.

Trisha sat back in her chair and placed her coffee on the table. "That poor girl," she said while her facial expression and tone suggested these were just platitudes she felt must be said.

"Although, it's hardly surprising, really. I mean, given everything she got up to. She was bound to piss the wrong person off eventually."

Was Trisha actually suggesting that Jessica deserved to be killed and left to rot in the woods?

I opened my mouth to muster some defense but was cut off.

"You don't think," Kyra exclaimed, grabbing Trisha's arm. "It's all starting up again?"

Trisha's eyes grew wide, and she reached for her coffee. "I didn't even think about that. God, I hope not. What a nightmare that all was."

"What nightmare?" I asked.

Kyra and Trisha were finally silent when I wanted them to speak up. Trisha shook her head, and Kyra held her coffee between both hands and sipped it. Several times, I looked from one to the other before Trisha finally spoke up.

"A few years ago—"

"And for several years," Kyra interjected.

Trisha nodded. "There was a time when every woman in this town was terrified to go out after dark or even go out alone."

"Why?" I asked, even though I sensed where they were heading.

"There was a string of murders. All women from the area," Trisha said.

"Some were just missing persons," Kyra added.

"But only because their bodies were never found," Trisha said.

"It's been what? Two years?" Kyra asked.

"I think so," Trisha said. "I allowed myself to think it was all over. That whoever it was killing those poor girls had either died or moved on."

"How many women?" I asked.

"Not including Jessica?" Trisha asked. "Four. But those were just the bodies that were found. Two other women went missing and were never seen again."

CHAPTER 63

When I pulled up to the police station to pick Jacob up, I saw two officers lead Crawford in handcuffs from their cruiser's backseat to the station's front entrance. On their way, they passed within feet of the Jeep. As they did, Crawford turned his head and made eye contact with me.

I tried to read his expression, but it was blank. Almost resolute. It was impossible to say if it was because he knew he was guilty and resigned to his fate. Or because he was innocent but broken to know that his beloved Jessica was dead.

Whichever the case, I hoped the police would work hard to ensure they had the right man.

I knew, from personal experience, that the police made mistakes. Arrested the wrong people. Destroyed families' lives. It was the reason I struggled to trust them.

My father and I had been through hell after my mother died.

Jacob pushed through the station front doors and passed by

Crawford and the officers with him. When Crawford saw Jacob, he stumbled and had to be held up by the two officers with him before they could continue walking. Clearly, Crawford recognized Jacob North and was very surprised to see him.

But Jacob didn't seem to even register Crawford's presence, never mind recognize him. Jacob passed by Crawford and the three officers as if they weren't even there. When he reached the Jeep, he opened the passenger door, slid onto the seat, and immediately reclined several inches back.

He didn't say a single word. Not to me. Not to the boys. He just turned his head toward the passenger window and closed his eyes.

I stared at him for several seconds, a series of questions circling in my head. But, given his state when I woke him up this morning, Jacob was either incredibly hungover or maybe even still drunk.

Had Riteman noticed this? It seemed highly unlikely he hadn't, but also strange that he would decide to question Jacob anyway. I shifted the Jeep into reverse and decided my questions could wait a while longer.

I assumed Jacob had passed out within the first few minutes of the forty-five-minute drive, but when I pulled into the garage, he unbuckled his seatbelt before I'd even stopped the car. He was out his door and back inside the house before I had the engine shut off. I suspected he was heading straight to his office again—I could only hope it wasn't also to another bottle of Jack.

Obviously, something was very, very wrong. Yes, I knew Jacob was taking Jessica's death hard. And yes, his drinking all night was making everything so much more awful. But I also now felt pretty confident that whatever Officer Riteman had said to Jacob today had him rattled.

I turned in my seat and faced both the boys, who hadn't uttered a sound or budged an inch since picking their father up from the station. "Want me to make some lunch?" I whispered.

They both nodded and looked slightly relieved for the opportunity to focus on something as everyday and banal as lunch.

"All right, then," I breathed. "Let's do that."

I had just placed the plates of grilled cheese and bowls of tomato soup in front of the boys when I felt my phone vibrate in my back pocket. I pulled it out and checked the caller ID—Gilliam County Police Department.

"I'll be right back," I told the boys, headed down the hall to the dining room, and answered, "Hello?"

"Ms. Luck?" I recognized his voice.

"Yes, hello, Officer Riteman."

"Quick question. You told me last night that you had given Crawford Allen Jessica York's cell phone. Is that correct?"

"Yes."

"When we brought him in today, he didn't have it. In fact, he didn't have anything. Not a single possession."

"Did you check the shelter? Maybe his stuff is there? He had a backpack when I met with him. He put the phone inside it."

"Yep. The shelter is where my guys picked him up from. The woman at the front desk said he had checked himself in this morning and didn't have anything with him."

"So, what, he just left his stuff somewhere else?" I asked.

"I can't say. When I asked him about the phone, he claimed

to have no idea what I was talking about and that he had no idea who you were."

"But—"

"I know he's lying. I even showed him the video of him breaking into the Jeep, and he claimed it wasn't him. I'm still working on this, but is there any chance you know where he might have stashed his bag and that phone?"

I blew out a long breath.

"Did he mention anything to you the other day about other places he may be camping or even staying? Someone else who may be helping him out?"

"No. I mean, I only knew about the shelter. I'm sorry I can't be more helpful."

"It was a long shot, but I thought I'd try anyway. Sometimes, people remember stuff later, so call me if anything occurs to you. No matter how small, okay?"

"I will."

"Thank you, Ms. Luck," he said and hung up.

I lowered my phone and stared at the screen, knowing I had, yet again, told the police another lie.

CHAPTER 64

I had no sooner hung up with Riteman that my phone rang again. And again, the call was coming from the Gilliam County Police Department. My heart raced, certain that Riteman had somehow detected my dishonesty.

I considered not answering.

As an adult, I knew my behavior was likely not rational. But my distrust of police was not created by rational thoughts. It was embedded in my childhood trauma. Emotional foundations not easily uprooted by reason.

I was eight years old when I found my mother's body. I had entered our apartment after school, just like every other day. Only that day, my mother wasn't seated on the couch in front of the television watching the end of *As the World Turns*. She wasn't in the kitchen, standing in front of the open fridge wondering what she would make for dinner. And she wasn't on our small balcony, cigarette in hand, staring into the middle distance of the flat, brown grass horizon our apartment was situated at the edge of.

She was not in the bathroom.

She was not putting my laundry away in my room.

My mother, her body, was sprawled across her own bed. Her dress pulled up over her head. Her underwear hanging from her left foot.

I remember the sound of my scream filling the room.

In school, they teach you to call 911. So, I ran to the phone mounted on the wall in our kitchen, lifted the receiver, and pressed the square plastic buttons we'd rehearsed when two men from the fire department had visited our classroom in second grade.

I have no memory of what I said or of what I did until the police pounded on our door later.

When my father arrived, he pulled me from underneath my bed. Our small home swarmed with people in uniform. A rolling gurney passed through the narrow hall from my parents' bedroom to the front door with a black zippered back on top of it.

As I sat on the couch, staring at the television, my father was speaking with two armed police officers near the front door and was then placed in handcuffs. He called to me, told me everything would be okay, asked me to be a big girl, stop screaming, and go with the two women who were holding me back.

I didn't know it at the time, I was too young—but it's always the husband.

At least, that's what everyone always thinks.

Except, my father didn't do it. His entire life, and the rest of my childhood, was destroyed by my mother's murder and his false accusation. In a small town, it can be impossible to shake labels once they've been assigned. To many in our town, my father was forever the man who killed his wife and got away with it. He'd lost his wife, his job, his reputation, his health. Finally, even his self-respect.

I was all my father had left in this world. Which was why, now, I could never abandon him and allow him to believe he'd lost me too.

My phone continued to ring. There was no point ignoring it, so I swiped to answer the call.

I figured Riteman had thought of another angle or line of questioning he wanted to press me on, so I was surprised when the voice on the other end wasn't his.

"Hello?"

"Libby!" he said, his voice strangled and desperate. "Is it true?"

"Crawford?"

"Yes! Tell me, please. Is it true?"

I turned toward the dining room window and stared out at the woods across the lawn. I could hear his ragged breath through the receiver.

"Crawford…I'm sorry."

"No…it's not true. It's impossible. They don't know her. Not like I do. Jessica can't possibly be dead. She's a fucking survivor!" he yelled, his voice cracking into sobs at the end. "She can't be dead…she's all I have. The only fucking person in this whole fucked up world."

I stood silent, listening to Crawford cry while watching the trees outside blow in the wind. Right now, the police were out there working to remove Jessica's body from the ground and collect whatever evidence they could find. I didn't have the heart to tell Crawford any of this.

"They made a mistake," he whispered.

"Crawford, she was wearing a gold necklace with her name on it," I whispered back. I let the image sink in. It felt harsh to share a detail that would abolish the hope he was clinging to, but it felt doubly cruel to allow him to continue hanging onto an impossibility. "The police called me," I added. "They're looking for her phone to see if it can help them catch the person responsible. I told them I gave it to you…why did you lie to them?" I asked.

"Fucking Jacob North gave her that necklace. All of this…it's all their fucking fault, and the police think I killed her!" he yelled.

"But you didn't…right?"

"Now you think I did?" he asked. His voice had changed from broken to vicious in the blink of an eye. This, I realized, was what made Crawford so scary. His emotional swings were both erratic and violent.

"Of course not," I lied. In truth, I didn't think Crawford probably did it, but I also didn't think he *couldn't* do it. It wasn't hard to imagine his intense feelings and obsession with Jessica turning dark and violent in an instant.

Love led to death for women every day—I knew this firsthand.

"But why keep her phone from them? Maybe it could—"

"It's safe. They'll never find it," he said and hung up the phone.

I held my phone to my ear for several more seconds before

returning it to my back pocket. He wouldn't tell me, but I thought I probably knew exactly where Crawford had stashed his backpack and Jessica's phone. The question was, should I call Riteman and tell him or go look for it myself?

"Libby?" Garrett said.

I turned and saw him standing in the doorway to the dining room. Everything about him seemed different from the kid I thought he was. In the aftermath of everything that had taken place, Garrett had transformed from the rude and defiant kid I thought he was into the scared and insecure child before me.

"Hey," I said and walked toward him. On an instinct to care, I placed my hand on his shoulder—he didn't pull away. "Everything okay?"

"Daniel and I are going to watch TV…would you…stay with us?"

Garrett asking me this; it was earth-shattering. It was also a testament to exactly how shaken up he was. I didn't make a big deal about it. "Of course. I'll make some popcorn and get us some drinks."

He nodded once, then continued down the hall to the family room.

Before heading to the kitchen, I stopped at Jacob's closed office door and knocked twice. When he didn't answer, I tried the handle—it was locked. "Jacob?" I called. "I need to speak with you." I had several questions that I wanted answered about his visit to the police station, and after my conversation with Crawford, I now had one more.

Jessica's necklace didn't seem like the sort of thing a boss would buy for an employee. It was her name in script between two diamond hearts—did Jacob really buy that for her?

And if so, what exactly was his relationship with Jessica York?

"Jacob?" I tried again and rattled the door handle. "Please open the door. I need to speak with you."

I waited a few seconds. I imagined he had pulled another bottle from some secret liquor cabinet he kept in there.

"Jacob!" I yelled.

"Not now, Libby! I need to be left the fuck alone!"

I fell back a step. Stunned by his anger. It practically radiated through the closed door.

I had never heard Jacob like this.

It was a side of him I didn't know.

CHAPTER 65

I put the boys to bed. Jacob had still not emerged from his office, and Daniel had asked to stay with his brother for the night again.

In my own rooms, I suddenly felt both alone and very confused. For the first time since I had arrived, I wondered if I should stay. Everything had turned completely upside down. Jacob hadn't told me anything about his conversation with Alexi yesterday. But surely, given the extreme circumstances, she would come home as soon as possible. Affairs and impending divorce aside—her children needed her.

Even if she was on the other side of the world with her new boyfriend, Chad, deep at work on her new film, she would probably be here sometime tomorrow or the next day at the latest.

Maybe it was about time for me to think about moving on from all this?

I switched on the table lamp beside my couch, sat down, and

opened my laptop. Surely, there would be some other nanny position listed on the agency's website I could consider. I couldn't afford to not work for very long, but I had managed to save up some of the money I'd been making and wasn't as desperate as I'd been when I'd jumped at this job. I typed in the web address and began scanning the jobs available when another idea occurred.

I opened a new tab and typed.

missing or dead women new hampshire

I wasn't expecting to find anything about Jessica. The police hadn't released the information to the press or the public yet. And while I was worried about the fact that Trisha now knew, I doubted very much that even she, with her vast network of interconnected gossips, could insert her theories into the serious news cycle in under twelve hours.

No, what I was looking for was information about what Kyra and Trisha had shared with me. The fact that Jessica was not the first woman in these parts to die under suspicious circumstances.

I hit enter on the search and saw that the entire first page of results was filled with story after story of both missing women and the bodies that had been found over the years. It was far more than just the four Trisha had mentioned. I scanned the headlines carefully. Some articles were ten to fifteen years old.

I retyped my search, added a date range for the last ten years, and scanned the results. I clicked on the headline for an article that was three years old.

The remains of 21-year-old Abigail Evans, whose family reported her missing in early July, were found forty miles from where she attended the University of Eastbridge. She was last seen by her dorm roommate...

I returned to the results and selected another article.

The body of 26-year-old Felicia Newton, was discovered late Tuesday evening two miles from the Crest Canyon Trailhead outside Walford, New Hampshire. She had been missing since early August and was last seen leaving the Starbucks on Fourth and Main in Deerfield, where she had worked as a barista for the last two years.

The hairs at the back of my neck stood up. They hadn't mentioned the university explicitly, but the town where Felicia had worked was where it was located.

After reading a third article, I closed my laptop and sat back on the couch, completely stunned.

The body of missing University of Eastbridge student, 20-year-old Amy Davis, was recovered Monday after hikers reported finding what appeared to be human remains in the back woods of....

All three of these women had connections to the university where Jacob worked. Had he known them? Even if he didn't, three dead women from the same community in as many years was likely a shock to the university community. This had to have something to do with the way Jacob was reacting. Obviously, he would be experiencing both shock and grief over Jessica's death, but was it doubly hard for him because he'd been through it before with his campus community.

Was he like Trisha and Kyra, allowing themselves to believe that the worst was behind them and now again afraid that whoever was responsible for the deaths was at it again?

Was it any wonder the man was utterly wrecked psychologically and physically? Especially if he had also known any of these other women? I covered my face with my hands and rubbed my exhausted eyes. Tomorrow I would try harder to approach him with less judgement and more empathy. He needed someone to talk to, not another bottle to drown himself in.

I could be that someone for Jacob…at least until Alexi got home.

CHAPTER 66

When I knocked on Jacob's office door the next morning, he didn't answer. I imagined he'd spent yet another night drunk and alone in his grief. "Jacob," I called through the door. "Please let me in. You can talk to me."

Assuming he was passed out on his couch, I expected more silence. So, when I heard the door unlock, I was hopeful my words had gotten through to him…until he yanked the door open, and I came face to face with his angry expression. His eyes were bloodshot and ringed in dark, exhausted circles. He hadn't shaved or showered in days. He looked haggard and smelled sour.

"You cannot begin to imagine what I'm dealing with right now," he spat. "Is it too much to ask that you just leave me the fuck alone right now while I try and figure out what the hell I'm going to do?"

My mouth fell open. His words felt like a slap. Before I could utter a single word, Jacob slammed the door in my face.

Stunned, I stood staring at the door for several more seconds while my brain worked to figure out both what had happened and what I should do next.

In my heart, the Jacob I knew was hurting, overwhelmed, and needed me.

In my head, I realized this was a man I barely knew, and he was taking whatever he was feeling out on me.

I wasn't sure how to help or what to do about Jacob. I did know I wouldn't be able to figure it out at this moment while I was both angry and hurt. I turned away from the door and returned to the kitchen, where both boys were eating the breakfast I had made them. "When you're done, I need you both to get dressed. We're going into town."

WHEN I STOPPED the Jeep and put it in park, Garrett asked, "What are we doing?"

His question was genuine, without a hint of the sarcasm or snark I'd come to know him for. Since the other night in the woods, Garrett's entire attitude and demeanor toward me had completely changed. I turned in my seat to look at both him and Daniel.

While Garrett's change was surprising but not at all unwelcome, Daniel's was more concerning.

I watched him stare out the window. He'd hardly spoken since we'd found Jessica's body in the woods.

I wished I'd known how close she would be. I wished I'd made him wait for Garrett and me on the trail. I wished his six-year-old brain had never seen anything so gruesome and horrifying as the sight of his beloved nanny's dead body.

In all the confusion and shock, Jacob and I hadn't done much to make sure the boys were okay. Jacob, their own father, had completely checked out.

"Have either of you spoken with your mom?" I was reluctant to add since we found Jessica. I hoped it was implied, and the boys would know what I meant.

Garrett shook his head. Daniel continued to stare out the window like he hadn't heard me.

"I did get a text from her," Garrett said.

"Did she say when she'd be home?" I asked.

He shook his head. "She didn't say she was coming home," he said. "She just asked if we were okay and how we were feeling?"

"In a text?"

He nodded.

"Anything else?"

"She said her new movie is really coming along."

I stared at him for a second and felt my mouth go dry. I turned back around before my expression could give away my feelings.

Why the hell wasn't Alexi rushing to be with her kids as fast as possible right now?

I pressed my fingers to my eyes and refocused on why we were here.

"There's something I'm looking for. It should only take me a few minutes."

"Do you need help?" Garrett asked.

I was about to say no and that he could wait in the car with Daniel. But the truth was, I could use his help. "Actually, yes." I glanced back at him. "Thank you."

"Where are we going?"

I pointed out the windshield. "That old building. I think it might be in there or possibly in the bushes out front."

"What are we looking for," Garrett asked as he unbuckled his seatbelt and opened his door.

"A backpack."

CHAPTER 67

We first looked through all the bushes I'd seen Crawford emerge from the day I'd met him here with Jessica's phone—nothing.

"I don't think someone would leave a backpack just in the bushes," Garrett said. "It'd get wet or stolen too easily."

I nodded. He made a rational point. "I think the person would sometimes stay in this building. It's abandoned, but I can't see a way to get in."

Garrett quickly scanned the exterior of the building all around us. "There's not even a broken window," he said. "Wait a second!" he added, excited by an idea.

I watched, and he strode back into the bushes. "Yeah! Over here!" he called.

When I joined him, fighting my way through a tangle of dead winter vines and juniper bushes, Garrett pointed to a spot at the base of the building. "Look."

It was a small, grimy, basement-level window that looked

like it opened and closed on a hinge. The frame moved inward when Garrett reached down and pressed on the glass.

It wasn't a big opening, but I could see how a rather thin person like Crawford, who was highly motivated to find shelter from the cold and elements, would make this work.

"I'm too big, but I think you could fit down there," Garrett said. "If not, we could always use Daniel."

I gave Garrett a sidelong look. To imagine asking little Daniel to shimmy down into the dark basement of an abandoned building under even normal circumstances was terrible.

"Okay, not Daniel," Garrett said. "But I bet you'd fit," he said again.

I moved closer to the window and turned on my phone's flashlight. Most of the light reflected off the dirty windowpane —I couldn't see a thing. I pushed my hand and phone through the opening in the window and tried tilting my head to get a better look.

I'm sure Garrett was right. This was most likely the place Crawford had been staying, and his bag was probably here...but the thought of entering this space without knowing what I'd be getting into was terrifying.

Sure, Crawford was in jail right now, but what if he wasn't the only person staying here?

The light from the phone wasn't great—what I wouldn't give for one of those large, high-beamed, police-issued flashlights right now—but I could see a thin mat with a sleeping bag in the corner. And there, right next to Crawford's depressing bed, I saw it.

"There it is," I said.

Garrett and I crouched in front of the window and stared

into the darkness between us and the bag. As the seconds ticked by, and I didn't make any moves, my determination shrank in the face of my fear.

Did I really need to go down there just to get Crawford's backpack? Sure, Jessica's old phone was in there, but I already knew it had basically been wiped. What else could possibly be in there? Crawford's change of underwear? Spare socks? I was about to suggest we give up and head back to the Jeep when Garrett broke the silence.

"Well, are you going to go get it?" His tone hinted at the attitude I'd come to expect from him.

"I'm not sure that's such a good idea."

"It's right there!" Garrett said, sounding exasperated at the prospect of walking away now. "It'll take less than two minutes."

"What if I get down there and can't get back out? What if I fall and break a leg? What if I get down there and there's...I don't know...someone else?"

Garrett seemed to seriously consider these possibilities. "Why do you want it, anyway? What's in there?"

I focused on the window in front of us while I considered telling him. Only two days ago, I thought he hated my guts... and I hadn't liked him very much either. But since finding Jessica's body, it was like he was a different kid. "I'm not sure I should tell you," I said.

I felt his eyes on my face while he thought about this. "You can trust me, Libby."

I turned and met his gaze. He looked sincere, but who knew which of the Garretts was real? The truth was, I wanted to trust him, and I was glad this version of Garrett was with me right now. Even though he was just a kid, his presence made me feel less alone.

"Jessica's old cell phone is in there," I said.

Garrett's eyes grew wide with surprise.

"I'm not sure what else might be in there, but the person who owns it may be the one who killed her."

"Shouldn't we call the police?" he asked.

I bit my bottom lip. "Yes, we should probably call the police." I thought about Crawford, distraught and broken, insisting that he didn't have anything to do with Jessica's death. In fact, he sounded absolutely wrecked and heartbroken to learn she was gone. "But it's also possible that the person who owns that bag is being wrongfully accused of killing her. If the police take it, and they find Jessica's phone in there.... With evidence like that, he's not the sort of person who will be able to defend himself."

Garrett considered what I was saying. "So, he's a guy that's easy to blame for stuff, even if he didn't do the stuff." He stared down at the depressing living conditions this guy was living in. "If that bag has clues about what happened to Jessica, we need to go get it," Garrett whispered.

I sat back on my heels and let out a deep sigh. "Okay," I said, resigning myself to the idea of squeezing my body through the crack before me. "But." I turned and looked him in the face. "Don't leave me," I said. "Stay right here. I'm going to need you to help me back out."

Garrett sat all the way down, the butt of his jeans in the cold dirt, and crossed his legs in front of him. "I'll be right here," he said. "But you should leave me your phone in case something happens."

"Where's your phone?" I asked.

"Dad took it…that night, after what happened at school. He hasn't given it back."

I furrowed my brow. I still didn't know what had happened at school, why Garrett had such a huge file, or that Jacob had decreed any sort of punishment for whatever it was that Garrett had done. The last few days had been a complete blur. A nightmare that just kept unfolding. I slid my phone from my back pocket and handed it to Garrett.

He stared down at the screen in his hands. "What's the code?" he asked.

I hesitated, but only for a second. Of course, he would need the code to unlock the phone to make a call. I gave it to him, watched as he keyed it in, and then nodded when it worked. "Okay. Ready to go?" he asked.

I watched as he slid my phone into the pocket of his hoodie, and a feeling of dread settled into my gut. I couldn't help but feel like I was making a mistake. Like maybe there was more at stake here than simply risking a broken leg or getting trapped in an abandoned basement.

When I looked into Garrett's face, his expression seemed sincere. Like he really did want and intended to help. I wanted a better relationship with him. I wanted to trust him. That couldn't happen if I never gave him the chance to be trusted. I moved toward the window and pulled it open as far as it would go. I had one leg through and was shifting my body to angle my hips and torso to fit.

To my relief, my foot made contact with something solid pushed against the wall on the inside. When I looked down, I saw it was a rickety and worn table. This was obviously what Crawford had used to help himself in and out of this place.

Feeling more confident, I swung my other leg down and stood on the table, smiling at Garrett through the grimy glass between us.

Even if I couldn't yet one hundred percent trust him, I did trust my ability to get out of here on my own with the help of this table.

"Don't go anywhere," I said.

Garrett shook his head. "I won't."

I knelt, stepped down off the table, and turned around. The basement was dark, cold, and smelled musty. The concrete floor had a layer of dirt. Broken cobwebs swung from the ceiling and crowded every window corner. And now that I was down here, I heard the distinct sound of rodents scurrying within the walls. My whole body shivered with revulsion, but I resisted the urge to crawl back onto the table and out the window.

It would take me only seconds to grab Crawford's backpack. I would be out of here, above ground, and in daylight within a minute. I focused all my attention on the bag and didn't allow my mind to wonder what, or who might also be down in this creepy space with me.

Ten steps, that's all it took. Purposeful and direct, I controlled the fear that threatened to make me run. When I reached it, I grabbed the bag with one hand and turned back. My steps were quicker, and I was a little panicked. Did I hear something in the distance? The rest of the basement stretched away and into darkness. It was possibly another room.

The sound, I heard it again. Was that a door opening?

Someone was down here with me.

I ran the last few feet to the table and jumped on top of it.

"Garrett," I hissed, terrified if I spoke any louder, it would draw the attention of whoever was down here. The table rocked beneath my feet, and the rotten wooden legs shifted beneath my weight. "Garrett?" I called as loud as I dared. He wasn't there.

I grabbed the window's edge with my free hand and swung the backpack through the small opening.

It landed in the dirt outside right as the table collapsed beneath me.

I stared up at the window, now far beyond my reach, and listened to the sound of footsteps rushing across the concrete toward me.

"Garrett!" I screamed and felt a hand grab my shoulder.

I pulled away and turned, crawling backward as fast as I could.

"Libby," they said. "It's me. It's okay."

I stared back into Garrett's worried face.

"Garrett?" I said as my hand flew to my throat in relief. "What…how did you…I told you not to move!" I finished as anger rushed in behind my terror.

"I'm sorry." He held up both his hands. "I saw a door."

"What door?" I snapped.

"When I was sitting in the dirt, so close to the building, I could see to the left that there was like a cellar door hidden underneath the bushes. I didn't think it would be unlocked, but it was. So, I just came down here because I figured it'd be easier than you trying to climb out the window."

My heart still felt like a hammer in my chest, but I forced myself to take a deep breath. "You scared the crap out of me."

Garrett shook his head. "I didn't mean to. I swear." He

stepped toward me and reached out his hand to help me up. "I'm really sorry."

I took his hand and let him pull me to standing. The table was a heap of scrap wood beneath my feet.

"Careful," Garrett said, pointing to a piece jutting up like a stake.

"Thanks," I said and brushed off my backside.

He glanced around the room. "It's gross down here."

"Yes."

"And kinda creepy," he added.

"Definitely creepy."

He scrunched up his face. "It probably *really* scared you when—"

"Yes, Garrett. I was *really* scared."

He smiled, and I glared at him.

"I swear!" he laughed. "I didn't *mean* to."

"Right," I said and nodded, but I couldn't help but smile back. "How about you just show me where this secret hidden door is, and we get out of here."

CHAPTER 68

I wasn't sure what I'd find or what kind of condition it would be in, so I laid one of the old towels Jacob kept in the garage out on my bedroom floor and emptied the contents of Crawford's backpack onto it. As everything spilled out before me, the stench of dried sweat, mildew, and dirt rose up. My hand flew to cover my nose and mouth. This was the extent of Crawford's life. I knew whatever was in the bag would be personal and private, but the smell made the violation feel much more intimate. As if I was about to rummage through his dirty clothes hamper.

I pushed the thought away and focused on what was before me.

There was Jessica's phone, but also another one. It must be Crawford's, I reasoned. I picked it up and turned it over in my hand several times. It was slightly newer than Jessica's but even more battered. The screen was so severely shattered I wondered if it was even functional. The edges were scratched and worn, and the port looked clogged with dirt. When I tried to power it on, nothing happened. It was either broken or dead. Either way, I set it aside.

In the pile were two crumpled and thin black t-shirts, a single sock, and a package of men's underwear that hadn't been opened. I used a ballpoint pen from the pile to push all this to the far side of the towel. What was left was two dollars and forty-two cents in loose change, a charging cable and block, a worn black nylon wallet with Crawford's driver's license and a few photos, and a bent and beaten spiral-bound notebook.

It reminded me of something you used in middle school. It was what you bought in the back-to-school section of Walmart, filled with notes during the first few weeks of school, then left discarded and forgotten at the bottom of your locker until it was time to clean it out at the end of the year. I opened the cover and flipped through the pages.

This was not a notebook Crawford had forgotten to use. When I saw the first few pages were filled, top to bottom, with a tiny, neat script, I quickly flipped through the entire notebook. Only the last few pages were blank.

I glanced at the pen I'd used to push his clothes to the side. This was what he had used with the notebook.

It looked like a journal because all the entries were dated. But when I began reading what he wrote, I realized this wasn't an account of Crawford's life or how he felt.

This was a tracking log.

4/7 12:16 PM

S left Carol's Diner with to-go pickup. Walking, took food back to work.

4/7 5:30 PM

S left work. Driving. Followed until they arrived at apartment on 16th.

4/7 8:57 PM

S left apartment. Picked up by an unknown female in blue Honda. Drove to Kings Court bar on Winston Street. Stayed inside until 11:12 PM when S and unknown female walked two blocks to Benton's (dance club). Stayed until 2:14 AM. Appeared intoxicated when they left. Spoke with two unknown males from Benton's on street for thirteen minutes. S kissed one of the males but left with the unknown female. They drove back to S's apartment where she was dropped off and entered alone at 2:42 AM. End observation.

There were multiple entries like this. Crawford followed S from her apartment to her work. From her work to the grocery store. There were entries detailing her nights out, her days at school, and her runs at a nearby park.

I turned several more pages and discovered that whoever this S was, she wasn't the only one. He followed and logged the comings and goings of someone he identified as M. Someone else identified as R. At the very end of the notebook, he had been following someone he labeled L.

I flipped through the entire notebook again and looked for a letter I didn't see on my first quick pass. I scanned the pages more carefully but still didn't see her.

There wasn't any mention of, or detailed log for, anyone he'd labeled J. Assuming the letters represented individuals' first names, none were about Jessica. Of course, the letters could be a less obvious way to label the people, but none of the described lives sounded like the one Jessica had lived. She didn't live in an apartment, a house she shared with four other women, a sorority, or with her parents as these women had. Given the mentions about campus, libraries, and frat parties, these people all seemed to be living college lives.

Regardless, Crawford had obviously been stalking these people. It was damning evidence considering the fact he was currently sitting in a jail cell as a person of interest in Jessica's death. I was about to close the notebook when an entry caught my eye. It was the last one for a person he'd labeled, L.

8:32 AM. L arrived in town and parked in front of Coffee Klatch. Inside until 9:05 AM drinking coffee speaking with unknown female who works there. Believe they are friends.

I froze and felt my heartbeat quicken as I searched for more. L was the very last person in his book, and there were only two recordings, both dated in September.

9/7 8:40 AM. L parked on Main Street and entered Coffee Klatch. Came out at 9:17 AM. Unable to access Jeep to check for cell. Unable to follow further without access to another vehicle. Next steps?

This was the last recording in Crawford's notebook. And while I wasn't sure whether or not he'd been following Jessica prior to her death, one thing was crystal clear.

He'd been following me.

CHAPTER 69

Tomorrow, I would head to the police station, hand all of this over to Officer Riteman, and pray that he didn't arrest me, too, for tampering with evidence. Whatever I had been thinking about giving Crawford the benefit of the doubt or trying to protect him from an unjust system evaporated the second I saw my presence in his book.

What had happened to all these other women, I wondered?

Then it hit me. All at once and hard.

The women Kyra and Trisha had told me about. The ones who had gone missing or who had been found dead. There weren't any years attached to Crawford's observations, but I would bet money that if I compared the contents in this notebook to the news articles about the missing or dead women, they would fit together like a perfect puzzle.

I felt sick and sad all at once. I thought about my close calls with Crawford and the time we had been alone in the Jeep—

Jesus, how close had I come to being yet another missing or dead woman? How could I have been so stupid? So careless?

I was relieved Crawford was behind bars. And this notebook would ensure he stayed there.

I closed it and returned it to the backpack—I wished I'd just left it where it was in the basement of that rundown building. It was irresponsible to try and take anything having to do with this into my own hands. What on earth had I been thinking? What if, by taking this, I was somehow jeopardizing the case against Crawford?

All I could do now was try and fix my huge mistake first thing tomorrow.

I picked up his wallet and was about to return it to the backpack when I noticed the worn edge of a piece of paper sticking up from the billfold. I opened the wallet to get a better look and saw that instead of money, Crawford had four old and worn photographs tucked inside.

One was the same photo I'd seen on Jessica's social media page. It was Crawford and Jessica sitting on the picnic table underneath the banner for their middle school graduation from McFadden Middle School. The other three were all of Jessica alone. One that must have been taken also in middle school. Jessica looked just as hungry with extra worn, too-large clothes and a feral look in her eyes. She was sitting on green grass that stretched out all around her. It must have been taken on a school field trip because I could see other same-aged students in the background, and The Gateway Arch rose high into the sky behind her.

I racked my brain about what I could remember about that

arch from my grade school days. Growing up in Nebraska, we had spent several weeks in fourth grade learning about the Lewis and Clark expedition. The explorers had traveled the Missouri River through Omaha—an important footnote in my home state's history. But the arch was in St Louis, Missouri, next to the Mississippi River.

Was this where Jessica and Crawford were from?

I flipped through the other two pictures. These were more recent. One was the two of them again, arms slung around each other's shoulders, standing on a street of some indiscernible city. They had grown up. Jessica looked more put together. Her clothes fit, her hair was styled, and she looked healthy. Whatever her childhood had been, she looked like she had figured out how to leave it behind her.

Crawford stood beside her in stark contrast. Still skinny and with the same haunted look around his eyes, he was taller and older in this photo, but it was easy to see how his particular path was leading him away from hers. Using drugs, living on the streets, and now in jail as a person of interest in a murder case.

I ran my thumb over Jessica's image—her murder case.

The last photo was of Jessica alone. She was walking down a wooded path, the sun glinting through the trees around her. The image was captured right as she looked back at the photographer behind her. Her hair fanned out, her eyes sparkled, and she was laughing. The image reminded me of several others I had seen on her sparse social media page. Jessica had enjoyed hiking in the woods—she probably never imagined she'd die in them.

I flipped to the picture of Jessica from middle school sitting on the lawn in front of the Gateway Arch, stood up, and grabbed my laptop.

CHAPTER 70

It popped up right away. McFadden Middle School wasn't in St. Louis but in a small town about two hours away. The first search results were for the school's web page and then online reports about its rankings. I had no idea this was a thing, but apparently, even schools were not immune from star ratings and user reviews.

Based on its score of two out of ten, if McFadden Middle School were a restaurant, I wouldn't eat there.

So now I knew where Jessica and Crawford had come from, a little town in the middle of nowhere America.

Just like me.

I wondered if Jessica still had family there that would soon be finding out about her death. Were her parents, right now, sitting in matching rocker recliners, TV remote in hand, flipping through channels, utterly unaware of the freight train of news that would soon be broadcast on their own local news channel.

Jessica York, a former resident of Farmington, was found dead on…

I imagined that since they had grown up together and were obviously friends, Jessica's parents knew Crawford. What would that feel like? To know your child was taken by someone who had been circling around her since she was a child and that you were unable to predict or prevent her tragic end. It made me sad for her family, and it felt strange to know that I currently had more information about their daughter and her killer than they did.

I had the idea that I would dig deeper with another search and see if I could learn the names of Jessica's parents. I was just about to open a new tab when an article near the bottom of the search page caught my attention.

Missing girl's body found in woods near school

I clicked the link. It was an old news story, but after scanning it for a few seconds, I realized why it had popped up in my search. Ruth Warren, a fourteen-year-old girl, had been reported missing three days prior by her family. Her body was recovered in the woods behind her middle school, where she had been a student for three years.

McFadden Middle School.

I checked the date on the article and heard my sharp intake of breath. This girl, Ruth Warren, had gone missing and died the month and year that Jessica and Crawford had graduated from McFadden.

She had been in their class.

CHAPTER 71

When I pulled up to the police station the next morning, I was ready to tell Officer Riteman everything I knew and had learned. I had packed Crawford's backpack and contents into a brown grocery bag. I spent the forty-five-minute drive trying to think of what I could say to explain exactly why I had it in my possession.

As I sat in the driver's seat, staring out the windshield at the low-slung brick building in front of me, I still hadn't come up with a logical reason. There wasn't one. I should have come to Riteman sooner. I should have told him everything I knew the minute he'd contacted me. And I certainly never should have shimmied through the cracked window of a derelict building and taken evidence that could help his investigation.

My fingers gripped the rolled top of the paper sack on my lap, and I let out a sigh. I needed to prepare myself for whatever the consequences would be for my obfuscation. I had no idea if that would be a look of disappointment, a lecture, or criminal charges…but I doubted very seriously it would be nothing.

Ready to get it over with, I reached for the door handle when movement near the building caught my attention. I looked out the windshield and saw the front doors opening… and Crawford Allen walking out.

His hair was wet and combed straight back like he'd recently had a shower. His clothes were nothing fancy, but the clean T-shirt and jeans were undoubtedly nicer than anything I'd ever seen him in before. I sat back in my seat, both waiting for and dreading the moment he looked up and made eye contact with me sitting in this bright white Jeep that he knew so well.

But he shoved his hands into the front pockets of his new jeans and kept his eyes focused on the cracked concrete beneath his shoes as he descended the stairs and took a left turn at the sidewalk. I watched him as he crossed the parking lot and the street behind me. I lost sight of him once he rounded the corner at the intersection.

Stunned, I couldn't believe what I'd just seen. They let him go?

I closed my eyes as a sinking realization washed over me—they let him go because they didn't know what I did. They let him go because I'd kept vital information and evidence from them.

They let him go because I let my past childhood fears interfere with what I should have done as a present and reasoning adult.

For some reason, I didn't imagine Officer Riteman was going to give two shits about my childhood trauma once he realized he'd just let a serial killer walk out the front door.

CHAPTER 72

When I walked into his office, Officer Riteman kept his expression neutral, but I could tell he was surprised to see me.

"Funny you should show up here," he said. "I was just about to call you and see if you could come in today. I have a few questions for you." He motioned to the chairs in front of his desk.

I ignored the invitation to sit. "You let Crawford go," I said as I walked straight to his desk and placed the paper sack on his closed laptop. "You can't do that. You need to send a patrol car right now to pick him up. Like three minutes ago, I watched him take a right onto Howard Street. He can't have gotten too far walking and—"

"Stop," Riteman said, holding up his palm like a crossing guard directing traffic. "I can see you have a lot you want to tell me. So, take a seat, and I'll see what you've brought me here." He gestured to the bag before him. "We'll have a conversation about what's bothering you...and me."

"You don't understand," I pleaded. "I've made a huge mistake. I kept information I should have shared. I took evidence!" I reached for the bag. I would open it and show him. Pull out the notebook. "Crawford had been stalking not just Jessica but other women as well, even me. Those other missing and dead women? Crawford's the one responsible. He's been doing this for years!"

Now, Riteman stood up from his desk. Finally, he was going to take some action and get Crawford back behind bars where he belonged before he could hurt anyone else.

Except, that's not what he did. Riteman pulled the paper bag from my manic and fumbling hands and leveled his gaze at me. "Sit. Down," he commanded. "Now."

His tone froze me to the spot.

"I want to speak with you. Hear everything you have to say. But first, I need you to calm down. So please, sit. Take a breath. I'll have someone bring you some water. And then, the two of us can have a long chat."

My hands flew to my head, my fingers pressed into my temples. He wasn't listening. He didn't realize. Crawford was getting away, it was all my fault, and the one person who could do anything about it was asking me to calm down!

The frustration and panic bloomed inside me like a volcano, ready to erupt.

Officer Riteman just looked at me, his expression neutral, and waited for me to do what he asked.

I closed my eyes and clenched my fists at my sides—if I

wanted him to listen, I needed to do what he asked. I pulled out one of the chairs and forced myself to sit down.

"Good, thank you." He picked up the paper bag, placed it to the side, and then called someone to bring me a bottle of water. He took a deep breath, let it out, then picked up his pen and positioned his notepad in front of him.

"I realize you have a lot of critical information you want to share with me. And I promise we will get to all of it. But please realize that I'm in the middle of an investigation here, and I have my own questions that need answering first."

Every second we wasted here, Crawford got farther and farther away, but I clenched my teeth and nodded once.

"Perfect. Now, it has occurred to me, given some of your behaviors." He gestured to the bag I'd brought him. "That perhaps you don't trust me or my judgment."

I didn't know what to make of this statement, so I just kept my eyes trained on his notepad and waited for him to make his point.

"Now, maybe some would be offended. Being mistrusted, outright and with no obvious cause, by a stranger..." Riteman nodded several times. "It can be upsetting to some. But in my experience, when a person who doesn't know me doesn't trust me, it usually has more to do with the uniform I wear than the person I am."

I glanced up at his face but couldn't read his expression. What the hell was he—

"I'm sorry about what happened to your mother."

I stared at him. His words were so unexpected I had no idea how to respond. And was he empathizing because he knew she was dead, because he knew she was murdered, or because he knew—"

"Anyone in your situation would hate the police."

I sat back in my chair and felt my shoulders slump. He had done his research. That much was clear.

"The officer that killed your mother…he's still in prison?"

I nodded.

"Did he know her?"

"They dated in high school."

Riteman furrowed his brow and shook his head like he couldn't quite figure out how the information connected.

I sighed and closed my eyes. "Apparently, they had started seeing each other…having an affair." My voice was a whisper. "He wanted her to leave my dad. She decided not to. From what I know…things got worse when she tried to stop seeing him at all." I took a deep breath. "When he couldn't have her…he killed her."

"And pointed the investigation toward your father," Riteman added.

I nodded.

It was Riteman's turn to sit back in his chair as silence settled between us. Several seconds passed before he continued. "Something like that…honestly I guess I wouldn't surprise me if you never believed anything any cop ever said to you again."

I shook my head. "I was a child."

"Seems like that would make it all the harder to move past."

I turned my gaze to the paper bag I'd brought in. Every second we spent discussing my mother's murder and the cop that tried to get away with it was another second Crawford was getting away. "Look, thank you, I guess, for trying to understand. But I imagine this isn't everything you wanted to tell me?"

"No." Riteman leaned forward, picked up his pencil, and tapped the eraser several times against his legal pad. "I asked you once before what you knew about Jessica York and the Norths prior to taking the position with them."

I nodded.

"Were you aware, or do you now know, that the youngest son, Daniel North, is not Alexi North's biological son?"

What? I sat up straighter and stared at him. "I...no, I didn't know that."

Riteman nodded and jotted a few notes on his paper. "So, it would stand to reason that you were unaware that Jessica York was, in fact, Daniel's biological mother?"

"What?" My mouth gaped open.

"That Jessica York was originally hired as a surrogate, but then the Norths kept her on as the nanny after Daniel's birth?"

He kept phrasing his words as questions, but they all felt like bombs to me.

"Ms. Luck, when was the last time you spoke with Alexi North? I have some questions I'd like to ask her."

CHAPTER 73

I hadn't spoken with Jacob since we'd returned from his questioning at the station. He had locked himself away in his office then yelled at me when I'd tried to help him.

His behavior had surprised me, but I had chalked it up to all the stress he was under and the grief he must be feeling about Jessica's death.

But after my discussion with Office Riteman today, my mind was working to find answers for the more complicated questions I now had.

First and foremost, why had the Norths not told me that Jessica was Daniel's biological mother?

And second, and possibly much more troubling, was Jacob the biological father? And if he was…how exactly did the three of them decide to go about creating the pregnancy?

The questions tumbled in my mind the whole drive home, each collecting small pieces of circumstantial evidence until I pulled the Jeep into the garage and felt pretty sure I already knew the truth.

There was the shape and color of Daniel's eyes—unmistakably Jacob's. There were Trisha and Kyra's reports about Jessica's alleged history with married men—this wasn't something she *wouldn't* do. There was her necklace, the one she was still wearing when Garrett found her body in the woods—an unusually personal present from Jacob. There was Crawford's testament—Jessica had completely lost herself to the Norths. And the fact that Daniel had such a strong attachment to Jessica, one that Garrett didn't seem to share.

And finally, and most uncomfortably, there was the speed at which Jacob had fallen into my bed.

Jessica's old bed.

Like a man trying to get back to the comfort and familiarity of a personal relationship he'd recently lost.

As I opened the door to the Jeep, I felt certain I already knew the answer to every question I had. But I also knew that I would absolutely make Jacob confess every single detail to me himself.

Inside the house, it was quiet. I imagined both boys were either in their bedrooms or the living room, zoning out and trying to forget their present reality in front of the TV. I would check on them later. I headed through the kitchen, down the hall, and into the foyer. As I had hoped, Jacob's keys were exactly where he always left them, in the carved wooden bowl on the entryway table.

I snatched them up and kept my determined stride toward his office.

There would be no knocking today. I was not about to plead with him through a closed door.

I shuffled through several keys until I found three that were most probably to an interior door. The first key I slid into the lock didn't budge, but I felt the lock twist under my hand with the second.

I pushed the door open without any announcement. It would probably be better to catch Jacob off guard and surprise him. It would be harder for him to think up any lies to my many accusations.

I scanned the room quickly but didn't see any sign of him.

What I did discover quickly was the stench in the room.

"What the hell?" I said and raised my hand to my nose and mouth. "Jacob!" I called out. The door had been locked from the inside—he had to be here.

When I was halfway into the room, I realized I was right. He was here. He was also the reason the room smelled so bad.

He was passed out on his couch. Wearing only a sweat-stained white T-shirt and his boxer briefs, a greasy sheen coated his skin and hair. He hadn't showered in days.

The collection of empty Jack Daniel's bottles had grown considerably since the last time I'd been in here. The horrific smell was in part due to Jacob's body odor but mostly because of the three piles of vomit. One on the table, spilling down the side. One on the rug next to the couch—like he'd simply rolled over in his sleep, threw up, then rolled back. And the third was several feet away at the base of one of the massive bookshelves.

"Jacob," I said. When he didn't respond or even stir, I tried again louder. "Jacob!"

Nothing. Not even a flinch.

I didn't want to touch him, but I needed him to wake up—now. I stepped closer, careful to avoid the ejected contents of his stomach all over the floor, and reached for his shoulder. I shook it gently at first, then harder, and even harder still when he didn't respond. For a moment, fear shot through me—was he even breathing? I lowered my head as close to his as I dared, then shouted directly into his ear at the top of my lungs. "Jacob!"

His eyes opened. They were unfocused, bleary, and bloodshot, but they met mine, and a moment later, a smile spread across his lips. "Jessica?" he asked with so much hope in his voice it was like hearing his heart crack open.

I shook my head and stood up. Speechless, all I could do was stand there and stare at him and his colossal mess. Bearing direct witness to this overwhelming display of utter and complete breakdown, I realized I was both disgusted and afraid. Jacob had fallen apart, things were completely out of hand, and now, the one person I had been hoping would soon arrive to take control and provide guidance and direction, Alexi, was nowhere to be found.

There were two children somewhere in this house that needed the adults in their lives to pull their shit together. And if what Office Riteman had suggested, even if he hadn't outright stated it, was true, then their little lives were about to be completely turned over--again.

"No," I snapped at him. “It's not Jessica, it's *Libby*." I waited a moment for him to return to our present reality. The one in which Jessica was dead. "Jacob," I said firmly. "I need you to listen to me."

He was struggling to sit up. "Libby?" he asked.

"Yes, it's Libby. I need you to answer some questions for me —and I want the *truth*."

He sat with his elbows on his knees, his hands cradling his head. Given the evidence in the room, I imagined he felt like his brains were exploding inside his skull. "I can't," he said. "Not now."

Watching him struggle, I almost backed off. But my mind returned to my conversation with Officer Riteman and all it implied. "Yes, Jacob. Right now. I've just come back from the police station. They are looking for Alexi."

He looked up and met my gaze. His brow furrowed like he was working to process this new thread. "Alexi?"

My hands moved to my hips, and I shifted my jaw. "Where is she?"

CHAPTER 74

I sat opposite Jacob and listened as he confirmed everything Officer Riteman had told me, and more.

After Garrett was born, Alexi had dug in her heels about having any more children. But Jacob, who had grown up an only child, didn't want that for his son. "I kept pressing her, practically begging." He shook his head. "I didn't realize it at the time. I thought she was being irrational and unfair to both me and Garrett…I called her selfish," he said in a whisper.

He was ashamed of his behavior…now. That much was clear. But it had gotten so much worse than that.

"Alexi's career," he looked up and met my gaze. "It was everything to her. And it was taking off in ways neither of us had ever dreamed of. She was always gone, meeting with film industry professionals all over the world…do you know she won an Academy Award?" he asked.

I did know, but I didn't say so. Even now, I didn't want to admit just how much I'd investigated Alexi online.

Jacob's head fell forward. "I was jealous," he breathed. "It was bad. Coming out of my own skin, actually. It was like watching this woman, my wife…a partner I'd started with, make this stratospheric leap, light years ahead of me. Completely beyond me into a world so much more glamorous than the one we'd built together."

"Wait," I said. "You were jealous because she was seeing other people back then? Or you were afraid she would?"

Jacob took a deep breath and shook his head. "I was jealous of her career. Her success. The life she was building for herself…it was like she suddenly existed in this completely separate universe." He sat back against the couch cushions and closed his eyes. "I didn't know how to be a part of that world. Or if she even wanted me to anymore. Every time she'd get home from California, or Paris, or Brazil, or fucking anywhere, it felt like all she wanted to do was leave again. Go back to work as soon as possible. To that world of other people who lived in the same universe as her."

He looked up and met my eyes. I could see his shame radiating from his gaze. "When we first had Garrett, she stayed home with us for months after. She still wanted to work, so we expanded her office and turned it into a studio so she could." Jacob shook his head. "I was so happy. I thought we had figured it out." He laughed, but the sound was hollow and sad. "I guess I was stupid enough to imagine that a remodel and a few thousand dollars of computer and video equipment was the solution to Alexi's unhappiness here." He took a deep breath. "It lasted five months. Then, she got a call from the producer she worked with on her last film. He wanted her to fly to Colorado. He'd secured an interview with Reggie Hollister at the supermax facility where he was being held. It was a delicate agreement that could fall apart over the smallest detail…Alexi was the only person he wanted to handle it."

My eyes grew wide. Reggie Hollister—everyone on the planet knew who he was and what he had done to the forty-three girls and women he had killed over three decades. I suddenly realized it was mainly due to Alexi's film that Reggie was a household name and a cautionary tale.

"She packed a bag and was gone the next morning…I should have known right then," he finished in a whisper.

"Should have known?" I asked.

Jacob sighed and ran his fingers through his greasy hair. "That she was already gone. She had already left this life, this house, me, Garrett…emotionally, she was already gone. She just hadn't yet figured out how to handle the physical part." He shook his head. "Hindsight's twenty-twenty." He scrubbed his bloodshot eyes with the pads of his fingertips. "So instead of realizing that, instead of letting her go, moving on, getting my own life back, I spent the next six years grasping at her, trying to hold onto the ghosts of our past life. I didn't consciously realize it," he said. "I argued that Garrett needed a sibling. That she had no idea how painful being an only child could be. I even resorted to accusing her of lying to me before we were married and claimed that if I'd known she didn't want kids, I never would have married her in the first place. But the truth was, I was begging her for another child that would plant her back into this life with me and Garrett. I wanted her here, with me, with us…for some reason, having another baby became my desperate road to accomplishing that."

"So, she eventually gave in?"

Jacob nodded. "But only if we used a surrogate. I was so lost, fumbling for any way back to us...I thought it was a compromise."

"And you hired Jessica," I said.

Jacob wouldn't meet my gaze. He kept his eyes planted on the floor between his feet. "Yes," he whispered.

"So why did she stay? After Daniel was born, why would you and Alexi ask her to stay on as the nanny? Why would she even want to?"

Jacob shook his head. He wouldn't look up, but I could see he was crying. His abject misery was palpable—he radiated regret. "Please, Libby. Don't make me say it," he sobbed.

I stood before him, silent, processing, trying to make sense of how this family ended up in this awful place. It seemed clear to me that Jacob himself was primarily to blame. I decided I wouldn't press him further. I felt like I largely had figured out how things had proceeded after Jacob and Alexi had hired Jessica. I was going to leave him to his sorrows and his next bottle of Jack, but Jacob suddenly took a deep breath and sat up straight.

His face was puffy from drinking, his eyes bloodshot from dehydration and crying, but he rolled his neck and looked me in the eyes.

"I'll tell you," he said, shaking his head once. "The truth is, I need to tell someone. Keeping it in...it's been killing me for years. What happened...it ruined everything. It destroyed my life and whatever may have remained of my marriage. It's fucked my kids, this house, and nearly cost me my own career. Getting involved with Jessica York was a cataclysmic mistake."

He swallowed and stood up.

"She was a wrecking ball. She took and destroyed everything I ever truly loved in this world. And if I'm honest, Libby... part of me is maybe relieved to know she's dead."

CHAPTER 75

"We tried insemination four times. Alexi's egg fertilized by my sperm in a petri dish and placed inside Jessica's body. It just wouldn't take. It cost us a fortune, hundreds of thousands of dollars. Jessica was taking hormones, Alexi was having eggs harvested, I was ejaculating into cups. All because I wanted my wife back. I wanted to be closer to her while absolutely everything we were doing on this path I'd placed us on was only driving her farther and farther away from me."

Jacob glanced around his office as if just now seeing what absolute filth he'd been creating and living in for the past several days. A look of disgust settled on his face. "Jesus Christ," he said and closed his eyes. "I'm a fucking disaster." He ran both his hands through his hair, walked over to his desk, and picked up a half-filled glass of water.

I watched as he chugged it and carefully placed it back on

the desk. He kept his back to me, sighed loudly, and kept talking.

"The thing was, Alexi didn't have to be anywhere near me or our life for Jessica to get pregnant." He let out a bitter laugh. "So, while I was driving Jessica to the clinic, watching her take pregnancy tests, and trying to comfort and convince her she wasn't a failure for not getting pregnant, Alexi just kept on working and traveling and living the life she had been living. Away from me, our home, and Garrett." He placed both his hands flat on his desk and leaned over. "Please know, I never meant it to happen. I don't think I even wanted it...I was so lonely, Libby. And I know that's no excuse, and there are a million other, better decisions I should have made...but it was Jessica and me alone in this house. She helped me take care of Garrett, ate meals with me, watched television with me...she would sit and talk with me over coffee in the morning."

He lifted his hands off the desk and straightened his spine. "We started sleeping together. And I don't mean sex, at least, not at first. We just started falling asleep together. The first time was on the couch in the living room. We had been up late watching a movie. I guess I fell asleep, and when I woke up in the middle of the night, Jessica was curled next to me, her arms wrapped around my neck."

He turned around and faced me.

"Believe me, Libby. I knew I should have got up, gone to my own room, and had a serious conversation with Jessica the next morning. But I didn't realize how absolutely starved for any sort of affection I had become by that point."

"So you stayed," I said.

"I stayed. I wrapped my arms around her, and I held her

back. And then the next night, when she asked if I'd sleep in her bed *just to keep her company*, I did. Night after night after night until one night—"

"I get it," I said, unable to hear any more about how his relationship with Jessica began.

Jacob took a breath. "Right, sorry. I just want you to know the truth. I think it's important for us, for our future. I don't want us to continue with any secrets between us."

Us? I couldn't even say the word out loud right now. Everything had changed, and I had no idea how I felt about any of it —including him. Couldn't he see that? But I didn't want to address any of that right now. Right now, I only wanted to know one thing. "So, when Jessica got pregnant?"

Jacob hung his head again. "Daniel is her biological son. Not a single implantation would take, but as soon as we began... well, yes, then she did get pregnant."

"And Alexi, she knew?"

Jacob didn't answer me. He stood there, staring at me, looking like he'd aged ten years in the past three days. Finally, he shook his head.

I could not believe it. "You didn't tell Alexi? You let her believe...you let her think that the baby Jessica was pregnant with was yours and hers?"

Jacob placed his hands on his head and closed his eyes. "We panicked," he said. "No." He opened his eyes and turned to face his desk again. "I panicked. Jessica, she wanted to tell Alexi the truth. Right from the beginning. She tried to convince me to tell Alexi what had happened. That we were in love. That Jessica and I would raise the baby and Garrett. She wanted us to be a family."

"So why didn't you tell Alexi?"

Jacob turned back around and faced me again. "Because I didn't want to lose her completely." Tears ran down his face. "Which was so stupid because any fool could see that she had left me long ago. But if I told her that Jessica and I were sleeping together, that the baby was Jessica's, not Alexi's, I knew whatever loose thread still connected me to her would be clipped that instant."

"You lied to her."

"Yes."

"But, I mean, she must have eventually figured it out."

"Yes."

"When? When Daniel was born? Before?"

Jacob shook his head. "Alexi found out…the day Jessica left."

CHAPTER 76

Six years. That's how long Jacob and Jessica kept their secret from Alexi. Longer, actually, including the months Jessica was pregnant.

And the day Alexi found out the truth...that was the day Jessica left.

Or was it actually the day Jessica died?

This was the reason Officer Riteman let Crawford go. Alexi was the number one suspect in Jessica's death. I saw it all now. The last time anyone saw Jessica alive was also the day Alexi found out the truth about her husband, their nanny, and the child she had always believed to be hers.

Alexi had a motive.

She also, given the nature of her work with serial killers, probably knew exactly how to both do the job and get away with it.

After Jacob confessed all his secrets to me, he crossed his office and reached to pull me into his arms.

On instinct, I recoiled.

The hurt this caused him was evident on his face. I was surprised to discover I didn't care. I didn't want him to touch me. I didn't want to be near him. I didn't want to be in this room, this house, entangled in this life. I wanted to figure out a way to get as far away from the Norths' messy lives as quickly as I could.

I didn't say any of this.

"The smell," I said to explain my distance from him. After all, he hadn't showered in days, and this room was permeated with his stench and the contents of his stomach. "You need to clean yourself up, Jacob," I said as I walked to the door. I reached for the door handle but paused before turning it. "The boys need you," I reminded him. "If Alexi did…if what the police think is correct, if she isn't coming back…you need to start thinking about the boys, Jacob." With my back to him and my hand resting on the door handle, I hesitated and considered my next words. They were harsh, but it needed to be said.

"If Alexi is guilty, if she is going to jail for killing Jessica, you're going to need to do a lot better than this."

Behind me, I heard an exhausted sob escape from Jacob, but I didn't turn around to witness the further devastation my words had created. "Start with a shower," I said, then turned the handle and left.

I closed the door behind me and rested my left palm against the warm wood.

In my right hand, I still held Jacob's keys. I used my thumb to fan them apart as I considered which one was most likely to open the door I would enter next.

CHAPTER 77

Alexi's office looked exactly the same as it had the first time I'd been in here.

But now, my perspective had completely changed.

Her personal and family problems aside, I had admired Alexi North. Her talents, her skills, her single-minded focus on her highly successful career—she was a woman who knew what she wanted and went out into the world and took it. Of course, there were costs. There are costs for any and every very successful person. Alexi had made choices. According to Jacob, her choices did not include motherhood and an isolated home life in New Hampshire.

Weeks ago, when I entered her private office for the first time, this was what I'd thought. I was standing amongst the evidence a highly successful person leaves behind. All these notes, photos, files, all the stuff littering this small space was a testament to the woman who'd created it and built her path to the top of her field.

The Academy Award on her shelf, the golden statue now gathering dust, stood sentinel over all the process that had delivered it into Alexi's hands.

Now, knowing what I did, knowing what she had done to Jessica, Alexi's office was framed through a new lens for me.

My hand reached and fanned out tens of highly disturbing photographs left abandoned on her desk. I flipped through her sloppy handwritten notes detailing the most graphic and gruesome crimes ever perpetrated. I glanced at her bulletin board of horror, the faces of criminals, their victims, settings, scenes, circumstances—all research.

Or so I had first thought.

I closed my eyes against it as a new vision of Alexi formed in my mind's eye. Alexi wasn't a woman trying to do what she could for the voiceless victims—women who were tortured, brutalized, and left for dead. She wasn't bringing some small justice to the families who had suffered. Alexi was never acting as their champion.

I thought about what Jacob had once said to me, about how Alexi had a gift for getting the killers to talk to her. Open up in ways not even their lawyers or psychiatrists could. This was, in part, why her films were so successful. Alexi's films humanized the animals capable of even the most egregious human transgressions.

Because Alexi understood them.

She knew what questions to ask, the emotional levers to pull, where all the psychological buttons were located. She knew how and, more importantly, when to press them because she *empathized* with the killers she interviewed.

As I looked around her office, her shrine of terror, I

suddenly understood—Alexi worshiped here. The killers were her gods. The victims? No more than necessary sacrifices.

There was so much material here, and it was stacked and splayed about in such a haphazard way; I felt sure that there had to be something, some piece of evidence, that would link Alexi to Jessica's death and prove she not only studied murder but had committed it herself.

After my earlier discussion with Jacob, I knew he wouldn't come looking for me for quite some time, certainly not until after he had cleaned up and sobered up. I had plenty of time to investigate.

I was about to reach for a stack of notebooks when my hand froze midair. Did my experience with Crawford's backpack teach me nothing? I snatched my hand back and held it against my chest as I shook my head.

No. I would leave the search for evidence to the professionals. Given what Officer Riteman had shared with me today, I felt confident that he and his team were probably working on a search warrant for the Norths' home anyway. Instead of complicating the matter, like I had with Crawford's stuff, I would call Riteman and make sure he knew about some of the things he might find here.

I turned around, ready to leave and lock the door behind me, when something caught my attention and stopped me cold.

It had not been visible the first time I'd been in here. And, given my position in the room today, I didn't notice it until I turned to leave. But as I stared at it now, I could feel my heart speed up as fear and adrenaline swept through my body and made my limbs feel weak.

It was the bookshelf, the one that held an array of books,

souvenirs from Alexi's travels, a few framed photos of the kids and her film crews, and her Academy Award. The last time I was here, the shelf was flush with the wall behind it.

Now, there was a two-inch crack between the shelf and the wall.

It wasn't only a shelf, I realized. It was also a hidden door.

CHAPTER 78

I stared at the black crack running the length of the hidden door and willed myself to move. Whatever was back there, it was dark.

I took a breath, pulled my phone from my pocket, turned on the flashlight, and pulled the shelf several more inches toward me. The hidden door was heavy, but the weight shifted smoothly. I held my phone in my shaking hand, trying to see what I could. I had no idea what to expect.

Was someone, maybe even Alexi, hiding in here? Was I about to get attacked? Was I only seconds away from ending up like Jessica?

I pulled the shelf until it stopped, and I heard a loud thump. Startled, I jumped back several inches and held my free hand to my chest while I used the light from my phone to scan the area before me. When nothing else happened, and no one rushed out of the darkroom to kill me, I realized I'd heard that exact sound before.

Several times, in fact.

It was the same loud thump I'd heard before, echoing throughout the house from this room.

It came from the hidden door itself, I realized. I pulled on the large shelf, trying to move it closed this time—it wouldn't budge. I aimed my light at where the shelf was hinged to the wall. A large, metal locking mechanism had sprung into a bolted position when the hidden door was fully open.

Did it prevent the door from swinging shut behind someone? I didn't see any handles on the back side of the shelf—could a person end up locked inside this room?

Or could a person be *purposefully* locked within this room?

The thought gave me a chill and made me rethink my investigation. Even though the door was now secured open, I still imagined the feel and sound of it swinging shut behind me. No one knew where I was or what I was doing.

How long would it take for Jacob to find me in here?

From the safety of Alexi's office, I lifted my phone light and directed it into the room. There didn't seem to be much inside, but it was certainly larger than I thought it would be. When I lifted my phone higher, the beam reflected back off what looked like a television monitor. When I shifted the beam to the right, I could see it happen again, then again.

I stepped forward enough to run my hand along the inside of the hidden room's wall—there was a switch. I flipped it, and the room's dark mystery evaporated instantly.

The opposite wall had rows and rows of monitors.

CHAPTER 79

With the lights on, I felt brave enough to step inside the room. It was fairly large. Compared to the grandeur of the rest of the house, I had been surprised by how small Alexi's office was. Now I knew it was because I had only seen a fraction of it.

The rest was hidden behind the shelf.

Looking around, I also now understood several other things.

Like the smell—electrical, plastic, and static--that reminded me so much of my high school's audio, video, and computer room. And the sound, the electrical hum I'd heard when I was in Alexi's office before. All of it was emanating from this hidden room.

Half of one wall consisted of rack upon rack of computer equipment. I was no expert, but I thought these were maybe servers or digital storage of some kind. The far wall, the one my flashlight had bounced off, had a grid of monitors, four by four, mounted to it. Beneath the monitors was a wide desk with a computer, chair, and a set of black notebooks, perfectly placed with their identical spines all aligned.

Suddenly, it all made sense.

I had never really considered the fact that, while Alexi was a documentary filmmaker, her office space, what I had known of it, had primarily consisted of photographs and paper notes.

In this room, the whole picture came into focus for me.

Aside from the servers and monitors, the glass cabinet to my right was filled with numerous high-end cameras, video cameras, lenses, microphones, cables, lighting equipment, and other devices I couldn't identify. This room held all the technology that would obviously go hand in hand with Alexi's career.

And all of it made perfect sense to me—except for the twin mattress and tangle of blankets that were pushed into the farthest corner of this room.

Why on earth, regardless of her feelings about Jacob, and given the multitude of comfortable and beautifully appointed bedrooms in this house, would Alexi ever need to sleep in here and like that?

I glanced over my shoulder to check the door; it was still secured open. I didn't honestly think it was possible for it to swing shut and trap me inside, but even imagining it made my skin crawl. Of course, it was exactly as I'd left it. Wide open and secured by the locking mechanism.

I returned my attention to the bed in the corner. It had been weeks and weeks since Alexi had left the house, but there was something about the untidy heap of blankets and sheets that gave me the impression that this bed had been recently slept in.

The blankets looked like they had been tossed aside this morning, not sitting here collecting dust for over a month.

When I stood right at the foot of the mattress, I noticed something else—a glass of water. Tucked between the corner of the wall and the mattress. I bent over, grabbed the glass from its place, and lifted it to get a better look—it shocked me. So much so, I nearly dropped it.

It was fresh, cold to the touch. It even had the last remnants of melting ice cubes floating on the surface. I placed the glass on the desk and stepped away from it like it was somehow capable of causing me harm.

She was here, I realized, somewhere in this house. At least she had been within the last several hours. Alexi was running from the law and hiding right here, under our noses all along.

I thought about the night Garrett had pulled me into the woods. The night Jessica's body was found. I had felt sure that someone had been watching us. I had even seen someone, or thought I had, at the edge of the woods. The person had disappeared into the trees, and I doubted my eyes. Afraid that I was seeing things after being so shocked and afraid after finding Jessica's body.

Now I knew. I hadn't imagined it. Alexi was here, not in some far-flung country or off the grid. She was here, watching everything play out.

I stared at the cold glass and wondered what I should do next.

CHAPTER 80

My first thought? *I need to tell Jacob.*

My very next thought? *What if Jacob already knows?*

I stared at the cold glass of water before me and wondered, for the first time, if Jacob could possibly already know what his wife had done. His words about Jessica's death, spoken less than an hour ago, came back to me.

"She was a wrecking ball. She took and destroyed everything I ever truly loved in this world. And if I'm honest, Libby...part of me is maybe relieved to know she's dead."

I hadn't fully digested the weight of what Jacob was expressing at the time. Now, as I sat staring at what felt like direct evidence of Alexi's very near presence, his words felt like a confession.

There were other things, now in the bright glare of my new suspicions, about Jacob's behavior that seemed particularly damning. Like the night Garrett showed me Jessica's body, a body I had seen with my own two adult eyes, and Jacob's reluctance to believe me. His unwillingness to investigate or call the police. Was it because he already knew what we had found? Was it because he already knew Jessica was dead, lying in a shallow, earthen grave, and that his wife was responsible?

Or...had Jacob helped Alexi?

The thought made me double over. I planted my palms on my knees for support while I considered the possibility that Jacob, the man I had become romantically involved with, was capable of being a part of such a heinous crime. I closed my eyes and took a breath.

I needed to think.

I opened my eyes and stared at the water again—I couldn't think straight in this insulated, windowless, claustrophobic room. I stood up, prepared to leave, when my eyes shifted to the computer, keyboard, and mouse on the desk beneath all those monitors. Alexi had been here very recently.

Would she have used the computer in this room? Was there possibly something on it that could help Officer Riteman in his investigation? And if so, if I just left now, would Alexi somehow find out I now knew about her secret room and erase something vital?

I stepped toward the desk, reached for the mouse, and shook it twice.

Tiny white lights illuminated the bottom corners of all the monitors on the wall. Several seconds later, they all came to life at once.

"Oh my God," I breathed, hardly able to either believe or comprehend what I was watching.

The sixteen screens before me showed sixteen different

video feeds from all over the house. There was the kitchen, the dining room, the pool and spa, and the family room where Garrett and Daniel sat watching the big screen television. There was Jacob's office, his bedroom, and his bathroom, where I could clearly see he was presently taking a shower. There was the front door entrance, the garage, both of the boys' bedrooms, and of course, my own bedroom, sitting room, and bathroom.

The last two cameras showed Alexi's office next door and the very room I was now standing in. I raised my hand and watched as the television me raised her hand too. On the screen, the view was of my back—the camera was behind me.

But when I turned to scan the wall and ceiling behind me, I couldn't see a thing.

I raised my hand again and looked over my shoulder at the view on the monitor while I moved closer to the wall and homed in on the camera's location. It was up high, beyond my reach, so I couldn't cover it with my hand and tell for sure. When I reached the wall, much of my body disappeared from view in the monitor, but I could tell—the camera must be mounted right where the ceiling and wall met. I gazed up, squinting and straining my eyes to try and figure out where it could possibly be—and then I saw it.

Painted exactly the same color as the wall and ceiling, a practically undetectable mound rose less than a fraction of an inch away from the ceiling. I never, not in a million years, would have ever noticed it if I hadn't realized the camera must be somewhere. At the center of the mound, there was a pinprick-sized dark circle. I grabbed the chair from in front of the desk and dragged it over until it was beneath the camera. I stood on the chair, then up on my tiptoes, and reached as close to the camera as possible as I waved my hand back in front of what I thought was the lens.

I watched my hand in the monitor across the room—this was it. I had found it.

I lowered my arm and stared up into the camera above me. These tiny, undetectable cameras were all over this house. And they were in places, like bathrooms, where most normal people would never place surveillance cameras.

There was even one in my own bedroom.

Jessica's bedroom.

How long had Alexi watched absolutely everything her husband did with the nanny?

I stared at the block of monitors before me, then shifted my gaze to the racks of computer equipment.

And how long had she been recording it all?

CHAPTER 81

I lay on my bed and stared at the camera in my room. Now that I knew exactly what I was looking for and where I would find it based on the view from the monitor, I was able to locate the cameras in here, my sitting room, and my bathroom in a few minutes.

I knew exactly where they were—I just didn't have any idea what I should do about it.

All those times, Jacob and me, naked in this bed. The things he'd done to me—private, personal, vulnerable things.

I glared at the pinprick camera on the ceiling with a perfect view of my bed.

Alexi had seen everything.

My first instinct was to storm down to the garage, find a hammer, and smash all the tiny cameras all over this house into shards of useless plastic, wires, and glass.

But that would be colossally stupid. I closed my eyes and forced myself to take a breath. I needed to think this through carefully. Even though I had found Alexi's hidden room and discovered that nearly every square inch of this house was under surveillance, I needed to play my cards right.

What did I know for sure? I knew Jessica was dead. I knew Jessica was Daniel's biological mother. I knew Alexi had found out she wasn't Daniel's mother the very same day Jessica *left* this house.

I also knew Jacob had communicated with Alexi.

I also knew Jacob's behavior was becoming more and more erratic.

I couldn't know for sure, but I highly suspected Jacob knew much more than he was telling me. I glanced up at the camera. Because how would it even be possible for Alexi to have a whole private room and this entire home wired for surveillance without him knowing anything about it?

Someone knocked at my door.

I sat up on my bed and stared through the double doors leading to my sitting room. On the bed next to me, the entire set of black notebooks I had taken from the hidden room were spread out before me. My plan was to read through them and see if I could find any evidence of what Alexi had done, but I'd only read through a few pages so far. I gathered them up and shoved them behind the decorative pillows leaning against my headboard. "Yes?" I called out and headed for the door. "Who is it?"

I hoped it was just one of the boys, but in my gut, I knew it wasn't. The door opened before I reached it. Standing before me was a freshly showered and decidedly sorry-looking Jacob North. He'd put on a clean pair of jeans and a fresh black T-shirt. His hair was still wet, and he'd combed it back, away from his face. He rested one hand high on the door frame while his other nervously ran through his wet hair. His questioning eyes met mine.

"Can I come in?"

Speechless, I stared at him for several seconds. When he was like this, clean, mostly sober, and with what looked like genuine sorrow in his eyes, it was easy for me to see why I had fallen so hard into his arms and into a bed with him. When Jacob was like this, a massive part of me begged my suspicious mind to let all my questions go. I wanted to believe him. I wanted to trust him. I wanted to go back to the way it was before I knew poor Jessica had been left for dead in the woods less than a mile from this house.

What I wanted was a fairytale.

I pulled the door open wider and stepped aside, both inviting him in and giving him room to do so. I had no idea what I would do or say, but I realized it was very, very important to try and act as normal as possible around Jacob.

If he had nothing whatsoever to do with Jessica's death, I still wanted to believe there was a way back for us.

And if he did have anything to do with Jessica's death... It was vital to not tip him off in any way.

Once in my room, he closed the door gently behind him and faced me with his head hung.

"Libby, I know I don't deserve it. But I'm here to beg you, please, you have to please try and forgive me."

A chill ran down my spine. I ignored it and stood silent, waiting patiently for him to tell me what I should forgive him for. How big was the infraction? Getting drunk and falling apart? Acting like a shitty dad when his kids needed him the most?

Or did he somehow imagine it was in my power to grant forgiveness for something as unforgivable as taking another life?

"Please don't look at me like that," he said.

"Like what?" I asked.

Jacob shook his head and closed his eyes. "Like I'm the worst person on the planet. Like the very sight of me is now detestable, and you can hardly stand to do it." He opened his eyes and gazed at me. "Nobody knows better than me how much I have completely fucked everything up. And I don't just mean these last few days." He gestured with his hand toward the door as if indicating everything he had mismanaged was right outside this room. "This whole last year… Hell, who am I kidding? I've screwed up the last decade of my life, Libby. I know that." He shook his head. "I should have let her go. Years and years ago. I should have let Alexi go. I should have listened to her. If I had really loved her, I would have wanted her happiness more than my own. I know that…now." He placed both his hands on his head. "And Jesus Christ, the entire shit show with Jessica? Believe me when I tell you, I wasn't thinking at all. I was drowning in my own fears and loneliness. And I know it's not an excuse, and I know absolutely everything I did was wrong. I used Jessica. I knew she loved me. I knew she would've done anything for me. And I was so desperate and broken, I allowed it and hung onto her like a life preserver. I never should've done that, Libby. I know that. You have to believe me."

I watched him, broken and begging, hating the fact that a huge part of me wanted nothing more than to go to him. To pull him into my arms and just allow the press of his body against mine to erase every horrible fact that had come to light over the last several days.

"Honestly, Jacob, I don't know what to think right now. It's all so much. Too much. The fact that Daniel is Jessica's biological child? You hid that from your wife for over six years. And now Jessica is dead?" I swallowed hard, willing myself not to say more or reveal any of my real suspicions. "I'm just really confused right now, Jacob. And I'm also really frightened." All of which was easy to say, because it was absolutely true. "The police. They're looking for Alexi. They think she...do you think she...hurt Jessica?"

He had shifted his hands to the front pockets of his jeans. He stood before me, his gaze locked onto mine like he was searching for something. Seconds passed, and the silence in the room grew so loud between us, it felt like it was speaking the truth Jacob couldn't.

Jacob's eyes shifted to the glass doors behind me. "I don't know," he said.

But I knew he was lying.

CHAPTER 82

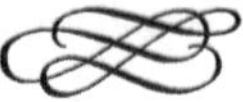

Jacob stayed out of his office and sober for the rest of the day. He stayed with the boys all day and did not once leave their side. He made their lunch and their dinner. He sat with them in the family room, watching movie after movie. Distraction after distraction to keep their heads and his own off the impossible to ignore tragedies that had upended their lives.

When I had come to get Daniel ready for bed, Jacob pulled me aside and shook his head. "You've done so much these last few days. You somehow managed to keep us all afloat. I'll get the boys to bed. I want you to try to relax. Have a few more moments to yourself."

I didn't argue with him. I nodded and returned to my rooms and my own spinning thoughts. All day, I'd been trying to make up my mind about what to do next. While Jacob worked to try to convince his boys he wasn't a terrible father and completely falling apart under all the pressure, I had sat staring out windows all day, wondering if Alexi was hiding in the woods or lurking somewhere within the house. I was frozen with both fear and indecision. Terrified of making the wrong move that would either implicate or alienate Jacob.

Now, back alone in my bedroom, I wished more than anything that I could slip into a hot bath, let my mind settle, and finally decide how I would handle everything tomorrow.

But now that I knew about all the cameras, there was no way possible for me to relax. Certainly not naked and in my surveilled tub.

Everything was always being recorded.

I settled for washing my face and brushing my teeth, then climbed into bed in the clothes I'd been wearing all day. Tomorrow, I would make up an excuse and head into town on my own. I had no idea what to make of anything. I had no way of knowing for sure if Jacob was an innocent bystander or a guilty accomplice to Alexi's crimes.

That would be up to Officer Reitman to decide. As I lay flat on my back, staring at my darkening ceiling, I decided it wasn't my responsibility to figure out Jacob's fate. None of this was my mess. And no matter how I felt about him, confusing as that was right now, he would have to work this out on his own.

Because after I had spoken with Officer Reitman, I was going to head straight to the airport and book myself on the first flight back to Nebraska.

I pulled the black notebooks from behind my pillows and settled in to read a few of them before bed. They were Alexi's. The handwriting matched all her notes in her main office. And like those notes, these books seemed to also be research about victims. But I wondered why these books had been kept separate and hidden in her secret room.

Until I read her notes about Amy Davis. A University of Eastbridge student whose body was found in a shallow grave deep in the woods—and it all clicked into place. I recognized other names from my internet search, Abigail Evans and Felicia Newton—these were local women.

Was Alexi researching another serial killer, one in her own backyard?

Or were these notebooks something else? A carefully organized and meticulous record of her own crimes?

Whatever they were, there were missing pages. Whole sections had been ripped from every book. The books were only details and facts about each woman, their lives, and their horrendous deaths. If Alexi had written any conclusions or confessions, she'd destroyed them.

Suddenly exhausted, I stacked the books together, placed them in the bottom drawer of my dresser, and crawled into bed. I was just beginning to doze off when I heard a light knock at my door and the sound of it opening.

I sat up just as Jacob came through the double doors separating my sitting room from the bedroom.

"Are you still awake?" He asked.

"Yes," I said.

"Can I… be in here with you?" He asked. "Both boys are in bed, and I don't want to be alone right now."

I didn't know what to say, so I said nothing. Instead, I pulled the sheet and comforter back on the empty space beside me. An invitation for him to join me. I knew it wasn't smart. Or what I should do. But I didn't want to be alone right now, either. And while Jacob didn't know it, this would be our last night together. Because even if he had nothing whatsoever to do with Jessica's death, everything that he had done and not done leading up to that tragedy was simply too much for me to look past.

But for tonight, and for just one more night, I would lie in his arms and pretend nothing had changed and that I wouldn't be walking out of his life tomorrow forever.

Jacob slid onto the mattress beside me, wrapped his arm around my waist, and pulled me until my back was curled against his chest. I felt his lips warm and hot against my neck. He rested them there and held me as we breathed and tried to anchor ourselves in this moment.

"I can't—"

"I know," he whispered. "I just want to be near you. I just want to feel you in my arms as I fall asleep. Nothing else."

And with this, I allowed my body to fully relax into his, my hand moving to join and hold his wrapped around my waist. I would worry about tomorrow, tomorrow.

"Good night, Libby," he whispered into my ear.

"Good night," I whispered back.

I WAS LOST. Far from the house, in the woods, and nowhere near a trail. I kept changing directions, running through dense trees, my arms flailing, panic rising in my chest along with the feeling that I was never, ever going to find my way out.

Someone else was in the woods. Someone looking for me.

Hunting me. I knew that if I couldn't get away, couldn't find my way back to the house, I would end up like Jessica. In my own shallow grave, discarded and forgotten. No one would know what had happened to me. More terrifying, no one would even care.

They were behind me, in the distance, and hard to see, but I felt their presence. Their intent. They were out for blood—mine.

On a surge of fear, I opened my eyes to the dark. It was hard to see, but it only took me a moment to realize it was a nightmare. I was in my bed, in my room, and I could hear Jacob's sleep-heavy breathing beside me. I let out a sigh, sat up...

And saw a person standing at the end of the bed.

I froze, flooded with fear.

I stared at the dark silhouette, not ten feet away but impossible to make out. I wanted to scream, but my voice was locked tight in my throat.

I reached for Jacob, my hand sliding slowly across the mattress between us as my mind grasped for rational explanations.

Was it Garrett?

Could it be Daniel?

I knew it wasn't. The silhouette was too tall, too slender to be either of the kids. The confirmation came to me on the wave of a panicked sob. "Jacob!" I cried as my hand grasped his arm and shook it hard.

But my eyes never left the person before us, shrouded in the dark.

Jacob stirred beside me. "Hmm?" he asked and tried to roll over.

"Jacob," I hissed, squeezing and shaking his arm harder.

The person tilted their head. It was hard to see. My eyes strained to catch their every movement. They raised a single finger to their lips and said, "Shhh." Then turned, and walked out of the room.

CHAPTER 83

Jacob didn't believe me.

Once he finally woke up, and I'd managed to explain what I'd seen through my tears and shaking breath, he'd rushed from the bed and searched the entire house.

When he'd cleared the hallway, I got up from the bed and checked on the boys. They were both sound asleep in Garret's bed. I stood over them, watching their chests rise and fall, their faces slack—whoever it had been, it was definitely not either of them.

Ten minutes later, when Jacob returned to my bedroom, I was standing in the sitting room with every light blazing bright. When he saw me, arms crossed over my stomach, still shivering from fear, he came to me and pulled me into his arms.

"There isn't anyone in the house."

"I saw them, Jacob. Right there." I pointed at the exact place, next to my bed, where the person had stood staring at us while we slept.

He sighed, and I felt his arms tighten around me. "Every door and window in this house is locked tight. And the alarm wasn't triggered." He then pulled back and looked into my eyes. "If someone had tried to break in, believe me, we would know it."

"And what if they were already inside the house?" I blurted without thinking.

Jacob furrowed his brow. He released me from his grasp and dropped his hands to his sides. "What? Libby...that doesn't even—"

"Don't tell me it doesn't make sense when you and Alexi have a whole hidden room attached to her office." I pointed to the door. Jacob's placating disbelief had whipped my fear into anger. My words poured from my mouth faster than my brain could consider the consequences. "I found it, Jacob. The secret room with all the surveillance equipment. There are cameras all over this house! There are cameras in my bedroom...my bath, even." I shook my head and stepped away from him. "The invasion...how could you?"

He just stood there, staring at me. His expression blank and unreadable.

This was a mistake.

I shut my mouth, fast, and stood staring at the floor in front of me as my brain raced to work out what I should do next. Because what if Jacob was everything I feared he might be? What if Jacob had helped Alexi murder Jessica?

What if Jacob already knew his wife was hiding in the house and was trying to keep her secret?

I glanced at the door to the hallway behind him. It was open, but there wasn't any way I could get past him if he tried to stop me.

"Libby," Jacob said. "What are you talking about?" His words came out slow, as if he were measuring each one.

Like he was being careful to not say anything to make me even more suspicious than I already was. When I met his gaze, his eyes were so laser-focused on mine...it felt like he could read my thoughts. "Libby?"

I shifted my jaw. "Jacob?"

"What cameras?"

I narrowed my eyes at him. Maybe I should play along? Maybe this was my way out? If I could keep Jacob from suspecting that I suspected him just a little longer, I could make a run for the front door and get out of this house. I shrugged. "It's what I saw. In Alexi's office behind the hidden door." I didn't say anything more about finding the bed she was keeping in there or the fresh glass of cold water.

Jacob's brow furrowed even deeper. "Wait here," he said. "I'll be right back."

CHAPTER 84

The second Jacob turned the corner at the end of the hallway, I ran. I was exhausted and scared and had no idea if what I was thinking was even correct, but every cell in my body told me I was in danger.

I needed to get out of this house now.

When I reached the end of the hall, I stopped. I didn't know where Jacob had gone or how long I had before he returned—I could run straight into him at any moment. I peered around the corner and listened for any sounds. When I didn't hear or see anything, I took a right and rushed for the nearest staircase.

Halfway down, I stopped dead. I'd left both my shoes and my phone back in my room. I glanced back up the stairs, gauging the risk of going back for them against running from the house without them. It only took me a second to decide.

I ran down the remaining stairs, across the wood floors, past the dining room, through the foyer, and reached for the front door. I was about to throw back the deadbolt and pull open the door when another thought stopped me.

The alarm.

If I was careful, Jacob might spend several minutes looking for me throughout the house before realizing I'd run away. Those minutes would help me get farther away and closer to help.

I turned to the alarm panel, keyed in the disarm code, saw the green light illuminate, and turned back to the door. With every second that passed, I felt sure I would hear Jacob's voice calling out for me to stop or the weight of his hand grabbing my arm.

My hands shook as I turned the lock, then the doorknob. When I opened the door, I dared a glance backward and then up to the landing above me, expecting to see Jacob there, glaring at me and ordering me to come back.

But the house was silent.

Not a person in sight.

I slipped through the door, closed it slow and quiet behind me, then ran across the cement driveway to the dirt road that would lead me to the highway.

Miles from where I was now.

The moment my feet hit the dirt road, I stopped and stared down at the expanse of gravel flanked by the dark forest on either side. It only took one glance at my bare feet to realize I wouldn't make it. I rushed out of the house in a blind panic without a good plan or even common sense. How could I expect to make it several miles down a rough road without even a pair of flip-flops?

"Libby!" I heard Jacob call out behind me, and a cold shiver of dread ran through me. I turned around, expecting to see him charging toward me, angry and out for blood.

But he was standing at the open garage door with both hands on his head. He looked more worried than murderous. Then he lifted one of his hands, and I could see he was holding his cell phone. "Officer Riteman is on the phone! He wants to speak with you!"

I stood in the dark, processing his words, wondering what to do next. Was it a trick? Was Jacob trying to lure me back inside with a lie? When I didn't say anything or move in any way, Jacob shook the phone in the air. "Are you okay?" he asked, his voice edged with the same hysteria I felt. He began walking toward me, and my mind raced. Should I make a run for it?

"Libby, I have to go," he said when he was halfway across the driveway. "Riteman wants me down at the station as soon as possible."

What. "Why?" I asked, still unwilling to let go of my suspicions. Was Riteman also onto Jacob?

Jacob shook his head and held his phone out to me as he approached. Now that he was closer, I could see the distress etched onto his face. "Somethings wrong," he said. "Something about...the body," he finished as he reached me, lifted my hand from my side, and placed his phone in my hand. "I'm sorry, and I know you're freaked out by what you think you saw, but can you stay here with the boys? I promise, I'll try to get back as soon as possible."

He didn't wait for me to respond. Jacob turned back toward the house. "I'm going to grab my wallet and keys," he said as he hurried back toward the house. "I'll get my phone back on my way out."

Confused, I wasn't sure what to make of any of this. Was I just overreacting? Letting my imagination run wild and away from me? I raised the phone to my ear and watched Jacob jog toward the house, back into the garage, and through the door.

"Hello?" I asked.

"Libby?" Officer Riteman said. "Listen to me. I need you to do exactly what I say."

A second later, Jacob emerged from the house again—he was holding something.

"Libby," Riteman continued in my ear. "You're in danger."

CHAPTER 85

"I've asked Jacob to come into the station. Right now," Riteman said.

I watched Jacob walk to his truck. The headlights blinked when he unlocked it. "He said something was wrong," I said. "Something to do with Jessica's body?"

"Yes. Now, listen carefully. Is he anywhere near you right now?"

"No."

"The DNA results came back today. That body you and the boys found in the woods? That's *not* Jessica York."

"What?" I asked. "Well…then…." I tried to make sense of what Riteman was saying.

"When I submitted the genetic testing request, I had a few other questions. Given what I'd learned about the Norths' marriage and the maternity of their youngest son, I'd asked for the body to be compared with another suspect as well. Is Jacob back yet?"

"He's starting his truck. He'll be here soon," I said.

"The last few years around here, young women have gone missing. Some have turned up dead. When we thought it was Jessica out there in the woods, I decided to pull those old cases too. Take a look with fresh eyes that included Jessica as one of the victims. I don't have time to go into the details, but Jacob North has ties to each and every one of those women. Now, as far as I can tell, he hasn't figured out he's a suspect. So you need to play it smart, Libby. Don't do or say anything that could possibly tip him off. But you should know that body in the woods…it's Alexi North. It's her body you and the boys found out there. I have a patrol car on its way to you right now, but I didn't want to risk wasting any time. Jacob North is now our suspect number one. I asked him to come in this evening to get him as far away from you as quickly as possible."

"He's here," I said as Jacob pulled his truck up next to where I was standing.

"Stay calm," Riteman said as I hung up the phone and Jacob rolled down the truck's passenger window.

I hesitated for a moment as I quickly took in all I had just learned and Riteman's warning—I wasn't crazy. I was right to be suspicious of Jacob. I stepped toward the open window and held out Jacob's phone. I was prepared to try and play it cool as if nothing had changed, but my entire body was shaking from head to toe. I worried Jacob would see right through me.

Turns out, I didn't need to.

Jacob put the truck in park, leaned across the seat, and took his phone from my outstretched hand. He was obviously worried—the fear showed clearly on his face and in his distracted behavior. "I'll get back as soon as I can," he said, his eyes never meeting mine as he took his phone from my hand, threw the truck into drive, then accelerated onto the dirt road. I watched him pull away, his tires throwing dust up in their wake. My eyes never left his tailgate, worrying he would have some sudden epiphany or suspicion about Riteman's request, and I would see the bright red of his break lights beaming in the dark.

But he just kept driving. Within seconds, he was so far down the road, it was like the entire vehicle had been swallowed by the night.

That didn't mean there wasn't time on the forty-five-minute drive into town for his mind to mull things over and decide to turn his truck around. I would need to act fast. I turned and ran back to the house. As quickly as possible, I would grab only what I really needed. Shoes, my phone, computer, and a change of clothes. I would worry about exactly what I would do next later. Right now, I just needed to do exactly what Riteman told me.

Get out.

It wasn't until I reached the mudroom that I stopped in my tracks.

I would get the essentials, and also the boys, I realized. Because there simply wasn't any way I could leave them here alone. Whatever their relationship had been, their mother was dead. What's worse, they had both seen her remains carelessly discarded less than a mile from their home. And now...it was highly probable that their father was the one responsible for killing her.

Based on Riteman's warning, he must have enough evidence to arrest Jacob. There wasn't any way I could leave the boys to wake up alone and in an empty house. I would need to get them up and pack their bags.

It would take longer, and I risked losing the time. But what choice did I have? Maybe the police officer Riteman had sent out would arrive soon. I hoped so. They would know what to do.

I closed the door to the garage, rushed through the mudroom, and was halfway across the kitchen when I both heard and felt a loud ringing. On instinct, I raised my hand to the back of my head as my eyesight blurred and wave after wave of radiating pain exploded across my skull in conjunction with everything sinking into blackness.

What happened?

Why was my head wet…sticky…and…

I barely felt the impact of my cheek hitting the floor.

CHAPTER 86

My body was vibrating. Rattling so violently, the discomfort was pulling me from a deep and dreamless sleep.

My mind fought against it. It wished the shaking to stop, vanish as quickly from my foggy awareness as it had arrived.

But *why* was I shaking? It was an annoyingly rational question that demanded an answer. I would have preferred to remain in the deep, dark, unthinking abyss of my unconscious.

Except, there was also pain. Dull. Aching…at first. But this persistent, rising awareness was coming on and bringing a skull-shattering, intense drum beat of agony with it.

Because I was hurt. Seriously. Badly. And some instinctual part of me knew I needed help.

I opened my eyes to a dark and unfamiliar place. I was not in my bed. The space beneath me was hard, ridged, and uncomfortable. Another large bump bounced my body up several inches, then back down hard against the unforgiving surface beneath me.

I reached up and felt a solid form above me, only a few inches from my face. In fact, I was surrounded on all sides. And this awareness. New knowledge. This brought my conscious mind screaming to the forefront. Fully aware, focused.

I was inside a box—trapped.

What was happening? I tried to remember. The phone call from Riteman. Jacob's truck disappearing up the road.

I wanted to get the boys and get out of the house, fast, because I knew I was in danger. Now I was here, and it must be real danger because why would anyone…

I heard it. Distinctive and familiar, the sound of car tires humming down a paved road. It wasn't a box…I was in the trunk of a car. I felt the scream rise in my throat. It took shape in my chest and flew from my mouth. Hysterical, unhinged, terrified, the sound bounced off the metal walls of my tiny moving cage and rang back into my own ears.

I felt the car's trajectory jerk left, and the sound of gravel, rough and much louder than the road, kicked up under the wheels. It was only for a second, then whoever was driving, whoever had kidnapped me, corrected course and returned the car to the road.

They had heard me. "Let me out!" I screamed, unable to help the hot tears that ran down my face. "Please!" I begged. "Please, let me out!" I kicked out the best I could against the side of the trunk beneath my feet. But I was so curled up and cramped--it was impossible to send any real force through my legs. "Please!" I begged again. "I can't breathe!"

And it was true. The air around me was suddenly hot. It felt thin. I gasped and gasped, unable to catch my breath around the knot of pure panic logged in my chest.

"Shut up!" I heard someone yell. Their voice was muffled by the back seat that separated me from them, but I could tell it was a man.

This was him. This was the person responsible for abducting and killing all those women who had gone missing or been found dead. This was the person who had killed Alexi and left her buried barely a mile from her own home and family. And now, it was the person who was going to kill me, too.

I closed my eyes and did the best I could to choke back the hysteria I felt. It wouldn't help. This tornado of out-of-control fear was paralyzing. If I wanted any hope of getting out of this, I would need a clear head and the ability to think.

Eventually, he would stop this car and drag me from this trunk. And if watching all of Alexi's horrific documentaries had taught me anything, it was that serial killers often had killing routines. The other women in the area had been found deep in the woods. And while I had no idea how big or strong this guy was, I would bet that he hadn't killed them first, then carried all that weight for miles into the middle of nowhere—that would be harder.

No. He must have either lured them, somehow, or forced them to walk into the woods on their own, then killed and buried them.

Which meant I might still have time and chances to get away from him. I clenched my fists until I could feel my nails digging into my palms and willed myself to take deeper, slower breaths. I had no idea if I would get a chance to escape, but I needed to be as prepared as possible to take the advantage if I could.

I began to take stock. Both my hands were bound, but not my feet. This led me to believe I may be right and that my kidnapper intended to make me walk to my death. I felt around the trunk with my hands as much as I could. Maybe there was something I could use. Something sharp. Something I could swing. Could he have possibly overlooked and left something I could use as a weapon against him when he eventually opened the trunk?

No. There wasn't a single thing in here besides my own body.

Maybe if I could position myself, turn a bit more, I'd be able to kick him right in his face the moment the trunk opened.

Which would possibly have worked if I hadn't already screamed out and let him know that I was very much conscious, awake, and aware that I had been abducted. He likely expected a fight now and would be more than ready when he popped that trunk.

After all—this wasn't his first time.

The sound of the wheels on the road changed, and I could feel the car decelerating. We nearly stopped then I felt us take a right turn. Immediately, I could tell the difference. We were on a dirt road now, unfinished and uneven. The jolts my body took against the sides of the trunk intensified and were more painful.

I imagined we had turned onto one of the many roads off the highways that led into the depths of the thick forests, just like the one that led to the Norths' house. He was leaving the world and their prying eyes behind so he would have the time, space, and privacy to do with me what he liked.

We were getting closer, either to my death or my escape. I only had minutes left before I would need to fight for my life.

Or die trying.

CHAPTER 87

The car stopped, and he cut the engine. I heard him open his door and then slam it shut.

This was happening. Every muscle in my body tensed and was ready.

But then, I heard a second door…open and slam shut.

Did he get something from the backseat? Or—

"She's awake, so be ready," someone said.

"What if—" I heard the guy say.

"I told you what the plan is. We're not deviating. Understand?" This other person…it was a woman.

There were two people, and one was a woman.

Before I had time to figure out how to get away from them both, the car trunk popped open, and a bright and blinding light was shone directly into my face.

I couldn't see a thing.

"Get her out," the woman said.

"I just think we should—" the man said.

"Now!" she commanded.

Seconds later, hands grasped my upper arms and pulled me up. The woman must be the one keeping the flashlight in my eyes. It prevented me from seeing their faces, but now that the trunk was open and I could hear him clearly, I recognized the man's voice.

"Crawford?" I cried. At the mention of his name, I felt his hands slip, but it only took a second for him to regain his grip on me. He hauled my upper body out of the trunk and dragged me until my legs cleared the edge and flopped to the ground. I tried to fight him, twisting and turning, swinging my bound fists and thrashing my legs—but I was so weak. My limbs were flailing and landing without any real force. My head swam with the effort, and I felt like I might black out again.

They had hit me over the head, I realized. Hard enough to knock me clean out. Hard enough that I was still not okay.

Outside the trunk, I found that my legs couldn't hold my own weight. I buckled to my knees the moment Crawford let me go. The light shifted away from my face, and after a few moments, my eyes adjusted to the darkness. Their forms came into focus, the ground beneath me, the trees around us, and the blood. My shirt was covered in blood. And my hands, they were caked in it. It was my blood, I realized. The crack to my head had split it wide open.

I knelt there, unable to stand, losing faith in my ridiculous belief that I would escape this situation alive, and began to cry. All those other women—had they felt this? Terrified and hopeless, knowing that they were about to die—powerless to do anything to stop it. I knelt there, my shoulders slumped as hot tears ran down my face. "Please," I begged. "Please don't do this."

"*Please don't do this,*" the woman mocked me. "You disgust me," she said, her words conveying a hatred for me that I didn't understand. "You're so fucking weak. Kneeling there, crying and begging...what the fuck does he even see in you? You're nothing. A nobody. You think you deserve this life you've fallen into? What a joke. I've *worked* for this life. I've put in the time—years and years of my *life*. No one as absolutely pathetic as you could ever replace me."

I lifted my gaze to meet her eyes. As my vision continued to clear, her facial features came into focus. "You're Jessica," I whispered.

To my surprise and horror, she smiled at me. "So, there are some functioning brain cells in that sweet little head. Congratulations, Sherlock." Her eyes grew wide, and she splayed her hands, palms out like she was part of a stage show. "You've cracked the case." Then, a vicious sneer instantly replaced her smile, and her eyes filled with disgust. I didn't see it coming. I only felt her fist striking my face hard and fast. The force of it knocked me sideways and into the dirt.

"Get the fuck up," Jessica barked.

But I didn't get up. I didn't move an inch. I lay there, my cheek pressed into the sharp gravel and stared at Jessica's hiking boots. They had thick soles and red cord laces that snaked through metal eyelets. It reminded me that my own feet were bare.

Jessica was in charge. She was prepared for what was going to happen next. If I had imagined finding an opportunity to escape and make a run for it, that fantasy evaporated entirely as I lay there, already broken, staring at those boots.

I was going to die today.

"I said, get the fuck up!" Jessica shouted. And I watched as one of her boots pulled back and then came flying back at me, full force. The first kick landed in my stomach, knocking the wind from me.

I would have done what she said. I would have sat up, stood up, and marched into the woods and my death. But her boots kept coming. She stomped my hip, my ribs, I felt her laces connect with the back of head. My vision swam again. One more blow and I was going to pass out.

And I wished I would. No part of me wanted to be present for any of this.

"Jessica!" Crawford said, and the blows to my body stopped.

"You're going to end up killing her right here. You need her to walk—"

"I'll drag this bitch if I have to."

"It's messier. You know that," he reasoned.

"Then get her ass up!" she screamed. "I'm tired of this shit!"

CHAPTER 88

I could barely stand—walking felt impossible. Crawford dragged me to my feet and then had to hold me up as we followed Jessica into the woods. When we lagged too far behind her, she would turn back and threaten to "Slit your fucking throat right here if you don't hurry up."

And part of me wished she would because walking miles along a rough path with bare feet and a broken body was just a torture march to my inevitable death anyway.

Why should I care if Jessica did it twenty feet from the road or twenty miles—the end would be the same for me.

But not her. This march deep into the woods was for her benefit. It ensured that my body would take a long time to find. If it was ever found at all. She was counting on that. She would need the time to completely distance herself from her crime, just like she had with all the other women she had murdered over the years.

Including Alexi North. Alexi who had spent her life interviewing and making a career off serial killers, just like Jessica. I didn't know if it was irony or destiny that Alexi would end up dying just like all the victims she had studied over the years, but it did make me wonder how it had happened.

I tripped over a small rock on the path and felt the flesh on my big toe rip open. I cried out on instinct, but the pain was hardly noticeable compared to the agony the rest of my body was in.

To my surprise, Crawford stopped walking and called out, "Jessica! Stop."

"What?" she asked, clearly annoyed as she turned to face us.

"We need to take a break," he said.

"What? No. We keep moving. We're not even half a mile in yet."

"Yeah, well, she can barely move, and I'm the one doing all the lifting here. Unless you want to be the one to—"

"Fine!" Jessica snapped. "Five minutes," she said and walked back to join us on the path.

When Crawford released my body, I fell back against a large boulder on the side of the path. It was precariously placed, right at the edge of a steep embankment. I thought I could maybe hear the rush of water in the distance.

I had spent the last several months watching Alexi's documentaries and interviews with convicted serial killers. In almost every one, she got the killers to talk about their victims who had managed to escape. Some had talked their way out of their fate, some fought back, others found an opportunity and ran. Regardless of their strategy, only a very small percentage of victims were able to save their own lives. Still, I had to try, and I didn't think running or fighting would end well for me.

"Why are you doing this?" I asked. My voice shook and came out barely above a whisper.

Crawford was turned away from me, staring into the forest next to the path. He either didn't hear me or was pretending not to, but Jessica turned the full force of her attention to me.

"Why?" She shook her head like I had just asked the dumbest question in the world. "Oh, I don't know. Because I can? Because you deserve it? Because for my whole fucking life, I've been sick of watching the world bend over backward and simply hand over everything good to stupid fucking idiots like you while people like Crawford and me are shit on over and over and over. There are never any breaks for *us*. No handouts or hand-ups. Which, you know what? Turns out that's just fine. My life taught me how to survive. To take what I wanted and what I deserve. But the thing is, it's never enough to just get your hands on what's yours. You have to fight like a fucking animal to keep it. You and every other bitch I've ever killed—you're only getting what you deserve for trying to take what's mine in the first place."

I thought about what Riteman had told me on the phone. About how he'd made the connection that all the women in the area who had died or gone missing were connected to Jacob in some way. "This is because of Jacob?" I asked.

Jessica's face shone with rage as she took four strides to separate the distance between us until her face was inches from mine. "Not just Jacob," she hissed. "I built this whole fucking life here. This is my world, my house, my land, and yes, my fucking man that happens to be the lynchpin keeping it all together. So, if you think for one second I was going to let some entitled, idiotic graduate student with nice tits or a fucking blond barista with a tight ass come along and distract him from the life we've built...no, absolutely not. There isn't any way in hell I'm going back to the life I had before." Just then, Jessica glanced over to Crawford, but he was still staring into the forest like he wasn't listening or couldn't hear every word she said.

"Nobody knows how bad we had it," she said to Crawford's back, but he still didn't turn around.

"But Alexi," I said. "This was her life first. And you stole—"

Jessica's fist smashed into my mouth, ending my words mid-sentence.

"You don't know shit," Jessica hissed. "If I'd been smarter, I would've killed that bitch in New York."

CHAPTER 89

I lifted my hand to my now split lip and felt the blood.

"Alexi didn't want this life," Jessica spat in my face. "She abandoned it. Everyone and everything in it. So, I made it my own. She doesn't get to just change her mind and try to come back after years of throwing it all away."

"*You* told her Daniel wasn't hers."

"Yes, I told her. I thought it would finally drive her off for good. But when she threatened to take him from me...I protect what's mine."

I thought about the notes in Alexi's office—the ones I'd found about Jessica. "But why all those other women?"

Jessica glanced away, and I thought she would just ignore my question. But then she said, "They were distractions. *Potential problems.* Just like how you have become a *potential problem.*"

She meant Jacob, of course, and she was letting me know I was hardly the first woman he'd had an affair with.

"She figured it out," I said. "Alexi knew what you were, what you were doing to all those other women."

Jessica leaned back several inches and licked her lips. "I never said she wasn't good at her job."

I shook my head. "But you didn't start here, in New Hampshire. This wasn't your first time."

Jessica narrowed her eyes at me, and Crawford turned around.

"I don't know what you're talking about," Jessica said.

"That girl. When you were in middle school. You and Crawford...you've been doing this long before you ever came to work for the Norths."

"What girl?" Crawford asked.

Jessica's jaw shifted but she didn't say a word.

I focused on Crawford, but his gaze shifted to Jessica. He stared at her a long time before he said anything else. "You didn't," he finally said.

Jessica glared at him as if daring him to defy her complete authority over everything and everyone. "And what if I did? That's ancient history, Crawford. We were kids."

He stood, his arms hanging limp at his sides, his expression completely unreadable. "Why?" he whispered. "She was the only person—"

"*I* was the only person!" she screamed. "Ruth Warren was just another entitled, spoiled, fake, stupid bitch. She didn't give two shits about you. *I* did!"

Crawford didn't say anything else. Defeated, he turned away and faced the forest again. Seeing him this way, entirely under Jessica's thumb, it was hard to imagine that I ever thought he could be the one who was a danger to *her*. It was clear to me now that Jessica was a master manipulator, and Crawford was her subservient lap dog. She had controlled him for years.

"Break's over," Jessica commanded. "Get her up."

Crawford hesitated for a second, and part of me wondered if he was thinking about not doing it or forming some additional argument, but when Jessica yelled. "Are you fucking deaf? I said get her up." He turned around immediately, grabbed my arm, and yanked me up from the rock I was perched on.

Jessica stormed down the trail ahead of us at a pace much too quick for my failing legs to keep up with. When she was several yards away, Crawford stopped walking. He just stood in the middle of the trail, holding me up, as Jessica got farther and farther away.

He held me with one hand while he reached into the pocket of his hoodie with the other and pulled out a set of keys. He placed the keys into my bound hands and lowered his mouth to my ear. "Run," he whispered. "I'll hold her back."

I looked into his eyes and saw every one of his regrets. I didn't know why Crawford would suddenly go against Jessica now or why I should be the one he finally decided to try and help, but I didn't think it would matter. I could barely move, never mind run. "I can't," I cried.

"You have to." He pushed me gently away from him. "Go, now," he hissed and glanced over his shoulder. Jessica was still walking away from us and hadn't yet noticed we were no longer following her.

I stumbled backward, my steps uneven and weak, somehow more terrified now that I had a chance to escape. Even though my pace was agonizingly slow, my heart raced. How far could I possibly get before Jessica turned around and saw that Crawford had allowed me to get away?

I wasn't ten feet away from Crawford when Jessica stopped and turned. "What the hell!" she yelled. In an instant, she was racing back along the path toward us. "Crawford, grab her! What the hell are you doing?"

"Run! Now!" he shouted at me.

And even though I was terrified, broken, and could already imagine what Jessica would do to me the moment she got her hands on me, I turned my back on them and forced my legs to move as fast as they could.

Behind me, I could hear their feet slipping, scrabbling in the dirt as Crawford grabbed hold of Jessica and tried to give me a chance.

"What the fuck! Crawford!" Jessica screamed. "You let her go?"

"Stop!" Crawford said.

"What is wrong with you? We have a plan!"

"*You* have a plan. It's always been about you! No!...It's always about him! It's always going to be about *him*!"

"Let me go!" Jessica screamed.

I dared to glance back over my shoulder. I hoped to see that I had gained some distance. That Crawford had Jessica in a secure hold. What I actually saw was that Jessica would catch me in seconds, and she was now holding a knife.

She pulled back her arm.

I stopped, stunned by what was coming next. She thrust the blade forward, plunging it deep into Crawford's stomach.

I screamed.

Jessica pulled the bloody knife from Crawford's gut and

pushed him away. He clutched the wound, fell back several steps, and collapsed hard into the dirt.

Jessica didn't stop. She turned, ran toward me, knife in hand. She was ready to finish me right here, right now.

I watched her, coming fast, gaining on me. Her bloody knife poised to cut me the instant she reached me. I needed to move, act, be ready to fight.

But I was paralyzed with fear.

CHAPTER 90

I couldn't outrun Jessica. I couldn't fight her off, either. Any moment, I would feel that blade plunge into my own flesh. And not only once, like Crawford. Jessica would release every ounce of rage she felt into me again, and again, and again with that knife. No part of my body would be spared.

Like so many victims Alexi had documented, I would be yet another who had suffered twenty, thirty…fifty stab wounds. I knew this. I could see the murderous blood rage written across Jessica's savage face.

And still, I couldn't move.

She was fifteen feet away, ten feet, five—she pulled back the knife, ready to strike.

I was going to die. And still, I couldn't move.

So…I fell instead.

My brain could not think of a solution, so my body found

one. I took a single step toward the steep embankment and collapsed into a fall.

One second, Jessica was within inches of taking my life. The next, I was far from her and her knife, tumbling down the steep hill, crashing through brush and tree limbs that cut my flesh. Slamming into rocks and boulders that bludgeoned and bruised my body.

I tried to slow my descent, but every branch I reached for ripped through my palms, and my bare feet couldn't find purchase long enough in the loose dirt, leaves, and bushes to stop or even slow my body down.

I fell faster.

I was out of control and had no idea what danger I was heading for. If my body was tumbling toward a sheer cliff, was that better or worse than being cut to shreds by Jessica?

I tried harder. Desperate to slow down and grab hold of anything I could, terrified that at any moment, I'd find myself free-falling through open air and plummeting to my death.

My back hit a large boulder that knocked the wind from my lungs, and then, the ground disappeared. I was falling, falling, falling away from a sheer cliff. I couldn't even scream because I couldn't take a breath.

The impact, would I feel it? Would it hurt?

But before I could process my fear of hitting the earth, everything stopped. For a second, there was no feeling, no sound, no sight. Then, all at once, I felt the frigid lighting flash of cold, the chaos of current, the lack of air. An icy, wet chill swallowed my body. Filled my nose. My mouth.

Disoriented, submerged, I couldn't see. All I heard was the fast-rushing water. My body was swept downstream by a current so fast, it was impossible to claw myself to the surface. I couldn't catch a breath.

I was going to drown.

But I didn't want to die. The desire to fight, push, pull, kick —I needed to survive this. I had somehow given myself a chance to escape Jessica, a chance at life. I couldn't give up now.

The current was too strong. The riverbed uneven and littered with large rocks that sent the water rushing one direction, then the next. It knocked me into a tornado of arms and legs, soft limbs useless against the water's force. I caught one breath, then was sucked back down. My hip slammed into a rock. The current pushed my body over a small waterfall. My head bobbed to the surface. I sputtered and coughed. Water had lodged in my chest. I couldn't catch a breath before I was forced down again.

I needed air. My lungs burned. My mind was shutting down —I was going to pass out.

But taking a breath now meant death.

I clawed for the surface. Kicked as hard as I could.

Another large rock slammed into my skull.

CHAPTER 91

I opened my eyes and was blinded by light.

I couldn't feel anything. My whole body was numb.

Was this death?

"Mom!" a girl screamed. "Mom! Mom! There's a body!"

I heard another voice in the distance, but it was too far away to make out.

"By the river!"

The light hurt my eyes, so I closed them again.

"No! It's a woman!"

The next time I opened my eyes, people were standing over me. This was good. They blocked the bright light so I could see now. I didn't know these people. I didn't think I did. Nothing felt clear. I didn't know where I was.

They were all talking.

One woman touched me…I couldn't feel her hands.

One man spoke into a cell phone…I couldn't hear his words.
They were trying to help me.
My eyes slid shut.

CHAPTER 92

I opened my eyes, and it was dark.

My eyesight was blurry, but I was inside. There was a ceiling above. I was lying in a bed. And my body—it wasn't numb anymore. No. Every inch of me radiated pain—it was the agony that woke me up.

I took a breath, even my lungs burned. I tried swallowing and felt the dry, swollen pressure at the back of my throat—I was so thirsty.

"Libby?" someone asked. "You're awake?"

I shifted my gaze and saw someone moving toward me on my left. Their features were out of focus until their face was only inches above mine.

"Jacob?" I asked, my voice weak and raspy.

He nodded, and I saw the smile break across his face. "You're awake. Thank God you're awake," he said, and I felt his large hand slide over mine on the bed beside me. "I'll call the nurse," he said.

I turned my palm over and grasped his hand before he could leave. "Jessica," I whispered. "It's Jessica."

Jacob stared into my eyes. "I know…everyone knows. Not long after you were brought into the hospital, Crawford Allen was found on the trail. He was bleeding out…it was bad. But when the rescuers asked him who had stabbed him, he managed to whisper Jessica's name before he lost consciousness."

I could picture Crawford, lying there in the dirt, staring at the sky as his life drained away from him. How long had he waited before help found him? I didn't want to know. "Is he here too?" I asked.

Jacob shook his head. "He'd lost too much blood. He died on the way to the hospital."

I shook my head. The news made me feel both sad and confused. "He…helped me. I wouldn't have gotten away without him."

Jacob's brow furrowed like he was trying to figure this bit of information into what he already knew about Jessica and Crawford's crimes. He shook his head and said, "And you wouldn't have even been in the situation in the first place if he hadn't helped Jessica. Riteman is handling all the details. You shouldn't worry about anything except healing right now." He stood up to go get the nurse, but I squeezed his hand harder, and he turned back again.

"Where's Jessica?"

Jacob didn't answer me right away, and I could tell he was trying to decide how or if he should tell me.

"Please?" I asked. "I need to know."

Jacob ran his free hand through his hair. "They'll find her,

Libby. Riteman has the whole state mobilized. The FBI is getting involved now. It won't take long." He leaned forward and kissed me once, gently on my forehead, careful not to inflict any more pain.

I watched him walk out the door. I hoped he was right, but felt certain he was wrong.

I didn't know much about Jessica York, and I realized now that was by design. She had spent her life becoming an expert at being an unsolved mystery that left death in her wake.

I had watched enough of Alexi's documentaries to know that the police were unlikely to find Jessica. At least not until she was driven to kill again.

CHAPTER 93

I stood on the balcony of my old bedroom and watched Jacob swim his laps in the pool below. I rested one hand on my growing belly as I sipped the hot tea I held in the other.

Jacob reached the end of the pool, executed a perfect flip turn, and headed back across the pool. My eyes lifted from him to the forest beyond the lawn. It had been seven months since Jessica had tried to kill me, and I still kept an ever-watchful eye out for her.

I always expected to see her standing at the forest's edge just before she slipped into the darkness.

As I had feared, the police had not yet found her.

Jacob continued to reassure me. Before I even returned from the hospital, he had professionals come in to inspect the current home surveillance system, explain how it worked, and make modifications, including removing the cameras from all the bedrooms and bathrooms. They were apparently astonished that he, as the homeowner, had no idea that when they'd installed the alarm system, cameras had been mounted as well.

"Alexi handled and oversaw the whole thing. She must have done it because she had suspicions about my relationship with Jessica," Jacob said. "I've made so many mistakes," he confessed to me one morning as we lay in bed together before he left for work.

"It's behind us," I whispered into his ear, and he ran his hand over my belly and the baby we had made together.

"Well, I don't want to make anymore," he said, turning to face me. "I know everything is happening fast, but I believe that's because *this* was meant to be. Marry me, Libby. Let's make this *our* home for *our* family."

I had kissed him. "Yes," I said. "Let's make everything right."

We applied for a license and were married the next week, with both boys and Kyra standing beside us before the judge.

I lifted my left hand now and admired the sparkle of my wedding ring set in the morning light. I had left Luck behind and become Mrs. Libby North. Our baby, a girl, was due at the end of the summer.

Below me, Jacob had finished his laps and was toweling off on the deck. I needed to see if the boys were ready to leave for school. Only two weeks were left, and they were both ready for the summer break and the family trip we had planned to Orlando.

My life had become everything I had ever dreamed it could be. It was nearly perfect.

If only the police could locate and finally arrest Jessica, I could stop being afraid, looking over my shoulder, and scouring the house every day for any sign that she was back and somehow hiding in the house again.

With all the new security measures Jacob had installed, I knew it was impossible. Jessica had access to the old systems, codes, and keys, which was why she had been able to hide among us for so many weeks before. But everything was new now. Doors, locks, cameras—the entire system had been overhauled and designed to keep anyone, specifically her, out.

I just needed her to be found and put away where she belonged. Only then would I be able to finally relax and enjoy the life Jacob and I were building. I sometimes worried I might never get that closure. I knew from watching Alexi's documentaries that killers were often never found. Or they were able to successfully avoid detection for years and years.

Jacob kept telling me we were safe and that Jessica couldn't hurt us now, but I didn't believe it. I couldn't allow myself to believe it. Not now, when there was so much on the line, and I had so much to lose.

Every day, once Jacob left for work, and I'd dropped the boys off at school, I spent most of my day combing the internet for Jessica. Collecting anything I could about her past, digging for anything I might find that may point the way to where she could be hiding now.

I was just about to click on the link with Jessica's parents' home address, one I'd visited at least twenty times before, when my phone rang.

It was Officer Riteman.

"Hello?"

"Libby. Hey, Riteman here. Are you sitting down?"

I sat back in my chair, my heart racing. Riteman didn't just call me for no reason. I closed my eyes, hoping I was about to hear the words I'd been waiting months for. "Yes," I said.

"Okay, well, this is not official information. Nothing is being announced and disclosed to the public, so I'm asking you to keep this to yourself for now."

"Yes," I breathed, willing him to say it. Just say what I so desperately needed to hear.

"We found her," he said. "I know what you've been through and what this means to you, so I wanted you to know right away. You don't have to worry about Jessica York ever again."

My eyes flew open, and I couldn't help the tears of relief that ran down my face. It was like being released from a crushing weight. I was finally free from an agonizing pain that had been lingering in my bones. "Where was she?" I asked. "How did you find her? Is she there now? In the jail? Or another state?" I had imagined so many scenarios over the last seven months. Places she might hide, new lives she may have started, or that she might even still be in our own backyard.

"No," Riteman said. "She's in the morgue. We found her body, Libby. Jessica York is dead."

CHAPTER 94

I sat, both hands on my belly, on my baby girl, and closed my eyes. At first, I felt exactly what Riteman hoped I would—an overwhelming sense of relief. So, I sat there at the kitchen table in front of my open laptop, relishing my new sense of freedom.

Finally, finally, we were free of her.

Finally, I could get on with my life and start the process of letting all the trauma she had inflicted on both my mind and body go.

Except, something still bothered me.

How had Jessica died? Because having faced her that day in the woods, it seemed unlikely that it would have happened by accident.

Someone killed Jessica.

I stood up so fast, I knocked over my chair. I left it and headed for the stairs, taking them two at a time, ignoring the way my heart raced, and my lungs burned.

Why hadn't I thought to look at it before now?

I rushed down the hall and through the door to Alexi's old office. Over the past seven months, Jacob and I had both worked to pack up all her notes and photos, carefully boxing them up to preserve her work. Instead of a horror room of real-life terror, the space now looked like a small, unused office. I passed through the small office quickly and headed straight for what we now called the surveillance room. The hidden room behind the bookshelf door.

The mattress Jessica had slept on while she'd been hiding in the house had been cleared away months ago after the police had finished collecting all the evidence they thought was relevant. All that was here was the desk and the computer connected to the surveillance system. Even all the monitors and racks of servers had been removed when the system had been updated.

It now reminded me of what my old bosses, Nicola and Damion, had installed in their Park Ave apartment.

I pulled out the chair in front of the desk and shook the mouse until the computer monitor came to life. The system was new, but all the old files, the ones that hadn't been deleted by Jessica, were still preserved and organized by date. I found the file labeled September of last year and opened the date that matched the day Nicola fired me.

There were subfiles labeled by camera location. I clicked the one I was looking for: Jacob's Office.

I opened the video file and fast-forwarded to the time I needed to see.

I'd been sitting in the coffee shop in Manhattan for three hours—the interview had been scheduled for eleven thirty. But

Jacob had been a little early to our video call. I remembered he was already on screen when I'd logged on. From my vantage point in the coffee shop, I could barely make out his face because of the window behind his office desk.

Now, looking at the footage from the angle of the surveillance camera, I could see everything that had happened in his office that day. I remembered wondering about what or who Jacob and Daniel had been looking at during the interview —now I knew.

Jacob sat at this desk, interviewing me on his computer. And sitting on the other side of his desk, behind the monitor and out of view with Daniel on her lap, was Jessica York. I watched the video as she signaled to him, then sent Daniel over to his father's lap when she likely suspected I felt uncomfortable about the interview.

Jacob had said Jessica had quit weeks before, but she had been there the whole time.

And Jessica was the one I had seen. That night, when I'd first arrived, through the crack in Alexi's office door. Jacob had said it was Alexi packing for her trip, but that was a lie. It had been Jessica. It had always been Jessica.

Jacob had known and been lying to me about it the entire time.

Because Alexi was already dead and decomposing in the woods less than a mile from the house before I'd even arrived.

In the video, I watched Jacob end the interview and send Daniel out of the office. Once the door was closed, Jessica stood up from her chair, walked over to Jacob, and tried to put her arms around his neck.

He dodged her embrace and pushed her hands away.

I turned up the volume on the video.

"We don't need her," Jessica said.

Jacob nodded. "Yes, Jessica, we do need her. We need her because you broke the rules. You decided to take matters into your own hands. You fucked up!"

Jessica's shoulders slumped and her arms hung limp at her sides. "I had no choice."

"There's always a *choice*," Jacob hissed.

Jessica shook her head. It was hard to tell from the angle of the camera, but I thought she might be crying. "Alexi was going to take everything from me!" she pleaded and tried again to grab for Jacob's hand.

He yanked free of her grasp. "And who's fault is that? You *told* her about Daniel."

"She would have guessed!" Jessica yelled. "She found out about us, didn't she? How long do you honestly think it would have taken her to figure out that Daniel is *my son*?"

Angry, Jacob turned on Jessica. In one lightning-fast move, I saw him grab her by the throat. "And how *exactly* did she find out about us?"

I watched Jessica struggle, but her small hands were no match for Jacob's ironclad grip.

He held her for several seconds, his furious face inches from hers as he watched her fight for air. She shook her head, was trying to speak, but all I could hear were her thin gasps for air.

Right when I thought she would lose all consciousness, Jacob released his hold and pushed her away. Jessica stumbled backward several steps then collapsed on the floor. She held her neck in one hand and coughed several times before she could form any words.

"I didn't…tell her. I don't know how she figured it out. It wasn't me." She shook her head. "I swear."

Jacob folded his arms across his chest and glared at her. "You were always jealous of Alexi. Of my love for my *wife*. From the day I found her you've wanted her gone."

"She didn't deserve you!" Jessica cried out. "She never even really knew you, did she? Not like I know you. Not like I've *always* known you, Jacob. I love you for who you really are. I know what you want, what you *need*. I'm the one who helps you, don't I? You think Alexi could ever do for you what I've done over the years."

"She would have understood. If I'd told her, explained it… she understands people like me. She's crafted her entire world around people like me."

Jessica shook her head. "Do you honestly believe that if Alexi ever found out what you've done…what we've done, that she wouldn't make sure you were put behind bars for the rest of your life? Do you honestly think she would still live with you? Love you? Can you imagine Alexi ever allowing you to see Garrett or Daniel ever again?"

"Alexi understands!"

"Alexi has made people like you into a fucking sideshow for entertainment," Jessica whispered. "I'm the only person who will ever love you for exactly who you are."

Jacob turned away from her. "Well, thanks to you, I'll never know the truth now. You've taken the one woman I've ever truly loved away from me and ruined everything. She was my fucking wife. How long do you think it will take for me to be named as a suspect once people realize she's gone?"

"That won't happen," Jessica said.

"Of course it's going to happen. The husband is the first person they suspect. How long until they start to connect the dots that link me to all the others?"

Jessica shook her head. "I have a plan. Someone else... Crawford—"

"Crawford Allen?" Jacob looked surprised. "That kid you hung out with in school?"

Jessica nodded.

"How?...Do you even know where the hell he is?"

Jessica nodded again. "You have to trust me. I've been doing this, doing this for you...for us, for years. I *know* what I'm doing, Jacob. I know exactly how to make this all go away. They are never going to suspect you. Or me. Crawford's going to take the fall for Alexi...for all of them. It will finally, finally just be us...if you'll have me."

Jacob turned away from her. Jessica couldn't see the way he clenched his fists into two hard rocks in front of him or the look of utter fury on his face...but I could. Seeing him this way, and knowing now what he was capable of, it wouldn't have surprised me to see Jacob kill Jessica right then and there.

But he didn't. Because he still needed her.

"You're going to fix this."

"Yes," Jessica said. "I swear. And fast, so you don't even need that woman—"

"No," Jacob composed himself and turned back around. "You're going to fix this, but not in this house. The new nanny is coming. As far as anyone else is concerned, Alexi left me for someone else, and you quit. I'm rebuilding my life with my boys, and I need help. That's my story. You do whatever you need to do to fix the mess you created. And you better do it fast.

But you're not doing it here. It needs to look like there's been a clean break and that you're long gone. The last thing we want is for people to start wondering if I killed my wife just so I could fuck our nanny." He shook his head in disgust.

A phone rang. Jacob reached into his pocket and took out his cell. "It's her," he said. "Keep your mouth shut," he ordered and swiped to answer the phone.

"Hello?" he said to me on the other end.

I was telling him I would take the job.

"That's great news," he said.

I remembered thinking his tone of voice was flat and didn't sound like he actually thought it was great at all. I had been confused because, based on our previous conversation, I thought he'd be thrilled.

Now I knew why his demeanor had changed so drastically. After his fight with Jessica, he was having a hard time faking it.

"Give me a few minutes, and I'll email you the itinerary and ticket," he said. I listened as he asked me about my car. I remembered feeling panicked that I sounded too frantic and was ruining my opportunity.

"Well," he said, looking directly at Jessica. "It sounds like everything has worked out for us all then."

He hung up the phone. "She'll be here tonight. Pack up your shit and be sure you're gone before I get back with her."

Jessica shook her head. "For how long? When can I come back?"

"Fix the problems you've created. I'm not discussing anything else until then."

Jessica was still sitting in a heap on the floor. Dejected and broken, her expression looked just as lost as it did in the pictures of her as a kid. When she didn't immediately get up and move, Jacob flung his arms wide and barked at her. "Get moving!"

When I saw Jessica drag herself up from the floor and leave the room, I shut the computer down, rested my elbows on the desk, and pressed my palms to my eyes as this new perspective of Jacob came into a sudden and startling focus for me.

And all the pieces fell into place.

Yes, it was Jessica all along.

But only because Jacob wanted it.

CHAPTER 95

The boys didn't get to go to Orlando that summer. They barely left the house for three months.

When I shared with Officer Riteman what I'd discovered, spelled out the twisted relationship between Jacob and Jessica, he'd had a team of officers at Jacob's university arresting him in the middle of his lecture before the day was over. Once I was able to give them that first clue, the evidence linking Jacob not only to Jessica's death but also to Alexi's and every other woman who had gone missing and or died in the area for the last ten years came into sharp relief.

As part of her work to pin all her and Jacob's crimes on Crawford, Jessica had scrubbed her social media posts except for the photos of her hiking in the woods. Photos that at first glance appeared innocuous enough, until the police realized they were the locations of where she and Jacob had lured other women to their deaths. Trophy posts. Each one careful to reference or thank Crawford for showing her *another gorgeous location!*

But it was so much worse than that.

Once the FBI had their man, they were able to link Jacob to the deaths of women across the course of his life, beginning with what they believed was the first. An eighth-grade girl, Ruth Warren, who was a student at the middle school where Jacob worked as a student teacher in the English department at McFadden Middle School.

That was the year he'd met and groomed the young girl who would become the accomplice to his crimes, Jessica York. A girl who'd grown up in and been bounced around by the foster care system. A girl who was easy prey for the charming, handsome, and enigmatic young English teacher who took her under his wing.

When the police arrested Jacob, the entire sordid and ugly truth swept through the town, then the state, and eventually the whole country. Thanks to Alexi's fame and her Netflix documentaries, there was never-ending public speculation. The entire world wondered: How could *Alexi North* not have known? Many people believed she had and somehow played a part in the deaths. They reasoned she had everything to gain by harboring a serial killer herself.

The churn and noise were unbearable for all of us. For the first time ever, I was thankful that the house was in the middle of nowhere and that, because of Alexi's fame, they'd worked to keep their address private.

Still, the boys and I couldn't hide forever. And my due date was now only weeks away. Their father was in jail, both their mothers were dead, and I didn't even know if the boys should or would continue to stay with me. I didn't even know how to bring the subject up with them. Jacob's parents were dead. Alexi only had her mother, a woman already in her seventies who lived in Australia and had not expressed any interest in taking on two young boys—who would very likely be suffering from severe emotional trauma for years to come.

I had no idea what was best for them. At least, I didn't until they both came to me about a week before the baby was born.

I was sitting at the kitchen table, staring out the sliding glass door into the dark, when I felt a small hand on my arm. I turned and saw both Garrett and Daniel standing beside me.

"We wanted to ask you something," Garrett said.

"What's up?" I asked, trying my best to smile and be reassuring.

"Do you know..." Garrett started but was having a hard time finding the words. "I mean...what happens to us now? Do you know?"

"Are you going to leave?" Daniel asked and started crying immediately.

I looked at them both, my mouth open, but no words would come.

"Please, Libby," Garrett said, and I could see that even he was on the verge of tears. "We don't want to...I mean, there isn't anyone else, so we'd have to go, right? Like, live with other people we don't know."

"Do you want to stay with me?" I asked.

And when they both nodded, I opened my arms, and they rushed into me. "I'll do what I can. I promise, okay. I'll try to keep us all together."

As it turned out, because Jacob and I had gotten married,

and no one else was jumping up to claim the boys, getting legal guardianship of them was pretty straightforward. The state of New Hampshire was more than happy not to have another set of foster kids needing placement on their hands.

With that settled, and after their new sister, Mary Beth, was born, we all tried to lead as normal of a life as possible while we all waited for Jacob's trial and for this horrific chapter of life to finally pass. We hunkered down, watched a lot of television, and ate too many microwavable meals. It wasn't until I received a notice from the school that I realized we had somehow made it to mid-September, and neither of the boys had returned to school yet.

"I can't go back there," Garrett said.

"No," I agreed. "But you guys need to go to school," I said as I rocked Mary Beth on my shoulder.

"We could move," Garrett said, and I could hear the hope in his voice. He was desperate to get out from under the weight of this town and start over.

We all were.

"Where would we go?" I asked.

"Anywhere they don't know us or our names," he said.

I had to smile at this. "I don't know if that place exists."

"We could change our names," Garrett suggested.

I nodded. People did this. Especially the innocent people connected to such heinous people. "Okay. Yes. That makes a lot of sense. We'll move, change our names—"

"Become new people," Garrett said as he reached out and ran his hand gently over his baby sister's head.

"New people. Where do we go?" I asked.

"Somewhere busy. Somewhere we don't stand out. Los Angeles, San Francisco...New York."

"Not New York," I said.

"Okay...San Francisco, then."

I nodded and imagined walking along the sidewalks in that city, sitting at coffee shops, living in a small house with a beautiful view. "Yes," I agreed. "San Francisco. But what about our name? Who should we become."

"That one's easy," he said. "I want to be Garrett Luck."

"Luck? Really?"

"Yeah, I mean...I'd like to be named after the woman who saved us."

THE END

A NOTE FROM REBECCA

If you enjoyed reading *The Last Nanny,* please leave a review. It makes a huge difference. Thank you!

Thank you for reading *The Last Nanny.* This is the tenth book I've written and second once I've released since I returned to indie publishing. If you enjoyed it, you may want to check out one of my other titles:

Once Upon a Lie
The Secret Next Door
Her Perfect Life

Writing stories, creating books, and connecting with readers is definitely a passion of mine. I am profoundly grateful that I get to do this for a living. That's not to say my journey to get here has been easy. Certainly not. Most of my writing has coincided with also working full time and raising a family. For years I used to get up at four in the morning to get a couple hours of writing done before my kids woke up and it was time to get all of us ready to go to school—I worked as a school psychologist at the time.

I always loved my life, and all that I wanted to do with it. But as I'm sure you can imagine, it was difficult to juggle it all. Sometimes the writing took a backseat—but I never let it go.

I firmly believe that if you keep working for a dream, it can and will happen. It may not look exactly as you imagined, but that's okay. It comes down to loving the journey and the process and not getting overly attached to end results. I'm never afraid that I'll regret trying—but I know for a fact I'll always regret giving up.

So I don't. And that's how and why this book has come to you. If you enjoyed reading *The Last Nanny,* please leave a review. I know many readers don't think they are a big deal or make much difference, but reader reviews are the number one reason new readers will take a chance on an author or book they may feel on the fence about trying. To say they are paramount to the success of indie authors is not an overstatement. Reader reviews and recommendations are the #1 most effective resource authors have to help reach more readers. Just leave the star rating you feel is appropriate along with one or two lines about what you honestly thought about the book. I read them all and I'm extremely grateful for each and every one.

You can also find a complete list of titles by me on my website along with links to your favorite store. Please visit rebeccataylorbooks.com.

Would you like to receive my monthly newsletter with updates about my current projects, travels, and life in general? If so, you can sign up at rebeccataylorbooks.com. I value my reader's trust and NEVER share your personal email information with anyone.

And finally, I LOVE to hear from readers directly. If you'd like to drop me an email, or share a picture of yourself and/or your pet reading one of my books, feel free to email me directly at readers@rrtaylor.com. If you give your permission, I may feature your photo either in my newsletter or on my social media sites.

Facebook: RebeccaTaylorPage

Instagram: RebeccaTaylorBooks

Youtube: RebeccaTaylorBooks

Website: www.rebeccataylorbooks.com

ACKNOWLEDGMENTS

I am exceedingly lucky to have some amazing friends and first round readers who generously offer up their time to review and provide feedback on early versions of my manuscripts. They are instrumental in helping in the creation of my books by catching errors, making excellent suggestions, and basically being a huge source of support. I would like to give a very special thank you to: Liz Clark, Rod Taylor, Jill Arnhold, Lisa Sundling, and Alison Migala for being the best beta readers an author could hope for. Thank you for your time, your attention to detail, and for being such fantastic people.

www.ingramcontent.com/pod-product-compliance
Lightning Source LLC
Chambersburg PA
CBHW030550310726
48979CB00011B/2096/J
* 9 7 8 0 9 7 9 7 3 5 3 9 4 *